California Street

By Thomas A. Curtis

Copyright © 2006 by Thomas A. Curtis

ISBN 0-7414-2953-5

Published by:

INFINITY
PUBLISHING.COM

1094 New DeHaven Street, Suite 100
West Conshohocken, PA 19428-2713
Info@buybooksontheweb.com
www.buybooksontheweb.com
Toll-free (877) BUY BOOK
Local Phone (610) 941-9999
Fax (610) 941-9959

Printed in the United States of America

Printed on Recycled Paper

Published February 2006

ACKNOWLEDGMENTS

Front & Back Cover Photography, Minnie Burkhardt
Front & Back Cover Lay Out & Graphic Design, Bernie Beckloff
War time stills of Bougainville, Torpedoed destroyer, The History Place
War time shot of SS-310, USS Batfish at sea, the Official Batfish Website

DEDICATION

To a warrior, great American Patriot, hero, and beloved friend

Wiley V. Davis

(USN, USAF [ret.])

Preface

War changes people and World War Two changed every person on the planet. When World War Two started, some fifty million people existed–primarily in Europe and Asia–who imagined they lived in peace. They were wrong. Men, women, children, villages, and entire cities on two continents were immolated in the conflagration. Those fifty million people perished over six years of bloodshed the like of which the human race had never seen.

The United States was caught unprepared for the magnitude of the conflict. When hostilities broke out in both Europe and the Far East the United States was still flying World War I era planes and using plywood tanks to stage war games. President Roosevelt had managed to pass draft legislation by only a single vote in the Congress in 1940 and Washington D.C. was awash in foreign spies and diplomats who wanted to see the United States continue operating under an isolationist foreign policy.

The President and the Speaker of the House, Sam Rayburn, both knew war was coming. They managed to pass the referenced draft act and lend–lease legislation over stiff opposition in the Congress. The Japanese, in turn, made a terrible strategic blunder by attacking Pearl Harbor in December of 1941. The Japanese Imperial Staff greatly overestimated the ability of the United States Navy to implement Plan Orange against the Japanese offensive in the Pacific. The attack on Pearl hastened the entry of the United States into the war and brought the industrial might and manpower of the United States into play on behalf of a beleaguered Great Britain and attendant allies.

Fighting a global conflict on two fronts created enormous social upheaval in American society. Americans were forced to acknowledge certain truths that had always existed, but were largely ignored in the prewar era. Among these, women were competent, trustworthy, talented workers. Blacks or African-Americans, if you so prefer, were loyal Americans; notwithstanding the blatant, harrowing racism prevalent in American society at the time.

As a result of the war, the privileged or moneyed classes would no longer hold a complete monopoly on the distribution of the wealth the American economy generated. A huge new middle class in America would be created out of the chaos and the mayhem of the war.

While I strive to talk about the referenced issues to one degree or another, this book is still a work of fiction woven within the context of history. Where the protagonist, Wilson Davis, is concerned, some of the events portrayed are taken from real life. However, I emphasize that all of the townspeople in my Gainesville Texas are fictitious and are not intended to portray any actual person living or dead. This is so for the rest of the novel too.

The exception to this disclaimer is, of course, the historic figures portrayed. While each historic figure invoked (e.g. President Roosevelt, then Congressman Johnson, The Speaker, Mr. Rayburn, various American and Japanese Navy Admirals etc) played actual roles in World War Two, the dialogue and roles created for them in this work are wholly fictitious. I consulted several historical sources in crafting fictional dialogue for specific historic figures so as to try and ensure their dialogue fit their actual place in history. However, no one should take anything the historical characters say within the confines of this book as having any historic weight or historic value. Any error made, historically speaking, in terms of the role of any historical figure or the actual sequence of events at any point in time, place, battle etc is wholly my own and is not to be attributed to any other actual person living or dead.

I note too that I severely condensed the complexity of several battles in order to fit them within the plot line of the book. For those readers wanting historical depictions of either people or events mentioned in the book, the good news is that the historical record on World War Two is immense. Four of my favorite historical works for purposes of obtaining a topical overview of various aspects of World War Two are: *The Two-Ocean War–A Short History of the United States Navy in the Second World War,* by Samuel Eliot Morison; *Washington Goes to War,* by David Brinkley; *War in the Boats,* by Capt William J. Ruhe, USN (ret.); and *At Dawn We Slept: The Untold Story of Pearl Harbor,* by Gordon W. Prange.

I hope my book provides a window into our vanishing past. A vanishing past wherein Americans overcame their societal shortcomings and accomplished on a vast scale the one thing that truly has made America great. The ability to answer the cry of a despairing world requiring release from the grip of evil incarnate.

Thomas A. Curtis
Denison, Texas
November, 2005

Chapter 1
Sitting above the Shoals

"Colder than a well digger's butt in a deep pit," I mumble as my eyes open. The night sky blazes with starlight–vast and impersonal, but awe inspiring nonetheless. I quit stargazing and force myself out of my bedroll. As I listen to the sound of my joints creaking, I decide to take a whack at raking the banked coals of the fire I had built the night before. As I gather fallen mesquite branches to toss on the coals, I prick my left thumb on a thorn and suck off the blood as the dry mesquite ignites. Fire up a cigarette and get my bum knee as close to the flames as I can without torching myself.

The cat is out in the brush; she's been prowling around since I made camp. She was moving closer when the fire was banked. Now she's backed off again. This old feline knows my scent. Even though she knows me she doesn't like me camping in her domain.

"No worries old girl," I tell her. "I've come to see you."

I lean against an old tree stump, recollecting when I first saw a mountain lion along the Red River.

"Definitely before the war," I mumble to myself.

I smoke, watching a faint light glow in the east. Down below the sandstone shelf I am camped on, the river sloshes along. Nothing at all like the Pacific Ocean I think. The sea is majestic and terrifying in equal measure. During a dead calm the surface is polished glass as far as you can see in any direction. The salt water whispers and coos like a mother singing a lullaby. As soon as you think you've made your peace with it, the sea unleashes its fury. You conclude that hell is filled with emerald green banshees.

Mind you, I grew up in Gainesville Texas and didn't know jack shit about the ocean. I thought I understood life in my own town. But I was wrong about that too. Until the war started and I joined the Navy, I'd never thought much about the ocean, even less about war and combat. Now, I'm old and have given combat, and the ocean some thought. I shift positions to ease my knee and to take stock of the mountain lion. She's stalking up slope of me.

The ocean doesn't think or care about you. The ocean simply is. A rattlesnake is indifferent too. A rattler will strike you if you corner it or step on it but it doesn't hate you. Be a Jew, be a Negro, be lily white. Religion doesn't matter. Catch a rattler or the ocean at the wrong time, and you're in a world of hurt.

People are different. They're in a league all by themselves. Many people will kill you for no reason at all. This is a hard thing to get your mind around. Saying people have murderous natures probably isn't proper fodder for the book publishing reception that I'll be speaking to later in the day. I sigh. Reluctantly, I pack up and head home. The lion trails me down onto the shoals …being tracked is comforting routine.

The wife knots my tie and kisses me on the cheek.
"Wilson, you still smell like wood smoke even after a shower."
"If I'm going to act like a ham, I should smell the part."
She regards me with those intriguing eyes, those eyes that haven't changed since I first met her.
"Did you see her?"

"Who?"

She knots my tie tighter.

I feign gagging.

"Yes, I saw her. I took down a deer for her. She thanked me by yowling all night and stalking me down onto the shoals."

My wife is wearing her best pearls against an emerald green dress. She's a looker.

"I don't suppose me telling you that you're too old to go out onto that snake-infested river to hang out with a cranky old lioness will do me a bit of good."

"Hell yes I'm too old. I'm too old to run. She's too old to care. Feel like all the iron has left my pecker, turned to lead and sunk to my ass."

"Ah, you're displaying such nice language and a pleasant disposition to boot. Perhaps we'll test this metal theory later. Get things ... ironed out."

She giggles as she smoothes out my jacket. Maybe I will have some iron left for her. We head for the civic center.

Camera lights bother me on the rare occasions when I am asked to speak about the war. I find my wife in the front row and focus on her. I look at the prompter gizmo as a bead of sweat trickles down the side of my face. I fight off the panic welling up inside and I start in. I tell myself for the hundredth time that this talk is no different than all of my other talks.

"A television reporter wrote a book calling my generation the greatest generation. That was a nice thing to say about our lot. Guess I suffer from a lack of perspective - having lived through the war era. Speaking only for myself, I can't say with certainty that there was anything special about us before the war began. We were young and full of piss and vinegar. But, then, I'm sure my young friends that many of you all are too."

3

I take a sip of water and grin out at the audience.

"I, myself, could personally curdle cold milk with a glance. Least ways that's how I remember myself and I'm bound to all of my youthful exploits by what some people call experience. But, really, what binds me to the past is a rapidly failing memory.

In Gainesville, as in the rest of the country, we believed that if you worked hard, you could make your own way in the world and everyone did work hard to make their own way because a buck was tough to come by. Our work ethic didn't make us peaches though."

I pause to take another sip of water from the glass on the lectern. "What I'm trying to say is that I want everyone to stop looking at 'my generation' through rose-colored glasses. Mean, stupid, drunk, bigoted and cruel people existed aplenty before World War Two. Just as they do today.

Here's the main thing. People pretend cruelty surprises them. Truth is people have always been cruel given proper opportunity. People have always maimed, raped and killed each other. Read your Bible; don't take my word for this sorry state of affairs. Sometimes, people engage in killing each other like murder was a spectator sport. A sport where men, women, and children all end up laying dead in heaps like discarded bits of wood waiting for someone to come along and sweep them up."

I pause and stare out. People are squirming. They hadn't expected to hear such blunt remarks.

"Humans maintain the illusion that we are a peace-loving species. We pretend to be surprised when war and killing waltz. We pretended a lot before the war too. In 1939 and 1940, the United States was busily maintaining this illusion of a peaceable planet. In 1940, the Congress passed mandatory military draft legislation by one vote, thanks to Sam Rayburn of Bonham, Texas. The politicians also wanted the peaceable planet illusion maintained. Our system of government and the oceans saved us.

Our country came together as a nation, not easy to do, by the way. Usually you can't get two people to agree on the time of day, much less convince a whole nation that we need to help a bunch of foreign folks clear across the ocean. The oceans kept our enemies at bay long enough for us to arm, after we got really pissed. We, of course, can thank Japan for that. Just in the nick of time, we armed our allies and ourselves.

We were Americans. We understood Joe Di-Maggio. Tojo and Hitler were irritating enigmas operating outside our daily existence. This naiveté came to a rapid close. By the time the war ended in 1945 virtually every person I knew had experienced combat in one form or another. Many listened to dying men screaming in agony and fear.

My friends and I did not feel unique about having acquired this horrid knowledge; we felt lucky… to still be alive at the end of each day and alive when the war ended. But, time has passed. I've garnered some insight." Unexpectedly, I feel emotion rising within me. My shirt is drenched in sweat. I hear nothing from the audience. Off of the teleprompter now, I am on my own.

"The war inflicted incomprehensible loss upon all of us. My story is not unique among my peers. Still, something simple but vital demands our continued attention to what happened in the nineteen forties. You can't change the past - but you can learn from it. I have learned this. Evil is patient and persistent. Evil waits. Then, suddenly, evil squats and shits where it will, usually where you least expect. Someone must always be ready to clean up the mess."

"In World War Two, my friends and I left Gainesville behind for combat. Our lives changed forever because of the war. The war provided me with a certain perspective. I came home. Many did not, including some people, who were and still are special to me, even though they have been dead for nigh on half a century. This book is my story and theirs."

I lean out over the lectern and say, "time is precious. If all the honored dead were here, they would tell us to spend as much time with the butterflies in the clover as we can spare, but to keep the eyes in the back of our heads open and alert. We don't have to leave home to be in a combat zone. War travels. We have recently learned this painful lesson again with the events in New York City and in London."

I am talked out. The silence is shocking. I wait for the rotten tomatoes to fly. My wife is crying in the front row. I hear noise and see people on their feet clapping. I feel relief for the future. Maybe young Americans do understand that freedom is always paid for in the hard currency of blood.

As I come down off of the stage, people are holding copies of my book out to be signed. I oblige as many of them as I can. I sign more at a table set up outside of the auditorium. My hand aches and throbs with the strain of the work.

Later, when we're home again and after my wife has determined that all my iron isn't gone just yet. "Think any of those folks will read the blamed thing or will they use it as a door stop?" I ask.

She runs her left hand over my chest. Her right eyebrow arches as she leans over me,

"I think that you wrote the book is enough. You can't control who reads it. Do me a favor though."

"What?"

"Read me some of it. Start at the beginning."

I laugh.

"Having trouble sleeping?"

"Come on, Will."

I'm secretly pleased she wants me to read to her. I grab a copy off of the floor. This is all a bit silly. She knows I want to read to her. I begin.

Chapter 2

Home Base

My mother didn't intend to raise a fool for a son. She reminded me of this fact on more occasions than I care to remember. When I was born, she named me Wilson Pickett Davis proclaiming it was a name any man could be proud of. Guess she figured right off the bat that I was headed for fame, fortune, politics, jail, or maybe all of the above. Throughout my life I've avoided politics. Although, politics seems like an interesting option when you are trying to figure a way into a life that doesn't include subsistence farming or oil rough–necking, that is, until you meet some of the people controlling access to the political machinery.

I wouldn't have been the first politician to hail from Gainesville, if I had decided to live or die by the ballot. The history of Gainesville is dotted with some fairly prominent political figures. In the 1920 democratic gubernatorial primary former Senator Joe Bailey and Ewing Thomason squared off against each other. Both were from Gainesville. Many who knew Bailey said he could have been elected President earlier in the century if only he could have controlled his temper.

Crime was not a prominent concern in 1940. Bad behavior usually amounted to getting caught with a pack of Lucky Strikes and a couple of bottles of beer that the Baptists hadn't destroyed or drunk themselves, preferably after a sweat-soaked summer night getting their faith revitalized under a tent.

My mom, however, had determined I was on Satan's A-list. She'd often say, "Wilson, the Lord does not tolerate fools within the boundaries of paradise."

I always wanted to respond saying, "He seemed to like Job okay," but instead I'd say, "yes, mother."

Don't get me wrong. I loved my mom and I miss her, we just didn't see eye to eye on everything. When I was young, the main thing was my conduct. In this regard 1940 was a pretty normal year for me. Mom didn't approve of my goings on, many of my friends, or some of the gossip she'd heard. You couldn't spit on the street at midnight or tramp around in someone's garden looking for a lost baseball without word getting back to her. On the other hand war was far away. The war was something you listened to on the radio, usually Walter Winchell speaking to 'Mr. and Mrs. America and all the ships at sea.'

My best buddy, Danny Ludlow - Dud for short - always said my mama could wield willow better than any man he ever knew. Mom liked Dud well enough, but didn't much cotton to his no-account family. True, Dud wasn't to blame for the fact that his daddy was a drunk and his mama was weak. That didn't matter one whit. Dud was admitted to the local no-account club, his dues already paid in full.

Mind you I only now realize what the score was as I sit here swatting at the cobwebs in my head trying to get all the facts right in my mind. When I was a young man, there was a pecking order and Dud and I understood we were near the bottom. Dud wasn't singled out or picked on by respectable folk; he just wasn't given any more consideration than the local coloreds. Come to think of it, he hardly rated higher than the prisoners working on the chain gang; the ones that laid oil down on the roads to keep the dust down. I was a rung or two up only because my mom was known to be a hard working, God fearing woman.

Still, we had life pretty good. We spent the summers hunting coons and fishing off the shoals of the Red River. Winter barn dances, quilting bees, and hog butchering parties were all worthy events. The Babe had retired but Joe DiMaggio was making a name for himself, as was Ted Williams. Dud and me knew who Hitler was from the radio and reading Amazing Man comics. We weren't paying too much attention to Tojo - yet. We should have been because things were happening around the world in exotic places. World events were fixing to reach out and touch all of us. The summer of 1940 was a dividing line for me. All stories start somewhere and end somewhere else. Mine starts that summer.

"Want to head on down to the train station?"
Dud and I usually hung out by the train station on California Street on Saturday nights.
"I don't know Will. I hear some pretty mean hobos been hanging around down there lately."
I bounced a hard rubber ball off the hallway wall. I missed it on its return and hit a window pane.
"Will," my mom yelled, "if you break a window with that ball, I'll tan your hide till you can't sit. Now get on out of the house until you can behave better than cattle on the hoof."
She didn't need to tell me twice, my mom would switch me at the drop of a hat. As we headed out of the house, Dud said, "I wonder if Bob Sullivan is out tonight?"

"No big deal if he is," I said. "Besides, Bob's alright. That is, so long as you don't bait him."
"Can't help baiting him," Dud said as he stopped to scrape chewing gum off the bottom of his shoe with a stick. "Like my old man, he brings out the worst in me."

"Then consider what my dad says about smarting off," I puffed out my chest and imitated my dad's slouch. "Son," I said, pointing at Dud, "a little manure can go a long way, especially on a hot day."

Dud laughed at the imitation and said, "smart man, your dad." Dud pointed. "There's Bob now." Whip-thin, jet hair gleaming in the lamplight, Bob was the spitting image of cool, leaning up against the side of the station, lighting up a butt.

"What do you think, Will?"

"He looks like he wants to be left alone."

Dud ignored me and walked up to Bob.

"Got a smoke, Bob?"

"Yeah, Dud, I got a smoke. Not that it'll do you a damn bit of good. You and your buddy Davis there only owe me about a hundred smokes already. Might as well piss on 'em as give 'em to you two and where in holy hell did you get that cowboy hat? You ain't ever roped a thing in your life."

"Maybe not but I aim to start. Wearing the hat gets me halfway home. All I need now is some boots and a saddle."

Bob snorted derisively. "Rid 'em cowboy."

"Davis and I have something important to tell you, if you'll lay off of my hat for a second. Once you hear us out, I'm guessing we'll be even on the smokes."

"That so, Dud? What in hell do you have to say to me that'll make us even?"

Bob got up in Dud's face as he said this. I winced. Dealing with Bob Sullivan in a good mood was an iffy proposition.

Bob was a loader in the rail yard and had arms like jackhammers. Rumor had it he was in Gainesville because he'd been run off from the Denison textile mill after beating up his foreman over back wages Bob was supposedly owed. Personally, if Bob had told me I owed him money, I'd have paid up on the spot - even if it meant being bare-assed broke for three months.

"Me and Davis here have seen Louis DeWitt stepping out to the State Theater last night with Betty Stevens. Now if I'm not mistaken, ain't they showing the latest Eddie Cantor flick there?"

"Bob," I added, "I even heard that he paraded her right down Lindsay Street in front of all those other swells living in the big houses."

Bob's face reddened and the veins in his neck bulged, but he wasn't gonna let us know we'd hit pay dirt. He backed away from Dud, then, leaned against the wall, pulling a drag on his cigarette. Exhaling the smoke, he threw the butt down and ground it under his boot.

"Who gives a damn about Eddie Cantor," he said. "Ain't like he was takin' her to see Jimmy Cagney or that John Wayne fella."

Bob stared into space for a moment.

"Doesn't she live on Lindsay?"

Dud responded, "yeah, but they visited every dang house on the block. I call that parading."

Bob continued to stare out into space for another moment. Dud and I could hear him grating his teeth. He suddenly stood straight up and threw a half pack of camels our way.

"If you boys are lying to me, I'll hang you both in the park where they swung those Yankee lovers back during the war of northern aggression."

Dud and me believed him. The only thing Bob hated more than Louis at that point was Yankees.

"Whoa there Bob," Dud said. "Davis and I aren't aiming to get in dutch with you. We thought you might like to know where things stand."

"Looks like I'm good for a laugh or two and a couple milkshakes and burgers down at Hicks', but that's where the party ends for Bob Sullivan. I have no real money, no automobile, and apparently no girl. I'm telling you boys, Yankees are going to be the death of the country - and DeWitt is from a money-grubbing, carpet-bagging Yankee family …or my name isn't Bob Sullivan."

"I don't know, Bob. Hardly seems Christian to love everyone on Sunday, then, hate 'em the rest of the week."

Bob shot me a steely-eyed glare.

"Are you a bible thumper, Davis?"

"Only enough to stay on my mom's good side."

Bob smoothed out the dirt and then bent over to examine a rock.

"You have to keep your mama happy, but stop peddling that Jesus crap around me. If God wants to love Louis DeWitt, and Yankees that's His business but it doesn't mean I have to like' em and if I catch DeWitt on a Sunday I will still beat his ass black and blue. Now scram. Oh yeah, hey Davis, one more thing!"

I reluctantly turned around. "Yeah, Bob?"

"Thanks for helping me rewire my boss's car last weekend. You saved my fanny after I shot off my big mouth and told him I could fix it."

I recalled the previous weekend. He'd asked for help by yelling, "Davis get your sorry ass over here" - from half a block away. Turning him down never occurred to me.

"No sweat, Bob. That clicking noise was the clue - voltage problem." "Good job. Fixed that rat trap in ten minutes flat, without shorting out a thing."

"Easy. I once rewired our entire house while my dad napped on the front porch." I laughed at the memory. "Once and awhile, he'd wake up and holler out, 'things going okay, Will? Need any help?' I'd say, "Nah dad stay put.' Believe me, the car was no problem at all."

"Okay, but at least you came over when I asked. I appreciated the help. See you around. Leave that sorry ass buddy–and his cowboy hat - home next time though - you hear?"

"Jeepers Bob, you have no idea how much that hurts me." Dud sniffled and rubbed his eyes.

"Damn, there you go, pissing me off again."

We didn't need a further hint. Dud and I hot-footed our way back down California Street towards home.

I yelled. "Sorry to trouble you. Thanks for the smokes."

We slowed our pace as we put distance between Bob and ourselves. I quit running and put my hands on my knees, as we rounded the corner onto Dixon.

Dud looked back at me.

"You gotta cut down on the smokes Davis," he said, as he stopped too. "You should be able to run all the way to Denton from here."

"Don't worry, Dud, I'll live to dance on your grave. Damn it, I warned you about baiting Bob like that. If he catches Louis, he'll beat him like he said he would."

"Probably but did you consider what the Sheriff would do to Bob in retaliation?"

"The Sheriff'd lock Bob up quicker than you can blink." Dud considered further. "And that's too damn bad because that shit-cake Louis is more dangerous than Bob."

"So, why'd you go pissing on Bob's oatmeal?"

Dud shrugged. "What's done is done. Besides, that slick dick darling DeWitt hangs out with the Klan on Saturday night, then, attends the Methodist socials on Sunday afternoon. Do him good to take a licking, even if Bob does spend a night or two in jail."

I ran a stick along the Milner's picket fence, just to hear the *whaaaacka whaaaacka* sound.

"Louis hates more people than Bob does sure enough, but that doesn't mean setting Bob up to take a fall is righteous."

"Okay, so I shot my mouth off. I just can't stand the way Louis struts around like Jay Gatsby and people love it. He's nothing but mullet bait and maggot food all rolled into one nasty package and people don't see who he really is."

"Agreed," I said. "Louis hates everyone, including poor white trash like us."

"Hey Davis! I resent being called white trash."

"What would you prefer? Mr. Ludlow?"

Dud stuck is chest out. "I'm an American like Charley Lindbergh and Wendell Wilkie."

"We'll call them tomorrow so you can pay your respects, Dud, American-to-American."

"Great! Maybe Charley will take me up for a ride."

"Come on Mr. America. Let's head for the house. Dad should have the radio tuned into Jack Benny. Winchell should be off the air by now."

As we headed home I was still worried. Egging Bob on about Betty Stevens was wrong. I was glad I hadn't told anyone about Bob coming into where I worked and buying a nice suit to wear to take Betty to Dallas in.

Waiting on Bob had been like trick or treating when I was four – scary, real scary. He'd stomped in the door wearing overalls. He was caked in engine grease and dirt from the top of his boots to the brim of his billed hat. He'd spotted me trying to hide behind and down under the counter, hoping Mr. Chaney would show up. He looked at me like he'd never seen me before.

"You work here Davis?"
"Yes sir I do."

Bob stepped back and looked around to see whom I was calling 'sir'.

"Quit calling me sir, Davis. In case you forgot, I'm Bob Sullivan and I need a suit. I don't need credit. I can pay cash money."

He began to pull his wallet out.

"Bob, I don't need to see your wallet. I'll take you at your word that you have cash money. My boss, Mr. Chaney, usually handles our customers who desire to purchase a new suit. He should be back in a few minutes."

"I'm in a hurry. You'll do. Show me what you have."

What the hell should I do now? I thought. Mr. Chaney'll shit a whole flat of bricks when he sees me working suits with a grimy, Irish working stiff.

"What is the suit for, Bob?"

"Why the hell do you need to know that?"

"Different suits for different occasions. If it's for business and you're going to be moving around a lot, you'll probably want something that will hold up like gabardine or something lighter like cotton twill. On the other hand, if you intend to go more formal you may want something that has a nicer cut and won't show the wrinkles like pure wool or a wool cashmere blend."

Bob glared at me like I was a rabid skunk that needed shooting. He stared at me for twenty seconds or so. Finally he made up his mind about something.

"Will, I've never bought a fine suit in my life. I don't know jack shit about what I need. A high-tone blonde has asked me to take her to some play called 'Canary' and I don't want to look like a hick when we go."

He placed his hands on the counter and said, "I can spend fifty dollars. Can you help me out or not?"

16

"Mr. Sullivan, for much less than that, we can put you in a perfectly cut suit that will dazzle your lady."

Bob spun on his heels.

I jumped.

We had not heard Mr. Chaney come in.

Mr. Chaney took Bob by the arm and led him away from the counter.

Speaking, as he walked, he said, "I have a nice dark navy. The navy will work well for you over a white cotton dress shirt. In the dark environs of the theatre it will pass for black and look even more formal. May I also suggest that we look at shoes Mr. Sullivan? The swells in Dallas always check shoes. Many times a man will get the suit right and the shoes will give him away. Bob was stunned and stood there shifting his weight back and forth. His clothes gave off puffs of dust while he fidgeted. Mr. Chaney eyed him for another thirty seconds.

"I think dark blue silk will work for the tie. What's your opinion, Mr. Davis?"

I was tongue-tied.

"His eyes?" I said.

"Yes. Precisely why blue is the way to go here."

"Mr. Sullivan, I propose that we…," he waved his hand in my direction, "outfit you for; shall we say -"

Mr. Chaney wrote a figure down on a white tab of paper that he discretely handed to Bob.

Bob was still speechless. He looked at the figure on the paper and nodded.

"That's a right fair price, Mr. Chaney. How do we, I mean, what do we do next?"

"Mr. Davis will procure an appropriate suit out of our stock. Mr. Davis, I think we will start with a 42 long. Bring me the Ellis McClain navy. The McClain is cut a little broader through the shoulders. Now Mr. Sullivan shall we proceed to the fitting room?"

Bob allowed himself to be led to the fitting room like he was a lamb in a manger.

I saw him three or four days later wearing the whole affair. He looked like a movie star. When I saw him, I thought. "Oh man, she's gonna go for him like he was an ice cream cone on a Saturday night in July."

Yes, all in all, I was glad I'd kept Bob's secret and was on the good side in his ledger.

When we got back to my house, dad was sitting on the front porch with my little brother, Ralph, who was twelve and a pain. I guess he wouldn't have been my kid brother if he weren't. They were listening to the radio through the front window.

"How's your back tonight Daddy." I asked.

Dad had injured himself working as an oilfield roughneck on the Walnut Bend wellhead site.

"Will, the ol' back is feeling pretty fair tonight. I can stand and walk around. Don't think I'm ready to take your mother dancing though - even if she'd go. How are you boys doing tonight? Staying out of trouble?"

"Yes sir, we are. Thought we'd listen to the radio with you all if you don't mind."

"We don't mind at all." He ran his fingers through Ralph's hair. As he did this, I caught a hint of his Old Spice after-shave on the breeze.

"Fibber McGee is fixing to come on. As I matter of fact, here's two bits in case you all wanted to head on down to the soda fountain before the show starts."

I knew immediately that dad must have had a good night at the wagering tables. After he had recovered from his oilfield injury, he started gambling to bring in some money. Gambling was not a steady source of income. Depending on his luck, dad was either flush or flat broke.

"Daddy, can I have something from Watts too?"

"Sure Ralph, I don't think your brother and Dud will mind if you tag along."

I glared at Ralph when dad wasn't looking. Dad gave me another quarter for Ralph's soda.

Before we left the porch, I said, "Winchell have anything interesting to say tonight, daddy?"

"Son, Mr. Winchell spent a fair amount of time talking about the trouble brewing in Europe. Poland's not faring well under Hitler and the Nazi regime."

"Do you think America will fight, daddy?"

"Think we will eventually - but I don't much like that answer. I won't be doing the fighting. You, Dud, and even Ralph, perhaps, will be going."

"Mr. Davis, I don't know about Will here, but I'm ready to fight the Nazis. War has got to be more exciting than hanging around this one - horse town."

Dad got a faraway look in his eyes as he rolled himself a cigarette. "Don't bite off more adventure than you can handle, Danny."

I laughed and said, "yeah, Dud. Those Nazis might make Bob Sullivan look friendly."

"Laugh all you want, Will. If a war comes along, I'm going. A big war doesn't come down the pike everyday. Maybe I'll finally see the world outside Cooke County."

"This is shaping up to be another war to end all wars," dad said, as he leaned back in the rocker, pulling on his cigarette. "If America gets involved, I don't think the damned mess will be fought here. Although, after the disaster at Dunkirk, I don't know where the Germans can be stopped. Hitler may attack England any day now - and if the Brits fall we're in serious trouble."

The locusts crooned and my dad smoked. After a moment or two, he continued his thought. "The Germans crashed through the Ardenne Forest like the forest was paper maché. How a slaughter was avoided at Dunkirk is beyond me.   The French didn't even slow the Wehrmacht down with their macerated defensive line."

"Mrs. Billings says we need to look out for fifth column activities around here," Ralph said. "She told us in class the other day that German spies are all around us and that we should round up every foreigner in the county and lock them in the jail."

"Lots of folks agree with Mrs. Billings, Ralph." The rocker creaked as my dad spoke.

"However, I find it's usually prudent to avoid locking people up before they've done anything."

"We have plenty of problems right here in the US of A to take care of. We don't need to take on people's problems from across the ocean."

We all looked toward the front parlor window. My mom took in seamstress work. She was working her foot treadle sewing machine in the living room as she spoke.

"Elizabeth, I didn't know you had an opinion on Chancellor Hitler and his schemes of conquest." My dad grinned as he waited for her response.

"Mason, I have views on many things, including smoking and gambling. Mainly, your smoking and gambling. The Germans elected themselves a fool to run their country. I fail to see why their foolishness affects us. Why should we go running off to fix the situation? My Uncle Hurley got himself killed in the Great War, died in the mud in the Argonne. He never did come home. So I don't want to hear any prattling on about another war coming."

Dad sighed, having heard about Uncle Hurley on many occasions. "Go on down and get those sodas boys," he said. "It'll give me some quiet time with her."

As we were walking out of the yard, I heard him saying, "Elizabeth no one around here wants to see..." His voice trailed off into the sounds of locusts and rustling leaves.

"How bad do you think your mama will ride your Daddy?"

"Not too bad at all, Dud. She wasn't even upset."

"I don't get your folks at all. If my mom spoke to my daddy like that he would have hauled off and knocked her upside the head. Course my mama doesn't know enough about wars and such to have any opinion to voice."

"Our mom has strong views on about everything. I'd be making greenbacks hand over fist if she hadn't forbidden Daddy to get me oil patch work. Daddy could have gotten me work all the way from here to Kilgore."

"Mom doesn't want you losing your life before you turn twenty, Will," Ralph said. He and Dud both laughed.

"Kinda hard to turn twenty, if you're dead in some acid pit," Dud said.

"That would be a sight alright, a Davis earning money from a days honest labor. Course, the acid pit part was alright."

I recognized the nasal tone and wheeled my stool around. Louis DeWitt and his sidekick Rob Franklin had come up behind us. Dud, Ralph, and I slid off our stools. As we stood toe to toe with the interlopers, Watts' got real quiet. Everyone sitting along the aisle looked up to see what the commotion was about. Rob spoke to Ray Watts over our heads.

"Ray, I didn't know you let scum in here. Louis and I hate to see the unwashed masses dirtying up our reserved stools."

"Rob, these boys paid for their sodas and are minding their own business. Can't really say the same about you."

"Its okay, we're leaving anyway," I said.

Ralph looked at Rob and said, "Who asked you to butt in anyway?" Rob grabbed Ralph by the front of his shirt collar. Dud inserted himself between Louis and Rob. I sidled off my stool and spoke very softly to Rob.

"Nothing has happened here yet, Rob. But if you don't let my brother go right now I'm going to break something on your body off and beat you with it."

Essentially a coward, Rob stepped back. His eyes cut to Louis. Louis was busy eyeing Dud's right hand–it held a sock filled with ball bearings.

Ray Watts walked up and said, "boys, take it outside or I'll get Dave Reilly in here to settle the issue."

Patrolman Reilly walked the downtown beat.

Rob let Ralph go.

"Dud come on," I said.

Louis yelled when Dud flicked the sock by his ear and then pocketed it. Everyone in Watts laughed–except Rob and Louis. I heard someone say, "Louis best go to the restroom and pit-stop. Make sure Dud didn't scare you too much."

We walked backwards between the stools and the green padded booths towards the door. No one tried to stop us. Our eyes stayed on Louis and Rob. As we exited, I looked at Louis and sneered, "Bob Sullivan is looking for you. See you again real soon."

The bell over the frosted glass door of the drugstore jingled as I slammed the door on the Saturday night crowd.

"I wanted to leave Louis puking on the floor," Dud said.

"Think on this a minute, Dud," I said.

"If we do that, who gets blamed? Rob? Louis?"

We walked on. Finally, Dud said, "we do."

I said, "that's right. There's a time and a place for everything. We'll take care of Louis and Rob, but not in Watts' on a Saturday night. Especially when Ralph is with us."

"Awww, I could of held my end up. They called us scum, Will."

"Ralph, no public fights if we can avoid them. Keep the eyes in the back of your head open though. Understand me?"

"Sure big brother I got it."

I put my arm around him and squeezed him to make sure he knew I was serious. He pretended to be embarrassed and said, "golly Will." He didn't shrug my arm off though. The three of us walked home. We thanked dad for the soda money when we got there.

Chapter 3
Revival Survival

Early the next morning, the sun hung low on the horizon like a fuzzy orange ball. I tugged at my shirt collar when my mom wasn't looking. We were at a sunrise revival service, but it was already hot and sticky. No matter, my mom and the preacher were already filled with the Holy Spirit.

"The Lord God did command the rock and the rock did bring forth water and the water was of the spirit. Now friends we know that water will wash the dust from our bodies. So why do we doubt that the Holy Spirit will cleanse us of sin and save us from hell!"

"Amen Brother Bill, save us!" yelled my mom and about 30 other moms and grandmas.

The young adults, and the few men, who'd been dragged to the service, held their peace and tried to stay awake. I was in this group.

"When do you think he'll quit talking and get to the wet stuff?" Benny Reavis hissed at me through clenched teeth.

"I hightailed my butt out to the river, because you said brother Bill was going to conduct a ditch knocking."

"Be still, you whiner," I shot back. The ladies aren't gonna get wet with the preacher until they're filled with the Holy Spirit."

The air was hazy. You could see steam rising off the cow pasture we were standing in. The Indian Paintbrushes stood straight up; you couldn't buy a whisper of breeze. I looked around my mom's back to see what Ralph was up to. He had a frog in his hands and was tormenting one of the Milner twins with it. I couldn't see which one. The tormented twin was going to scream any second. Mom would slap him in the back of the head. Yep, a typical revival.

Brother Bill came down off the wooden dais that he had been preaching from and proceeded to walk thirty feet or so over to the small pond where he would play John the Baptist. The pasture grass was damp. He was filled with the Spirit and forgot God made damp grass treacherous for men with leather brogans. As we all solemnly watched him wade into the muddy shallows, he slipped, and fell backwards. His skinny legs pointed skyward, the offending brogans shook themselves at Heaven. Benny Reavis and I let out guffaws. My mother grabbed the back of my neck to shut me up. But, she had to let go to cover her own mouth so she wouldn't burst out laughing too.

Two church elders helped Preacher Bill to his feet. He looked around as a grin spread across his face.
"You wouldn't let your spiritual leader be wet all by himself would you?"
The congregation decided not and ran into that pond wearing their Sunday best. I waded out to where Mindy stood. Ralph followed me.
"Don't you dunk or splash me Will," Mindy said.
"Wouldn't dream of it."
"Will wouldn't dunk you Mindy, he's sweet on you," Ralph chortled.
I turned around. "Shut up Ralph. I won't dunk Mindy but I might drown you," I said.
"Wilson, please quit flirting with the young woman and bullying your brother. I could use some help."
I looked to my left and saw my mother standing waist-deep in the pond with her hat at half-mast.
"Yes ma'am," I said.

I carried my mother to a spot on the bank where the pasture rough was thick enough so her dress wouldn't be muddied.

"Ralph, run on home and get my bath started," she said.

"Yes ma'am." Ralph sprinted in the direction of our house; frog still clutched in his left hand. Mindy called out from the pond, "Will, may I have your assistance as well?"

I glanced at my mom, sitting on the bank dumping water out of her best pumps, she shrugged and said, "Be quick about it son. The lady is waiting."

So I scooped Mindy up and set her gently on the grass next to my mother.

My mother held out her hand, "nice to see you again Mindy."

Mindy took her hand. "The pleasure is mine Missus Davis. Was that your work I saw on Corrine Bryant's dress? The embroidery was truly something to behold. I have not seen better work anywhere, including New York."

My mom's eyes sparkled.

"I'm glad someone has an eye keen enough to spot good stitch work. The good Lord knows Corrine surely can't see it. She asked me to add that stitch work so that her dress would be truly unique."

My mom stood up and laughed. "Had the gall to be upset because I charged her an additional five dollars for the work."

My mother looked directly at Mindy. She said, "don't misunderstand me. Corrine is a valuable customer, but she has sorely tried my Christian patience."

Mindy smiled as she also stood. Her dress clung to her like paint. She shrugged and said, "Corrine Bryant could try the patience of all the saints in heaven. Why should you be immune to her inability to employ either tact or charm?"

My stern, God - fearing mother smiled so broadly I thought her face would crack. She clasped Mindy's left hand in her right hand and whispered, "I know the Davis family isn't much in this town. But, I want you to know you are welcome in my home and I will remember your kindness." She turned my way and said, "son, walk me home."

We received a lot of strange looks heading back through town. My mother, with her head held high, nodded to her friends who happened to be out. Some took note of our "damp passage".

My mother would only say, "Today was a good day for the Lord."

Chapter 4
Opportunity and the Anti-Christ

Like I said, my mother didn't want me working in the oilfield during school. But, she had no objection to my picking up a summer job, so long as the work didn't involve playing cards or rattling dice with Daddy. That's how I had ended up learning the clothing business; selling suits to guys like Bob.

I was lucky. Daddy was a friend of George Chaney. Mr. Chaney owned a clothing and dry goods store called Smyth & Mark. He claimed the name sounded very English and very Protestant. Mr. Chaney was Jewish. But, the last thing he wanted was to remind people of that erstwhile fact while conducting business in Gainesville, Texas. The fancy name was shortened by his customers to Smitty's. Smitty's sat in a prime location next to the Kress 5 &10 on the corner of Commerce and California. We called this corner Kress' corner–the corner was the main spot to meet up with folks, especially on a Saturday night. Daddy had once loaned Mr. Chaney money when business was bad, even though Mr. Chaney was a Jew. Daddy called in his marker. Mr. Chaney gave me a job during the summer of 1940 updating his stock inventory sheets.

Mr. Chaney was gregarious. He liked to hold court with his patrons on current issues. He'd hold forth most days, even if the store was empty. When he really got wound up, he would take off his glasses and wipe them on his breast pocket hanky–he never came to work in anything other than a double-breasted suit. Like my dad, he was worried about events in Europe. He too thought that war was around the corner. His patrons started rolling their eyes whenever he started in on the war. The thought of America caught up in another European conflict distressed most folks.

By the end of July I had worked for Mr. Chaney for the better part of two months. He liked that I didn't talk much unless someone spoke to me first. Gave him center stage so to speak. On the Monday morning after my adventure at the Sunday revival, Mr. Chaney and I were putting up stock. Mr. Chaney was excited because some War Department official in Washington had been in the store. He had let it slip out that Gainesville was being considered as a site for a new Army training post.

"Imagine the money if the store is filled with Army trainees, Will. Money burning holes in their olive drab pants." Mr. Chaney spoke as he continued working the stock.

"So, tell me Mr. Davis is Hitler the Anti-Christ or is he just a schmuck who thinks he'd like to be the Anti-Christ?"

"I had no idea you cared about the anti-Christ sir," I said.

"Yes, Will I know," he said. "I'm Jewish and, therefore, am a heathen non-believer whose entire race has already rejected Christ."

"That being the case," I said, "isn't the Anti-Christ completely off your pie plate?"

Mr. Chaney sighed and got this faraway look in his eyes.

"A sense of humor is a good thing Will but where Hitler is concerned, the Baptists' use of the Anti-Christ label is apt. He is from hell and whether from Christian hell or Jewish gehenna is of no consequence."

"Certainly loves hearing himself talk," I said. "Lots of folks like him though. He's picked the Germans up off the ground and put 'em to work. Course, he did invade Czechoslovakia, France and Poland. Now, he's doing his level best to whip England. Invading other countries doesn't seem right."

"Ahh Poland. Have you have ever been to War-saw or even seen a picture?"

"Sir, I've never even been to Austin or Oklahoma City. Warsaw is pretty far down on my list."

"Yes, of course. Here, put these socks in that bin next to those flannel shirts. I highly recommend putting Warsaw on the top of your travel list."

Mr. Chaney stopped long enough to wipe off his glasses.

He stared out the front window of the shop and said, "whatever happens to the thugs and the black hats, the world will never be the same again. Warsaw is one of the world's great cities. Jews and Christians have lived side by side in that wondrous city for centuries and both religions have prospered from the experience. I love America but she is young. Most if not all of the buildings and churches on Krawkowskie are older than America by several centuries. Now, Hitler is turning the city into a prison and blood is running in the streets. I'm afraid Warsaw is lost to me."

Mr. Chaney continued to stare out the window. I accidentally dropped a packing crate. He started as if I had lit a firecracker under him.

"I talk too much and am silly enough to pay you to listen. I don't know why I am telling you this."

"I'm sorry sir. I didn't mean to upset you," I said.

"Not you my young friend. Here in America, people are easily lulled into thinking they're removed from the rest of the World. This is not so. Evil is coming. The world is already on fire and Americans play baseball. I do not criticize here. I only note that America is … preoccupied."

As he finished talking he suddenly reached up to the bridge of his nose and grabbed hold of his glasses again, as if they were burning his nose. "You are to excuse me now. Please finish stocking and don't get the woolen socks mixed in with the cotton ones."

His shoes echoed on the hardwood floor as he hurried off. His spectacles still clenched in his right hand.

"My dad says Mr. Roosevelt is already spending too much to support England," a soft voice behind me, said.

I turned around.

Mindy reached over the counter and brushed some lint off my shirt. I jumped. Her touch jolted me like an electric current. She giggled, "you need to relax, Wilson, or you're going to hurt yourself." The sunlight was behind her. Her hair was copper flame.

"You heard us?"

"Yes, didn't think I should interrupt," she said.

"He surprises me," I said.

"How so?"

"He loves to talk about things that extend beyond the weather, cotton prices, oil prices, and baseball. Left me on my heels though - the way he talked about Poland."

"Good to know someone is paying attention Will," Mindy said. "You all are certainly more interesting than listening to my mother talk about her blue damask."

"Okay, I'm with you now," I said. "You're here to pick up fabric."

"Maybe yes, maybe no. I might also be here to interview you for the circus, can you juggle?"

"Wool socks. I'm great with wool socks," I said. "I'll check on the damask."

"Still, I think you have a future in red tights." Mindy straightened up as she said this. Her dress hitched up to her thighs. She made no attempt to straighten the skirt. I turned away and said, "I'll check the stockroom."

"Do that, Will. I'll wait right here. The lipsticks look interesting. Looks like you have the right colors. I always wear pale pink—even when I'm fishing."

I brought the damask out of the stockroom and rang the fabric up.

"Expensive stuff, mind if I ask what it's for?"

"Wallpaper—mom is going to take this lovely material and hang it in the formal dining room."

"Wow!" I blurted out.

"Crazy, isn't it? She's bringing a man all the way from Dallas to hang the stuff. Her garden club will be green with envy for a month. How much for these lipsticks?"

"The red is fifty cents. The pale pink is seventy-five cents."

"Tell me, Will. Do you think Betty will like the red?"

I considered. Betty Stevens and Mindy hung around together like the North Star and the Big Dipper. Betty's blonde features favored red lipstick. Besides, I thought, Betty was easy on the eyes when she was wearing red.

"No doubt. Red is Betty's color. You, on the other hand, should always wear the pink, goes with that stunning hair – even when you're wearing clothes."

Her cheeks colored. I'd actually surprised her. She leaned over the counter again and whispered. "Hurry, before someone comes in, kiss me hard on the mouth."

I did.

She tasted like lemons.

She let go of me and marched out the door, keeping a firm grip on the damask. When she arrived at the threshold, she said, "you're the only man, other than my dad, who has any idea about the color of my lips." She closed the door. The bell tinkled. Her taste was still on my mouth.

Word gets out in a small town. The day after Mindy picked up her mom's damask, I was closing the door to my school locker, when Louis DeWitt walked up and leaned against the locker next to mine.

"What do you want? You black hole," I said.

"What I want is to light you up, dim bulb, but today I'll settle for a short chat out on the bleachers."

As we walked out, I noticed Louis had on white flannel pants and a blue button down that was worth two months of my salary.

"Reading too much Fitzgerald again, Louis?" I sneered.

"What the hell are you talking about, you tin thug?"

I lit a cigarette as we reached the bleachers.

"Louis, I don't know why we're out here but you picked the wrong damn day to mess with me."

"Mess with you? I don't even want to be seen with you, Davis. I'm slumming because I hear you been dipping your wick where it isn't wanted."

"DeWitt, save me the effort of trying to decide whether you're smart enough to be retarded or not. What the hell are you talking about?"

"I'm talking about you doing the nasty with Mindy Hulen."

"DeWitt there are no Martians. Orson Welles made it all up. Why do you think Mindy would even give me the time of day?"

"That part is right as rain. I wouldn't have believed it either if Benny hadn't told me that you jumped her over at Smitty's. Wonder what Mr. Chaney would think of that?"

I looked around. No one else was near. We were alone. I inhaled on my cigarette to get the tip good and hot. I took it out of my mouth and before Louis could move, I burned him on the forearm with it. I clamped my free hand over his mouth to muffle his scream. I threw the cigarette away and with my other hand pushed Louis down flat onto the bleacher.

"Louis," I said, "you and I are going to have us a one-sided conversation. I don't give a shit what you do or who you do. Get this straight though you mouthy asshole, if you want to survive long enough to inherit your dad's money, you'll never mention Mindy Hulen and me together in the same sentence again–to anyone."

I let him up. He grabbed his arm and winced in pain.

"This isn't over you prick," he hissed.

"This town is mine and Mindy is mine," he said as he walked back towards the school.

"Right," I said. "Betty is yours too I suppose? By the way, don't ever try to make points off of me again in public. Call me out again like you did in Watts' and you will be eating food through a tube."

"I've warned you Davis. Scum like you and that Sullivan thug don't get it."

"Louis you really gotta be more careful around cigarettes. Hold the lit end away from yourself."

I watched him limp back into the school and then I got up off the bench and watched the sky for a moment. The wind was picking up and the temperature had dropped ten degrees. A blue norther was blowing in for sure. Time for one I thought. We were late into October. The football season was well under way. The practice field was nothing now but ruts, mud puddles and dead wet grass. Cleats ripped up a wet field in a hurry.

I laughed as I thought about my dad's favorite refrain while watching the Leopards play Paris in a 21-0 loss two weeks earlier. He'd lowered his head and said, "the damn school board. Why couldn't they find a guy like Tyson down in Waco to coach? The morons we have coaching couldn't defense a wing back option if it bit 'em in the ass. How can the boys play when they aren't prepared?"

You could change the team we played and the week, even the month; but if Gainesville was losing, my dad's refrain stayed the same.

I stuffed my hands in my coat pockets, kicking up clods of wet sod along the way, as I headed back to Mrs. Kelso's English class. "Now is the winter of my discontent," I said.

"Since you arrived late Will, I'm sure you've had extra time to study. So tell us, what is the central message of King Richard the Third?" Mrs. Kelso asked as I came through the door. Didn't even give me a chance to sit down.

I imagined DeWitt crying for a horse as I caved his face in with a mace. Richard the Third was mean and unrepentant to the end. I liked him. I sat down and answered Mrs. Kelso's question.

"Richmond kicks Richard's ass and takes the throne because Richard was a murderous cretin. Cruelty works in small doses but brains usually bring home the bacon and Richmond was smarter than Richard."

Mrs. Kelso stared at me along with the rest of the class. Finally, she spoke. "Class, Will's answer is somewhat abrupt but correct. Richard was evil. We will consider Shakespeare's general view of evil tomorrow. Will, stay after class please."

When I reported for detention, Dud was already there.

"What did you do today?" I whispered, watching Mr. Roget, my science teacher and current detention monitor nod off.

"I farted out loud in Miss Spencer's geometry class. Then I was caught smoking in the restroom when I was supposed to be visiting with the principal concerning my failure to keep my noxious bodily functions in check."

Dud rolled his eyes skyward. "Can you believe this? I'm in detention for a full school week, just for farting and smoking."

"Next time, you should split it up. You know, fart one day then smoke the next."

Dud's face ballooned up and turned bright red. Mr. Roget gave him a heavy-lidded stare before nodding off again.

"What're you here for anyway? You never get detention."

"I was late for class because DeWitt and I had a disagreement about Mindy out by the bleachers. Poor guy burned himself with his own butt," I said.

Dud stretched and said, "nothing good ever came of getting involved with society women, even by accident. Sorry I missed DeWitt getting burned with a butt."

"Don't worry. He'll mess up again and require correction again and when this happens, I'll make sure you're present for the party."

"Okay, wish I'd been there today though," Dud said. "I'd have burned him in a couple of other spots too. Damn, I'm bored out of my bucket. Think I'll wake the professor and see if he needs the erasers cleaned." Mr. Roget was so moved by his gesture, everyone got out of detention thirty minutes early.

Benny Reavis caught up with Dud and I as we were leaving detention.

"Man, you are one cool customer," he said.

"Benny, why did you open your pie hole to DeWitt about seeing Mindy talking to me in Smitty's?"

We stopped on the school's front steps.

"Hey," he said. "I can put two and two together. First, you rescue Mindy from the fishpond. She can't bear it anymore and comes running into Smitty's to horse collar you. Damn, she was a sight for sore eyes waltzing in there in that see through white number. Man, I wish I could have watched you two go at it."

He sighed, a hangdog look of regret crossing his face as he let out a long breath. "My old man came along though and kicked me in the ass for not getting all the feed sacks thrown in the back of the truck."

I sighed too. "Is everyone delusional? Does the entire school have nothing better to do than conjure up visions of me doing it with Mindy while I'm working? You shooting your mouth off got me in a snit with DeWitt today. Benny, I'm sorry, but you're going to have to take back the rumor you've spread about Mindy and me."

"Jesus, Will. Don't get pissed. I didn't mean nothing by it."

"Maybe not, but, if Mr. Chaney hears this crap, I'm done for."

I put my arm around him while Dud shuffled his feet on the steps in a manner suggesting that he had to pee in the next 10 seconds or die. "Benny, I ain't exactly Jack Armstrong, right?" I said.

Benny's brow creased in deep thought - which didn't come easy to Benny.

"Right, I think."

"Who's more important in this town - Mindy's dad or President Roosevelt?" I asked.

"Mindy's dad."

Dud picked up a garter snake and began to fiddle with the small green serpent. Benny stopped to admire it.

"What happens when her dad finds out she's sweet on a boy who plays football with the colored boys?"

Benny took the darting snake from Dud. His brow still creased in thought as he watched the snake wrap itself around his arm.

The light went on.

"Crap in a basket, Will. You might have to move away."

"Bingo, Benny. You win the door prize. Spread the word. Louis is building castles in the air."

Benny stood on one foot, then the other and said, "Huh?"

I laughed. "Start telling people that Louis should stop gossiping about the Hulens. Everyone knows that a Hulen and a Davis wouldn't socialize outside of church or school."

"I don't know Will," Dud said. "You sorta sound like Armstrong or at least the narrator. I caught *White Sultan* on the radio the other night. Jack Armstrong is a pretty cool character," Dud said.

"I like him better than *Tarzan,*" Benny said.

"Besides, I really don't know what you're upset about Will," Dud said. "I'd root through a mile of pig slop just to smell Mindy's stockings, or even the stockings of her buddy, Betty."

Dud paused, turning the image of Betty over in his head.

"Dang she's a hot number," Dud said, as he tried to feed the snake a grasshopper.

"Wow," Benny said. "Creepers jeepers Dud, would you really smell their stockings? I always wondered what those two smelled like myself."

"You two shut your pie holes. Didn't you all hear a thing I said?"

"Sure, Benny and me heard you," Dud said. "You don't want the entire town to know you want to chew on Mindy's underpants."

"Dud," I said, "have you read or even thought about anything lately that doesn't involve a bodily function or a girl's clothing?"

He looked at me like I was made of green cheese.

"Sure, I know all the swells who look down their noses at us still buy my dad's corn liquor."

Benny was trying to control himself. He thought Dud's mentioning Mindy's underwear in public was just about the funniest thing he'd heard. As we walked away leaving Benny rolling on the steps, he said, "I think I peed myself."

"I'm glad you find Dud's humor amusing Benny, even if it's a little twisted. Just remember what we've talked about," I said.

I picked up a rock off of Lindsay Street and skimmed it off of a puddle that had pooled next to a clogged sewer grate.

"Remember back in July when we had that conversation with my daddy on my front porch?" I asked.

"Damn Will, we've had a ton of conversations with your daddy on that porch."

"This one took place the night we had that run in with Louis and Rob down at Watts' fountain."

"Isn't that the night your mom got all riled and started talking about some uncle?"

"That's the one."

"What about it?"

"Remember our talking about whether we'd get involved in the war?"

"Sure we talked about the war, so what?"

"Think the Brits can hold back the Nazis?"

Dud stopped dead in his tracks and looked directly at me. "What's eating you?"

"Come on Dud, tell me what you think."

"If the Nazis are half as mean as those German farmers near Muenster then the Brits will have their hands full. All they have going for them is the water. The latest *Amazing Man* comic I read told me them Nazis can't figure a way over that Channel - the Brits kicked the Krauts' butts over the channel in June."

We turned left at the corner of California and Lindsay.

"Makes sense to me," I said. "I sure can't see bailing the Europeans out again."

"Maybe not, Will, but that Hitler fella is crazy and he is not finished by a long sight. He and that Italian fella ain't gonna quit; they've both signed a pact with the Japs."

Dud stopped to pick up a stick. He drew a circle in a muddy patch next to the walk. It had rained earlier that day and the sky held the promise of more to come.

"Look at a globe, for crying out loud. We're the only place that hasn't been invaded." He drew the United States as a distinct X.

"And England," I added. Another X was drawn by Dud to account for England.

Dud looked at me, then down at the muddy circle.

"I know people think I'm a clown and a dunce–mostly everyone but you and your dad. But even I can see where this is leading. We fight because we have to. The only question is when."

I squatted by Dud's circle, feeling like General Marshall.

"Aren't there really two questions, Dud? When will we fight? And when we do, will we win?"

Dud's face turned stony.

"The second question doesn't exist, Will. Maybe you haven't been reading the paper closely. Losing is not an option."

He threw the stick like a boomerang. The branch twirled across Lindsay and hit a lamppost.

"Remember the brown and white terrier that lived across the street?"

I didn't say anything for a minute.

"Yes," I said. "I remember the howling noise he made…even after we caught him and put the flames out. Why in God's name did you bring him up?"

"Police still can't say for sure who tied those cans to his tail and lit him," Dud replied.

"So?"

"I hear those cans late at night, Will. Dream about catching whoever did it–just before they light that awful match."

"Me too," I said.

"The Nazis are fire starters. So are the Japs. We see the match. We hear the cans...and we ... wait."

Chapter 5
Rolling Along the River

We were lying on a sand bar in the middle of a shallow, sluggish, frigid Red River. Dud and I had our fishing poles and our sleeping bags. They were Army surplus bags Mr. Chaney had given to me as a bonus for staying up all night putting together a new inventory control system for him. The trees on the riverbank shimmered with russet, gold, and burnt orange. They rustled in a breeze that couldn't be felt where we were.

Dud broke the silence. "November is the best time of the year."

"Why?" I asked.

"Comfortable out. Bugs aren't eating us. Snakes are hibernating. Air is crisp."

"Got it," I replied.

"I read an interesting article in the paper today," Dud said.

"Yeah?"

"Article said the government has increased draft quotas for the next ninety days."

I turned over on my side and looked at him closely.

"Reading the newspaper, Dud? What has gotten into you?"

"Decided to start that day you burned Louis with the cigarette and told Benny to quit flapping his yap about Mindy."

"Anything else catching your eye—other than the draft?" I asked.

"Don't know why you're worried ain't a damn thing you can do about any of it. Just wanted to let you know that I'm keeping my eye on the situation though since you're all concerned."

"Read some myself," I said. "The Brits caught a major break when the krauts couldn't pound them to powder from the air. Don't know how long the Brits can go it alone though. I don't think they can hold Gibraltar or Egypt or Libya or anywhere else in North Africa without us."

I lit a cigarette and blew a cloud of smoke away from Dud.

"Strange place to fight–North Africa," I added.

"Can I have a drag on the butt or are you getting selfish and horny in your old age?" I passed the cigarette to Dud. He too blew a cloud of smoke into the night air.

"Oil, Will. The eyeties and the krauts need oil. Can't fight a war without lots of gas," Dud said. "We have a more pressing concern than oil though."

"What's that?"

"How we're going to keep Wat Eakins from kicking our asses tomorrow over to Lindsay Park."

"Wat scares the hell outta me. I admit it," I said.

"Should," Dud said. "He's bigger than Zeus, faster than Mercury, and meaner than Conroy's old jackass Beulah, when he's playing ball."

"Got an ace in the hole though," I said.

"Yeah right," Dud snorted.

"Sure enough, Bob Sullivan agreed to come play with us."

"How in God's blue heaven did you get Bob to agree to come play ball against the colored boys?" Dud asked.

I grinned.

"Bob was pleased as punch when I told him I burned DeWitt with a cigarette. Told me he owed me one. So, I called the marker in right on the spot. He called me a pissant and asked me what time I wanted him there."

"Hot damn, Davis, you're slick. Getting Bob to play ball against the colored boys was inspired."

I put my hands under my head and shifted position.

"I can't get comfortable. I'm headed up river before I hit the hay, you coming?"

"Go on with you Davis. Get mosquito bit if you feel like it. I'll keep the fire stoked."

I took off my shoes and crossed a shoal in the river. I had to be careful. As the sun fell behind the bluffs, it became harder to spot quicksand and mud holes, damn things could suck you under in a blink.

I wanted to find a nearby overlook where an old Indian camping ground once sat. I slogged out of the shoal and wound around and over a huge pink and red sandstone outcropping. After I tramped through a thick stand of green briar and stubby mesquite, I knew I was in the right spot. The trail narrowed to something a goat wouldn't walk on. I pressed my face up against a wind blasted rock wall and said to myself, "Will, if you miss your step, you're going to drop fifty feet." I pictured myself hitting the riverbed. If I fell I hoped someone would find enough of me to bury. When I came to the end of the narrow traverse, there was a spot where erosion had etched a deep gully in the neck of land that connected the promontory overlook with the rest of the bluff. The jump was only three feet or so, but if you misjudged it you were going to fall here too.

I peered into the crevasse. I could see some stunted underbrush growing over and through the hard scrabble and boulders that had piled up over several years of intermittent gully washers at the bottom of the crevasse.

The destination was worth the journey. Once you made the jump, you had a high bluff behind you, dense brush in the form of green briar and a mesquite thicket on three sides and the river in front of and below you. Some truly fine arrowheads and even intact pottery was buried in the mix of sand and clay that had settled on the top edge of the overlook. A mountain lion lived here. We'd stared at each other across a heap of coiled briar more than once.

The last time I'd been up on the bluff, I'd noticed him thirty feet below me and to my left. His eyes glowed green. I could smell him. His yellow fangs looked sharp enough to rip the shit right out of me. If he had decided to try and climb up after me I would have been in a world of hurt. I guess he finally decided there wasn't enough meat on me to justify a romp through the briar. He snarled at me, sniffed the air and padded off in search of prey more easily acquired.

I had marked the overlook by stacking a rounded piece of rock on top of three flat stones. Didn't want to forget where the spot was. I liked knowing about a piece of the river that probably hadn't been seen by a living breathing human since the Apache and the Comanche had hunted here a hundred years ago.

I walked over and sat on the marker I had built. Except for the wind there was no noise. A couple of deer were drinking out of the river. I sat on the bluff listening for the yowl of the cat or the whispering of long dead Apache spirits. When the night became dark enough that I could no longer see light reflecting off the river, I headed back to camp. When I got back, Dud was sleeping. The fire was still going though. I crouched down and warmed my hands near the embers.

Without turning over Dud spoke.

"Any sign of the cat?"

"No yowl. No print, not even a whiff of him."

"Better luck next time."

"Guess I'll turn in. Big day tomorrow."

"If Wat hits you, you'll wish you'd got hold of the mountain lion instead."

"Thanks for the vote of confidence, Dud."

"Anytime, Will."

Next day, I was lined up on the left side of the defensive line. Bob was lined up on the right. Wat and his brother Paulie "the Pancake" Eakins were huddled up on the other side of the ball. I could tell from the way they stood that they were pissed off.

"We losing by 5 points to a bunch of no account white trash ghosts." Wat hissed to his brother.

"That don't bother me none," Pancake replied. "What bother me is that big boy there talkin' about jungle bunnies not knowing shit about football. Don't think I like being called no bunny."

"How much longer you boys going to huddle?" Dud said. "While you're huddled though, I've got a riddle for you. How many jungle bunnies does it take to screw in a light bulb?"

"Shut up, Dud," I said.

Bob stopped laughing long enough to scream, "how many?"

"I don't know but it don't matter because the bunnies don't have any electricity in their shacks anyway."

"Dud, the electricity isn't on at your house right now either," I said to him, as the colored boys broke their huddle.

"That's different," he whispered back. "My dad drank up the light bill money."

"My dad does that a lot too," Benny said, as he lined up across from the ball on my right side.

The colored boys were on our 20-yard line. This was the game. If they ran out of downs and didn't score

46

we'd win. The center snapped the ball to Pancake. Pancake turned left with the ball and began sprinting down the line with Wat sprinting behind him in the tailback slot. When Bob sliced through his block to grab hold of Pancake, Pancake pitched the ball to Wat. I was standing between Wat and the goal line. I had anticipated the play and left my end of the line early and sprinted to get in position to make the tackle. I crouched low to take Wat down around his knees and ankles.

He wasn't buying it. He knocked the crap out of me. One second I was crouched to grab him, next thing I knew, I was on my back watching pinwheels and stars, then nothing. His right knee hit me in the head as he mowed over me. Dud told me later that he never even slowed down. I didn't see the score because I'd already been knocked unconscious.

"Who won?" I wasn't sure where or who I was, but the question seemed important.

"The colored boys won by a point."

Someone threw a bucket of water on me and said, "Walk it off."

"Mama, this possum sure is ugly. I don't think we should eat him."

I was picked up and carried like a sack of potatoes.

We jounced pleasantly along for awhile.

"What on God's green earth are you doing with my son, Robert Sullivan?"

"Afternoon, Mrs. Davis. Sorry, Will here got his bell rung playing football."

"Goodness gracious, boys and football, why don't you all take up tennis or something?"

I was no longer jouncing along.

"Hey, I'm home!" I said to no one in particular.

"Welcome home, moron," Ralph hissed into my ear; at least I think it was Ralph.

"A colored boy smacked him upside the head for talking trash in a football game, Mrs. Davis." Truth was never Bob's strong suit.

"He never saw the hit coming."

"Maybe this will teach him something useful. I doubt it though. Can I get you anything to drink, Mr. Sullivan?"

"No thanks, I have to be going. Hope his noggin is okay."

I was at least aware that I was home now. Something plinked my right ear; something hit me in the back of the head. I looked around and I felt like I was trying to move under water. A sunflower seed hit me in the nose. Ralph was spitting them at me from behind the couch. I turned around in time to see Bob, hands deep in the coveralls pockets, striding down the sidewalk. He whistled *Dixie* as he strolled.

Still rooting for the wrong side you big sap, I thought.

Later that night I was lying awake staring at the ceiling in my room. A big brown water stain ran lengthwise across my ceiling. The dark stain looked like an enormous cockroach.

"I am going to die someday," I said to myself. "Don't know how or when, but sooner or later, the grim reaper will knock me upside the head like Wat had."

I shifted on the bed, so that I couldn't see the stain. Doesn't matter where you live, how you dress, or who you love. We are all brown-skinned nomads riding the desert on borrowed time, I thought.

"Hope I die somewhere other than here, looking at that stain on the ceiling," I said as I nodded off.

Two weeks after the game, I ran into Wat Eakins at Leonard Park.

"What's going on, steam train?"

He grinned and said, "baby boy, for a ghost, you're an alright ball player. You may be even better than the old West brothers."

"Right, everyone in town thinks so too. Maybe that's why they get written up in the paper every week and I get carried home over Bob Sullivan's shoulder."

"Lord, Lord you speak the truth. The paper sure do love to talk about those white boys."

I took a yo-yo out of my pocket and 'walked the dog'. Wat watched this for a minute and then took the yo-yo from me and made a triangle with the string, he then 'walked the dog into its house.'

"Damn Wat, you can work a yo-yo even better than you play football. Are you playing over here today?"

"Nah, the circus troupe is looking for some niggers to shovel elephant poop. You know, work that no self-respecting white boy would do. Pay's pretty good though. The clincher was when they saw I could fill out an application and sign my name to it. Guess there's always a place behind the elephants for a smart nigger like me."

"Wat there's a whole world waiting on a smart guy like you, nigger or not. Texas or even the South isn't the whole world."

"Come on over and teeter-totter with me, Will Davis."

We sauntered over to the playground equipment. Big ruts had been worn into the ground on either side of the red slat. Who knows how many kids had bobbed up and down on the board to wear the ground down like that? I got on my end. We bounced each other up and down. I could feel the splinters working their way through the backside of my threadbare overalls.

"I work at the best clothing store in town, I ought to get some new overalls," I said.

"If you buy new ones, give me those. I'll get some use out of 'im."

"Sure, no sweat."

"Sorry about that hit we put on you the other day. We really wanted to knock the crap out of that cracker Sullivan. Didn't count on you being so quick."

"I could tell you were tired of Bob and Dud popping off."

Wat shrugged. "Dud's alright, when he ain't with that Klan cracker."

I thought on this for a moment and said, "Wat, are you just talking or is Bob really in?"

Wat looked around to make sure we were alone, then, said, "I don't talk shit when it comes to the Klan. Never seen him in a robe or a hood, but he acts and talks like he's tight with the grand dragon. To tell the truth, we were afraid something would happen when you got hurt. Pancake and me, we laid real low until we heard you was okay."

"Wat, I didn't take it personally, and I'd never do anything to hurt you or your family."

Wat stopped the teeter-totter. We both got off.

Wat put his hands on my shoulders and said, "sometimes, baby boy, it doesn't matter what you do, only who you are."

Chapter 6
Football and Sex

Early in the morning the day after the football game at Leonard Park, the mist hung below the trees, like translucent silk. The yard was white with frost. My mother and I were on the porch snapping beans in preparation for Thanksgiving. The sun was just catching the edge of our sight line.

"How does your head feel, son?"

"I'm okay. Wat Eakins hit me hard but I made the mistake of getting in his way when he was mad at Bob."

"Learned a cheap lesson didn't you?"

"Never step in front of a moving train?"

"Something like that. Avoid getting mixed up in other peoples' hatred."

"Mom it was football."

"Maybe it was and maybe it wasn't. People can be downright mean and contrary when they get angry and Bob is one contrary cuss. Anyway, I fail to see what enjoyment you take from playing ball with the colored boys."

"They're good mom. I got Bob to play so that we wouldn't get stomped."

"The town is small son. I can't expect you to stay away from people, but you'd be smart to keep your distance from Bob and the coloreds."

I knew when to keep my mouth shut. Any response was going to dig me a deeper hole. Snapping bean pods was the only sound on the porch for several minutes.

"There's something else I want to take up with you this morning, Wilson. I know full well that you are fond of Mindy Hulen in the manner God intended men to be fond of women; that is, women they wish to procreate with."

I groaned inwardly while straining to keep my face impassive. Talking about sex with my mother ranked low on my list.

"Mom, we aren't doing anything. She comes into the store now and again. We talk."

"Wilson you're growing up. Nothing I can do about that, short of killing you outright. I'm not going to follow you around to see whom you're courting or rolling in the hay with. I couldn't keep up with your comings and goings even if I was of a mind to try."

"Okay, I like Mindy. I don't see why everyone has to bend my ear about it."

Mom put the bowl of green beans down on the porch. She then fluffed out her apron and rocked for an eternity. Finally, she turned her chair so that she faced me. She held out her hands, "see these?" She asked. Her fingers were long - elegant hands, but scarred–callused over by hard work. She picked up a gnarled, green bean pod and snapped it between her index finger and thumb. "What are these hands, Wilson?"

"They're working hands," I said.

"That's right, son," she said. "Mindy Hulen comes from money and will return to money. Her hands will never look like mine. Even if she likes you, the pressure to associate with her own kind will always be immense. Don't get hurt or humiliated by something you can't control."

She got up and walked over to the porch rail. She leaned on the weathered rail with one hand and pointed with the other. "Now, fetch me that basket of peas over there under the tree. I have some more shelling to do before it gets too late. I have to be down to the church no later than ten to help spruce it up for the Thanksgiving service. Go wake up your brother after you've brought me the peas - he's going with me to church. Tell him to scrub his head good before he shows himself."

I fetched the peas wordlessly, and then I went in to wake up Ralph. He was already awake. A huge grin spread across his face as I walked into the bedroom.

"Heard Mom bending your ears about Mindy."

I tipped his bed over.

He rolled into the wall in a mass of tangled bed covers and jumped up madder than a wet hen. I wasn't worried–too much. I had thirty five pounds and four years on Ralph. He knew I would pound him if he pulled anything.

"God bless it, Will, you're gonna wake up some night with a snake snoozing on your chest!"

I didn't much care for that. I proffered a peace pipe.

"Sorry, Ralph. I didn't mean anything. Tired of being teased about Mindy, truce?"

"Yeah, I'm sorry too."

"Okay, if you heard the conversation then you also heard that mom wants you up and scrubbed clean so you can take her to church at ten. Don't forget your ears. Mom'll check them."

Ralph rolled his eyes, "Lord Almighty, I swear mom loves Jesus twice as much as the rest of us."

He headed for the bathroom. I went back out on the porch.

"Ralph's up."

"I know, I heard. You know, boy; what Ralph said isn't so. I know Jesus - and he's close to my heart - but he's not closer than you and your brother."

She'd left dad out of her confession. I let it go. We shelled peas on the shade porch for another twenty minutes or so.

After Ralph and Mom returned from church, Ralph and I got on the roof to replace worn tiles. Dad climbed up the ladder to fix a cornice out front when he hit his thumb with the hammer and climbed down to take a look at it.

"Never was any good with tools." He shook his left hand up and down as he spoke.

"Good time for a break, Ralph," I said. "Let's climb down too. We all sat down together on the stoop to drink the lemonade my mother brought us.

Ralph looked at dad side ways and said, "dad, you worked in the oil fields, how could you be so lousy with tools?"

"I'm not out there anymore." He grinned and put his right arm around my shoulders and his left arm around Ralph. Mom peered through the porch window. "I never saw three more worthless goat heels in all my life." We looked over our shoulders at her.

Still grinning, dad said, "My God, your mother is right. We're worthless goat heels. What in the world will become of us?" We laughed for five minutes. My mom brought out some ice for my dad's hand.

"Man, oh man. Is the rain going to drop on us forever?"

"No, Ralphie…only for football games."

I pointed at the big mud pie doubling as our football field–Leeper Stadium.

"Game might be better with everyone rooting around in the mud," I said. "We'd kill Denison if we played 'em on a dry field."

We were sitting in the student section about 4 rows up on the twenty-yard line. Out on the field, West went up to catch a pass from Mercer. The pass was high.

"Why is Lester calling for a pass on such a wet field?" I said.

"Look at West! He's using his face for a mop." Ralph pointed as he spoke. West slid six feet or so before sloshing to a stop. The ball splashed down about five yards further down the field.

Dud stood up and yelled, "hey West, you'd make a great ballerina!"

West shot Dud the Italian salute while heading back to the huddle.

"West and his brother might decide they both want to kick your ass Monday morning," I said.

"You know if our coach had a brain in his head he'd figure a way to get Wat, Pancake, and some of them other nigger ball players from over to Booker T. on his team. Wat would have mangled Paris single-handedly."

"Maybe so, Dud," I said. "Still, all the muddy white guys down there could twist you like a pretzel."

Ralph laughed. "Dud, the magical, mysterious pretzel boy–the world's eighth wonder." A couple of Ralph's buddies guffawed. The Leopards punted. Denison got the ball around midfield. The rain started to come down a little harder.

I stood up. The wind gusted. A wet, soppy hot dog wrapper plastered my face. I peeled the nasty thing off my mug, wadded it up and threw it out onto the field. "Colder than an Eskimo's butt," I said.

"So much for moving game time from Saturday to Thursday. How'd that wrapper taste?" Dud said.

"Like your mom's cooking," I said. "Gonna hit the restrooms. My butt can't take the bleachers another minute." I wandered down the ramp and turned left under the seats, dodging puddles, discarded popcorn bags, and the occasional abandoned candied apple.

The wind whistled as it funneled under the bleachers. Other refugees from the bleachers were standing around in the gloomy underbelly of the stadium. I went into the restroom. Two men I didn't know were finishing up. The one guy was saying, "I'm telling you if Greenberg gets one more hit the Series goes the other way."

The other guy zipped up his pants and said, "if, *ifs* and *buts* were cherries and nuts we'd all have a Merry

Christmas, Jack. Derringer toasted the Tigers' oats in game seven and that my friend is that."

They nodded to me as they went out. The men's room stank. I urinated and then washed my hands at the cracked basin. Only the cold water tap worked.

"Wonder if the woman's room smells any better," I said to myself.

I had a brand new pack of Chesterfields in my shirt pocket. As, I walked out of the men's room, I unwrapped the pack and tapped it against a steel support girder. The crowd roared. The roar was coming from the far side of the field - not a good sign for our local heroes. As it turned out later, Denison had just run the ball for 28 yards - their only decent play the entire game. I gazed through the chain mesh fence at the parking lot. Rain was still dropping. Something caught my eye. I didn't know if movement or color or both attracted my attention. I stuffed the Chesterfields back into my shirt pocket and decided to take a closer look at the parking lot.

The lot was poorly lit. Had to watch my footing. I heard them before I saw them. Bob Sullivan and Betty Stevens were standing close together next to Betty's car. Betty was talking. "I don't care if we do it out here," she said. "But, I don't want to get my panties wet."

Bob spoke. "Here give 'em to me Bet, I'll put them in the car."

There was the sound of a car door opening and closing.

"Hurry, Bobby. I'll be missed if I don't get back soon."

The right thing to do, I thought, would be to turn around and walk away. So, I crept forward. I heard labored breathing. I peeked around the back end of a black Lincoln Zephyr. Bob's hands were on her shoulders. They were leaning against Betty's red Mercury. The red coupe was parked in front of the Zephyr.

Bob spoke, "you sure about this Betts? Cold as hell out here and someone might see us."

Betty got up on her toes and kissed him.
"Yes, I'm sure. We can't do it in the car. Mom gets in after I've driven it and sniffs around for cigarette smoke, beer, or you know–man stuff. She'd spot any kind of stain. Besides, look around, do you see anyone? No one's coming out here in this mess."

She turned slowly, lifting her pleated skirt over her hips. Even in the wind and rain, her moves were tawny, seductive. Bob unzipped. Betty braced herself against the fender of her car as Bob entered her from behind.
She gasped, and said, "push - hard."

That big red Mercury moved as Bob and Betty found their rhythm. I'd seen enough. No good could come from my remaining. I headed back to the stadium. Approaching the turnstiles, I saw Mindy and Angela Culpepper looking out in my direction.
Mindy said, "hi, Will."
Angela smiled and said, "hey, Will Davis."
I bowed deeply and said, "ladies, I'm at your service."
"Good. Maybe you can tell us if you know where Betty went off to. She said she was going to the restroom but she's not there. We're getting a little worried."
I looked right into Mindy's eyes and lied. "Yeah I saw her about ten minutes ago. She was headed over to the other side of the field to meet the Denison cheerleaders. Said she'd meet up with you all after the game at Hicks' place."
"Thanks, Will." She pecked me on the cheek. Angela surprised me by kissing me on the cheek as well. They turned and walked off. I decided to wait Bob and Betty out. I needed to let Betty know she was missed. I lit up the cigarette I'd meant to smoke earlier. Ten minutes or so passed. I fidgeted, pacing back and forth

on the cratered, pocked concrete. If they didn't show soon, Mindy and Angela would be back or Dud and Ralph would come looking for me.

Suddenly, I saw them. They were approaching the stadium from different spots in the lot. Betty got back to the gate first. I didn't make eye contact with her, kept my eyes on Bob as I spoke.

"Mindy and Angela are looking for you. They left for the visitor's side of the field about ten minutes ago. I told them you went over there to talk with the girls on the Denison cheerleader squad."

I took a quick glance at her. She looked dazed, like a deer that's been shot. Bob strode up, menace flashed in his eyes.

Betty said quietly, "everything's okay, Bobby. Will has done me a favor."

I gave my handkerchief to Bob.

"Betty," I said. "Be sure to fix your lipstick before you meet up with them at Hick's - it's a little smudged."

Bob's face was also smeared bright red. Bob didn't say a word. He stood his ground, swaying slightly. Betty took the handkerchief and began to wipe his right cheek off.

Finally, he said, "alright Betty that's enough. People are gonna see this and start asking questions. I can get the rest. Go on now. Don't keep your friends waiting."

She turned and walked into the gloom under the bleachers. I hoped she had remembered to put her panties back on. I sure as hell wasn't going to ask. I handed Bob a cigarette. He put it into his mouth. He pulled his Zippo out of his battered, scuffed jacket and cupped the lighter's flame in the palms of his hands.

"What did you see Davis?" He asked.

"Enough to get you ran out of town or thrown in jail - if I was a rat."

He blew out a cloud of smoke and absently played with the zipper of his leather jacket. "You aren't a rat, though are you, Davis?"

"Not even close Bob, not even close."

Bob leaned up against a girder and took another drag on his smoke. He looked around to see if anyone else was nearby. When he was satisfied no one was; he squatted down and stared out into space.

"I love her more than I loved my mother, Will - I have no idea what I'm going to do about that."

This was the first time he'd ever used my first name.

"Guess you'll do whatever she wants…that's how it works, isn't it?"

"I couldn't resist her. Knew we were doing something stupid, did it anyway."

"Bob, my right palm is the only thing I've ever had sex with," I said. "So, take this for what its worth, you're going to continue to love her and let all the related crap take care of itself. Could end badly for you. Look at Romeo and Juliet."

"Davis, I wonder about you sometimes. No one else I know would mistake Betty and me for characters in a play, especially one where the men wear tights. Don't let too many people know you have brains. People won't like you anymore."

"All I'm saying Bob is that things don't always take care of themselves."

"Right. *Things* probably will go south with Betty. I don't give a crap. My mom's been dead for five years. Not one soul on this planet has cared whether I lived or died since she left. I have no choice here. I'm holding onto her if she'll let me."

He snubbed his cigarette butt out. He got up out of his crouch.

"I won't forget this Davis." He walked off into the gloom. I climbed back up into the stands.

Chapter 7
Physics

The Professor was on a roll. Half my physical science class was asleep and the other half was stupefied–convinced time had halted. Professor Roget, my science instructor, chose the last class before Christmas break to extol the genius of a scientist in Leipzig, Germany and another scientist at Princeton who disagreed with him.

"Now my young friends consider this."

The Professor rolled the chalk between his hands as he warmed up his lecture topic. "Newton was the most elegant thinker of his day," Mr. Roget said. "He provided us with the answer to the question I am about to pose."

Mr. Roget put the chalk down and took a string out of his pocket. A small rock was tied to one end of the string. He stepped around the front of his desk and began to swing the rock around his head. He kept swinging until the string and the rock was merely a blur. The front row kids kept their heads down. We all thought he had gone completely nuts. Mr. Roget finally stopped the rock and placed it on his desk.

"Take note. The rock didn't hit me. There is a reason why. Over the holidays, write down your thoughts about what you observed." I groaned along with everybody else in class.

"Turning in a blank sheet is not acceptable, even though in some cases, this probably is honest."

He turned and picked up the chalk. The elbows of his tweed jacket were white with chalk. I also thought he had chalk on his pants, until I realized I was looking at a sliver of his skivvies poking through the seam. Some of my classmates were sniggering at him out loud, some quietly behind cupped hands. I scribbled him a note saying his pants were dead and suggested he come down and see me at Smyth & Marks. Said that I could put him in a brand spanking new tweed suit for less than 10 bucks. I slipped the note into his grade book after class.

"I will give you all a clue. The basic Newtonian formula for the rock's behavior is $F=MA$." He wrote this on the board.

"As you contemplate this formula, be prepared to discuss what effect, if any, Professor Einstein's work has on Newton's laws. I will be grading you on creativity and participation not accuracy. Happy Holidays, Ladies and Gentlemen."

"Happy Holidays, my butt," Benny Reavis said. "Was he speaking English or what? I didn't understand one second out of the last ten minutes of his class."

"Damn, Benny," I said. "You should be happy. That was the Professor's *final* class of the semester!"

Benny shook his head while we walked through a swirl of paper left in the hallway. Lockers clanged shut all around as my classmates abandoned the school for the rest of 1940.

"Gonna get anything for Christmas, Benny?" I asked.

"You bet. A 24 carat hard time from my old man—gift wrapped inside a knuckle sandwich. He's probably getting good and drunk right now, just so he'll be ready to participate in all of our planned festivities."

"Head home with me if you want Benny. My mom won't care."

"Won't help. If I don't go home, my old man'll just take his frustration out on my mom. Thanks, though. I'll drop by in a day or so; once my dad conks out and sleeps off his holiday bender."

I had time on my hands. Dud had already left for Sulfur Springs. I was working over the holidays. Mr. Chaney had asked me to keep an eye on the prices at Levines and at Bomars over the break. I thought I'd go ahead and look at prices while shopping for mom.

The night was going to be cold and clear. The night before, Thursday, had been foggy. The fog had been like wet cotton candy and so thick it hadn't burned off until 11 this morning. The weather felt like snow now. I wrapped my muffler around my mouth and nose and pulled my cap more firmly down onto my head.

As I walked along I saw something glinting in the late afternoon sun. Light was reflecting off two Royal Crown Cola bottles lying in the grass next to the walk. Had to be rich kids. No self-respecting poor kid would throw a dime away. Those beauties were worth a nickel apiece.

I ran them up to Thrashers Grocery and collected my two nickels; then I headed over to Hicks' restaurant before I went shopping. Hicks' was a great place, a pure grease pit. You could smell it, especially on a cold day for several blocks in every direction. Gravel crunched under my shoes as I waltzed through a parking lot laced with water-filled potholes. These would be iced over as evening came on. Hicks' was crowded with kids and with farmers and ranchers, who'd been working since four in the morning and were ready for coffee and conversation.

I wedged myself into a booth with Dave Mercer, Louise Balgruder, Elmer Graf and Ruthie Svensen. They accepted my company with grudging grace. I ordered three hamburgers, and then looked across at Dave.

"Tough loss to Paris, Dave, but you all rebounded against Arlington Heights and Denison."

"Like you care Davis. Save the hair oil for some other sucker. I saw you in the stands with that rat turd Dud Ludlow."

"Honest Injun, Dave," I said. "I can't control Dud's mouth. I told him to stop the guff about you all looking like ballerinas."

"Tell Ludlow that anytime he wants to come out for the team, I'll put a word in for him with the coach. We need tackling dummies real bad."

Elmer looked over at me. He was a big kid. He could toss 75 - pound hay bales around like feathers. He put his huge mitts on the table and pushed himself around to eyeball me.

"Davis, you related to Elvis Davis?"

I fought the urge to bolt and kept the expression on my face neutral.

"I don't know, Elmer," I said. "I have lots of cousins. Let's see there's Alvin...Emory, and ... don't recall an Elvis."

"I know Alvin," Elmer said. "No offense, but he's a polecat too. My daddy is short about thirty chickens out to our place on 82. Seems an old boy named Elvis Davis has been trying to sell some hens to a butcher over to Saint Jo."

My stomach turned. Couldn't even eat a burger in peace without hearing something negative about some member of my extended family. I listened. *Ezekiel Saw de Wheel* was playing on a radio somewhere. Christmas lights ringed the restaurant windows, giving off a cheery glow.

"Elmer, I swear I know nothing about any hens or roosters. If I hear anything at all, I will turn the information over to Officer Reilly or Sheriff Williams."

Elmer eyed me for a moment and said, "okay, Davis. You ain't a polecat like some of your cousins. Now what's this about you and Mindy Hulen?"

I wished a host of angels would carry me off ... I lost my appetite.

Chapter 8
Holiday Cheer and Bone White China

"Wendell Wilkie understands this country. I can't believe this county went 3 to 1 for that nefarious Roosevelt. The man is becoming a menace to a free society."

"Well, sir, I understand your concern, but you'd still better ante up if you want to see my hand."

Chester Harris eyed my dad through the blue haze created by his Havana short. "Damn it Davis, I'm the only bank president in this town. As such, I think I am entitled to know what you're holding."

"Chesty, it'll cost you ten bucks to call and another five to raise me, even if you're God."

"Alright, by damn, we'll see what kind of metal you're made of, I call." Fifty dollars lay in the pot. Dad and the offended bank president were the last two players in the hand.

"Full-House, Ace high."

The banker threw his cards onto the table and said, "no one is that lucky. These cards are marked."

My dad stood up. Sheriff Williams said, "take it easy Mason. He's had too much to drink, and so have you. Everyone here, including Chesty, knows the deck is new."

"Chesty, seeing as how you're a Republican and, therefore, feeling some pain right now; here's my contribution to your Christmas fund." My dad wafted five dollars back across the table at Harris.

Harris grew red-faced and began to sputter, "why you…"

"Careful, Chesty, my son has come to take me home - and it is Christmas Eve. Merry Christmas to all and to all a goodnight. Son, please retrieve our winnings from the table."

With that, my dad did an about-face, then pitched and yawed through the salon door of the Turner Hotel. I watched him go. 'Jeez Louise, I thought, I hope he's headed home.'

"Boy, get the money and get out of here. What kind of family allows a boy to be out at eleven in the evening on Christmas Eve?"

I gathered the cash and looked at President Harris. "Sir, I guess we're a family who cares about where their dad is. Ralph and I do. I 'm the eldest, so here I am." I looked around.

"Where's your son?"

Laughter erupted from the card players.

Mr. Hunter spoke. "You got him, son, but I recommend getting away now while you're still ahead."

"Yes sir. I reckon so."

I left slowly, stuffing crumpled bills into my pockets. I heard the remaining men discussing whether to play another hand before retiring to their respective homes.

"Young Davis!"

I turned. Harris was beckoning me. I returned to the table. The other men stared at Harris. Harris spread his arms wide and, then, said, "look, I'm sorry I was short with you. I have a proposition."

"Yes sir?"

"I'm wondering whether you're as lucky as your old man."

I waited for an explanation.

Lars Regelschorn, a local dairyman interceded. He was one of Chester Harris' largest banking clients. "Chesty whatever you're up to, I warn you, it can't come out well. Need I remind you again that you're drunk, and that Will here is a young man. I'll not stand by and watch him be taken advantage of."

Sheriff Williams nodded in agreement.

"Oh come now. I'm not taking advantage. I merely want to see if Will wants to make a little extra Christmas money."

"Wouldn't be smart to gamble with my dad's money, sir."

"Nonsense boy. Your dad trusts you. Here's my proposition. I will go double or nothing with you for the money in your pocket. If you lose, I'll personally write your father a note explaining the circumstances and I will extend a $45.00 line of credit to your family at Thrashers grocery over my signature."

"Don't, son," Mr. Regelschorn spoke to me. "You're old enough to make your own decision, but I don't want to see you take a licking on Christmas if you lose."

"I agree. Walk away, Will." A voice behind me spoke out of the darkness. I jumped.

Mr. Hulen was sitting in a dark corner, an invisible observer. He must have sat the last hand out; I could see only the lit tip of his cigar.

"Chesty here got his feelings hurt. You don't need to give him any reason to feel better," Mr. Hulen said.

"Leave the boy alone. He knows his own mind."

"Yes, I do sir. I accept your proposition."

"Good man!" Bellowed Chesty. "I like a boy with spunk. I'll let you decide who shuffles."

I pointed to Mr. Regelschorn. He picked up the deck and rapidly shuffled the cards. He placed the shuffled deck in the center of the green felt. I tapped the deck and pointed to Mr. Harris. He tapped the deck as well. Mr. Hulen drew his chair up to the table to view the outcome. Mr. Harris offered me first draw. I declined. He picked up the upper half of the deck and turned over the exposed card–a Jack.

"Tough to beat, Will," Mr. Hulen murmured.

Mr. Regelschorn reshuffled the deck. President Harris cut the deck. I picked up the upper half of the deck and turned over the exposed card–an Ace.

No one spoke.

Chesty Harris looked at me and said, "may I write you a check?"

"I'll pay Will in cash, Chesty," Mr. Hulen said. "You can write me a check."

He took out his wallet and handed me two twenties and two fives. He looked at me and whispered, "better get on home, Will. I'll tell Mindy you said 'hey'."

I took the money and left the salon. I knew Harris' card playing well enough to know that he would slip himself a face card. Figured he would try for the jack or the queen so as to leave me some chance. What I hadn't counted on was Mr. Regelschorn discreetly marking the Ace for my benefit.

Harris isn't going to forgive or forget this evening. I thought. Won't occur to him when he's sober that he had no one to blame but himself either. He'll come after my dad and me.

"Let me skip church this morning mom".
"Christmas celebrates the Lord's virgin birth."
"I'll start Christmas dinner, it'll save time."

Mom pursed her lips and tapped her shoe on the floor. I had learned to cook to get on her good side. On several occasions I had been allowed to leave church after Sunday school by promising to get Sunday dinner ready. The first time she'd allowed me to leave church early, she had warned me that if peanut butter and jelly sandwiches were on the table, she'd switch me right on into Monday. When she came home and found a warm, baked ham on the table and an apple pie on the sideboard, an unspoken agreement was reached–I could cook–rather than pray.

"Cooking is not natural for a boy, especially one of your age and temperament. I've never seen the like of it. Satan is behind this offer."

She waited.

"Thank Lucinda Piper, Mom - not Satan."

"Lucinda Piper? How do you know her?"

"She's Wat Eakins' Aunt. On his mother's side," I added.

"She gives me recipes when she comes into Smittys on colored night."

"Isn't she the night cook over at the Turner?"

"Yes ma'am, she is," I answered.

"That explains your skill in the kitchen. She's been teaching you how to cook while you wait for Mason, hasn't she?"

"Was a fair trade mom. She taught me how to use a real stove and I did the room service dishes and mopped floors."

"Will, I've told you to stay away from colored folks. You do us no good befriending coloreds."

"Mom," I said quietly. "We believe in Jesus, a Jew, as the savior. Still, people hate Jews. A black woman has taught me how to cook on a stove. You telling me we'll be hurt by having these people as friends?"

"Never said hating coloreds or Jews was right. If you want to live here though, a certain...distance is required."

"Mom, a lot of people in town think Mr. Chaney is a dirty Christ killing Jew. How much distance should I keep?"

"Everyone needs someone to look down on son," mom said, as she reached into the sideboard. She pulled the good china out. Only mom was allowed to touch the china. The bone was so fine that the rims of the plates were translucent. Everyone was afraid to eat off of them for fear of breaking the edges.

"You, boy, are taking life lessons from two people who belong to races the lowest of the low love to spit upon. Stay home. Cook dinner. I'll set the table when I get home."

I heard her yell for dad and Ralph. The front door slammed. I pulled the Christmas goose out of the oven. There was a lot of hot grease in the bottom of the roasting pan. I was careful about taking the goose out of the pan, so as not to splash any on myself. After checking the goose I went down to the cellar to grab some berry preserves. When I got back to the kitchen, mom was pounding the daylights out of the potatoes with a masher. She threw a half-cup of butter into the big clay crockery bowl with the spuds.

"Mom, what're you doing?"

"Mashing potatoes."

"No, you know what I mean."

"Do your dad and Ralph good to attend church without me. I wanted to finish with you."

"What're we finishing?"

"You thinking I'm a hateful woman."

"I don't mom. I just don't see a thing wrong with Lucinda or Mr. Chaney."

"There is nothing wrong with them Will, that's my point. I can't help that the coloreds and the Jews are mashed together into a big lump, sort of like I'm trying to do with these potatoes. Lucinda teaching you how to cook doesn't matter. What matters is being seen in her company, and treating her as an equal."

"What about Mr. Chaney?"

Mom poured the mashed potatoes into a serving bowl and said, "Like you mentioned earlier, he's tainted…a killer of Christ. His good works will not alter who he is, son. We're not talking about Gainesville alone here. Go to New York or Boston or Atlanta - same story."

Discretion being the better part of valor, I kept my mouth shut in response. We finished cooking Christmas dinner in silence.

Chapter 9
Between Us Girls

"Bett, this is nuts."

"I know, Mindy."

"Then tell me why we're here."

"Because, we can talk here and not be overheard."

"Maybe but we might be seen and that could be as bad," Mindy said. "I can see the look on my dad's face if he hears from some old goat, 'Walt, saw your daughter out on the river yesterday.' 'That so, Ed? What was she doing?'

'Walt, funny thing. She was standing buck naked on a shoal of the river netting minnows with another naked girl. But, she had her waders on; January is cold on the river after all.'"

Betty laughed hard and dropped her end of the net.

"Don't fall into the river," Mindy said. Betty wobbled on the rocks. Mindy grabbed her arm at the last second.

"Thanks Mindy. Don't ever mimic your Dad again while we're standing like this in the middle of the river."

"Bett, I swear," Mindy said. "You're so clumsy, and that water looks cold."

Betty and Mindy got the net untangled and threw it back into the current.

Betty giggled.

"What?" Mindy asked.

"Remember the time Wilson Pickett Davis sat up on that bluff yonder and watched us for a good hour. He must have smoked an entire pack of butts."

"Smoking butts while watching butts," Mindy replied. "He knew that we knew he was there; made enough noise to wake the dead. Would have left if he thought he was truly spying. Anyway, he knows how to keep his mouth shut. Never told a soul about seeing us out here in our birthday suits."

"You know, Mindy, he's loved you for a long time. He loved you long before he saw you naked."

"Are you suggesting someone has to see you naked before they can love you?"

"No," Betty giggled. "But, it doesn't hurt."

"Louis has seen you naked. Does he love you? Bobby Sullivan has seen you naked. Does he love you?"

The minnows in the net caught the sunlight and glinted red, gold, and violet in the midst of their thrashing.

"Jesus, Mindy!"

"When are you going to spill the beans, Bett?"

"You can tell already?"

"I can. Doubt anyone else will notice for awhile yet. Who is it? Louis or Bobby?"

Having secured the catch, the girls folded up the net, pulled off their waders and stretched out on some warm rocks.

"Amazing isn't it? I mean that the weather is so warm in January."

Betty finally answered.

"You know who the father is already."

"Do I?"

"If you don't, Mindy, than you don't know me very well after all."

"Your parents will be thunderstruck when you walk through the door some evening with Bob in tow."

Betty let her breath out in a long sigh.

"Can't change what my parents think. Don't care to try. They're in love with DeWitt money." Betty turned onto her stomach and moved closer.

"Problem is; I can't stand Louis. He's so…infantile. Mindy - he couldn't even get hard the one time I let him …play around with me… he was awful. I had to spank him and whisper, 'mommy still loves you'."

Mindy's jaw dropped. "You're kidding."

"Wish I was. I certainly wasn't playing Olivia de Havilland to his Errol Flynn."

Betty leaned back and gazed at a hawk that dropped down onto the river in the middle distance.

"He started by rubbing his thing on the bottom of my feet," she said. "Can you imagine? I wanted to stop right then. We were in his car, out toward Pilot Point, I think. So there was nowhere to run. He cried when I pulled my feet away. What he'd done was so awful, took me a second to realize what he was doing."

"Bett, you don't have to tell me this. I didn't mean to pry when I asked who it was. I was being nosy."

Tears ran down Betty's cheeks.

"If I don't tell you who can I tell? My situation isn't even helped by the fact that I got myself into this, because this is something you can't get out of on your own. When the other kids find out, everyone will call me a whore. I'll be finished in my own home town."

Mindy reached over and hugged her.

"It'll be okay, Betts." Come on. Let's get dressed. Anyone happening along this inlet now is going to be treated to the sight of two naked girls on a rock embracing. Betty's face turned beet red as she pulled away and wiped her face with her T-shirt before putting it on.

"Louis scared the tar out of me Mindy. I had never tried to go all the way with a guy before and the first time I decide to give it a whirl the guy I pick is rubbing my feet with his thing and bawling. Finally, he stops crying and asks me to spank him for behaving so badly."

Betty grabbed her panties and her shorts. Then, dug around until she pulled a battered pack of cigarettes and a box of matches out of the back pocket of her shorts. She offered Mindy a battered cigarette. Mindy waved it off. Betty hiked her panties on over the curve in her hips, lit up the smoke and inhaled deeply.

"Better," she said. "I would have done anything to get him to agree to take me home. Finally, I told him that I'd whack his fanny for him just this once. I also told him that I never wanted to be alone with him again. He agreed."

Betty took another drag off the cigarette and splashed her feet in the river.

"I was put out with him. So, I whaled him. Went on for a full minute. Seemed like damn near forever. He was moaning to wake the dead. Kept saying, "sorry, mommy" the whole time I was whacking his ass. Finally, he kind of jerked and flopped around. I felt something warm and sticky spreading over my thighs. The rat turd made a mess on the car seat and me. Thankfully, the car was his–but," she held up her right index finger and waggled it, "his stuff never got near my patch…not even close. Doesn't matter. Wouldn't marry Louis if he were the daddy. "

The girls dressed in silence. When they had gathered up the minnow bucket and net, Betty said, "when I let Bobby screw me, he thought I was using him, maybe I was. I know how that feels after spending time with Louis. Once the fact that I'm pregnant is out - and it will get out - everyone will think its Louis. Louis knows its Bobby, but will say it's his baby."

"How will Louis know its Bobby?"

"I told him."

"Oh Lord, Betty! That was a big mistake."

"Maybe, but he's being quiet for the moment because he thinks this puts me and Bobby under his thumb. I want him thinking he's got us where he wants us until I get this all figured out."

Betty's plan worked - for about a week. Then, Louise Balgruder cornered Mindy in the girl's locker room.

She sat down beside her on a gym bench and whispered in a smug confidential tone, "Mindy, I've heard something but I can't believe it."

"Believe what?"

She hissed, "Betty has a hot cross bun baking in the oven."

"Keep your voice down, here comes Miss. Pritchard."

"Okay, Mindy, but let's talk soon."

"Balgruder, you're such a snoop," Mindy said.

"Okay, I'll put a sock in it. Still, I don't know what would be worse to be ... you know, or to have tuberculosis like Jane's brother."

"What's the matter?" Mindy said. "Can't even say the word pregnant without turning red and giggling? You're eager enough though to hear about someone else's misery."

"Ladies get a move on, the locker room is not a social club and you two are already late for your next class." Miss Pritchard towered over the girls.

"Yes, Miss. Pritchard," Louise and Mindy said at the same time.

The PE teacher slammed a couple of open locker doors shut to emphasize her point and headed back into her office. Mindy stepped into her skirt. Louise zipped for her.

Mindy whispered, "Miss Pritchard was staring at your breasts Louise. Better get your brassiere on a little faster next time."

Louise gasped. "Really! Oh Mindy, don't even joke about something that awful."

"Could have been worse Louise. I mean what if we had still been in the shower. I understand coal black really gets her going."

Louise's' hands shot down between her legs.

"Oh God Mindy, I'm going straight home and shave."

Mindy fought the urge to burst out laughing. Good old Louise was as gullible as they came. She was so concerned about her own thatch she forgot to ask who'd been poking around in Betty's.

"I hope Louis makes an honest woman out of her."

"An honest woman Janet?" Mindy turned toward Janet on her stool. The group of girls having sodas at Watts grew quiet.

"Mindy, don't be coy. You're her friend, but you've got to admit she wouldn't have her little problem if she'd kept her legs closed."

"I agree Janet," Mindy said. "She should've used your method." Several people gasped. Ray Watts stopped mixing a seltzer in mid-stir.

"Whatever are you talking about?" Janet said. "I'm a virgin."

"Maybe so Janet but word has gotten around that you suck on more than soda with those lips of yours." Mindy watched as Janet's face went red up to the roots of her hair.

Mindy dumped her coke on Janet's head.

"Have my coke too Janet, extra syrup. It'll cool you off." As Janet sputtered and people around the two gasped, Mindy whispered, "Betty isn't the only girl with a soiled reputation, Janet. Word's out that you can suck the chrome off a bumper and I'm not talking about a Buick." Mindy turned and left Watts before Janet could react.

Mindy's dad was waiting when she got home.

"Mindy, wait in the study," he said. "Your mother and I want to speak with you."

Mindy's feet sank into the carpet as she walked across the room to 'her' chair. The carpet in the study was a rich forest green. The walls were lined with books, all of which her dad had read. As she waited for her parents to make their grand entrance, she studied the book jackets on the study's shelves.

Her eyes locked onto two books. The first was *An Inquiry into the Nature and Causes of the Wealth of Nations* by Adam Smith. The second was *Ulysses* by James Joyce. She was surprised. She recalled that Miss Lundy had called this particular book a filthy rag. "Hmmm, didn't tell us what made it so filthy though." Mindy read the book a few years later and concluded that Miss Lundy simply didn't understand Joyce's message, regarding things like nationalism, religion, class structure, and the intensity of human sexuality–all crammed into one day in Dublin.

Of course, Mindy read the book after the war. Joyce was pretty thin soup by then. Depictions of someone simultaneously pissing and menstruating into a chamber pot after you've stood ankle deep in the blood of a twenty year old with his intestines hanging out, screaming for his mother is banal. However, sitting that day in her dad's study, she was struck only by the notion that her father was an educated man. She hadn't any notion as to why this surprised her. He was an accountant and a lawyer. She reckoned she hadn't ever taken any time to picture him as a man who read for enrichment or pleasure.

Mindy's mother and father were not going to discuss the merits of literature on this day though. Her mother came into the study and sat in an easy chair positioned to her right. Her dad decided to lean on the corner of his desk and fiddle with a glass paperweight.

"Mindy, we try to stay out of your day-to-day affairs unless it appears your grades are deficient or your health is suffering, but we aren't going to continue ignoring your friendship with Betty."

Mindy gathered her skirt and repositioned herself in the wing chair. This was going to be a long go, she thought. She was now sitting face-to-face with her concerned mother. Her loafers and the toes of her mom's heels nearly met on the carpet. I wished I had the heels on, she thought. Mindy imagined clicking them three times and being whisked away.

Her dad spoke after her mom fell silent.
"We are well aware that you are not Betty and that her… hmm…pregnancy is not your problem."
"Then, why are we having this conversation?"
"Because, Wilhelmeana Rose," her mom said. "There is such a thing as guilt by association." Her mother came forward in her chair. The color in her cheeks was high. Her blue eyes were spitting sparks. "Your name is often mentioned in the same breath as hers. There is also talk about you and that no-account Davis boy. I will not tolerate this family's name being mentioned in the same breath as a slut and the son of a drunken card shark."
She sat back in her chair, crossing her arms as if this closed the matter.
"Elaine, we agreed we wouldn't base our concerns upon bridge club gossip."
"Walt, don't patronize me. You're already taking Mindy's side in this! This can ruin us, like the poor Stevens's."
"Dearest, this is not about sides and while I agree the Stevens's are both worried and heartbroken in roughly equal measure, I don't think they are ruined. Life goes on."

Mindy's dad stared out the window for a moment while he shifted the paperweight back and forth in his hands. He suddenly stopped and turned to Mindy.

"Your mom is upset by what happened to Betty, with good reason," he said. "Honey, we thank our lucky stars that this happened to Betty and not to you."

Mindy felt ire rise in her throat like molten lead. She leaned forward to respond.

Her dad held up his hand. He put the paperweight down.

"I'm implying nothing." He glanced at her mother and said, "we trust you."

Mindy's mom slowly nodded her agreement. Too slowly Mindy thought.

"Your mother is correct on our main point though. Your name is being linked with increasing frequency with both young Davis and of course Betty."

"So?" Mindy said. "This is a small town. Are you going to chain me up in my room and feed me through a slot in the door?"

"Don't be fresh young lady!"

"I hadn't thought of that," Walt Hulen said. He squatted down in front of his daughter. "I like young Davis. He's got some mettle. See him if you want to, but I won't tolerate any foolishness - from either of you. You're headed for a good school in the fall. Davis, unless he's lucky, is headed nowhere. His life is not fair, but that's tough. Don't force my hand on this. I'll send you away if I need to, to stop him from seeing you."

Mindy listened to the mantel clock ticking over the hearth. She thought back to the first time she could recall hearing it. She'd been six or seven at the time. Her dad had brought her into the study because her mom had caught her jumping off the roof of the house into some snowdrifts.

Her parents were still watching her. Seemed like hours had passed. She was fixed in place, so were her parents, like everyone was waiting for a cut sign from a director so that they could all move off of their marks. Mindy watched the sunlight play through the wooden shutters.

"I love you both dearly," Mindy said. "Always have and always will. I'm your daughter. I owe both of you everything but don't interfere with me where Will Davis is concerned. I'll walk out the front door and never sleep under this roof again, if you all interfere. I have the money Memaw left me and I will use it. I've done nothing to be ashamed of and do not intend to."

My mother rose, saying, "young lady…"

Mindy stood. "Enough, mother. Glass houses, beware of glass houses."

She sat down as if Mindy had struck her.

"Father, may I please be excused?" Mindy asked.

"Yes, Mindy you may," he said, as he packed his pipe.

As Mindy walked out, he spoke with his back to her so that she had to strain to hear. "Careful honey, sometimes there are simply no snowdrifts there, no drifts at all."

Chapter 10
A Walk in the Park

Bob's old man, Liam Sullivan, was a woman-hating drunk. Consequently, Bob didn't really understand women. Liam's only pronouncement concerning women, usually uttered when he was drunk, was "son, why do men die before their women do?"

Bob would answer, "I don't know pop, why do the men die first?"

Liam would laugh, slap his knee, and say, "because they want to."

Liam got his wish. He died ten years before Bob's mom. Did his fair share of damage before he left though. Bob's mom was left with a stack of debts and five hungry mouths to feed. She died of fatigue. Worked six days a week, 12 hours a day in a commercial laundry, washing and ironing hotel sheets to keep five kids alive.

Bob supposed she was better off. He often wondered how she had gone to work everyday knowing her job was washing pecker tracks off of sheets for carpetbaggers like Louis DeWitt. God rest her soul. She had lived long enough to make sure her kids got through school and found useful trades.

Bob was a mechanic. He had a talent for fixing machines, especially engines. Even the foreman, whose head he'd busted over in Denison, had grudgingly admitted that Bob could build a donk out of rusting blocks, shafts, and bolts. So, Bob was doing okay in Gainesville. He'd gotten himself a good job in the rail yard, wiping down trains and doing general maintenance for the yard boss. He was keeping his nose clean and his head down. Then, he'd met this blonde bombshell and within a month, his life was down the toilet.

"Hey you, know where Steve Walker is?"

He had turned around and saw this blonde girl leaning over the station railing eyeballing him. He forgot how pissed he was about being interrupted while trying to bust loose a rusted flange from a barrel shaft.

"Yes ma'am," he'd said. "Mr. Walker is the boss and right now, he's over at the freight office. Walk down that ramp and make a left and you'll see the door. He should be in there signing freight manifests."

He'd felt like a New Deal politician. Couldn't keep his mouth shut. If she'd asked, Bob thought, I'd have given her my wallet too … and thanked her for taking it.

"What's your name, mister?"

"Bob, Bob Sullivan."

"Thanks, Bobby. I'll tell Mr. Walker that you were most helpful. Bye now."

She turned to walk away but she wasn't really walking. She was gliding. Her hips swayed left-to-right, right-to-left and she wasn't even wearing heels. Heat had rolled off of Bob in slow sweaty waves. Suddenly, she had turned and smiled right at him. Her grin was large and humorous. "Steady Bobby," she'd said. "I never knew banging on a pipe could be so…exciting. Looks like more fun than walking in the park barefoot."

Bob had taken a red bandana out of his back pocket and mopped his face as she had sashayed on into the freight office. He'd stuffed the bandana back into his overalls and tried putting Blondie out of his mind. Wouldn't do to have a big woody knocking around in your overalls if the boss paid you a visit, he'd thought, as he banged away at the flange.

Chapter 11
Bob Meets his Match

By the time Davis had *ran* into Bob and Betty at the football game, Betty had already hit Bob like a meteor hits the atmosphere. She had come back to the yard as Bob was getting off work a few days after he'd first seen her and said, "I'm Betty Stevens, and you're Bobby Sullivan. Hello again."

Wiping off the wrench he was using on his coveralls, he had walked up close enough to smell her before he said, "I remember you Miss Stevens. You had that nice sweater on the other day when you came by to see Mr. Walker."

She had laughed. "Right. I could tell that my sweater is what you were thinking about too. Call me Betty or Blondie or 'hey girl.'" She smiled that 1000-watt smile at him and flounced her hair.

"Anything but Miss Stevens."

"Okay Blondie, what's up?"

"My dad is taking mom with him to some boring old convention in Austin. They can't take me to see 'Premiere for Great Britain' or even 'Hard Boiled Canary' this Saturday down to Fair Park. Would you mind taking me?"

"Blondie, you sure you want to be seen with me?"

"I don't know, Dagwood. Are you potty-trained?"

"Sure am. I can read and write too."

"We can take my car, the red two-door over there. Come on over and check it out."

As they walked to her car, she leaned into him and said, "I know men hate to shop for clothes, but if you talk to Will Davis over at Smitty's, next to the Kress 5&10? He'll fix you right up."

"I've never seen paint this color on a car before," Bob said, as he ran his hand over the hood and then wiped his prints off with a shop rag.

"Car is special order. Daddy had to pay for a special run of the paint. Upholstery is custom too."

"One honey of a car for sure," Bob said.

"Want to drive me around for awhile?"

"Give me a minute to get out of these overalls. Don't want to mess the seat up."

When he had returned minus his coveralls, he said, "that's a helluva long ways to go to see a play. We'd have to leave early and get back late."

He kicked the tires on the coupe, asking, "is the spare good?"

She came up behind him while his nose was stuck under the hood.

He felt the soft curve of her as she leaned into him and whispered, "better than good Bobby, never been used."

He straightened up without banging his head too hard on the raised hood.

"The car's brand spanking new. It'll make the trip with no flats. I'll go."

"Oh I don't know Bobby," she said. "Anything can happen in a car. We might break down in the middle of nowhere."

She stood beside the passenger door of the coupe and waited. He opened it for her. She got in. He ran around and got in on the driver's side.

"Blondie, do your parents know a strange older man is driving you all the way to Dallas?"

"Course not, Mr. Sullivan. They'd lock me in the cellar with the canned goods."

"I'd lock you up too," Bob said. The V-8 in the Merc purred like a well - fed lion when he turned the ignition key.

"I don't know if I like the shift on the steering column," he said. "I keep reaching for where the damn thing ought to be."

"Daddy says that's a new feature, easier to reach."

They drove off down California Street towards the park.

"Bobby that's a nice suit," Betty said. Bob glanced over at her. Her hair glowed in the moonlight as they headed home from the show in Dallas on 77.

"What's the matter Bett?" He said. "Don't think a yard mutt like me knows how to clean himself up?"

"Quit getting all riled up. I'm only trying to tell you how nice you look. If you yell every time I compliment you, what's gonna happen when I do something like this?"

A jolt of pure electricity ran through him. Betty put her hand under his shirt, and stroked his chest.

"Davis was right," he said.

"About what?"

"When you asked me to this 'Canary' play, I went to that clothing shop Davis works at like you said to. His boss fixed me up with these duds. That old guy, Chaney, treated me like a swell."

Betty slowly plucked the buttons open on Bob's shirt one by one. He felt her hot breath and soft wet tongue as she slowly licked his chest.

"Baby, you are a swell. All day in every way," she said.

He felt pretty swell.

While she licked, working her way lower and lower, she reached over and turned on the radio. A voice came out of the darkness crooning, "okay, lads and lassies that was *Moonlight Serenade* by Glenn Miller. We gonna jazz on the back side now with a new Decca cut called, *Is You Is or Is You Ain't My Baby* with Louis

Jordan on vocals with the Tympani Five. Watch the moonlight don't blind you now."

Betty stopped long enough to ask, "who's your baby, Bobby?"

"You're my baby, Bett. You are."

She was licking his belly button now, while slowly unzipping his pants. Bob pulled the car over into a copse of mesquite on the side of the road. Later, he couldn't remember how they'd gotten back to Gainesville.

Chapter 12
White Flannel

Sparks flew as the sledgehammer struck the rail. This is a contest of wills, thought Bob. He imagined the rail laughing at him, telling him to give up. "Straighten you whore." He muttered under his breath. The hot rail, glowing cherry in the grasp of the huge shop clamps, said nothing. Just as he was getting ready to give it another stroke, he heard someone behind him. His boss, Steve Walker, was standing behind him.

"Sullivan, I need to speak with you up to the shop office."

"Okay boss, let me straighten this rail before it cools though."

"It'll keep, Sullivan. What we need to talk about won't."

Bob's stomach dropped. He felt like he'd swallowed the damn rail. The steam heater hissing in the corner of Walker's office sounded like a kettle, and smelled like wet dog. Walker had cleaned up. Looked like he'd even dusted his desk. A single sheet of paper rested on it.

"Sullivan, you have any idea what this is about?"

"No sir, Mr. Walker, I don't."

"Have a seat, Bob."

Bob lowered himself into a worn green armchair; a spring poked him in the ass.

"You're a damn good worker, Bob. Show up on time, mostly sober - and you work your freaking butt off. I never have to worry about whether you're working or jacking off like that dumb shit Donaldsen."

"Are you firing me, boss?"

Walker stared at the ceiling, then, stood to look out into the yard.

"Did I ever tell you what I did before I landed a job with the railroad, Bob?"

"Never did, boss." I don't know what I did, Bob thought, but I'm screwed, and tattooed.

"I dug ditches for Buckeye pipeline up in Ohio. I was paid two bits an hour, rain or shine. My brother, God bless him, got me a card with the steamfitters union."

Walker turned and leaned over the back of his swivel chair.

"Got this job through the union. No one in the union and no one in management gives a shit about Gainesville, so long as the trains arrive and depart on schedule."

Walker plopped his butt down in his chair.

"I don't know who you pissed off, Sullivan and, frankly, I don't care. Got a telegram from Kansas City yesterday ordering me to pay you eight weeks severance, at time and a half your normal rate, so long as you agreed to leave without a fuss. They mentioned you by name, Bob."

"What else, Walker?"

"What do you mean what else?"

"Who's fucking me over? You know, you just aren't saying."

"Bob, if anything happens, I can't pay you the severance. If you don't leave quietly, the local cops will escort you out of the yard."

"Do yourself a favor, Steve," Bob said quietly. "Tell me what I want to know. If you don't, I'll break your nose. I'd feel bad about it too. Wouldn't be right, you having a broken nose, me in the local rat hole lock up. Some swell laughing his ass off at the both of us; who is screwing me Steve?"

Walker took a piece of paper out of his desk wrote something on it and stood up.

"I gotta take a leak real bad. When I get back if you or that piece of paper is still around, I'm calling the cops. If you're gone, your severance check will be at the post office tomorrow morning."

When he got to the door he stopped, keeping his back to Bob, he said, "I think your work is high-tone, Sullivan, but I never want to see you in this yard again. I can't do a thing more for you. Are we square, or do I need to watch my back when I leave here every night?"

"Damn Steve, take it easy here. You did right by me. I have no beef with you. We're square. If I ever see you again, I'll buy you a beer."

Walker's shoulders slumped and his head dropped.

"I'm fifty-five Bob. I need my pension."

"Go on, Steve," Bob said. "You're just doing someone else's dirty work because they didn't have the balls to come in and stand up for themselves. Take care of yourself."

Once the door shut behind him, Bob reached over and slid the piece of paper across the desk. Two names were written there. He pulled Steve's ashtray over to his side of the desk and lit the piece of paper with his Zippo. The names didn't surprise him.

"Eight weeks at time and a half," he said, grinning. "I'm surprised they thought so highly of me. In 1941, it's money. In 1841, it would've been tar and feathers for ol' Bob Sullivan."

The paper was black ash. Bob dumped it in the waste can and walked out. The weather was cold, but the weather wasn't going to interfere with his plans for that shit-for-brains DeWitt. The wind picked up. Bob considered leaving town immediately, catching up with

Bett in Ft. Worth, and heading west before anyone knew they were gone. But, he couldn't leave unfinished business behind. Steve Walker was doing his job. Robert Stevens was involved because he was pretending he cared about his daughter. Prather DeWitt though had helped screw him for one reason only - his son had wanted Betty and Betty had rejected him–in favor of Bob. Bob kept humming that Louis Jordan tune Bett and he had listened to on the way home from Dallas.

Bob shifted his legs under him. He was getting stiff crouched here waiting on the little Yankee bastard. If the son of a bitch loved her so much, why was he here in Leonard Park drinking moonshine with his snot-nose buddies, while she got hauled off to Ft Worth to a Home for Wayward Girls.

Bob flicked a glance at his watch. Nearly two in the morning and Bob's legs felt like lead from waiting close enough to know what the little jerks were saying and far enough away to remain hidden.

The conversation stank. They swapped lies about who had the bigger dick, and why Hitler was really a good guy because he'd square things with the Jews, and how Phil Rizzuto wasn't spit, even if he did get traded to the Yanks. Then Bob heard somebody say, "spit it out, Louis, how many times did you pump ol' Betty to light her oven?"

Bob's jaw clenched so tightly, he was sure he was going to break some teeth.

He heard DeWitt say, "oh boys you know how it is with us DeWitts - a little dab will do ya."

The pecker was the hit of the whole drunken soiree. Bob thought.

The moon was high overhead. The drunken shits wandered off in twos and threes. Some shitheap was staggering out of the park with DeWitt when fortune smiled on Bob.

"Hey Louis, wait up. I gotta piss."

"My car is parked up on the highway," DeWitt said. I'll give you two minutes, then, I'm leaving."

Bob considered hitting DeWitt from behind the first time so he couldn't be sure who got him. Then he thought for a moment. Hitting Louis from behind defeated his purpose. Bob tapped the drunk pisser over the head so he wouldn't show up at an inconvenient moment. However, he didn't conk him until he was done pissing. He had nothing against him, besides being in the wrong place at the wrong time. Bob even caught him when he fell so he didn't hit his head on a rock.

He smelled DeWitt before he actually saw him. All you had to do was follow the alcohol fumes and cigarette smoke. He was leaning up against the car humming. Bob circled around the Packard down wind of him so DeWitt wouldn't hear him. Didn't want to give him a chance to bolt. Bob came up quick and put his left arm around DeWitt's shoulders. With his right hand he took the cigarette out of the punk's mouth, tossed it on the gravel, and stomped it out.

"Hey there, Louis, how the hell are you, man?"

Louis grinned back at Bob but his pupils widened when he recognized who'd grabbed him.

"Come back in this stand of trees with me, Louis. We don't want anyone coming up on us by accident, do we now?"

"I'd love to, Bob," DeWitt said, "but Rob'll be along any second now, and Jesus, it's got to be three in the morning."

Louis stumbled along as Bob half carried; half dragged him away from his car.

"Louis, you really shouldn't wear such nice clothes to a stag party. The jacket and pants are flannel, aren't they?"

Bob threw him against an old, stunted oak tree. His face was chalky in the moonlight.

"Hey Bob, come on now, you're beginning to scare me a little here. Rob'll begin to wonder where I am. If you like flannel, here, take the jacket, it's yours. I have thirty bucks on me. Take that too.

"Louis, for once in your fucking life, shut up. Rob is taking a little nap and I wouldn't take your money even if the alternative was a long cold stay in hell with your mother."

Louis began to sob.

"Oh God. Please Bob. Wasn't my idea, I swear."

"What, exactly, wasn't your idea?"

Bob slugged him hard in the gut. He went down like ten pounds of fertilizer in a five-pound bag.

"Don't get up ass wipe," Bob said. "Talk to me from the dirt–where you belong."

Bob kicked him hard in the ass and slightly less hard in the ribs.

Louis struggled to sit upright, against the trunk of the tree.

"Wasn't my idea to take your job, Sullivan. After this, my dad might want your life though."

"Louis, you're such a prick beating you isn't even fun. True, I didn't appreciate losing my job. That aggravated me a little, but what really burns me is how you can court Betty Stevens by knocking on her front door like a regular swell; then, you talk about her to your friends like she was a three-dollar whore."

He kicked Louis once in the head and once in the balls when he said, 'three-dollar whore', to emphasize his point.

"Suckers like you don't get it, Bob," Louis gasped. "All women are whores. Some take three dollars, some take thirty. Just have to find the right amount and guess what? I had my way with Betty and getting some didn't even take three dollars."

Louis grinned as blood ran out the side of his mouth. He tried to mop off blood from his mouth and the side of his head with a handkerchief.

"Let's clean you up Louis," Bob said. He unzipped and pissed on him. Louis sputtered some as the piss hit him in the face but he didn't budge from the base of the tree.

Zipping up, Bob said, "enjoyed our time together, Louis. Sorry, we can't chat longer. Got business elsewhere. I'm borrowing your dads' Packard for the morning, if you don't mind. No objection? Good. I'll leave it in Muenster or Sherman or, maybe, over in Denton. I haven't decided how far your goodwill is going to take me before the police get interested."

He kicked Louis square in the face.

Louis groaned. His nose looked broken. Bob couldn't decide if this made him feel better or worse. "I'd kill you now Louis," Bob said. "Unfortunately, you dead provides the police with too much motivation to come looking for me."

Bob left Louis propped up against a tree so he could breathe a little easier. Then he headed off, thinking about Betty in Ft Worth. He figured he could get Bett to the West Coast on what he had saved up and the generous severance check he had in his pocket. Steve had gotten his money to the post office even faster than he'd promised he would. He checked his watch again. The time was four-thirty a.m.. He had ground to cover and not much time. The coming day was going to be a long one.

He decided the Packard was too big a risk. The huge sedan would stick out like a negro at a Klan rally and he'd be stopped before he got five miles even at this hour. He'd have to hoof it. He stopped at the car long enough to bash the headlights and remove the distributor cap. He started hiking north, over the Red. Being in Oklahoma seemed much safer at the moment. He could double-back at some spot where John Law might not be so interested in his sorry carcass.

As he walked a tune came to him out of nowhere. "One sunny day, 'twas... no that ain't it. Okay yeah, *'Twas in the spring, one sunny day. My sweetheart left me, Lord, she went away. Now she's gone, gone, gone and I don't worry, cause I'm sittin' on top of the world."* Bob remembered. He'd heard the nigger musician Blind Lemon Jefferson play one time in Dallas. Was it Blind Lemon's tune he was butchering? "Coming for you, Blondie. Blind Lemon and me, darling, we coming now."

Chapter 13
A Season for Farewells

Ralph and I were taking our first pass at the lawn for the year. I was pushing the mower. Ralph was raking.

"Ralph," I said. "I hate April. I'm sweating like a dime a dance girl being chased by four drunk sailors."

"You're too ugly to charge a dime a dance; I wouldn't dance with you even if I was drunk," he replied. "Be okay if it wasn't so humid. Daddy got the better of us again, Will. We should've held out for more than two bucks apiece to get the place in order."

"Maybe we'll get something out of the sale proceeds," I said.

"If he manages to sell it. We'd better be right there at the closing."

"The extra money would be welcome," I said. "What extra money, Will?" Ralph said this as he threw a couple of tin cans on the metal heap we'd started. "Extra makes it sound like we've got plenty and anything more that comes along is gravy. Besides, you're flush even without the two bucks. You've got a real job."

"Trying to bank the money from Smittys for the future. I can use the two bucks to take Mindy downtown to see *Dark Command* with Roy Rogers and John Wayne. Don't want her offering to go Dutch. Drives me nuts when she does that."

Ralph leaned on his rake. "You poor sap. Trying to save and date a rich kid all at the same time." He turned his back on me and used the rake to search for more metal in the crawl space under the house.

Dud walked around the side of the house wearing a smug grin.

"Damn Dud, we're working here. You're the last person I expected to see."

"Shut the hell up, Will. Or I'll take my choice piece of gossip and leave." He pretended to turn and head out front. He had something big. He was bursting his buttons trying to keep his news inside.

"Ralph!" I yelled. "Watch for snakes and don't lay that tin on mom's sprouting tulip bulbs. Mash those tulips and she'll tan your hide for sure. Dud and me gonna take a short walk. I'll be back to finish mowing."

"Right big brother, I won't hold my breath."

He waved at us and peeked under the rusty tin to see if anything was wiggling before he stuck his hands under the old piece of scrap.

Dud and me sidled around the house on the grassed over flagstone path that went from the back to the front yard. We skirted a pair of unruly rose bushes that no one had seen fit to trim back over the summer. Dud yelped as his sleeve caught on a thorn covered branch.

"Christ, Will, when you gonna trim these things. That branch almost caught me in the face!"

"Dud, I'll fetch the hedge trimmers. They're ready anytime you are."

"Fat chance, you seen my yard lately?"

"It's a sty."

"Exactly. So why would I help in your lousy yard, when I won't work in my own."

"Point taken. Get to it. What gives?"

Dud plopped under the pecan tree in our front yard, where I'd already mowed. The scent of mown grass was heavy in the air.

"You really haven't heard, have you?"

"What's going on? Has the President died? Bob Feller been traded by Cleveland?"

"Better. Louis and Rob are both in the hospital. Rob'll probably get out today; he only has a bump on his head. Heard that Louis looks like he got trampled on by a herd of longhorns. He was found under a tree over in Leonard Park beaten half to death. He probably would have died except that Wat found him on the way home from work. The Chief wanted to arrest Wat for the beating." Dud paused to catch his breath. "Wat had an alibi though. He'd been cleaning cages for the community circus the entire night. The circus troupe vouched for him."

I stared at Dud. He stared at me. We said the same name at the same time, "Bob Sullivan."

"Sure enough appears so. Louis is still unconscious, so he ain't talking. Bob is missing, and that ain't all."

"Betty Stevens has turned up missing too from the home her parents packed her off to in Fort Worth. That's the rest of the story, isn't it?" I said.

Dud was impressed.

"How in the name of Houdini did you know that?" Dud cracked a pecan shell open on a flagstone and popped the meat into his mouth. "That part is being kept real quiet," he said. "The Tarrant County Sheriff may call the G-men in. Her parents and the Sheriff are calling her disappearance a kidnapping."

"Elementary, my dear Watson."

I lied by omission. I didn't see any point in explaining what I knew about Betty and Bob to Dud.

"Bob has been talking about Betty for a whole year. His anger became too much to deal with, so he blew."

"Okay, but who is this Watson guy?"

"Never mind, just say your line."

"What is my line?"

"Say, 'right again, Holmes.'"

"Right again, Holmes."

Dud shifted his position on the grass. Pecan shells were digging into his backside. We watched Bertha

Ferguson drive by the house in Ben's old model-T pickup truck. The truck had red mud stuck to the front wheel wells. The rest of the truck was covered in a thin film of red dust.

"Ben and Bertha been working their whiskey still again."

"Yep," Dud said. "They have. Bertha hasn't been drinking too much of the product though, her drivin' still looks pretty steady."

I laughed. "Needed to stay sober long enough to get into town and buy sugar and a case of mason jars."

"True," Dud said. "Doubt she's going temperance on us."

"What else did you overhear at the courthouse?" I asked.

Dud sat up and looked me in the eyes. "Piece of bad news. Only part that's important to you - and to me. He wasn't laughing now.

"Heard that Rob Franklin has been shooting his mouth off; seems that he told the Chief and the Sheriff that you picked a fight on a couple of occasions with Louis and that you're a big friend of Bob's."

I shrugged. "All of that's true. Except, usually, Louis is the one looking for trouble."

"The Sheriff asked about me too," Dud said. "Couldn't hear that part of the conversation very well. Seems their thinking on me is that I'm a punk acting only on your direction."

"So, if I drop my pants and tell you to smooch my butt, you're there, huh, Dud?"

"Yeah, I'm there with a baseball bat Davis. Go on and drop those sorry ass pants."

"Sorry, buddy. Guess that wasn't funny."

"You're entitled, under the circumstances. What you gonna do?"

"If I do get picked up, I'll lie and tell the truth, as appropriate. Guess what I have to do ultimately depends."

"On what?"

"On what Louis says when he wakes up."

"Sure," Dud said morosely. "*If* he wakes up."

"I'm impressed that you know *Gershwin,* Will."

"Don't be too impressed Mindy. We have a radio at my house and my mom is fond of *Rhapsody in Blue.* I recognize the tune."

"So, Mr. Davis, what kind of music do you listen to when your mom's not around? Are you a Mozart man?" She played a quick 16 beat Mozart riff at jazz tempo.

"You know jazz," I said. "Recognize this?" I sat down at the piano and played some Bird Parker.

"Will Davis, you do keep secrets. I'd no idea a musician was hiding behind those violet blue eyes."

I tapped my shoes on the wood parquet floor and listened to the muffled echoes of the rain, tapping on the house.

"Most jazz musicians are poor. Take Jelly Roll Morton or John Lee Hooker for example. Their music is written for hicks like me."

"Didn't mean to poke fun, Will."

"Listen to the rain, coming down harder, I'm afraid. The movie is looking hopeless."

"Roy and John will keep. Sitting here with you at the piano is better than a movie anyway."

"What about your parents?"

"What about them?"

"Won't they be upset to come home and find their daughter sitting in the dark with a suspected thug?"

"How romantic! I've always wanted to date a thug, especially one who has beaten Louis DeWitt."

I shoved her. She shoved back. I grabbed hold of the piano to avoid falling on the floor. I put my left hand on the nape of her neck and kissed her. She grabbed my face in her hands and kissed me back. Her breasts pressed into me. She gently pulled away; I could hear her raspy breathing.

"I have a question," she murmured.

"What is it?"

"What's your favorite Jelly Roll Morton riff?"

"Heard *King Porter Stomp* the other night."

"My, my, my, a street thug who knows his jazz." She broke into the piece. She used no sheet music. From the way she formed the notes I knew she'd played the piece many times before.

I walked across to the French doors that opened onto the Hulens' terraced backyard. No debris piles here. The only debris pile Walt and Elaine Hulen are concerned about is standing in their house, thinking about screwing their daughter. Lightening flashed. Four seconds later, thunder followed. Buckets, maybe even wheelbarrows of rain fell. I lit a cigarette and watched the rain while Mindy Hulen beat out Morton on the piano.

Chapter 14
The Ludlow Household

Dud's ears were ringing. His old man hit harder when he was liquored up.

"Now you listen you little shit heap and you listen good. I done seen the damn notice in the paper about the reward money. You been hangin' 'round with this Sullivan fella."

He slapped his folded leather belt against his left palm to emphasize his point.

"I could use that five hundred dollars real bad and I think you or your friend Davis knows where old Bob is hiding that Stevens bitch."

His dad cuffed him again with the belt. He just flicked him though, he didn't want to bruise him up or cause him to pass out while they were having an important conversation.

"Now Bert, be careful," Dud's mom said. "You've been drinkin' kinda heavy tonight. You could hurt him."

My mother, Dud thought, always the protective one.

"Shut up, Doris. Or, I'll belt you when I'm done with the shit heel here."

Dud's mom, her maternal obligations fulfilled, left the room to wherever she went when Dud was his old man's entertainment for the evening.

"Shit heap pop," Dud said. "I'm a shit heap."

"What the hell are you saying?"

"Keeping you straight pop. A minute ago you called me a shit heap, and then you called me a shit heel. I' m trying to keep you consistent."

"Why, you little fucker, I'll take some skin off tonight. Teach you to sass."

As he stretched back with the belt to let Dud have a hard slap with some mustard behind it, Dud pointed towards the doorway.

"Mom's back, pop."

When his dad turned to look, Dud grabbed his baseball bat. He'd positioned the bat by his chair after he'd heard his dads' tread in the hall. Dud hit his dad hard on the outside of his left knee as he was turning back around. His pop was drunk but his knee wasn't and it wasn't designed to take that kind of abuse. Fair is fair, Dud thought. My face wasn't meant to be slapped with a leather belt either. His dad fell into a heap on the floor. While he was down, Dud hit him in the ribs. His old man tried to block the blow but he wasn't quick enough. He yelped when the bat connected. Dud heard his mom coming down the hall. He stepped around pop, shut his door and turned the latch.

Pop eyed him from the floor. He grabbed the edge of the chair Dud had been sitting in. Pop was right handed and was using his left hand to hoist himself up. Dud slammed down the bat on his pop's left hand. He heard the bones crunching as they broke. They sounded like locusts being crunched on the sidewalk. Well, maybe a little louder.

"Dud!" His mom screamed through the door. "Open this door right now!"

Dud knelt by pop, who was now crying. "I understand pop. That hand has to hurt like a mother bear. I know. I've been on the receiving end lots."

"You little prick. I'm gonna kill you and then have you arrested."

"Pop, I know you have $125. taped inside the Penney's Christmas catalogue in your closet. I'm taking a hundred and your hunting rifle."

"Danny boy, let mommy into the room." She rattled the doorknob.

"Mom, give us a minute. Pop and me are having us a little chat."

"You nigger-loving little frog gigger, I'll skin you alive if you so much as touch that money...or my goddamn gun." He grabbed for Dud's bat with his good hand. Dud cracked his outstretched right arm with the bat.

Pop yelled, "Christ on a stick that hurt!"

"Pop, you aren't listening. I know you earned that money by running liquor for Ben Ferguson. Oh yeah, you've also been stealing poultry off of the Graf place. I bet the Sheriff would be very interested in talking with you."

"Damn boy, a man has to earn a living."

"Good for you, pop. You're free to go on about your business enterprises after I've left. I'm letting mom in now to sign my enlistment papers."

Pop rolled over. Dud cocked the bat.

He winced and said, "steady boy, steady now. I ain't gonna try and git up. What the hell makes you think the government is gonna let the likes of you in the Army?"

"I'm enlisting in the Marine Corps," Dud said. "They'll take me at seventeen, so long as I have a parent's signature on the paperwork."

Dud opened the door. His mom ran past him to comfort pop.

"Oh God, Danny! What have you done? Get me a wash cloth from the bathroom."

"Mom, leave pop be for a minute. I need you to sign my paperwork, and then you two can be alone to wash each other, hit each other, drink with and then hit each other–whatever you want."

Pop started to laugh, but stopped, grabbed his ribs and groaned.

"Doris, sign the kids' paperwork."

He watched me like he was watching spit fizzle on a hot griddle.

"If the government don't kill you, maybe you'll turn out better than your old man after all. Careful with the rifle, a round is chambered."

This was as close as Dud's old man ever came to expressing approval of Dud in his whole sorry life. His mom signed the paperwork and Dud gathered up his stuff. Before he started packing though, he made pop tie himself up. Dud stayed out of his reach even after he was trussed up.

"Danny, you want any supper before you go? I'll fix you eggs and bacon if you want."

"Mom don't bother. I'll catch something on my way out."

"Write us when you get where you're going, so we don't worry."

"Maybe. I'll have Will come over and let you all know how I'm doing. I'm going to have my mail sent to his place."

Dud gave his mom a cursory hug before grabbing his old canvas pack and pop's rifle at the door. "I'm going to pawn pop's rifle in Dallas if he wants to go looking for it." As he headed out the door for Will's house, he turned back to his mom and said, "If it gets too bad with pop, go to Wills'. I'll leave money for you there. Can't save you though, all I can do is save myself."

After he'd gone, his mom sat in the dark saying, "I know, baby boy, I know."

His pop, still trussed like a Christmas turkey, slept on the floor, snoring to wake the dead.

Chapter 15
A Voyage Begins

Someone or something was scratching on my windowsill. I kicked the blankets off and padded over to the window. Tripped on a baseball bat that Ralph had left propped against the window. I picked it up, considered hitting Ralph with it, and then propped it up in the corner. I went back to the window and looked out.

Dud was standing outside. He had his pack and his dad's rifle slung over his shoulder.
"What the hell is up with you?"
"Lots. Sorry to wake you up, I fell asleep myself waiting for your parents to go to bed."
"Crawl in here so we can shut the window. Cold out there."
He climbed in and I shut the window with a muffled bang.

"You awwright big bruuuther?" Ralph mumbled in his sleep.
I went over and smoothed the hair off his forehead.
"Fine Ralphie, go back to sleep."
"Want something to eat, Dud?"
"Sure, I'm hungry, what you got?"
"Left over fried chicken and a glass of milk?"
"That'll do. Nothing better than fried chicken."
"Maybe. It's my cooking," I said.
"Beggars can't be too picky. I'll still eat it."

We settled in at the kitchen table. I watched him slurp down a glass of milk, poured him another, and waited.

"I'm leaving, Will. I just finished beating up my old man. I'm headed to Dallas to join the Marines. If it's okay, my mail will come here. I don't want my parents knowing exactly where I am for awhile. I'll write you though."

My head was as empty as an Oklahoma farmer's bank account. I couldn't think of a thing to say. Finally, I managed to croak, "why? You won't graduate. School isn't over for another month and a half. Live here with us."

Dud gnawed on a chicken breast like he hadn't eaten in weeks. When he'd finished, he said, "can't, Will. I wasn't going to get the sheepskin anyway. I'm flunking everything but woodshop. Anyway, my old man'd come looking for me sooner or later and I figure the next time we meet, one of us will end up dead. He's sorrier than a rabid skunk but I don't want his blood on my hands and I don't want him catching me from behind when he's drunk," Dud grinned. "He'd bash my head in, then feel real bad about killing me when he sobered up."

"Dud, I ain't gonna slobber all over you about this. Guess you've already figured the angles. The Marines will own you once you enlist. You'll have to dig holes, hit beaches, and whatever else they can think up."

"I can't wait," Dud said. "At least there won't be anymore glares from people whispering the word 'trash' as they walk by me. Honestly, everyone in this town, except for your family and Bob Sullivan, can kiss my white butt."

We listened to the mantel clock chime five.

"Need any money, Dud?"

"Nah, my daddy was generous. The liquor business has been good to him lately."

I snorted out loud. "No doubt, took all your paw's liquor-running dough?"

"Every damn dollar. I lied and told him I was going to leave him twenty-five. I figured leaving twenty-five with you would be better. Buy my mom groceries with it?"

"Sure Dud, I'll check in on her. I promise."

Dud rose from the table, picking up his pack and his dads' rifle. He threw the money down like he handled that kind of money everyday.

"I'll send more as soon as I can. Thanks for everything, buddy."

"How are you getting out of town Dud?" I felt like I was talking with marbles in my mouth. Against my will, tears welled up in my eyes. I turned away, not wanting to cry in front of Dud.

His voice came to me from the front door.

"I'm jumping the six a.m. freighter. Bob showed me where to catch it a couple of weeks ago, so the rail bulls don't snag me. Be seeing you, Davis."

"Seeing you too, Dud. Keep your mouth shut and your eyes open."

I heard the door open and then shut again and then open again.

"Will?"

"Yeah, Danny?"

"Tell your mom and Ralph that, you know that I love them."

Tears poured down my face.

"I'll tell them. By the way, they love you too."

The door shut again. Danny Ludlow was gone.

"I love you too, Danny. I love you too," I whispered to the mantel clock.

I went back to bed wishing for the present to vanish. Here I was, only six weeks away from being only the second Davis in history to graduate from high school, but I was low, real low.

I got up again, padded over to Ralph's side of the room and turned his bed over just to hear him yell. I went back over to my side of the room, dodged a brogan that Ralph threw at me and said, "we need to trim the roses on the trellis on this side of the house after school today. We didn't get it done on Saturday."

"I'll trim the trellis alright Will! I'm going to stick the thorniest cutting I can find right up your butt!"

I looked over at him and said, "ouch!"

He started laughing and picked up his pillow and threw that at me too.

As I was about to return the favor, we both heard our mom. "If you two hooligans aren't ready for school in ten minutes, there'll be no breakfast served in this house!"

We headed for the bathroom. As our arcs intersected in the bathroom bowl, I told Ralph about Dud leaving.

"Jeepers Will, he only had to hang in there for another month to get his diploma. What's he gonna do?"

"He didn't believe his daddy would let him live for another month." I said. "He's going off to join the Marines."

I flushed the commode. "Indoor plumbing sure beats the outhouse we had when we lived on that hard scrabble farm out near Post."

"I don't remember that, Will."

"That's because you weren't born yet numb nuts. Mom would deny it now, but she was relieved when Daddy gave up dry land farming for the oil patch. Truth is she tolerates his gambling because gambling beats West Texas farming all to flinders."

Ralph combed his hair in the basin mirror. "Oh, I've heard this story," Ralph said. "This is dad's West Texas story. He loves to talk about how you all ended up out west for two years."

"Never tells the story when mom's around, does he?"

"Daddy isn't a complete lunatic, Will," Ralph said. "He never tells any stories when she's around, especially when the best part is his imitation of her." Ralph imitated daddy imitating mom. "Mason, you could get a new lease on life in West Texas. Your son will grow up respecting you as a working man, a man of integrity."

"You lucky stiff, Ralph," I said. "You've never had to worry about a bee or a wasp coming out of an outhouse pit to sting your ass."

"Man, I hope Dud has indoor plumbing when he gets where he's going," Ralph said, as he headed to the kitchen. We tore into grits with red-eye gravy, bacon, eggs, and fresh squeezed orange juice.

"I don't think the Marines care about plumbing," I said.

"Doesn't matter," Ralph said between bites. "Dud'll be too busy trying to stay alive to take time out for a crap anyway."

Chapter 16
Requiem

"Mason, you're out of your mind!"

I snapped to attention. My mom and dad were glaring at each other across the dinner table. I discretely held a finger up to my lips. Ralph nodded.

"Elizabeth, stop getting worked up. It'll only be two weeks and I'm not going by myself.

"Bless me Jesus!" She said. "My husband is going card sharking in Mexico, but he'll be okay, he's going with two pillars of the community."

As she said this, she raised her hands and eyes to the ceiling in angry appeal to God. She lowered her hands and said, "God loves a fool and you, Mason, are no exception. You are truly loved by the Lord."

My dad turned red. "I'm sorry," he said. "Easier to be a fool than a saint."

"Mason!" She said. "Are you mocking me in front of my children?"

"No, Elizabeth," he said, as he reached for the mashed potatoes. "I'm headed down to Monterrey to play cards. Chester Harris and Robert Stevens are paying my expenses. They tell me high rollers from L.A. play there. I'll make a killing."

"Call them on the phone, Mason," she said. "Tell them you've changed your mind."

SLAM. My dad's hand nearly broke the table in two. "Enough Elizabeth!" He said. "I'm going." He left the table. We ate the rest of our meal in silence.

Before dawn the next morning, dad was sitting on the porch, waiting for his buddies to come get him. My mother didn't get up to see him off, but I did.

"Dad?"

"Hey son! Good morning."

He was sitting on the porch stoop, enjoying his first smoke of the day. His tobacco pouch and rolling papers sat beside him on the stoop.

"Dad, are you really going to Mexico with Mr. Stevens and Mr. Harris?"

"I am," he said. "We're driving to San Antonio and then we'll take the train into Monterrey via Laredo."

"Daddy, I understand this is your business," I said. "But, have you forgotten what happened at Christmas?"

"No. I remember, Will." He shifted around to look at me straight on.

"Don't you think your old man can handle himself in the presence of his enemies?"

The morning sky was still dark. I couldn't read his expression in the predawn gloom.

"Dad, Mr. Harris is a mean, vengeful man," I said. "I don't know Mr. Stevens as well, but, he's Mr. Harris' best friend."

Dad took a long drag on his cigarette, and then looked into the middle distance.

"Don't worry, son." He wrapped his arm around my shoulder and said, "I hit a big score right after Christmas. A score that isn't on the table for this trip." He looked at me with a wide grin on his face. "Can't talk about it right now, too big, but, the arrangements are almost final. I'll save the surprise for when I get back. I will tell you this much though. This is my last hurrah at the gambling tables. When I get back, I'm done with cards for good."

Headlights came slicing around the corner making narrow cuts in the predawn darkness. A big, black Lincoln stopped in front of our house. The sedan looked like a pregnant beetle in the predawn light. Robert Stevens stepped out of the backseat.

"Come on, Mason," he said. "The cards wait for no man."

"There in a minute, Robert."

Dad stood and stretched. He had on traveling clothes. A gray felt Stetson sat atop his head. He had on a blue work shirt and gray linen pants. He also had his brown leather jacket. Years later, when I first saw the advertisements for the movie, *Raiders of the Lost Arc*, I was astonished by the resemblance between the lead actor and my dad. Before he started down the walk, he gave me a bear hug.

"Kiss your mom and little brother for me. I should be home in eight or nine days tops. Here, give this to your mother."

He handed me a thick white envelope.

"I'd have given this to her myself but she would have accused me of holding out on her. Mind your mother and stay out of trouble as best you can."

He got in the back of the Lincoln and Stevens got in after him. They drove off.

That morning was the last time I ever saw my dad alive.

I stayed on the porch until my mother came out for me.

I handed her the envelope.

"What's this?"

"I don't know. I didn't open it. My guess is that its cash. Dad said something about you accusing him of holding out and all."

She opened the envelope. … $500.00.

My mom dropped the envelope as if she'd been bitten. She did not pick it back up.

"Will, put that envelope someplace safe," she said. "Mr. Chaney maybe? Just don't bring it in the house. She walked back inside without giving the greenbacks another glance. We used all of the cash to pay for my father's funeral.

"In my distress I called to the Lord, and he answered me. O Lord, deliver me from lying lip, from treacherous tongue ... all too long have I dwelt with those who hate peace, those who rejoice in wars' desolation.

I lift up my eyes toward the mountains; whence shall help come to me?

My help is from the Lord, who made heaven and earth."

I lifted my eyes from the podium and focused on Mr. Chaney, who was wearing his yarmulke and prayer shawl in honor of my father. I saw him silently mouth, "*The word of the Lord.*" as I finished my reading. He then bent over and touched his head to the top of the pew in front of him. Many considered the presence of a Jew in our Baptist church sacrilegious. Brother Bill had stepped in and told the church board that if a Jew wanted to come into a Christian house of worship and pray for a poor sinner like Mason Davis, he was by God going to be let in, so long as he, William Nestor, was the pastor.

He won that battle. However, the congregation drew the line at blacks. Lucinda, Wat, their families and other negroes, including the Reverend James King, the minister of the local black Baptist church, were forced to stand outside the church to pray for my daddy's departed soul. Brother Bill's contract was not renewed the following year, 1942. Still, the day my daddy was buried, George Chaney begged the Lord to accept his soul into whatever heaven He could fit a murdered gambler.

My Daddy was stabbed to death and left in an alley. He'd been playing cards in a combination bodega and cathouse. Men came to play cards on the first floor and get other, more intimate, needs met on the second floor.

According to Chester Harris, my dad had been winning all night. He was up four hundred dollars and had decided to quit.

Harris and Stevens both signed statements to the local authorities saying they'd last seen him at five a.m. when he'd left the card table. He'd told them, according to the statements that he was going for a walk, maybe towards the Plaza Zaragoza to watch the sunrise over the Cathedral of Monterrey. When he wasn't at their hotel room when they returned from the bodega around nine the same morning, they contacted the local authorities.

Dad's body was found four hours later, stuffed haphazardly under some garbage in a barrio alley. He had been beaten, and then stabbed. His shoes, wallet, jacket, hat, and pants were gone. I knew Chester Harris was lying through his teeth. My dad didn't give a rat's ass about cathedrals. If he was winning, staying on trump, taking pots, cleaning out his fellow gamblers, he wouldn't have left the table to piss, let alone watch a sunrise.

I really knew Harris and Stevens were holding out when they both gave my mother checks. They claimed they were covering the amount my dad walked out the door of the bodega with. Bullshit. It was blood money. I had no proof. I only knew that my dad left with those two men knowing that he was in some danger, he'd underestimated how much. I didn't know why he ended up in an alley under a garbage pile. But, I vowed I'd find out.

We buried my dad at the beginning of May 1941. We buried him in a plain pine casket, in a blue suit that Mr. Chaney personally tailored for him. As I watched the attendants lower him into the ground I knew that if I stayed in Gainesville I'd have to kill two people.

Life in Gainesville was over for me. I'd be leaving soon.

"God, this is a nightmare you can't wake up from," Mindy said. "I don't know what to say or do."

"Nothing, Mindy," I replied. "Even if there was something to be done, this isn't your fight."

"The wind's cooling the bluff off, Will. Let's get in the sleeping bag together."

"Glad you agreed to come up here, Mindy. You didn't have to."

"Wilson Pickett Davis! Are you really that dense?"

"What are you all fired up about?"

"I'm fired up because you act like I'm doing you a favor, that I'm taking pity on you."

"Aren't you?"

We crammed ourselves into my sleeping bag. Mindy slapped my forehead.

"Ouch! That hurt."

"Good," she said. "Is that how you see yourself, someone deserving pity?" We leaned up against a log and stared into the fire we had built out of the plentiful brush. Heat was building inside the bag.

"I'm feeling sorry for myself," I said. "That's okay," Mindy said. "Just don't treat me like the consolation prize. I'm here because I care for you not because you're a stray puppy needing a home." She kissed the spot on my forehead where she'd bopped me.

"Do you really think Chester Harris arranged your Dad's murder?"

I let out a long sigh. "Yes, I do," I said. "Who's going to believe me though?" Mindy put her arms around me and leaned her head on my shoulder.

"Proof is the obvious problem," she said. "Without any, you're just a grief-stricken son grasping at straws."

"Exactly," I said. "Let's face facts. I could be mistaken. I admit this is so. I just know what I know. Harris was furious with Dad after that card game last December. My dad knew something was up before he left - he

114

couldn't resist the lure of easy pickings, even if going meant risk to himself. Dad also mentioned something about a big score the morning that he left. He was excited, but he wouldn't tell me what he was talking about."

We were both silent for a moment. "The implications are enormous Will," she said, as tears rolled down her face.

"Sorry, the way your daddy has been taken, it's just so…evil," she said. "No one can believe your dad died like he did."

I managed to free an arm and stroke her left cheek. She hiccupped. We both laughed. "Are there really mountain lions up here on the bluffs, Will?"

"Yes," I said. "One eyed me through the brambles once when I was here. Are you frightened?"

"No, intrigued is more like it. Could you shift a little? I think my right foot has gone to sleep." We shifted. I managed to put my left arm around her shoulders. I felt her right hand gently settle on my crotch.

"Are you okay, Will?"

"No darling. I may never be okay again. But, knowing you is a saving grace. I kissed her hard on the mouth. I loved the taste of her, the smell of Woodbury's soap in her hair with a tinge of wood smoke mixed in.

"Stop for a second, Will. Let's get organized."

She unzipped the sleeping bag and crawled out. She stood, silhouetted by the fire; she took her clothes off slowly, deliberately. When she was finished, she stood in front of me with her feet planted apart. The wind raised goose bumps on her skin. She placed her hands on her hips and said, "If you laugh, I'm going home."

"The goddess of the hunt comes forth," I said.

I got out of the bag, stood up, and started unbuttoning my own shirt. She stopped me and whispered, "let me." She reached over and tore my shirt off. She then bent over and stripped me of my pants and underwear in a rough downward yank. We faced each other. She placed my right hand between her legs. Her cleft was damp, yielding. I gasped. She then produced a little square packet with a feral grin, as she dropped to her knees and wet me with her mouth. I felt her slip whatever was in the packet over me. We fell in a heap onto the top of the sleeping bag.

Mindy was on top of me licking my face, kissing me, biting my ear lobes. Her scent overwhelmed me. I felt the brush of her pubic hair as she mounted me. The whole world narrowed to the singular feel of her raising and lowering herself. We probably lasted two minutes from beginning to end. She engulfed me physically and spiritually. If I could have gotten myself, whole, inside of her, I'd have done it. I gently grabbed hold of her throat with my teeth. Her whole body clenched, unclenched and then clenched again.

Later, after we'd gotten back inside the sleeping bag, we listened to the fire crackle and the distant howling of a coyote.
"Sorry about your shirt Will. I'll buy you a new one."
I nestled my head against her breasts.
"Mindy, my shirt is the least of my concerns."
"The whole world is changing, Wilson. Can you feel it?"
"Mine already has, darling. Way too fast for me."
"I didn't intend to add to the things you now have to wrestle with."
I kissed her breasts and said, "wrestling with you is the nicest thing I've ever done. I wasn't really thinking of us as change. To me, seems like we've always been right here, waiting for the rest of the world to catch up to us."
"And now the world has?"

"Yes, now it has."

"What happens to us now Will?"

"We're leaving."

"What?"

"We're going away."

"But, not together?"

"No, I don't think together is possible. I don't know why, but, something tells me we both have business elsewhere to take care of."

"Speaking of business elsewhere, where were we supposed to be tonight anyway," she said. "I forgot already."

"We were going to a piano competition in Ardmore. Louise is bringing you back a program to cover us. She's also supposed to shoot off her mouth about what a great time we all had together."

"The jazz musician, Bukka White, was going to be one of the judges," I said.

"Bukka puts smoke into his music. Wat let me listen to some stuff he waxed up in Chicago last year. Surprising he'd come to Oklahoma for a piano recital."

"Waxed?"

"Made into a record."

She rolled over on top of me.

"I don't know if I can...respond, again, this quickly."

"It'll be better this time," Mindy said. "You won't be able to pull the trigger as fast."

"How can I resist a line like that?"

"You can't," Mindy said, as she settled herself on me again. "We have to be careful this time, Will. I don't have any more pecker covers."

"Pecker covers?"

"One of those rubber things I put over your penis. I love you but we're not ready to have babies; and I'm not bunking with Betty at the home for wayward girls."

"Where did you even get the one?"

"My dad's sock drawer. I was lucky to find it. Those little rubber things are nearly impossible to find around here.

"He uses covers with your mom?"

"Oh, Will, don't be so provincial. My guess is that several young women in New York enjoy his company when he's in town."

"Your mother knows?"

"Probably." Mindy put her hands behind her head and arched her back. Constellations were racing across the sky over her head.

"Why would she put up with it?"

"Because the alternatives stink, Will."

"Did your mother approve of your father's gambling?" She ran her hands through my hair.

"No, she hated it."

"Yet, she stayed with him didn't she?"

"Yes."

"And she misses him now?"

"She's beside herself. Sent Ralph to our Aunt's place over to Wichita Falls. She threatened to send me too if I didn't leave her be for a couple of days."

"Why?"

"She said she couldn't bear being reminded how beautiful daddy was every time she looked into our faces."

I was bawling again.

Mindy put her arms around me.

"That's our predicament. When you're a woman, you get this feeling in the pit of your stomach about a man sometimes. The man can be a bucket of slop. He can be a drunk. Doesn't matter. If his key fits your lock, you're stuck."

We fell asleep.

I woke up with a start. Mindy was pushing my arm.

I tried to sit up.

"Whoa, sleepy head slow down!"

My neck had a crick in it. When I tried to look at her, a sharp pain caught me right below my ear.

"I'm afraid to ask, what time is it?"

"Good morning to you too."

"Mindy, I love you but we've bought a boat load of trouble. A piano recital isn't going to cover you standing on your welcome mat at daybreak."

She grinned and pressed those lovely breasts into my back, while kneading my temples with her hands. "Shush," she breathed. "You have whole wagon loads of good qualities Wilson Pickett, but I see waking up even-tempered isn't one of them."

"I'll go in with you when we get back. We'll think of something."

Mindy stood flat-footed, naked, in the morning chill. She was flawless.

"I can fight my own domestic battles Will," she said, as she pulled on her panties and her gray twill pants in one smooth motion. She regarded her brassiere distastefully and threw it on the ground, picked up her pullover sweater and slipped it over her head.

"Besides," she added. "If you were there, they might say something insulting to you. I won't allow that." She picked up my clothes and threw them at me. "Quit staring at me, you bad boy and get dressed," she said. "Men are so lucky."

"Why do you say that?" I asked, as I pulled my pants on.

"All your clothes button or zip or clasp in the front. If women could zip in the front and pee standing up, we'd rule the world."

"Do you think the world would be a better place if you did?"

"I'll tell you one thing for sure," she said as she paused to watch a goshawk catch it's breakfast off the river, "We wouldn't have people killing each other in Africa or in Asia like we do right now. And, she pointed to the used rubber laying wadded up in the dirt at her feet, "we sure as hell would have better birth control."

"I'll give credit where credit's due," I said. "If my dad had listened to my mom instead of those two worthless fucks he did listen to, he'd still be alive today."

I put my arms around her waist.

The hawk was screeing high above us. She folded her wings in and hurtled toward something only she could see. The sun streaked her plumage gold.

"She's marvelous."

"She's gorgeous, like you are," I said.

"Will, you do know how to lie."

"I don't think I've ever seen a goshawk this far south before."

"Right," I said. "No mountain lions live her any-more either. Even though one nearly ate me for lunch. Hey, maybe I was eaten. You were pretty ferocious."

She punched me for the second time in less than a day.

"Is hitting me becoming a habit?"

"I don't know. Are you going to keep saying dumb boy things?"

"Can I ask one more dumb boy question?"

"You can ask. I don't promise to answer."

"Why?" She put her hands over her brow to shield her eyes against the rising sun. The bluff glistened gold and silver in the dawn.

"We are running out of time," she said. "As you said last night, we're both leaving this place - soon. I wanted to spend time with you on the river before the opportunity passed. I've wanted to do so since that day you watched Betty and me seining in nothing but our waders." She pointed, "right down there."

"We might both be wrong," I said, as we began to work our way back down the bluff. "The war could be over in three months."

"Maybe, but I don't believe that and I don't think you do either. My dad has a college classmate who works at the State Department in Washington. He's telling daddy that the Americans don't know half of what's already happened. The Germans and the Japanese are murdering innocents in China and in central Europe. American isolationism is working to their advantage. Blood is running while we worry about...baseball."

We hiked back to her car hand-in-hand. When we came to the spot in Leonard Park where we'd hidden her car behind a hedge, I said, "we've wasted too much time. I've spent the last two years watching you walk around and I've never once thought about who you really are."

"Oh, Will, get in the car for crying out loud," she said, as she threw me her keys. "We haven't wasted any time. We're kids. Two months ago, we thought we had forever to circle around each other."

She squeezed my right thigh.

"Now, Betty and Dud are gone. Even that rough looking friend of yours is gone. Stop the car here at the corner. They'll come out and make a scene if we pull up front."

"Don't do this by yourself, Mindy. Let me go with you."

"You're a typical man in one sense - you don't listen." She tugged my right earlobe. "I know what to say to them. You'd just be a vulnerable target." She got out of the car. Her neck was bruised where I'd bitten her. She read my thoughts and smiled.

"That's not the only sore place on my body." She reached back and grabbed me behind my neck. She bit my lips, and then kissed me.

"I love you Wilson Pickett. If we had time, I'd let you do me again, right here in the backseat. Park the car on California Street. I'll find it later."

"I'll leave the keys under the driver's seat," I said.

She waved as she walked off. Guess she waved to signify that she'd heard me, but it sure looked like a good-bye wave. As I drove off, I figured I'd be arrested later that day for grand theft and probably rape. Walt Hulen would be gunning for me. I drove slowly. I wasn't in any hurry. My mother cried every time she saw me anyway.

Today was Sunday. Everything was closed. I headed to Smitty's, unlocked the store and went in. I washed myself off in the stockroom bath. Even when I was done, Mindy's scent still enveloped me. I slept soundly on a pile of cloth bales the rest of the day. I don't remember dreaming. I woke up once because I could have sworn someone had been standing in the aisle brushing my hair away from my forehead. When I woke up, no one was there. I smelled Old Spice in the air though.

"Dad?" I whispered.

No response.

Chapter 17
The Consequence of Acting

Will dropped me off at the perfect moment. Mindy thought. Her parents were in Ardmore, assisting the police in a massive search for the two of them. Acting nonchalant in front of Will had taken all of her strength. She'd wanted him next to her but knew keeping him around was a bad idea. The house was locked. A terse note on the back door stated that if she happened to come home, a key was under the geranium pot adjacent to the grape arbor in the back yard.

Mindy let herself in, undressed, and ran a hot bath. She eased herself into the tub, ducked her head under the water and came up sputtering. Lord, she ached all over. Will had worked her over. The ache was a good ache though. She couldn't resist imagining him here in the bathtub with her.

"Oh stop it," she said out loud. "Don't get side tracked. Will is one thing, a sweet thing to be sure. This getting away business is something else. My parents could get nasty."

As she soaked in her mom's rose scented bubble bath, she wondered how long the eerie calm would last, before the storm struck.

"I've completed my high school equivalency work," Mindy said. "Aunt Shannon is meeting my train in Philadelphia on Thursday."

"This is outrageous!" Elaine Hulen said. She stomped over to the window in the study and opened a window. "Walt, give me a cigarette." Mindy's dad opened his desk drawer and pulled out a cigarette case, flipped it open, and proffered her the open case.

"We can stop you Mindy," Walt Hulen said. "You're only seventeen."

"I start nursing school at Penn the third week of September," Mindy replied. "I'm already enrolled and my tuition is paid. Do you really want to try?"

"Walter, she's not living with Shannon."

Mindy's dad frowned but didn't respond. "Why'd you choose to leave this way?" He asked. "You could've came to me and asked for help."

"I wanted out of here quickly. Aunt Shannon has a lawyer who has rented an apartment and bought a piece of land in trust for me in Upper Darby."

Mindy's dad whistled softly. "So, you've already began establishing an independent residence. I admire the effort but I still don't understand why."

"Too many secrets," Mindy said. "Too many lies said and unsaid. I don't like this town and I want out–now."

Walt Hulen formed a steeple with his fingers and stared at her. Her mother continued to smoke and look out the window. She wouldn't even look at Mindy. "What's Shannon's angle?" Her dad asked.

"*Quid pro quo,*" Mindy said. "I'm going to help her resolve some legal issues; she's going to act as my guardian."

"Mindy's been looking in your safe, Walt," Elaine said. Her gaze didn't shift from the window.

"Dear God," Walt Hulen said. "Is this true, Mindy?"

"You were careless, dad," Mindy said. "I saw the … the pictures sticking out of an envelope on your desk."

"So, you used those pictures to blackmail your Aunt Shannon. Child, you're involving yourself in dangerous matters." He came around the desk, and gripped Mindy's arm. Steel permeated his voice. "Do you have any idea what you've…"

"You're hurting me dad," Mindy said. He released his grip. "The photos in your safe are copies," she said, as she rubbed her arm. "The originals are … elsewhere."

"I'm astounded," her dad said as he leaned against his desk. He staggered as if he'd been struck.

"Daddy," Mindy said. "I didn't even recognize Aunt Shannon at first in those awful pictures."

"I'm not staying here and listening to this any longer," Elaine Hulen said. "I don't know who this, this person is."

"That's okay, mom," Mindy retorted. "I didn't know we were one generation removed from being shanty Irish Catholic. Guess I didn't know who you were either. My aunt's predicament has been useful. I had a remarkable conversation with her after seeing the pictures."

Elaine Hulen froze with her hands on the doors of the study. "What did Shannon tell you?" Her dad asked. "And what have you done to this family?"

Mindy recounted her conversation with Aunt Shannon.

"Where is your dad?" Aunt Shannon asked.

"Out, they're both out."

"What makes you believe your parents will allow you to stay here and go to school. Jesus, Mary and Joseph, child, this is a long way from Texas."

"Aunt Shannon, I love talking to you," Mindy said. "Imagine what the old hens in Mom's garden club would say if they knew she was Irish Catholic, not English Presbyterian."

"Don't start something you can't be forgiven for later."

"Believe me, I've considered that."

"Have you now?"

"Well enough to know that it's a man's world unless you're brave enough to break the mold. So, tell me Aunt Shannon, did my father set you up?"

"Lord on high, the way you talk! What do you mean by that?"

"I've seen the pictures."

"Child, do you think so little of your father?"

"No," Mindy said. "Or, at least, I'm not sure. But, why does he have them?"

"I'm sorry you had to see those," Shannon said. "But, you're a meddling child. I owe you nothing."

"I'm coming to Philadelphia whether you help me or not."

"Why would you come here, knowing I can't keep you safe?"

"What did dad get you into?"

"Are you so eager to enter such an ugly world?"

"No," Mindy said. "On the other hand, I'd like to hit someone in the gut for you if you'd quit shadow boxing and tell me what happened."

"What the hell," Shannon said. "You want to hear this; I'll share the sordid burden with you. Your father convinced me to act as his agent and buy some land near the bay here. He was speculating. A rumor was afoot that the Navy was going to build a new test facility on the land. We bought the land at an inflated price. Deal fell through. Your Dad's business associates defaulted on the loan. The…principals for the other side were unhappy and took their unhappiness out on me."

"Why wasn't dad there, protecting you, talking to the cops?"

"You don't rat guys like these to the cops. He's trying, desperately, to convince these thugs that he's good for the debt."

"How much?"

"I've said too much already."

"Aunt Shannon, did you like having those scum spread you out like that over money? Did you have a good time?"

"Damnation! I should hang you up right now!"

"I have money," Mindy said, "lots of money, Aunt Shannon. Belongs to me, not my parents. Their money is gone. You've found that out the hard way. Let me help you. We'll hire lawyers, protection, and medical attention whatever you need."

"Bless me if I'm talking to a seventeen-year-old here. When did you get so tough?"

"Someday, we'll talk about things worse than those pictures, Auntie, but not tonight. Will you help me and allow me to help you?"

"May I not be cursed by being born a woman in my next life. Your grandda gave me a man's name from the old land to help protect me in the new and it hasn't done a bit of good. What do you want from me then?"

"Okay, here's what I need to get started..."

"So, you know everything," dad said.

"Yes," Mindy said. "That conversation took place three months ago."

Dad sat down at his desk and ran his fingers through his hair. Mom went over and stood behind him. "Mindy, I failed," he said. "I was horrified by what happened. I've never dealt with people who were willing to do what those people did to Shannon—for money." His shoulders sagged.

"You paid them off?" Mom asked.

"Yes," Mindy said. "Wasn't easy. The trustee and my lawyer went several rounds over the release of the money. My lawyer convinced him, finally, that this was an educational expense. The trustee wanted to involve you all of course. My lawyer threatened a law suit if he did."

Her dad was weeping onto the top of his desk. She turned her face away. She didn't want to cry too. "Twenty thousand dollars covered the debt," she said. "They won't get the chance to enjoy their money though," Mindy paused. "Arranging to have my aunt raped and beaten was not a nice way of asking for money. The counsel I retained in Philadelphia is an old school chum of the District Attorney. The D.A. has called certain businessmen and told them that a grand jury is being convened to investigate the aggravated rape of Shannon Cassidy. A good Philadelphia lawyer is, I have found out, worth his weight in gold."

Shannon's acquisition of property in Mindy's name and Mindy's enrollment in Penn proceeded without a hitch. Like Mindy had told her parents, nothing beats the assistance of a good Philadelphia lawyer on retainer. No one bothered Shannon a second time.

Mindy and her Aunt became best friends because they never wasted a moment of each other's time. They were tough broads and they had no time for foolishness.

Mindy and her dad burned the copied pictures. The originals went to the Philadelphia District Attorney. Mindy and her dad never said another word to each other about the queered land deal. What was there to say?

Chapter 18
Hey Boot!

We are the boots, Most stupid of recruits;
We love to eat but hate the chow;
We love to sleep, tonight or now;
We'd love to fight, but don't know how...
We are the boots...
We ride the range and scrub latrines;
We loathe the sight of pork and beans;
We are the lowest of Marines...
We are the boots!

"Sing it out, you maggots! I can't hear you!"

"That motherfucker can't hear us because of all the noise he's making."

"Shut the hell up, Louwicky, or we'll be scrubbing the cans for two solid weeks!" Dud hissed.

"Shut up yourself, Ludlow."

The mud squished beneath their feet, as they ran in place in the pouring rain. "Jesus, what a hellhole Parris Island is," Louwicky muttered. Dud silently agreed. In May of 1941, Parris Island, the Rock, was the butt hole of the known world.

"I hope you friggin greenhorns remembered to put pecker covers on your rifle barrels. I see rust in any rifle in this platoon; I will run you maggots until your sorry nuts are dragging. Now, what are you maggots?"

"We are boots, most stupid of recruits, the rain is wet and the mud is deep, we'd like to eat and we'd love to sleep; we growl like wolves, but obey like sheep; we are the lowest of Marines; we are the boots."

"All right, boots, stand down, chow formation in nine minutes. No mud in the hut, if I see mud, we'll party through the night to get it four-by-four."

"Aye, Aye, Drill Sergeant!"

Dud and the other recruits double-timed it to the communal showers and stripped down. Hughes and Dud had "bootie duty." They gathered the boots up for the entire platoon and took them around the shower to the exit, then raced back around the building in their skivvies to run through the shower and catch up with their buck-naked platoon brothers. DI Belzer, a.k.a. "Bucket butt", was exceedingly fond of watching his recruits mop the barracks with a small hand brush out of a bucket of foul smelling disinfectant. Bucket butt was a cleanliness fiend.

"Show me those feet girls," Bucket butt said. "Show up clean for evening chow and someone might decide you're officer material. Damn, I'd be glad to send you jerk-offs en masse to OCS. Every last mother's leg drip in this company is too worthless to remain enlisted in my Corps."

"DI Belzer is not a nice man," Dud said to Hughes, as they sprinted through the showers. "I like him though. He reminds me of my old man."

"Pathetic," Hughes said. As the squad jogged back to the barracks, something didn't feel quite right. Dud looked down and noticed he was wearing two left boots.

"Goddamn it Louwicky! You got my right boot on your left again."

"So? What's it to you Ludlow? Youse got two left feet anyway."

Dud was running behind Louwicky, so he grabbed Louwicky's nuts and squeezed.

Louwicky yelped and fell face first in the mud.

"Damn, Louwicky," Dud said. "A perfectly good shower shot to hell."

"Crap on a shingle, Ludlow," Hughes said. "What'd you rack up Louwicky for? We have inspection in five minutes."

"Quit whining Hughes," Dud said. "If we all piss on him, he's clean as a whistle."

The men were back at the hut. They had four minutes to chow call.

"Stand in the rain with your rifle at port arms," Dud said. "If anyone sees you, they'll think you're standing a punishment tour. I'll hand you a towel out the back."

"You flaming shit-brick," Louwicky said. "This better work."

"Wonder what Bucket butt will do when he sees Louwicky standing at port arms in the rain–buck-naked," Whitlock said.

"Doesn't bother you that you've probably bought us all a run down to Elliott beach tonight, does it?" Hughes said.

Dud bloused his left pant leg as he rested his boot on top of his footlocker. He wiped his footlocker off and stowed the rag. He secured the locker and came to attention in time to hear, "Attention boots. The Drill Instructor is on the deck!" Bucket butt marched slowly up one side of the hut and down the other. He looked constipated. Everyone's uniform was crisp and the hut was 4 x 4.

Stopping at Louwicky's bunk, he got happier. "Where is this boot?"

Silence reigned. Everyone knew the question was rhetorical. No one had been commanded to speak. Bucket butt strode up to Dud and stuck his face one-inch from Dud's.

"Speak, maggot! Where is the sorry excuse for the sack of shit that occupies that berth the Marine Corps so generously provided?"

"Drill Instructor, this Boot informs that the Boot the Drill Instructor seeks is standing close order drill on the port side of the hut. The Boot the Drill Instructor seeks is ashamed of his close order drill technique and is seeking to become a better marine, Drill Instructor!"

The DI marched to the rear entrance of the Quonset hut, stuck his head out and bellowed, "boot, front and center, on the double!"

Louwicky dutifully trotted around the corner and came to a halt with his rifle at port arms, naked to the world, except for his boots.

The DI stared at Louwicky for 5 seconds.

He turned about face and with no change in expression returned to his previous spot in front of Dud's face.

"Retrieve this maggot's poncho. The manual states that no marine shall stand post in the rain without donning his poncho. When you maggots return from chow, each boot shall stand guard in precisely the same attire for two hours until 0600 hours tomorrow morning. You, maggot, (his finger was on Dud's chest) will stand the 0200 to 0400 watch and the 0400 to 0600 watch. The boot standing watch now will also stand the 0400 to 0600 with you, understood?"

"Aye, aye Drill Instructor!"

"Proceed to chow call, you miserable boots. And you, sentry, return to your post until relieved."

Covered by his poncho, Louwicky, returned to his post.

"Yo, Ludlow, you awake?"

"Yeah, Louwicky," Dud said. "I'm as chipper as a rooster at dawn. What's on your mind?"

"When I left Brooklyn for this gig, I never thought I'd end up watching the stars while toting a gun and standing sentry duty bare-assed."

"Do me a favor, Louwicky, never call your rifle a gun again. For that, Bucket butt will have us pouring tea and peeling spuds for two weeks."

"Ludlow, youse alright. I know I'm a fuck-up, that is why I'm here. I didn't mean nothing by the boots thing, you know? We okay with each other?"

"We're gonna be fine, Louwicky," Dud said. "I don't agree with you about one thing though."

"What's that?"

"I don't think you're a fuck-up. I just think you gotta remember left from right."

"Left from right, I can handle that 4x4, Ludlow. I can."

The two men spent the rest of the sentry tour picking constellations out of the morning sky. The rain had stopped at eleven, revealing the diamond on velvet splendor above them. Louwicky never confused his boots with Dud's again.

Chapter 19
An Inexact Science

I sat on the stoop where I had last spoken to dad. I took a swig of orange soda out of the bottle sitting on the porch next to me. I hoisted the bottle toward the sunlight that was arching over the house and yelled, "orange soda, the breakfast of champions!" The prior week had been a blue ribbon award winner. I had received a note from Dud and a letter from Mindy. I decided to read both again before I headed off to school. Dud had placed the note inside an envelope with a picture showing him and three other guys covered in mud holding their rifles while standing ankle deep in what appeared to be a huge mud pit. The caption on the picture read, "humping it on the Rock." The card said,

Davis you wouldn't believe some of these people. Get a load of this - I'm one of the smart guys here. They've made me a platoon leader and gave me a stripe. Bucket butt (my DI) assures me that if war comes, this'll get me killed in a hurry. The SOB loves me like a son. Looks like we're shipping out to the West Coast in a week or so. I'll write again when I have a new temporary address. Tell my mom I'm okay, if you see her.

Dud

The letter from Mindy was longer. Makes sense, I thought. If your buddies in the Corps caught you writing long-winded letters to another guy they might begin to wonder which way you tossed your rifle. Mindy wrote:

Really miss you. My days here are taken up trying to remember which comes first out of the stomach, the

transverse or the descending colon. I want to be up on my anatomy when school starts. I'll enter Penn for the first summer term. I wanted to start in January, but the Dean said I needed some prep courses. Hope living in the same town with my parents isn't too big a pain. I know I have done nothing to make life there easier on you. The day after we...you know...a lot of family business was discussed, including you. When you came up in conversation, mom slapped me. I slapped her back and we haven't said word one to each other since I left the study that awful day. She didn't even go with dad and me to the train station the day I left for Philly.

They need me and they hate me for it. Wanted to see you at the station but the tension would have been too much to bear. Hope you understand.

I can't believe you're headed for the Navy in the fall. It'll be different that's for sure. Hope they send you someplace interesting - maybe, Marseilles. If you do end up there, describe the sun for me. I've read the sunlight on the French coast has a special quality. Aunt Shannon is a laugh a minute; she's no longer concerned that having me around is a disaster. Got to go, we're headed down to the market. I think of you often... If you ever make it up here, we'll go sculling on the Schuylkill. It may sound disloyal, but the Schuylkill is a better river than the Red–no rattlesnakes, no water moccasins. They know a little about music here too...bet we could find some Gershwin or even some Caruso to listen to. Tell Ralph and your mom I said hi. Hope this finds everyone well.

Love,
Mindy

P.S. Do you know the difference between the frontal lobe and the parietal lobe? Or what your spleen does? Don't feel bad. I don't know either. But I intend to change that!

"Mindy and Dud are out in the world having adventures and I'm still stuck in Gainesville, Texas," I said out loud. I held the letter up. Her scent was on the stationary, leaving me dizzy and disoriented. The scent hung heavy in the air like she was all around me. The memory of her wrapping her legs around me exploded in my head unbidden. My visceral need for her forced me to grab the porch railing. I had a raging hard on and was going to be late for school to top it off. Thankfully, Ralph had already left for school and mom had already headed down to the train station to ship some dresses off. No one was around to witness my predicament.

I picked up the letter and the card from where I'd just dropped them on the gray and weathered seat of the porch swing. No sound, no welcome smell of cigarette smoke, no essence of dad to save me from this dreary nightmare. I was leaving soon, but not soon enough.

I stood up and placing the letter and the card in my back pocket; went to my room and looked at the letter I'd received from the Department of the Navy for the umpteenth time.

The letter indicated that as a result of my aptitude scores, I was being routed to Iowa State University for motor mechanic school before reporting to New London Connecticut for sub school. I had to be at Iowa State by 22 September. They wanted me sooner, but I told them about my dad, so they moved my reporting date back 90 days. Truth be told, I was more concerned about Ralph than mom. I figured the extra time would help Ralph adjust. I was mystified by my assignment. I had expressed no interest in submarines to the navy recruiter who had visited the high school. I have since figured out that my wishes do not matter to the military.

On my way to school, I sauntered down California Street. I waved at Mr. Chaney, yelling, "I'll be in today after I finish up my science project."

He waved me over.

"Good morning, Mr. Chaney. I finished March's balance sheets last night."

"Yes, I wanted to tell you how much I appreciated you staying late on a school night to finish that up. When are you leaving us?"

"In a couple of months...after I graduate."

"Perhaps we go to Dallas or Oklahoma City with your mother and have dinner before you go. You are a dependable young man, Will Davis."

"I'd like that, sir."

"Do me a favor in the meantime."

"Yes sir?"

"Please, stay out of the way when Mrs. Hulen or one of her friends comes in to shop?"

"Yes, I can do that, sir," I said. "Hope my working for you hasn't hurt business. I'll quit now if you want me to."

"No boychik," he said, as he patted my shoulder. "We will salve their feelings by pretending you are in proverbial cathouse."

"Mr. Chaney, I think you meant - doghouse."

"Yes, yes just so. I do not wish to pry into your affairs, but I would like to call upon your mother to inquire after her health. Do you object?"

"No, Mr. Chaney," I said. "Call away. Don't expect too much though. My dad's death took the sap right out of her."

"Sorry, sap?"

"Yes, like how you feel about the krauts in Warsaw. You become very sad when you speak of it."

"Ahh, Ich verstehe dich. Well, perhaps, one sapless old trunk will speak to another."

"Sorry, sir, but I have to go. My science project still needs to be set up."

"Hurry on. I did not mean to hold you up for so long. May I ask what your project is?"

"I'm demonstrating the effect varying light levels have on fungus cultured in Petri dishes."

"Good, good - this is new science, I think. I wish you much luck my young friend."

Chapter 20
Power to Heal

"Thus, we are given to understand that lowly mold spores have the power to heal," Mr. Roget, my science teacher, said. "People understood by the late Middle Ages, for example, that poultices could often heal wounds already raw with infection for no apparent reason. Of course, they had no concept of infection. We ourselves are only beginning to understand the implications of Fleming and Chain's work.

Perhaps, Mr. Davis can isolate and stabilize the healing properties of what is now known as penicillin. If so, he may share the Nobel Prize that Fleming and Chain are almost certain to receive at some point in the near future."

Mr. Roget continued peering at the moldy culture dishes as if he expected the cultures to dance around the dish for him. He stood, tapped his head with a pencil for a moment, and then moved to the next project, a homemade radio set.

Benny leaned over and said, "oh man, you hit the jack-pot. Rocket Rojet looked like he wanted to jack-off into your Petri dishes. I never saw anyone get excited over mold before."

"Benny, your talent is wasted here," I replied. "You belong on the New York stage."

The bell rang.

"Saved by the bell," Benny said. "Davis, you better lock up your moldy dishes before the Rocket asks them out."

Benny's project consisted of three rocks in a box. The rocks had notes attached to them that said, *old rock, older rock,* and *oldest rock.* He had grandly called the three rocks, "a study of geologic time."

I gathered up my stuff. Mr. Roget waved me up to his desk.

"Yes, sir?"

Mr. Roget tossed chalk in the air as he leaned on the corner of his rickety desk.

"Mr. Davis, you think I'm nutty am I right?"

"Well now Mr. Roget, I–"

"It's okay Mr. Davis. My feelings aren't hurt. Nor am I mad. I do want you to think about something. I want you to think about the implications of your work."

"I'm sorry sir. I don't understand."

"Yes, you do, Wilson."

I sat my books down on the edge of his desk.

"Is my work sloppy or careless sir? I tried very hard to record my data and document my findings."

"Precisely my point. Your work is careful, thoughtful and demonstrates intellectual rigor. Your careful documentation of the fragility of the mold spores under varying temperature and lighting conditions is scientific work of the first order. This effort is impressive."

"Sir, I don't know what to say."

"Nothing further is required Mr. Davis," he said. "I live in this town. I know that you have had other things on your mind lately. I couldn't pass up the opportunity to complement you on such a strong effort when you could've plodded along with Mr. Reavis … and done nothing."

"Thanks, Mr. Roget."

"No, Mr. Davis, thank *you,*" he said. "You've re-minded me that my students do listen occasionally. And, now, excuse me."

After I left, Mr. Roget placed *Ode to Joy* on a turntable. He then entered an *A+* next to my name in the grade-book, a D next to Benny's name, and said, "my high and low parameters have been set."

The janitor disturbed him at a quarter past seven.

"Okay to mop now, Mr. Roget?"

"Sure, Al. I was getting ready to leave now anyway."

"Heard Charlie Parker on the phonograph from down the hall, Mr. Roget."

"You a bebop fan, Al?"

"Yes sir," Al said. "I am."

"Want me to leave the music on for you?"

"That's kind sir, but, no," he said. "I'm done after I finish in here."

"Al, I'm sorry. Hope I haven't kept you."

"No sir," Al said. "Truth is, enjoy the company when you work late. The music is a gift."

"I know," Mr. Roget said. "The rigor of science applied to the gift of genius."

"Amen," Al said.

"Amen," Mr. Roget agreed.

Chapter 21
A Milkshake on the Beach

"Southern Oklahoma is nothing but red clay and snakes," Bob said to himself. "Can't see jack-crap out here either." Bob reckoned he was 20 miles north of Gainesville. He pulled his ankle out of the stream he'd found. "That's ugly," he said. "Never saw anything that purple before." He'd made good time for the first two hours then he'd tripped on some sliding rock on an escarpment leading down to the stream. "Went ass over tea–kettle," Bob said. "Lucky that I only sprained my left ankle. Could've broken my frigging neck."

Bob gingerly dipped his purple ankle back into the stream to cut the pain and the swelling. Bob focused on a boulder across the stream from where he sat and said, "It'd be a damn shame to kill me now, Lord. Trying my best to do something right for a change. I'd like to see Betty and my kid before anything happens to me. So, I guess I'll just sit here and soak this foot until the sun gets up over the horizon and I can actually see where I'm going."

He leaned back and enjoyed the feel of the water rushing over his foot. "Not angry anymore at you Louis," he said. He felt strange. Then, reality hit him hard in the gut. "Damn, guess I'm just happy. Going to see my family." He whispered, "thank you, Lord. Reckon you've given me more than I deserve."

Bob pulled his foot out of the stream. The ankle was numb. "Numb is good," he said, as he eased his boot back onto his swollen foot. Bob foraged around and found a strong branch suitable for use as a staff and crutch. The sky was brilliant orange in the east. Guess I now have enough light to walk in without risking another potentially fatal tumble, Bob thought. Even have an outside chance of catching the afternoon bus from Ardmore to Durant.

"Well get on with it then shit-head," he mumbled to himself. "I don't see any angels or fairies coming to carry you on gossamer wings."

He chuckled again. "Gossamer wings? Where the hell did that come from? He was beginning to sound like Will Davis. Hope that boy is all right. Who knows, if Betty and me have a boy, I might just name the little cuss Will. Ohhhh damn, this ankle hurts."

"I'm totally sick of milk," Millie Dodson said. "If I never see another glass, I'll be content."

"You should have thought of that, Miss Mildred, before you got yourself pregnant."

"Shut your yap, Evans," Millie said. "Go play little miss tight britches on someone else. "You think I'm a slut? That's okay, because you're a stuck up bitch." "You bought yourself an adverse write-up with that remark Miss Mildred," Matron Evans said. "Rest assured the head mistress will hear of this behavior."

"A bun in the oven won't ever be your problem, Evans. Any man desperate enough to try and have sex with you won't be able to pry those skinny little legs open with a crow bar."

"That's nice Miss Mildred. I intend to ask for your expulsion."

"Go soak your head, Evans," Millie said. "My old man could buy and sell this place ten times over. You'll be fired and replaced twenty times before a rich, little pregnant girl like me is sent packing. Deal with it."

Matron-of-the-House Evans performed an about-face and left the dining room with as much dignity as she could muster for someone whose latest frontal assault had been completely decimated.

"Millie," Betty said. "Did the thought occur to you that she might cut your throat some night while you're asleep?"

Mildred Eloise Dodson studied her oatmeal carefully. Her brow furrowed. "I think the oatmeal would be greatly improved if we crushed several beetles and added them to the mix." She sighed and threw her spoon down. "Won't happen, Betty," Millie replied. "Underneath that ugly exterior beats the heart of a true coward. She hates me enough to kill me. Can't handle her fear though. Therefore, her approach is to try and suck the life out of me slowly."

Millie shoved the abandoned oatmeal across the table. Betty prevented the bowl from toppling over the edge and onto the parquet floor. Millie and Betty were alone at a breakfast table that could comfortably seat ten.

"Evans is like Bela Lugosi in those Dracula films," Millie said. "Dracula takes a little blood here, a little blood there, and before you know what has happened, you're chalk white, sleeping the day through, hoping that no one stops by with a stake made of sharpened holly."

"If that's the case," Betty said. "Sleep in armor and stay away from me. I'm trying to stay on her good side."

"I don't see what you're worried about. Your big, strong boyfriend is coming for you. I'm headed back to a stupefying boarding school in Boston to a chorus of whispers and snickers."

"Why? Are you the only rich kid this has ever happened to?"

"No," Millie said. "I was stupid. Used the wrong part of my anatomy to keep my boyfriend happy." She giggled. "My school chums, on the other hand, use their mouths to do more than gossip."

"Millie," Betty said. "You *really* are a poor little rich girl. Where will you be next year? Radcliffe? Rome perhaps?" Betty examined her chipped nails, and then said. "Oh, sorry, not Rome, the war and all. Guess you'll have to settle for Palm Beach. As for your kneeling debutante buddies, they probably gargle with rose water after they've...satisfied their prep school, horn-dog, boyfriends."

Millie looked at Betty over the top of her milk glass. Her eyes were blue china saucers - Spode saucers - a Brahmin princess. She deliberately put her milk on the table and steepled her fingers. As she stared at Betty over the tops of her long, manicured fingers, a wide grin broke across her face.

"Lemon water, maybe, but never rose," she said. "Rose water is for finger dipping."

Years later, when they spoke to each other, the opening line was always, "rose water". The response, "lemon water, and, by the by, how is Radcliffe?" The response, "I wouldn't know. I spent the term in Rome, or was that Palm Beach?"

Later that night, after the lights went out, Betty crept into Millie's room and crawled into bed with her. It was a tight fit. They were both getting rather large.

"Sorry, about breakfast," Millie said. "That's okay," Betty said. "I'm on edge too. I haven't heard from Bob in two weeks. I can't go home; it'd be bad, real bad. My mom has to call me from a pay phone, so my dad won't see the call on the phone bill. He hates me."

Millie cradled Betty's head against her chest.
"Men, even daddies, are amazing," she said. "They want their mommies when they're little and when they are old enough to mate, they do everything they can think of and then some to impregnate us."
"Problem is," Betty said. "Once they do, they go haywire."

"Ever wonder," Millie asked. "Why, sex is always our fault?"

"Strange, isn't it?" Betty said. "We give men what they want–they hate us. We hold back–they hate us."

I know!" Millie exclaimed. "We can't be ourselves. Men seem to control all the labels. We have to be wives or mommies."

"And, if we're not?" Betty said.

"Then, we're sluts or whores," Millie said. "We can't play bridge and we can't join the local garden club."

"This is depressing," Betty said, as she shifted her position on the narrow bed. "We can't win. We're pregnant or we bleed. Are you saying men need us, but they don't really like us?"

"Some do," Millie said. "But, I don't think I've met any real men yet. I think all I've met so far are boys. What about you?"

"Maybe I'm lucky," Betty said. "Knew from the moment I saw Bob, that I wanted him. I begged him to screw me - from behind."

"Wow! He got behind you?"

"Guess I should be ashamed, huh?"

"No," Millie said. "Feel happy. I tried to explain to the shit-for-brains who knocked me up what I wanted him to do, you know, with his mouth and with his fingers. Guess what his response was?"

"I have no earthly idea," Betty said.

He looks at me and he says, '"what are you, a nympho?"'

Then, he dresses in three seconds and leaves. After he'd spewed his stuff in me and on me, he couldn't get away from me fast enough. He didn't care about what I wanted."

"I know what I want right now," Betty said.
"What?"
"I'd love a frosty chocolate milkshake."
"I'd go for that," Millie said.

146

"I thought you were sick of milk."

"Milkshakes are exempt. If someone brought me a milkshake and a cigarette, there's no telling what I'd do."

"You sure sell out cheap for a Boston socialite."

We listened to the lonely sound of the wind knocking the branches of a big elm against the side of the house.

"You're right," Millie said. "A milkshake and a cigarette are small potatoes. What I really need..."

"Is?"

Millie didn't answer. She was asleep.

Chapter 22
Florence Nightingale Had Life Easy

"Nursing is service, a life of service to others. Much of your time is spent tending people who are in pain and who are dying. Often, you will be working on wards at night when you have had little or no sleep. The patients will often be querulous and the doctors sleep deprived."

The auditorium was quiet. The Dean sipped water from a glass on a small table adjacent to the podium. Then, before continuing she made eye contact with all forty-seven nursing students.

"This, ladies, is not a calling for the faint of heart or the weak - willed. Most doctors remain unenlightened about the role a well-trained nurse plays in healing. Most doctors think that nurses change bedpans–nothing more."

Clearing her throat, the Dean took another sip of water and continued.

"Idealism is a good thing. Idealism is what brought most of you here. But, high minded thought alone will not sustain you. Rid yourself of any starry-eyed visions you may have of being a white angel gliding across the floor with a lamp in your hand. Quit now if this is your expectation."

The Dean walked around to the front of the podium and stared hard at each of us before continuing.

"We here in the States kid ourselves, but our denial doesn't matter. We will soon be in this war. When it happens, we'll need nurses, lots of them. Those of you who survive our program are going to places that are incomprehensible. I was in France in 1918 with Black Jack Pershing during the Meuse-Argonne offensive. I spent days covered in blood, vomit, and worse. I watched young boys...."

The Dean suddenly stopped talking and dropped her head down onto her chest as if the weight of her thoughts were simply too heavy to bear. She suddenly raised up and with a defiant glint in her eyes, came closer to us. Some of the girls sitting in the front row actually flinched.

"Enough about me. I'll save the Argonne for another day. Stay with us here at Penn, if you dare. We'll make each of you first-rate nurses. Nursing is a noble profession. Don't pick up the torch on a whim however. If you aren't strong, this torch will burn you."

As we were filing out, the Dean whispered, "it will burn you even if you are."

Mindy didn't actually hear the Dean whisper the words about the torch. She was already out the door, making her way across the Quadrangle to catch a bus on Spruce Street. Her Aunt Shannon had recently taken a position at the Curtis Institute of Music. She controlled audition appointments for musicians seeking entry into the prestigious school.

The day was mild.

Mindy and Shannon had agreed to meet on the South side of Rittenhouse Square. They intended to eat their lunches outside, before listening to a student string quartet performance at the Institute.

Mindy's aunt had a brightly colored quilt already spread out on the grass in the square. Children were sailing toy boats in the square's pool not far from where they sat.

"Cucumber or hard salami, dear?"

"I'll go with the hard salami," Mindy said. "What do you have to go with it?"

"How about mustard on dark rye?"

"Sounds good to me. How are the auditions going?"

"I believe that auditions are the auditory equivalent of grading thirty-five essays... if you're an English teacher. I'll hear Purcell in my nightmares for the next three weeks. Still, the kind of musical talent this place attracts is amazing."

Mindy munched on her salami sandwich. The sandwich was delicious.

"Can you really discern a small variation in the way a piece is played? Seems like discriminating between two good piano players based solely on how they play the notes would be difficult."

"Sometimes musical discernment is difficult," Shannon said, warming to the subject. "We get a fair number of musicians at this level who can play a piece well, if they've practiced, but lack the innate ability to sight read."

She knitted her eyebrows, as she considered the question further and swallowed the final bite of her cucumber sandwich.

"Fairly esoteric considerations separate the good musicians from the great ones, or at least great enough to get into the Institute. The other day we accepted one student and rejected another because we liked the ability of the accepted child to play a piece with triple pianissimo while still separating the individual notes correctly and with legato - smoothly. The child we rejected played with great clarity but often rolled the notes. One gets admitted. One goes home."

"May I ask you a personal question, Aunt Shannon?"

She smiled as she stood up.

"Why not? You already know most of my deep dark secrets. Ask away. I may, however, lie in response."

"Which kind of piano player were you?"

Aunt Shannon stared off towards the Institute and replied, "You never beat around the bush, kid."

She took a cigarette out of her purse and fiddled with trying to find her lighter. She finally managed to light up and dropped her lighter back into her purse.

"Forget I asked."

"No, it's okay," Shannon blew out, cigarette smoke wafted away above their heads. "I ask myself that same question over and over. I've decided I was the worst kind of musician. I was someone who had talent and pissed it away; getting drunk and doped up in more juke joints than I care to remember."

"Hell, I'm flattering myself," She added. "I was a drunk and an addict who blamed my failures on others."

She took another deep drag on her cigarette and scattered the remnants of her sandwich on the ground for the birds to eat.

"I chose to fail. That about cinches it."

I stood up and kissed my Aunt on the cheek.

"You're okay now though, that's what matters."

"Yeah, darling, I'm okay now."

Chapter 23
Leaving California Street

"Will, war and combat is always the same. Young men go off to war and die in combat. These same young men come home in boxes. Old men like me weep and leave flowers on their graves, wondering why young men fight battles that old men start."

"Mr. Chaney, you're talking like I'm already dead, I'm only going to Iowa."

"Remember your prayers, Wilson. With due respect to Mr. Chaney, remember Jesus in your heart. Avoid the wicked."

"Mom, between you and Mr. Chaney, I'm about ready to run home and hide under my bed. Anything you care to add, Ralph?"

"Dang, Will, I wish I was old enough to go with you. Everyone is getting out of this one-horse town."

"Praise Jesus that you're too young to go anywhere except to church. Go get on that train Will, if you're of a mind to."

"Bye, mom."

I gave her a quick hug and a peck on the cheek. My mother wasn't much for displaying affection in public.

Mr. Chaney though bear-hugged me and wiped some tears from his eyes.

"You have been a good friend and a loyal employee, Wilson. I will pray fervently for your safe return. I also have something to give you. Please don't open the package until you reach your destination. All I will say for now is that this thing was my father's and his father's before that." He hurriedly pressed a pale blue box into my hands. The box was sealed around the edges with wax. Before I could respond, he turned and walked off the platform.

The train let go with a hair-raising whistle. Ralph jumped a foot off of the platform. "Guess maybe we ought to go down to the cemetery and see if that blast raised the dead," he said.

"Speaking blasphemy is no way to send your brother off."

"Sorry mom, I didn't mean anything by it."

"Hell is filled with people who didn't mean anything while they were alive. Wilson, write to me when you arrive. You have a good head on your shoulders. Use your mind often and your mouth as little as possible. Try as best you can to avoid the perils of sin. The gates of Hell are wrought by the sins of men. Go on now."

"Bye Ralph, bye mom." I leaped onto the stairwell of the day coach as the stationmaster called, "all aboard!"

I settled myself into my seat and looked at the box Mr. Chaney had pressed into my hand. I put the box in the breast pocket of my suit coat. I was alone. I propped my feet up on the seat facing me and stared out the window. The haul to Iowa was going to be a long one. After I changed trains in Dallas, I was going to make stops in Oklahoma City, Wichita, Kansas City, and Des Moines before reaching Ames. My orders allowed three days travel time. I reckoned we'd make it.

I was apprehensive about what was ahead of me. I didn't know why I was being diverted. A telegram from the Navy Yard in Washington had informed me that indoctrination and basic training in Green Bay Wisconsin was waived. I was reporting to a new program the Navy was implementing, called "V-6". The Navy said I had an aptitude for electronics and mathematics. Complete surprise to me. The Navy probably was going to need two days to figure out they had the wrong Wilson Davis, then I'd be in Green Bay with the rest of the seaman recruits. I rooted around in my valise for my copy of *The Grapes of Wrath*.

Mrs. Kelso, my high school English teacher, was fond of both John Steinbeck and William Faulkner. She considered them to be the greatest living American authors. I read - flipping pages as the scenery went by. I felt an involuntary shiver go down my backside. The book was gloomy. The despair of the Joad family wasn't what I needed right now. I put the book away and slept till we hit Dallas.

"Hey pal, wake up."

I sat up. A conductor was standing over me. I had no idea where I was for a good five seconds. The conductor helped me out.

"This train heads back up to Gainesville in about forty-five minutes. I reckon since you came from there, you weren't intending to head back right away?"

"That's right. I'm headed up to Ames, Iowa."

"You have a bit of a wait. That train leaves this platform in about two hours. There's a canteen on the mezzanine level. The coffee isn't bad and for Texas, the pastrami is pretty good too. Watch your wallet. Pickpockets watch for young guys like you. Act like you know what you're doing and where you're going, even if you don't."

"Thanks. Guess I am in the big city."

The conductor snorted. "Compared to where you came in from and where you're going I suppose it is. Truth is, Dallas doesn't know big from anything. Wait until you see the Big Apple or Chicago. Then we'll talk about big."

"Your accent - you aren't from Dallas or even Oklahoma City are you?"

The conductor laughed.

"No way, kid. I'm from Jersey. Hoboken to be exact." The conductor, who was younger than I'd first thought, looked down at his shoes.

"My dogs feel like I walked the whole way here. Come to think of it, I have walked the whole way here. Anyways, have a good trip up to Iowa kid. Remember what I said about your wallet."

Being alone on the Red River is different than being lonely when you're a long way from home, I thought as I hopped off the train onto the platform. I doubted the Navy would appreciate it if I telegraphed and said, "never mind."

I gathered my things and placed my wallet in my front pocket before heading off the platform and into the station. I tried hard not to gawk. The marble and the gilt edged ceiling tiles were a sight to remember. People were scurrying around. Everyone listened to the sound of train arrival and departure times being announced over the intercom.

You could fit every person in Gainesville in the lobby of Union Station, I thought. I saw an information booth and inquired about the location of the canteen. The lady at the booth also pointed out directions to the luggage storage kiosk.

The coffee was good, the roast beef sandwich with brown mushroom gravy was even better. I was sitting in a green booth wedged in between two or three other booths. Some moments after I tore into the roast beef sandwich I overheard the conversation of the two men in the booth behind me. The voices caused me to raise my eyebrows.

"Mr. Sam, I'm telling you that man is twenty pounds of horse manure in a ten-pound bag. The SOB hasn't got the sense the good Lord gave Adam."

"Lyndon, have you ever been in the Army?"

"Sir, you know that I haven't."

"Well then, do not underestimate the irrational love the Army has for horses."

I heard some shuffling of feet and then, "Mr. Sam, they can play polo on them ponies until their balls turn blue in the saddle for all I care. I just can't abide such obvious stupidity, even in an Army General."

"Lyndon, I'm aware Patton can't get his tanks repaired."

"Mr. Sam, even if he could, most are hopelessly antiquated anyway. New equipment is essential, yet, that goddamn idiot at Hood still wants to charge machine gun emplacements on horseback."

"Yes, I agree, that was even a bit much for me. We didn't witness modern tactics and strategy at Hood. Some of our commanders ended their education in the Crimea or even at the end of the Civil War."

"Hell, Mr. Sam if he had even studied those wars, he would know that the days of headlong cavalry charges are a thing of the past."

A man in a tie approached their table.

"Gentlemen, I came the moment I heard you all were here. Can I seat you somewhere more private perhaps?"

I got a shock. Suddenly, this huge face was peering around the corner at me. I recognized the face immediately. Lyndon Baines Johnson had the waviest black hair and the worst jug ears I'd seen.

"Son, this here man wants to move us the hell out of this booth. Are we bothering you? If we are, we will certainly move."

"No, sir. You all aren't bothering me. I do have something to say though."

"Shoot, young man."

"If what you all are saying about the Army is true, I sure am glad that I signed up with the Navy."

Johnson slapped his hands across his knees and guffawed loud enough to wake the dead.

"Come on around here, boy. Introduce yourself and meet Mr. Rayburn."

I stood up and turned around so that I was facing both men.

"I'm sorry, gentlemen. I didn't mean any disrespect."

Mr. Rayburn took a stubby cigar out of his mouth and said, "Boy, what you said wasn't disrespect. That remark was the cold, hard truth. Where you headed?"

"Sir, I'm headed up to the college in Ames, Iowa to study electronics. The Navy intends to put me on a submarine."

Mr. Rayburn studied his cigar for a moment and said, "lots of interesting things are happening at Iowa State. You must be a sharp young man to get into that program."

"You certainly have a dry wit," Said Congressman Johnson.

"I am surprised by the posting gentlemen. They tell me I scored extremely high on their electronics tests. The only real electrical work I've ever done is on our house in Gainesville and on a couple of cars."

"What's your name, son?" Asked Mr. Rayburn.

"Wilson Pickett Davis, sir."

"You're not Mason Davis' son are you?"

My eyes grew wide. "Yes sir I am. How in the world did you know that?"

Sam Rayburn waved his cigar in the air as if his naming my dad out of the blue sky were nothing.

"I heard about your daddy's untimely death awhile back. I used to play some cards with him. You bear a striking resemblance to him. He was a pretty fair card player, never cheated in order to win," Mr. Rayburn chuckled. "Or, if he did, I never caught him."

I lowered my eyes to the checkered linoleum floor. I was almost too choked up to speak.

"Thank you Mr. Rayburn." I said after a moment. "You can't imagine what you saying that means to me, sir. I'll remember this day forever."

"Think nothing of it son. Do your daddy and yourself proud. As a matter of fact, why don't you give me your address in Gainesville and I'll write your mom a note to let her know that I ran into you and that you're doing okay."

"Sure Mr. Rayburn, I'd be honored. My mom would be thrilled to hear from you."

Lyndon smiled and said, "Is it okay if I contact her on your behalf as well?"

"Of course, I'm sorry. I certainly didn't mean to imply she wouldn't be glad to hear from you as well, Mr. Johnson."

Lyndon Johnson laughed and pulled a couple of cards out of his vest pocket as he consulted his pocket watch.

"I'm afraid we will miss our train to Bonham if we don't hurry and that would be embarrassing because this train is being diverted for our use. Take these cards. If you ever get to Washington, call my office."

Mr. Rayburn placed his hands on my shoulders and said, "come see me too. Make sure Mr. Johnson here remembers to bring you around. I'll contact your mom. Write her. Mothers always worry about their sons. Your mama is no different."

The two men walked away. Both men were as good as their word. Throughout the war, my mom received regular notes from both of them.

The manager brought me out a fresh plate of food and told me the food was on the house, adding that if I was a friend of Mr. Sam's, my money was no good in his place. I hadn't even left Texas and my life was getting interesting. I wondered if Dud and Mindy were having adventures like this.

The rest of the ride up to Ames was not uneventful. I was sitting in one of the day coaches–daydreaming. Several sets of eyes, all female, I realized with a start, were staring at me from the aisle. One of the women stepped out from the others and said, "excuse me we don't mean to bother you but are these other seats taken?"

"No ma'am, they're not. Excuse my feet being up on the seat. I left my good manners at home on my dresser."

"Think nothing of it, Mr.....?"

"Davis, Miss, the name is Wilson Davis. My friends call me, Will."

"Our pleasure, Will. I'm Helen Trajan, this (she pointed to the Brunette over her left shoulder) is Eloise Kent, and this, (she pointed to a very pleasant looking red head over her right shoulder) is Janet Goldman."

The women made themselves comfortable.

"Are we crowding you?" Helen asked.

"No, Miss Trajan. I appreciate the company."

"Are you on the train for business or pleasure?" The red head asked, as she stowed her bag in the overhead. I tried to remember her name.

"Business, I've joined the Navy and I'm on my way to Ames."

Helen smiled. "Ames, Iowa is an awful long distance from an ocean. Aren't you from Dubuque, Eloise?" Helen sat down next to me as she spoke.

"We're right outside of town. Dad has a dairy farm there."

"Any water for Will to go sailing around on in Iowa?"

Eloise furrowed her brow in mock concentration and picked at a run in one of her stockings before answering.

"Nope. Ice skating maybe. No oceans though."

"Thanks for the geography lessons girls. Kind of figured I wasn't going to see any saltwater in Ames."

"Where are you three headed?"

"The Army does not require vast amounts of water. We're headed to the Army nursing school in Des Moines."

"I'm headed to electrician's school in Ames before heading over to New London–a place where you see lots of saltwater."

The red-headed girl kicked off her heels as she settled in across from me. Her toes brushed across my left knee. I heard the faint murmur of silk as her thighs crossed. I forced myself to look up from her legs. All three women were watching me watch her legs cross. I flushed right up to the roots of my hair. "Getting a tad warm in here," I said.

"Tell me Will; are you any good at it?" Asked the red head.

"Excuse me, good at what?"

She gave me a smile and leaned forward on her seat and said, "You know going down … in one of those submarine things. You could get wet in all that water. Can you even swim sailor?"

I remembered. The redhead's name was Janet. I leaned forward so that my face was only inches away from her own. She smelled like ripe peaches on a warm day.

"Janet, not only can I swim. I can dive pretty deep, hold my breath, and surface with breath left over."

"Impressive Will," Eloise said.

"Yes it is," agreed Helen. "For a second, I even thought you two were talking about the ocean."

Helen said this with one eyebrow arched.

The arched eyebrow cracked everyone up and released the tension of the moment.

Later that evening after the train was quiet and the only sound was the clacking of the cars moving over the track. I was drifting off when the berth curtains parted and Janet slid onto my bunk. The moonlight made her body look fluid in her diaphanous gown. As she lay down, I didn't speak. Her gown disappeared. Smooth, warm, she moved over me. Later, she said, "I was wrong about you Will Davis. You can swim. In fact, you could pass for a yeshiva boy." Then, she was gone. I went back to sleep with the scent of peaches all around me.

"Trouble sleeping?" Helen asked.

"Never slept on a train before. Strange experience–pleasant though."

"Is that all?"

I glanced across the compartment at Janet. She was concentrating on her 'Treatment and Care of Tropical Diseases' text.

"Pretty much, what about you?" I asked.

"Thankfully, I could sleep next to a working lumber mill. Good thing too, you're a noisy berth-mate." Helen replied.

"You were in the upper last night?"

"Yes, the evening was educational."

"Helen, you watched us?"

Helen giggled. "Only the part with, you know, with your toes, then her toes, people can be so creative."

"Janet, did you know she was there when you - you know?"

"Don't be mad, Will. Better Helen than some stranger."

"Helen, I've never heard a girl admit she watched before."

"Oh come on Will. Haven't you lived or worked on a farm? My daddy didn't believe in a woman's work and a man's work. I knew more about breeding and animal husbandry before I was ten than most men pick up in a lifetime. Still, I have to tell you, I've never seen a farm animal do what you did to Janet with your toes, I was astounded."

Janet turned red. Eloise opened the door and came in. "Morning everyone. Did I miss anything?"

"No. Helen, Will and I were just talking about animal husbandry." Janet replied."

"Let's get breakfast," I said.

"Yes," Janet said, as she jumped up. "I'm famished."

As Janet and I left, I noticed Eloise' puzzled look. I didn't look at Helen as we exited the compartment.

I had a three-minute egg, wheat toast, pancakes, and bacon. Janet had a three-minute egg, bran flakes, and coffee.

"If I packed food away like that, Will," Janet said. "I'd weigh two hundred pounds in a week."

"Well, he's still a growing boy, right Janet?" Helen said, as she walked up to the table.

"He needs to eat now," Janet said. "Once the war gets rolling, we all may remember meals like this with fondness. Hell, I may order a rasher of bacon just so I can say later on that I didn't pass up an opportunity to eat."

"That's depressing. Especially for someone who's adapting so well," Helen said.

"Put a sock in it Helen," Janet shot back. "Read the papers. The war is raging in Syria and North Africa. The Brits have bombed the Rohr Valley and the German Luftwaffe is bombing London. The Germans sank another American freighter yesterday. Do you think the United States is going to remain neutral?"

"Janet is right," whispered Eloise.

I jumped in my chair. We hadn't heard her arrive.

"Maybe we should all eat pancakes," Eloise suggested, "to, you know, celebrate our existence." The table became silent. All of us cloaked ourselves in our own thoughts. Helen broke the silence up.

"Guys I was thinking. This could be a small penis problem."

I choked on the wad of syrupy pancakes that I had stuffed in my mouth.

"Excuse me Miss Freud, you were saying?" retorted Janet.

"Napoleon Bonaparte was mortified by the fact that his dick was only four inches long - even stiff. Think about Hitler and Mussolini - those two characters have *small dick* written all over them."

I noticed how quiet our dining car had suddenly gotten. Our fellow diners were staring. We got up. Everyone was quiet until we completed our trek back to the day coach.

We settled in. Janet's forehead was wrinkled as she sat down.

"Helen," she said. "Even if the war is a small dick problem, it won't matter."

"Nope," Helen agreed. "Won't even be an issue."

"I'll bite," I said. "No pun intended. Why not?"

"Because," Eloise exclaimed. "They aren't women."

I rolled my eyes back in their sockets and stared at the coach ceiling. Doing so didn't save me. I was the resident male.

Janet bobbed her head up and down while saying, "If women behaved like these guys, men would gang up on them for acting crazy. They'd nod their heads, sagely, and say 'must be that time of the month."

"Look at Will here," Helen said. "If he could, he'd turn into a bug and crawl away. I'll bet when we were talking about penis length though, he was dying to go off somewhere private and measure his."

"Don't worry, Will," Janet snickered. "I can testify on your behalf. You aren't a member of the 'four-inch' club."

Helen smiled. "Yes, I'm sure he isn't. Everything is larger in Texas. Still, we could make you present your anatomy for immediate measurement."

"Yes," Eloise giggled. "We are nurses, Will. Our examination would be entirely in the interests of science."

"Enough of this," Helen said. "Sorry. I started this. Ladies, we're not going to talk about male anatomy or female monthlies for the rest of the trip."

"Okay, I guess," mused Janet.

"The male penis is an entertaining short subject though," observed Eloise.

When everyone had stopped laughing, I ventured. "Anyone read any good books lately?"

"Yes," Janet said. "I just finished two books that literally had to be smuggled into the States. I've read *Ulysses* and *Tropic of Cancer.*"

"Oh Lord, we'd be better off on the previous topic. Miller is absolutely grotesque and Joyce isn't much better. I can't believe you brought those awful books up Janet."

"Right Helen." Janet began ticking off things on her fingers. "Will here is going to probably end up working in a metal tube. The Army is recruiting nurses to tend to wounded and dying soldiers. There are rumors that the Japanese have murdered several thousand Chinese and that the Germans intend to treat Jews in occupied Europe the same way–with a bad case of death. So, don't sit there and tell me Joyce and Miller are grotesque. Their observations on the human condition are mild - compared to the reality we all now face!"

Tears began to roll down Janet's cheeks. She wept in silence. No one spoke. The train clicking and clacking along was the only sound.

Helen broke the silence.

"Perhaps, we have been unfair to you, Will. Allow us an explanation, we are cousins. We share one other bond too - in case you haven't already guessed."

"Yes," cried Janet. "We have flirted. And I? I've had sex with you without revealing my true identity! Am I a comic book superhero? No! I'm at the other end of the totem pole! I'm a Jew! We are all Jews! Don't you feel dirty?"

I sighed and said. "I'm Baptist. I don't care that you're Jewish. Remember Janet, you came to my berth. I wasn't looking for a cross or a Star of David."

"Yes," said Eloise. "We're wearing our burdens on our sleeves. Two days ago, you didn't even know we existed. Suddenly, we show up and envelope you in our lives."

Eloise stood up and stretched. Janet wiped her face on the sleeve of the blouse she was wearing.

"Oh I don't know, Ellie, Will seems to enjoy my envelope."

"Janet you're shameless! If our family knew of your behavior…"

"What El? What would they do? Send me home - to Warsaw?"

Eloise spoke while gazing out of the window. "Janet's parents are still in Poland."

"I haven't ´heard from them in several months." Janet said. She went and stood beside Eloise at the window. "State Department inquiries haven't yielded anything. We don't even know if they're…still…in Poland."

Helen spoke from the opposite corner of the day coach. Her face was in shadow and her voice was flat. "Last time we heard, my sister Hanna was trapped in Sarajevo."

I sidled over and sat next to Helen. I put my arm around her. She pushed it off. I placed it around her again and said, "listen to me for a moment." I whispered into her ear.

"Really?" She said.

"Really."

She laid her head on my shoulder and closed her eyes.

"I am truly sorry," she whispered.

"Don't be. I only wanted to let you know that I'm capable of comprehending loss, even if I am a gentile."

"Will," Janet said. "No one in this coach holds your Christianity against you."

"Jews, Gentiles, Hindi's, Christians, Buddhist's, Muslim's. Ever wonder why we tie ourselves into knots over the name of God?" I asked.

"Because God is so reticent about giving us guidance. In the Old Testament He was a real chatterbox, now not so talkative, not so free with his counsel," Janet said.

"Hmm," Eloise said as she shuffled a deck of cards. Anyone up for a couple of hands? Penny a point?"

"Still thinking about today?" Helen asked. She sat cross-legged on my bunk next to me. She had dropped feet first into my berth fifteen minutes earlier, saying, "sorry, didn't mean to be so forward. Am I interrupting anything important?"

"Helen, if the world was on fire, I'd have time for you," I'd said. She was wearing a nightgown the color of a blue flame. "Sounds stupid to say, but I feel I've known you, Janet, and Eloise forever. Today was painful because I feel so connected to your loss."

"I know. Strangers on a train and all of that, although I think the real reason for the confidences is you Will. You give off this aura."

"Aura? What the heck is that?"

"Can't really describe what I mean," Helen said. "All I know is that talking to you, getting near you, I get the same feeling I get when I'm drinking warm milk and eating cookies in my kitchen back home. The other girls get this same feeling about you as well. The sensation is strong, like smelling cinnamon or chocolate in the air."

"I don't know what you're talking about Helen. No one has ever told me I smell like chocolate or even cinnamon, but something weird is going on."

"Weirder than the last day and a half?"

"I want to show you something," I said. "My boss gave me this package as I was boarding the train." I held up the box in the dim light of the berth.

"May I?"

I handed her the package. She took the box and gently rattled it against her ear. Her breasts pressed gently against her gown as she rattled the box.

"Silk?" I asked.

"Yes," she said. "Do you want to touch the silk or, are my breasts really what you want to touch?" She picked up my right hand and placed it against her breasts.

"Doesn't the silk feel wonderful against your skin?" She whispered.

"Yes, it does."

She handed the box back. I forced myself to remove my hand from her breasts.

She came across the narrow berth and snuggled against me. I put my arms around her. Heat radiated off of her in waves. Unlike Janet, Helen smelled of exotic spice rather than peaches. No two women I have met have ever exuded such intoxicating odors as Janet and Helen.

"Do you want me to leave so you can look at whatever is in the box in private?"

"Are you kidding me? I wouldn't have shown you the box if I didn't want you to see what's inside. Besides, we're neighbors. Even if I opened it in private you'd know soon enough. I'm nervous though. Whatever is in here meant something to him. He told me what's inside was a family heirloom."

I undid the pale blue paper that had been meticulously wrapped around the bone white box and removed the lid. A square of cotton covered whatever was inside. Helen removed the cotton. The metal glinted in the light of the berth lamp.

"Oh Will, the Star is perfect," she said. "I knew there was a reason that we found you. Are you sure you're a goy? No self-respecting Jew would ever give this gift to a gentile."

Her tone was mocking. Still, there was truth in her words. The golden Star of David sparkled in the dim berth light.

"Are you going to wear this star, Will? Are you going to pronounce your link to the House of David? Or, will you tuck it away in your luggage?"

I placed the filigree chain around my neck. Helen kissed the Star and then kissed me.

"I'm going to take everything off you, except the Star of David, Will," she said. She was on her hands and knees. Her hands resting outside of my thighs. Her hands came up and in one fluid pull, removed my pajama bottoms. "No Will, you have been lying to us the last two days. You're not a goy, not at all."

The next morning, Helen was sitting cross-legged on the berth watching me when I opened my eyes.

"Been awake long?"

"You're such a strange boy. You make love like someone who has spent much time among the Hasidim."

She touched the Star that still hung around my neck.

"This is strange, very strange," she said. "When we decided to have a dalliance to defy our elders, we never intended to meet someone like you. Now, I must explain to Ellie why I stayed all night and didn't come wake her up."

I laughed.

"I' m upset," I said. "Are you insinuating that when you first saw me, you automatically assumed that I would be your pet project for the trip?"

Helen sat with her back against the berth wall. We heard movement in the corridor. Somewhere to our left, we heard the conductor yell, "Des Moines in one hour, Des Moines in one hour."

Helen nodded toward the voice, "a baritone in his church choir." "Or," I said. "A cantor at synagogue." She gathered her robe about her. She was divine. Her tousled hair made her look like a thunderstorm. "True, one can never tell from hearing a voice."

"Or even from seeing, most of the time," I responded.

"I have to go," she said. "In answer to your question. Your suspicions were correct. We decided to have an amorous adventure when we boarded. You were our victim."

She leaned over, pressed herself into me, and kissed me on my mouth. The kiss hurt a little. My lips were still sore from the previous night.

"We didn't bargain on getting you."

She cupped my face in her hands and looked directly at me.

"Please, write or call me Will. I do want to see you again."

"I will. I'll both call and write you. Given the chance, I will also ..."

"Stop right there mister," she laughed. "We'll save the *will also* discussion for another time."

Then, she was gone. By the time I'd cleaned up and headed back to the day coach, the train was pulling into Des Moines. The girls didn't show up. As I headed out onto the platform, to try and catch them, the conductor stopped me and said, "are you Mr. Will Davis by any chance?"

"I am."

"Well, fella, three attractive young ladies asked me to give this note to the good - looking, blue-eyed, Jewish guy in compartment 3-C."

He handed me a small, square envelope.

"Strange, mentioning you was Jewish," he said.

"Why?" I asked.

"The way they described you, I thought you'd be wearing a prayer shawl."

"What caused you to stop me? I wasn't."

"No, but I'm not completely ignorant. You don't see many gold stars like that one in Iowa. See them sometimes when I visit my sister in New York though. Figured you might be the guy. Especially after I saw your eyes."

I'd left the Star of David hanging outside of my shirt. The conductor was right. The icon gleamed in the morning sun.

"Thanks. I appreciate you tracking me down. Means a lot to me."

I got my wallet out to tip him. He held up his hands and said, "Forget it, if three beautiful dames ever wanted to give me something, you'd do the same for me."

With that, he turned and walked off to assist an elderly woman whose poodle had escaped his leash. The poodle, at least, seemed very happy.

I leaned against the station wall and opened the envelope. A short note was enclosed. At the bottom of the note were an address and a phone number where I could reach them in Des Moines. The note read:

Dear Will:

Hope you're not angry with us for leaving you so abruptly. We felt it would be more comfortable for you. My cousins were astonished by the story of the Star of

David. They both thought I was lying until they remembered seeing the package yesterday.

Please do not feel shy about calling us, we are all (I hope this isn't presumptuous on our part) fond of you and would be disappointed not to hear from you - especially me. Stay safe and do well in your work.

> *Your friend*
> *Helen*

I read the note several times. "Remarkable women" I murmured, as I pocketed the note and walked down the platform to find my grip.

Chapter 24
Prepare to Surface

I was finally in Ames Iowa. I'd made it to Ames on a late Sunday afternoon and wasn't required to report in until Monday; so, I had no sense of urgency. Although, as I bag dragged out onto what was West Main Street, I realized I was a long way from home. The weather was cool but the sky wasn't dropping any rain on me. I plopped down on top of my duffel bag and propped my valise up on end and deliberated my next move.

The Navy had provided no guidance on what to do if I arrived early. Two beetles did battle over a dead fly carcass. Their shiny carapaces' were colored forest green by the slanting sunlight. They made tiny clicking sounds as they bumped against each other in their pursuit of the fly.

"Need a ride, Mack?"

The voice startled me. I came up off the top of my duffel, stomping both beetles in the process. The cabbie observed me with good-natured humor. He had a scar that ran from his right ear to his chin. Gray stubble covered his face and a cigarette dangled out the side of his mouth.

"Don't worry, kid, I ain't as mean as I look. Caught a scythe with my head when I wasn't paying attention. I pay attention now." He wheezed as if this was the funniest thing he'd heard in a month.

"Sure, I could use a ride, except I don't know where I'm supposed to go. I report in with the Navy on Monday but today is ..."

"I know, kid. Today is Sunday. I swear if you boys were any greener you'd still be wearing diapers."

Then, he reached around and unlatched the cab's back door.

"Get in, son. The name's Sam, Sam Maxwell. I'm gonna run you up to Melinda Grey's boarding house on Thirteen and Grand. The fare will run you a dime. Melinda will board and feed you tonight for half a sawbuck. I'll pick you up at seven sharp tomorrow morning and run you over to the Navy billet on the campus."

I got in the cab and my stay in Ames began. After I'd left, flies landed on the smashed beetles.

The Petty Officer supervising our entry into the Navy may have been several thousand miles from an ocean but he came into the dorm at 0700 sharp every morning roaring the same oath. "You mother loving shave-tails better have this place looking battened down and shipshape or I'll run your skinny white butts till Jesus makes his second appearance!"

After inspection and calisthenics, he would usher us back into the dorms yelling, "don't pay too much attention to your peckers in the shower, ladies. If you mama's boys want to play with yourselves or with each other, we'll send you over to the damn Army. They love butt-hole bombardiers. Hell, they might even make freaking pilots out of you!"

The P.O. excepted, I enjoyed life in Friley Hall. We were billeted in a bay type setting. Eight guys were billeted in a bay. The shower facilities were located at one end of the hall. A couple of pay phones were located at the other end. There was a small lake sitting just to the east of the dorm. In the winter, we could skate on the frozen surface.

Our routine was the same everyday. After finishing breakfast, we were marched (double-time) across the commons, past the Campanile, to the Agronomy building for the days' instruction. We felt sorry for ourselves. We grumbled about being abused by our sadist Drill Instructor. We didn't understand that the Navy was handling us with 'kid gloves'. Uncle Sam was rushing us through school so we could build a submarine fleet. At the time, the United States was woefully behind both the Third Reich and Japan. We knew nothing of this though. We just didn't appreciate being yelled at because we couldn't bounce a quarter off our bunks. Fact is, we didn't know shit from Shinola, but we were fixing to learn.

Chief Delacroix creaked when he walked and scared the holy crap out of us. He had a patch over his left eye and an honest-to-God peg, where his right leg should have been. If he'd walked into the room with a parrot on his shoulder no one would have blinked.

Our first day with the Chief was memorable. He clomped into the hybrid lab/ warehouse/classroom that Iowa State had provided for our use and glared at us out of his one good eye. He puckered our sphincters with his stare alone. After looking slowly around, he said, "alright boys, what is the one singular most important thing to remember while on a pigboat, or on one of the new fleet boats some of you ladies will serve on?"

We all mumbled various replies ranging from remembering to dog the hatches down to not trying to drink torpedo juice, even filtered through bread.

"No. I'm only going to tell you this once, so listen up. When you use the head on the boat never, never, never use more than twenty pounds of air pressure to blow your shit out of the head into the ocean. If you do, you will learn what the word shithead really means."

We laughed at this advice in a nervous, jittery collective giggle.

"Now someone here will forget what I have said and catch a face full of shit. On a submarine, boys, that's one of the nicer things that can happen to you when you fuck up. Most of the time, you end up trying to breathe cold seawater. Right around the time you figure it ain't gonna work, your lungs implode from the pressure." He looked at each one of us and said, "this is all happening as your crumpled boat slides into Davy Jones' locker. You get no second chance, no reprieve, and no help from your mother. Take a look around. If we get into a shooting war with our good friends the Germans or our good buddies the Japanese, chances are, most of you greenhorns won't be alive when the fracas is over." The Chief struck a match against his peg leg and lit a cigarette. He blew a cloud of smoke over our heads.

"My first boat got shelled on the surface by a Chinese patrol boat disguised as a trawler. I was on deck and got blown clear of the boat by the blast. Everyone else is on eternal patrol. We were in the South China Sea when the attack happened. I lost my leg to a shark. I was lucky. I wasn't a fat seal, so, I wasn't worth a second pass."

The Chief tapped his leg against the floor in a syncopated jazz rhythm.

"After I lost my leg, I managed to pull my belt loose from my dungarees and tie the ragged stump off before I passed out. I had God and a cork life preserver for company. A tender operating out of Mindanao picked me up. I was only in the water a day. The Captain had telegraphed the boat's position before the pressure stove the hull in. I did not ask what his voice sounded like as the transmission faded into the depths. In case I'm not making myself clear, the sea doesn't give a shit about you. The sea ladies will watch you die with complete indifference."

He stood stock still for what seemed like twenty minutes but was probably only a minute or two before continuing. The floor appeared to undulate around and under him as if the lab had been transformed. I could taste the brine.

"We were on the surface because I'd given the all clear. You see, at that time I was all spit and polish. Thought I had the angles covered. The Captain relied upon me to spot potential adversaries. I saw the boat that killed us. The swells partially blocked my vision though and I discounted the danger the vessel represented. The shark that hit me came at me from below. Never saw him. Felt him ripping away at my flesh though.

I resigned my commission and requested continued duty in the enlisted ranks, even though the loss of my leg entitled me to a medical discharge. I couldn't take the discharge because my dues were not paid in full.

I lost my eye when I was assisting on the retrofit of a boat in port. A Bosun's mate wasn't paying attention and turned a valve the wrong way. I didn't react to his mistake in time to save him. A loose valve coupling busted loose. Blew a hole in his head the size of a coffee saucer and still had enough force to catch me in the eye. In my long tenure with the Navy, boys, I have fucked up just these two times. God spared me my miserable existence to bear witness to greenhorns like you."

He headed for the door. At the threshold, he said, "Tomorrow, I'll accept resignations from anyone who wants transferred. Those who decide to leave will be reassigned with the surface navy. The rest of you will study the power plant and gear reduction systems diagrammed in your manuals. Calculate how many amps of power the fully charged batteries should be able to produce over a ten-hour period. Also, make yourselves familiar with how many kilowatts the generators in your manuals produce at 720 rpm and 650 rpm respectively."

With that, he left.

Chapter 25
Pagoda on the Pacific

Millie, I can't begin to tell you how different life is out here. Bob is making good money down at the LA shipyards. He is working 12 on, 12 off, 4 days a week. If he goes in for an eight - hour shift on the fifth day or for at least four hours on a Sunday, he gets 12 hours of double - time pay. We have a wonderful walk-up on 5th Street off the Plaza in Oxnard. You can see the ocean from our front windows. Baby Conor is doing well. My heart melts when I watch his big old bruiser daddy dote on him.

Leaving Texas was a problem. My parents told the highway patrol that I'd been kidnapped. By the time the law caught up with us, we were married. My mother has already shipped me baby clothes, apparently against my father's wishes. Please be happy for me. I miss you terribly and hope that things are well with you. Write me soon.

Love
Betty

Betty raised her head from the writing table and listened. Then, walked across the dayroom to peer into the baby's nursery. He was still sleeping. She lowered the window so the room wouldn't be too cool for her sleeping son. She checked the clock on the stand by Conor's bed, ten till four. She would let the boy sleep for another thirty minutes. Any longer, he'd be up 'entertaining' his mother well into the night.

The room was awash in the soft buttery color of afternoon sunlight. She loved the way the windows caught the breeze and the sun at the right angle. She and Bobby had the second floor of a thirty year old Victorian home that was built by an executive at the local beet processing plant. The executive's widow, one Mrs. Wilkes, had recently renovated their floor. After they had signed the lease, she had said, "Thank goodness, I'm sick of carrying a mop bucket up these steps." She eyed Betty warily, as if she expected Betty to argue with her about who had cleaning responsibilities in the apartment.

Once Mrs. Wilkes saw that Betty was a competent housekeeper, she often came upstairs, saying, "I don't mean to impose, but if you need some free time dearie, I wouldn't mind sitting with that baby."

A tacit deal was struck. Betty kept the place so clean you could eat off the tongue and groove floors. Mrs. Wilkes spoiled Conor.

Betty smiled inwardly as she stared out her son's bedroom window. The lace curtains played about her face on the current created by the breeze still squeezing through the partially opened window. She thought about how Bobby loved them, but was wrapped up in a different world, a world of noise, tools, gears, boilers, levers, and bolts. Bobby rumbled through the door at 6:45. He loved routine. He would say the same thing in the same order everyday.

"Hey baby, love you to death, where's that son of mine? Any idea when we're gonna eat?"

Promptly at seven, she sat his dinner on the table and Conor on his left knee. Conor gratefully did his part by pulling on his dad's hair and nose. Bobby ate with his right hand while bouncing Conor on his left knee.

Most nights, Bobby was asleep in his easy chair by eight. If Conor's nap hadn't been too long, he, too, would be asleep - on his dad's chest, lulled to sleep by the rise and fall of his dad's breathing. She would sit across the room from them until nine or so reading or sewing. Sometimes, she would sit at the Secretary and pay some bills. Bobby enjoyed earning money. He had no interest in how the income was spent, so long as his family was doing okay. On those occasions when she mentioned something she had bought or intended to buy, his standard response was, "don't spend us into the street, Bett."

She made sure that a savings account was opened for emergencies and for Conor's future education. This amused Bobby.

"What are we gonna do Hon? Send a shanty Irishman's son to college?"

"That's exactly what we're going to do if we get the chance."

"By damn, what do you know, an educated Sullivan. Wouldn't that tickle my old man, God rest his soul."

He was interested though. At the beginning of every month, he always asked her if she'd put money into *his son's* account. Every month she looked back at him, and said, "of course, Bobby. We can't get him to Harvard if we don't save, can we?"

He'd grin back at her saying, "we sure as hell can't, baby."

The marvel of it all is that they were happy. As she headed back for the kitchen to prepare Conor's afternoon bottle, she whispered to herself, "who the hell would have thought such a nice deal would come from two people humping in a stadium parking lot."

Bob figured his number was up. He had been left alone to do his job as an engineering technician, his job title, here at Technodyne Corporation, for a whole six months. He tapped worriedly on the yellow note he had received from the shop steward. Via the union, Bob was being asked to meet with the plant manager. Bob hadn't even known the plant manager was aware of his existence and he liked it that way.

When he'd asked the Steward, Big Al Dawson, what management wanted, Big Al had shrugged saying, "hell, I don't know. Wasn't a disciplinary thing. They haven't notified the union of any allegations against you and you haven't filed any grievances against them, have you?"

"Hell no. I like it here. Best damn job I've ever had."

"Go to the meeting then and if they give you any crap, let me know. I'll request representation. Good luck, Bob."

Bob chuckled. Unions were shunned in Texas for reasons Bob didn't entirely understand, despised by management and workers alike. Bob paid $5.00 a month to the union and for that money he had a whole group of people standing between himself and the Man in the corner office. The union was a bargain.

Still, Bob didn't want to give Big Al the impression that he was afraid to meet the Man by himself. So, he puffed out his chest and said, "the SOB probably wants me to unscrew a light bulb for him. You can't tell with these fucking management types. They all think they're President Roosevelt."

"Fucking A Bob, you got that right. Give me a full report tomorrow before your shift starts."

Bob wasn't lying when he'd told Al that this was the best job he'd ever had, he loved it. The job was a real hoot and holler. In Texas they would have called him a journeyman apprentice electrician. Here, they had to sparkle his title up to let people know that California was a bit better than the rest of the country. In any event, he was making a whopping $4.75 an hour to keep the plant wiring in good order. He had a job, a wife who could cook and screw. He had a son to send to college. Life was good, but Bob didn't want to let too many people know. He could jinx himself in a flat minute if he dared to let people know he was a respectable citizen. Now, the Man in the suit could break Bob's balls, union or no union. No, a yellow slip from management did not brighten Bob's disposition, not in the frigging least.

"No, darling, I don't have any idea why the plant manager wants to meet with me. No dear, I haven't been drinking at work. No honey, I haven't cussed anyone or beat the crap out of one gosh darn soul." Bob cupped his hand over the phone so Betty wouldn't hear him laughing. His wife knew him all too well.

"No, I shouldn't be more than forty-five minutes beyond my normal time. Don't worry, even if they want to rip me a new one, they have to work through the union. I won't be on the street tomorrow. We'll be okay. I promise. Yeah spaghetti is fine. Kiss Conor for me. Bye, love you too."

Bob hung up the cafeteria pay phone. He wished he felt as upbeat as he had made himself sound to Bet. He went into the locker room and showered after tossing his work clothes in the laundry bin. The Company required work clothes to stay on site. The government, according to rumor, didn't want foreign agents identifying Technodyne workers.

Once he had dressed in his street clothes, he shaved for the second time that day, and slicked his hair back with some Bauers Tonic. He looked in the mirror, decided he wasn't getting any better looking while he stared and headed upstairs into management territory.

The reception area floor was decked out in wall-to-wall carpet. The lush stuff was some shade of dark green. Bob figured Bet would call the carpet 'forest green' if she saw it. Bob noticed that even though the time was getting on towards 5:30 the receptionist who'd told him to take a seat, showed no signs of leaving.

"Mr. Witherspoon will be with you in a moment. He asked me to tell you that he's sorry for the delay. He had to take a call from the Department of the Army out of Washington. May I get you something? Coffee? Soda Water?"

"No thanks. Nice of you to offer."

"You're the electronics wizard from downstairs, aren't you?"

"I work with the circuitry and fabricate different types of conduit to handle the wiring load but most of my work is ordinary everyday electrical wiring."

"Mr. Whitherspoon mentioned someone had finally figured out how to wire the lab B area to handle their power demands without constantly browning out the rest of the building."

"Those lab B fellas were sucking some serious juice from the grid. I had to reconfigure the wiring so that the power they were drawing was on separate circuitry than the rest of the building. Solving that didn't take more than a day once I'd figured out what was going on and then, a week or so to get the lab wired correctly. Took a whole week because I had to make sure the circuits were completely separate. Otherwise, you'd get arcing, bleed over, that sort of thing."

Her look told him she hadn't understood what he'd said. "I won't pretend to understand what you've explained. I do know that Mr. Whitherspoon said that having you on the payroll saved his timetable for the project."

Bob lowered his chin and mumbled, "thanks, but I was only working items on the punch list." He thought, no way am I going to tell her that once upon a time, I had to get Will Davis to help me fix the electrical system in a car.

Mr. Whitherspoon's door opened and he came towards Bob with a grin on his face and his hand out.

Good Lord, he wants to shake my hand. Bob couldn't have been more shocked if the man had thrown an angry rattler at him.

"Mr. Sullivan, I'm pleased to finally meet you. First of all, thank you. The speed and the accuracy with which you solved the electrical problem in Lab B was superb. Every time we ask who's working the knotty pine electrical issues we need resolved, your name pops up."

Bob's jaw dropped. The Man was not pissed off. The Man was not going to put Bob on the street. The Man was happy. Bob was speechless.

"Bob, I won't beat around the bushes, we've obtained several government contracts. Mind you, this is on the QT. Performing the work demands that we have someone in-house who knows what our physical plant is capable of. Mr. Morton tells me you look at a blueprint once and know what needs to be done and says you also understand how power behaves. I'm promoting you to plant electrician, if you're interested. Frankly, the job is more engineering and less hands on electrical work. Can't really call you the plant engineer though because you don't have a degree."

Mr. Whitherspoon tapped on his desk with a pencil, and then stared out the window at the cargo ships docked in the middle distance. "I've been authorized to offer you a thousand a month."

He faced Bob as he said this.

"We'll evaluate how you are doing in ninety days. If the new job isn't working out, you can have your current job back. If your progress is satisfactory and you like what you are doing, we'll take another look at your salary level. Is this something you'd be interested in?"

"Sure," Bob said.

"This isn't gravy Bob. You're management now. Some of the people you worked with today will report to you tomorrow. By the way, you'll need to resign from the union."

As he left Mr. Witherspoon's office, he felt like he was floating.

"How'd it go?"

"Huh?" He blurted. The receptionist was smiling at him. She said, "I asked how the meeting went."

Thoughts about his mom, his dad, his wife, and his son flashed through his mind. "Fine, the meeting went just fine."

Bob once again called home from the pay phone.

"Hi Bet. No, I'm not calling from a bar. No, dang it, Bet I'm not going to show up at home pissed off and drunk. Can I talk here for a second? Thanks. You know that blue silk number you bought two weeks back? Yeah the one I didn't like because you looked naked wearing it, even when you had a slip on underneath, that's the one. I changed my mind. Wear that naughty piece of fabric tonight. We're going out for lobster.

"What? No, I haven't gone around the bend. You're talking to the newly minted plant electrician. They like me. I'm going to get a flat grand a month to keep this place squared away."

Bob listened for a moment. His face turned beet red but he had a grin on his mug.

"Now who's being nasty. I don't think we could do that in the car, Bet. We'd get arrested for that. A football stadium, what do you want me to find a...? Ohhh, I got it. I'll be home in 45 minutes. Baby, we're gonna kick this town in the butt tonight."

"Ouch! That hurts Bet."

"Quit being so whiny Bobby. I think you have some pieces of glass stuck back here. Wiggling is only going to make cleaning the cuts up worse."

"Told you that football parking lot was bad news."

Betty giggled as she plucked a small piece of green glass out of her husband's backside. "We were fine until you rolled us off the car Bobby. Be still! You wiggled at the wrong time."

"I rolled us off because you—you know."

"I goosed you. Didn't expect you to fly through the air. Still, you did okay."

"What would we have said if the police had shown up, Bets?"

"Get ready. This is going to sting a little."

"Dang Bets! What the hell was that?"

"Whiskey Bobby. Works wonders down here too."

"Betty, if I ever get another promotion, we're not doing the stadium thing. We're respectable now."

Betty daubed some more whiskey on Bob's backside.

"Guess we'll cross that bridge when we come to it Bobby. I see another small piece of glass. Quit wiggling!"

Chapter 26
Higashi no Kaze, Ame

Tadeo Karawara once heard a drunken American Army officer describe Hawaii in Zen-like fashion. The quote went: "I love Hawaii. Today was like yesterday, and yesterday was like tomorrow." The American had provided him no useful intelligence. The quote was the only interesting thing he'd said all evening. The quote calmed Tadeo. He fervently prayed to all the gods that today, Friday, December 5th and tomorrow, December the 6th were truly the same as any other Hawaiian day for American Servicemen stationed on Oahu.

Tadeo was pissed because his country's so-called allies were not worth the price of a cheap dung bucket, much less the 15,000 American dollars he had paid his German contact in Honolulu. The money was *quid pro quo* for German supplied intelligence. The Germans were supposed to signal information to Japanese submarines on the movement of American Naval vessels in and out of Pearl Harbor. As of today, the Germans had supplied the Empire of Japan nothing. So here he was taking extravagant risk on behalf of his country. The Americans were fond of repeating the adage, "If you want something done, do it yourself." He agreed.

He waited for the geisha girls he had procured to board the seaplane. As he boarded, he gave the pilot a foolish grin and bowed several times. He sat next to the rear bulkhead window. As instructed, the girls were already paying the pilot a great deal of intimate attention. He wanted the pilot focused on anything but him.

He had paid for a tour that would take them on a huge loop around Oahu. He wanted to test wind conditions and snap pictures of the island from different altitudes and angles. Heading north by northeast, they would cross just to the east of Ewa and then right over Wheeler before turning in a wide loop that would bring them back over the top of Battleship Row. He had long since diagrammed the ships while sitting in Shunchoro on a tatami mat. He considered it the height of irony that he had gathered some of the best intelligence of this tense prewar period while never moving from the best Japanese restaurant on Oahu.

One time, he'd paid for a private room overlooking the harbor. He had allowed a Japanese courtesan from his home village to put her mouth on him while he diagrammed and ate marinated raw squid with cucumber. Her technique was exquisite. His emotional control, however, was such that he never stopped diagramming even when nature took its inevitable course. Yes, in some ways he would miss Hawaii. The island, and even American culture, had good points.

"Now girls, don't touch that. We don't want to flop over into the harbor do we?"

Tadeo glanced up. His plan was proceeding like clockwork.

"Oh, you girls aren't shy about getting friendly, are you? Sure, you can touch that if you want."

The pilot glanced back to check out Tadeo's interest in the events transpiring on the flight deck. Tadeo grinned at him and said, "Go Yankee!" in heavily accented English. This was, of course, absurd in the extreme. Tadeo had majored in English at UCLA.

While the pilot was being ministered to, Tadeo confirmed that the American carriers were not in port. He snapped some pictures, providing visual confirmation. The plane pitched a bit and then yawed to starboard about 5 degrees.

"How do you say it? Tubulence, Captain?"

"Naw, winds aloft are fairly calm. I got distracted is all. Sorry about the bumpy ride."

"Ah, just so. This is not a problem."

When they landed, Tadeo paid the women a bonus for their superior efforts and headed straight for the Japanese consulate.

When he got there, he had the rolls of film packed and placed in a diplomatic pouch. He then radioed Tokyo a coded message that informed the government about the missing carriers and about his assessment of American defensive preparations on the island. He noted in particular that there were still no barrage balloons aloft over the harbor entrance.

"Admiral Nagumo thanks you for your timely information Tadeo san." The attaché bowed.

"Please convey that I'm humbled to be of service to the empire."

"The decision to attack the Americans here was almost rescinded due to the quality of your intelligence." The attaché, Jenji Okusu, noted.

Tadeo halted in mid-stride. They were in the midst of the consulate gardens. He looked around as if his thoughts might be picked up and wafted to the American Navy by an evil spirit.

"The Admiral is concerned about the American carriers?" Tadeo asked.

"Yes, Tadeo-san. This was the issue."

Tadeo sat on a stone bench and stared at large carp in a reflecting pool placed next to the walkway.

"You said was. The attack is still on?"

"Yes. The general staff is unwilling to pass on this opportunity to weaken the Americans–they don't believe the carriers will survive if the fleet is other-wise…diminished."

"Just so." Said Tadeo, as he stood back up and exhaled. "I'm going home to prepare myself Jenji-san. I expect to be expelled, if not killed outright, on Monday, if I can't make it back to the embassy." He smiled. "My death poem is already written."

"With respect, Tadeo-san, isn't that somewhat dramatic?"

"Is it Jenji-san? The Americans will react to the attack with vigor. I have posted a copy of the poem to my parents, just in case." Tadeo recited the poem in his head. In English, the poem translated roughly as:

> *'Early summer nascent heat;*
> *Early winter nascent cold;*
> *But in the late autumn–*
> *Blossoms ascend unto heaven.'*

"Farewell for now Jenji-san. Please inform the consul that I'll stay in my apartment long enough to hear the code words."

"Of course Tadeo-san. Fare well."

"Be well, Jenji-san."

Chapter 27
Tea and War

Vice Admiral Chuichi Nagumo was not a politician or a fool. He was what he appeared–a naval tactician of the highest order.

"Forgive my intrusion into your thoughts Admiral. Would you care for a cup of tea? The Admiral ceased contemplating the North Pacific and focused on the yeoman who waited respectfully for his answer.

"Yes, Yoshi, a strong cup of tea is a good idea."

The yeoman bowed and said, "I will obtain the tea at once Admiral."

Admiral Nagumo again watched the light rain and sensed rather than saw the gray swells of the Pacific. 0430 in the morning, local time, was too early. The ocean reflected nothing at this hour. The weather had been foul since leaving port in the Kuriles. In all the weather was perfect. This moment, he thought, held the cruelest irony for him. He was commander of the fleet - poised to strike Japan's greatest potential enemy. He smiled grimly. Once they struck–the word potential would no longer apply. On the other hand, he was at sea executing a plan about which he had grave reservations.

"Your tea revered Admiral."

"Thank you, Yoshi," he said. "Please do not revere me too deeply. I have accomplished nothing of note."

"Sir, may I ask you a question, or is now a bad time?"

"You may ask me anything you choose, Yoshi; however, I reserve the right not to answer."

He slurped his English tea. English tea was one of the few indulgences he allowed himself while at sea.

"Are the Americans really so stupid as to leave their entire battle fleet unprotected at their Hawaiian Harbor?"

Nagumo considered the question, not an easy one to answer.

"The Americans are isolated from the world, which makes them unduly insular in their views. They lack perspective because they are a young people. Hence, they make faulty assumptions about our intentions and their own. That is why I am confident we will prevail...today. But no, they are by no means stupid. They are a formidable adversary."

"Just so, Admiral. I hope I have not offended you by asking such a question."

"No, Yoshi that question is a most difficult one. Figuring out the Americans is something our General Staff has failed to accomplish, so, we prepare to make war against a country we do not understand."

The yeoman was frozen in place. The Admiral had uttered words that if heard by the wrong person could be construed as disloyalty, or worse, treason.

The Admiral continued to sip his tea. When he spoke, he appeared to have read Yoshi's thoughts.

"Do not be alarmed, Yoshi. I have told the Imperial Headquarters Staff what I have said to you–and more besides. My thoughts did not sway them."

The Admiral smiled into his teacup. "Anymore than, I suspect, they have swayed you."

The yeoman, sensing that he was being politely dismissed, bowed and backed away.

Nagumo wondered if anyone on the American General Staff would appreciate the similarity between this coming engagement and the Confederate American Army General Lee's attempts to invade the Northern American States at some place called Antietam in 1862 and at Gettysburg in 1863. Both of those actions were essentially offensive rear-guard actions. So, too, was the intent here. Japan could ill afford the United States implementing their Plan Orange against Japanese forces attempting to consolidate their hold on Southeast Asian resources–especially the rubber plantations.

The problem was that even if they were successful in pressing the attack against Pearl Harbor, Nagumo knew Japan could not win an extended war of attrition against the United States. A settlement with the United States would have to be forged. But, this was not his concern.

He was a puppet of lesser men who controlled the apparatus of state. He had his orders. He would carry them out. He bowed his head slightly and said a prayer of silent thanks for the inclement weather that had masked this operation. His intelligence briefings indicated that the Americans still expected a strike at Singapore or in the Indies. They still didn't view Pearl as a vulnerable target. This was good, very good. He placed his empty teacup down and headed for his final mission briefing. The fleet would be at the mission launch point in approximately ninety minutes.

"If there was anyone else, you'd be in the brig today and standing mast tomorrow, you little Saturday night accident!" The duty Sergeant bellowed.

Damn his head hurt. Dud thought, as he was getting his ass chewed. He had to cut down on the hooch. Didn't pay to stay up, play cards, and drink all night with those artillery pukes out on Barber's Point.

"Showing up for guard duty three sheets to the wind is not going to further your career in my Corps! Do you read me!"
"Aye, aye Sergeant!"

At least, Dud thought, he'd managed to get back to the barracks in time to put a freshly pressed set of fatigues on. His rifle was spotless and his boots had a highly righteous sheen on them.

"Your uniform is wrinkled, I could grease my hair with your weapon, and your boots look like you polished them with shit. You're a damn disgrace!"

The duty Sergeant ran out of breath after another five minutes, saying, "If I catch you sleeping on post, I'll blow your brains out and send them to your mother in a gift-wrapped box." The Sergeant had left at 0600.

He looked at his watch. Damn! 0600 seemed like hours ago. Yet, his watch indicated the time was only 0745. The sun was still low on the eastern horizon as the morning rays struck the Waianae Mountains. He uncapped a thermos of coffee that the duty Sergeant had instructed him to drink and took a sip. He glanced around at his assigned station, Wheeler field, and thought, "Oh man, airfield guard duty on a Sunday morning and I thought Gainesville was boring."

As he replaced the thermos bottle in the guard hut, he heard a loud rumble from the mountains. He settled his rifle more comfortably on his shoulder and cupped his left hand over his eyes to see if he could tell where the rumble was coming from.

He immediately saw a tight flying V formation coming in through the valley just east of the mountains. He also saw a second formation coming around the mountains' southern edge. Both formations were getting larger by the second.

Dang, he thought. Those Army fly-boys are look-ing pretty serious about their training for a Sunday. Then, he heard someone screaming. He looked to his right, some officer was screaming at him to hit the klaxon switch. His last coherent thought before all hell broke loose was that he had screwed up. Did I forget a joint training exercise briefing? If I did my ass is truly in a sling.

Dud ran to the shed and hit the switch and looked up in time to see a line of machine gun rounds walking right toward him. "Sweet Mother of Jesus!" He dove out of the shack and buried his face in the tarmac. The guard shack exploded behind him. Most of the shack landed on him. Things went dark. Suddenly, he was being pulled out of the guardhouse debris. He heard someone saying, "Are you hit? Can you hear me?" Dud was vaguely aware that he was being dragged and that bad things were happening around him. KAAAWUUUUMP, KAWUURRMP He and whoever was dragging him were knocked over again by a series of blasts. He saw some explosions and could smell the pungent odor of burning aviation gas.

Whoever had dragged him out was now slapping him across the face.

Getting slapped pissed him off. "Would you knock it the hell off!"

His eyes focused on the Captain from the flight line. He was covered in mortar dust and sweat.

"Good, you're alright."

"What the hell kind of training is this? They damn near killed us and trashed our goddamn runway and planes."

The Captain grimaced. His right arm was covered in blood.

"Private, this is no frigging drill. Those were Zeke fighters from Japan. We are under a full-scale enemy attack, and we have barely caught a small taste. The main contingent was headed for Battleship Row at Pearl."

"Those little fuckers! Sorry sir, I meant no disrespect."

"No apology required, Private. You expressed my sentiments exactly. Come on, we need to see who and what we can muster to repel a secondary assault."

"The little shits are coming back?"

"I'd bet serious money we'll see a secondary assault within a half hour to forty-five minutes. Let's move, Private!"

"Aye, aye Captain."

The men galloped for the flight line. The Captain was yelling into a phone that hadn't gone dead.

"No, damn it! We're getting bombed and strafed. Our birds are sitting ducks for the enemy. We need mechanics and pilots out here ASAP to get these planes up. They're grouped so closely that one or two bombs could kill a squadron."

The Captain slammed the phone into its cradle.

"Half the damn planes on the tarmac have no fuel, the other half, no ordnance. If we don't get cracking, the Japs are going to make us pay dearly."

The Captain was a prophet. The Japs returned. They strafed the airfield repeatedly with both explosive and incendiary rounds.

"That fire truck isn't gonna make it." The Captain shouted.

"Damn brave of those guys," Dud said.

The two men watched helplessly from their slit trench as the fire truck went up in a fiery blossom. "Bastards," Dud said. "Can't even shoot at the pricks. Haven't got a round left."

Black smoke was rising everywhere. The air reeked with the acrid smell of burning fuel and rubber.

"Dear God," uttered the Captain.

"Amen," said someone else.

"Think the battleships made it out to sea, Captain?"

The Captain stared off toward Pearl before answering. Huge smoke plumes were rising from harbor.

"Private, the process for getting a battleship underway takes two hours, even under emergency conditions. May the Almighty forgive me, but I don't think they did. I think we're taking it in the shorts. The important question is did they get the dry docks and what are they going to do next?"

"Think they'll try to invade?"

The Captain climbed out of the trench. Wincing as he bumped his injured arm. Dud climbed out and helped him. "Sir, with respect, you need to have that looked at."

"In due course, Private. There are a lot of men and women who would be grateful to exchange my wounds for theirs right now."

"Just the same, let me sling it for you."

He sighed. "Yeah, go ahead."

Somehow, Dud had ended up with the first-aid kit that was stowed in the guard shack. He had no idea how he'd managed to hold onto it. As Dud bound his arm, the Captain said, "there will be panic and talk about an invasion, but I don't think that's their strategy. Logistics are too difficult. I think they struck us here to keep us off their flank in the Far East. Our embargo forces them to obtain rubber and crude oil from Burma and Malaysia."

Dud tightened the sling.

"Ow! Damn that hurts."

"Sorry, sir."

"Do you have a name, Private?"

"Danny, Danny Ludlow, sir. My friends call me Dud."

"My name is Chet, Chet Addler."

"A pleasure to make your acquaintance sir. Thanks too for hauling me out from under the guardhouse this morning," Dud said. "I didn't know which end was up when that thing landed on me."

The two men walked away from the trench with a group of bedraggled and dazed airmen.

Captain Addler laughed and said, "I know this isn't funny, but I caught the look on your face when those machine gun rounds headed your way. I've never seen anyone move so fast. I couldn't believe it when I pulled you out of that pile alive, you must be living right."

"Sir," Dud said, "the truth is I'm alive because I was still drunk when I showed up for duty. If all that stuff had landed on me when I was sober, I might have actually felt it."

As the Captain smiled grimly, his teeth made a startling contrast to his soot covered face. He looked like an actor playing a role in a demented minstrel show. Everyone did.

"Well, you're sober enough now aren't you, Private Ludlow?"

"Unfortunately I am, sir."

"Very well. Let's see if we can't establish some order here. At the moment, I'm the senior officer present. Until further notice, Private Ludlow, you're my acting executive assistant. Let's establish a *de facto* command post next to that barracks the Japs missed. Next to the command post have the injured men assembled for triage. Find some uninjured men and have them locate a field radio or any other communications gear that appears to be operable. Assign a second group of uninjured men to form a damage control party.

Finally, find me a coherent NCO and tell him to report to me on the double. We'll establish a perimeter defense, in case I'm wrong and we're confronted with a Jap invasion force. Any questions, Mr. Ludlow?"

Dud noted with pride that he had been addressed as a fellow officer.

"No sir," Dud said. "I understand."

"Move out, Mister."

Dud snapped off a salute, which the Captain smartly returned.

As he left to carry out the Captain's instructions, he thought; we're United States Marines by God. This was only the beginning. Dud began to smile. He smiled a smile filled with terrible menace - a smile of a marine who had lived through a horrible defeat that he would neither forgive nor forget.

Sunday Tea at Philadelphia's Winston hotel was a civilized if somewhat insipid affair, Mindy thought. The Earl Grey was first rate, as were the strawberry tarts and thinly sliced cucumber sandwiches. The Winston wanted its patrons to imagine themselves at London's Savoy or the Plaza in New York City. Presently, she was talking with a young pre-medical student about peritoneal lavage protocols in a patient presenting a gunshot wound to the abdomen.

"I wouldn't have believed it if I hadn't seen it myself. This poor guy was laid open on the table like a roast beef sandwich."

"Whitford, a little softer please. People are beginning to stare."

Brad Whitford looked around. "What's the problem?"

"Maybe tea isn't the place to discuss this particular subject."

"What's wrong with this particular subject?"

Mindy shrugged. Brad Whitford was hopeless. Brilliant by all accounts and good-looking despite his unkempt appearance, his social skills, nonetheless, were limited. Rumor was that his roommates had to prepare him for dates with cue cards; the cards helped him remember baseball scores, the war in Europe, and his date's name. "I'm as interested in surgical protocol as you are," Mindy said. "I, however, don't want to discuss protocols over tea."

"Sorry, hard not to pick your brain. I've heard you're holding the top grade in surgical anatomy."

"I can wield a scalpel Brad and I don't turn green and faint when a cadaver is wheeled out of the cooler," Mindy said.

"That's an understatement," Whitford retorted. "People are talking about your technique. The word flawless is being used and, no offense, but you're a nursing student."

Mindy struggled with her emotions for a moment. She wanted to toss her tea in his face.

"Feeling threatened Brad?" She hissed. "Is working with me beneath your dignity? Are you too good to train with mere nursing students? Listen to this rumor. I have information on good authority that when our anatomy class test scores came out, nurses were holding six of the top ten scores." What Mindy knew, but didn't say, is that she had the highest grade among the nurses and the third highest mark overall.

Brad buttered a muffin, saying, "I mouth stupid stuff to women all the time. I like you, so, my manners are worse than usual. I don't resent you. Seeing you work is–words can't describe it. A scalpel looks like an artist's brush in your hands. No one is used to seeing that kind of dexterity in a student."

"Especially a nurse?" Mindy said.

"No, from anyone. But from a young nursing student–well...no one has ever seen anything like you. That's what's going around the halls."

Mindy let him off the hook. "Tell me, what happened to Beakley during the practical yesterday."

Brad's face brightened immediately.

"We're in the teaching suite with Stokes and he asks Beakley if the bowel has been run thoroughly. Beakley responds with this self-assured, 'Yes Doctor, I have run the bowel twice.' Stokes looks at him for a second and says, 'ladies and gentlemen bowel injuries are quite tricky, especially when traumatic injuries inflicted by a firearm are presented.'"

As Brad told the story, I'd noticed an increase in the noise around us. People were getting up and talking loudly. I heard Hawaii mentioned, but I couldn't catch the context.

"So, sure enough, Stokes gets to the retroperitoneum and in the lining, up against the abdominal wall, he finds a pellet Beakley missed. Beakley turned so red I thought he'd blow a vessel right on the spot."

"Brad, something has happened."

"Huh?"

"Look around. People have started buzzing. Two minutes ago, other than you talking, you could've heard a pin drop in here."

An ashen-faced man, dressed in afternoon formal attire, walked into the tearoom. He clapped his hands together. People grew attentive at once.

"What the hell has happened?" Mindy wondered.

"Ladies and gentlemen, WTEL is reporting that the Empire of Japan has launched a surprise attack on our naval installation at Pearl Harbor in Hawaii. This is a recent event and information is still somewhat sketchy. But, my information indicates our losses are severe."

The man's head dropped onto his chest for a second. When he raised his head, tears were visible on his cheeks.

"A moment of silent prayer is appropriate. When approximately a moment had passed, the major domo raised his head and said, "God save the United States of America and President Roosevelt." He turned on his heel and left. The room was silent for 5 or 10 seconds. Then, someone began singing 'America the Beautiful'. Everyone joined in.

People were out on Market Street. Mindy and Brad followed a throng headed for Independence Hall on Chestnut. People were in shock but, were also angry. Word circulated that the Japanese had hit the harbor in

Hawaii with no declaration of war or any other advance warning.

While they were walking, Brad looked at Mindy and said, "Mindy, we're going to war now. Won't be any further debate."

Mindy replied, "One of my best friends is headed to submarine school at New London. He's got a friend stationed in Hawaii."

"Really, no shit?"

"Yeah," Mindy nodded.

"We'll be busy too once this gets rolling. The Army is going to need doctors and nurses in a big way."

People were all around them now which was okay. The sky was clear, but, the wind was chilly, a cold and blustery day in Philly.

"If we do get in a shooting war with Japan–and probably the Germans too, we'll get plenty of opportunities to practice lavage protocols," Mindy said.

"I hope you're wrong with all my heart, I really do," Brad said.

Mindy got on her toes and kissed him on the cheek.

"I hope I'm wrong too, Brad," Mindy said.

Brad took Mindy's left arm in his right arm. They continued toward Independence Hall. All the city's church bells were tolling for the men and women at Pearl Harbor.

Chapter 28
The Murky Depths

The good thing about being a raw recruit is your blissful ignorance. When you first join the submarine service, you don't know jack-shit about what you're getting involved in. First is the sea, awe-inspiring and terrifying in equal measure. During a dead calm, the surface is like polished glass for as far as you can see. The water whispers and coos to you like a mother singing a lullaby. Other times the cliffs of liquid granite crashing around you bring you to the conclusion that hell is filled with emerald green banshees made of salt water.

Second, there's the reality of life on board a combat submarine. I'll always remember the smell and the heat. Fuel oil mixed with sweat and cigarette smoke in heat that often-exceeded 130^{of} dominated. The smell and the heat were good things though. The severe discomfort meant that you were still alive. I am getting ahead of myself, but the middle explains the beginning.

Training started at Portsmouth.

"Haven't ever drowned before so I suppose it really ain't fair for me to criticize drowning as a way to go," the Chief said. "Still, if your choices are eternal patrol or trying the escape hatch, the escape hatch will look good. Don't kid yourselves though, boys. If the boat is seriously damaged and trim can't be maintained." He stretched his arms toward all of us sitting on the barge's edge–"Ain't none of you drips getting off alive."

The Chief, who was also the dive master, undogged the inner hatch. We were nervous. Leaving a perfectly good submarine for the deep cold murk of the Sound was not a natural act.

"The Navy requires all hands to master escape hatch training. You boys are the bravest or the most foolish. You volunteered to master a genuine escape from a real sub. Anyone can still back out. Let me remind you of the obvious. You aren't in the tower now. At this point, we're a full 40 fathoms down, two and a-half times deeper than your deepest tower dive. The idea is the same though. Follow the knotted rope topside. The knots are located every 2 fathoms. The Munsen Lung will supply you with 15 minutes of air. You'll hear a warning bell when you're down to your last minute. With the diving hood on, you won't be able to see anything when you leave the outer hatch. The water will be colder than a well digger's ass and blacker too. Don't let this panic you into rushing the ascent to the surface. Remember; make yourself stop at every knot on the way up to allow your body to adjust to the pressure variance. If you don't, you risk popping your lungs or giving yourself a real bad case of the bends. When you get to the top there will be men at the buoy to assist you. If you get in trouble, tug on the rope. 40 fathoms is a fair amount of water. The pressure will feel extreme at first. Give yourself a moment to acclimate before heading up. Okay, who's first?"

I couldn't stand waiting. "I'll go first Chief, if no one else wants to."

"Alright," the Chief said. "Davis is gonna show us he has brass ones. Remember; let the hatch fill completely so that the pressure is entirely equal before undogging the outer hatch."

"Aye, aye, Chief." I strapped on the air lung gear, and then checked the mouthpiece to make sure I was getting air. For the exercise, we were all in rubber suits. Once the inner hatch was dogged, the icy water filled the escape hatch. I had been told the water at this depth, depending on currents was around 65°ᶠ. The water felt like half that. I fought the panic rising within me to keep from going ape shit. The only thing that kept me from going over the edge was knowing I'd have to do the exercise again. I was more afraid of quitting than drowning. Finally, the hatch was flooded.

I undogged the outer hatch and groped around for the line. Finally, I managed to grab the line and the buoy release. I saw…nothing. I was in dark I'd never imagined. I was inside a huge cold ink spot. The pressure was forcing me toward the surface faster than I wanted to ascend. I lost my grasp and flailed around until I found and grabbed hold of the line again. I had no idea how many knots I had missed. I silently counted my blessings for managing to find the rope again before I'd become totally disoriented. I focused on slowing my breathing and commanding my legs to move; though I'm not sure they were. I was numb from the cold.

My hands hit a knot on the rope. I stopped and slowly counted to fifteen before continuing my ascent. The cold and disorientation caused me to lose all sense of time. The rope swayed in the water. The current was strong, took everything I had to hold on. The lung alarm went off. Jesus Christ! I'd already been at this for 15 minutes? I hastened my ascent and at the same time slowly counted down from thirty. I decided that when I reached zero, I'd let go and head for the surface, to hell with the bends. I hit a knot, but didn't stop. Just as I got to zero, I could see my hands in front of me. There was light! A second or two later I broke the water's surface. The red buoy bounced off my head. Two sailors watched me from their perches in a nearby whaleboat, they didn't seem too eager to help me out of the drink.

"Damn, Mac took you long enough. Have you got gills?"

"Thanks for the sentiment. Get me out of this stinking cold water."

They looked at each other, considering my response.

"Say 'please,' Mac."

I was in no position to argue. "Please, get me out of this stinking cold water."

They pulled me out, threw a blanket at me, and then gave me a cup of hot Navy joe.

"So how did you like seeing Davy Jones' locker up close and personal?"

"See? Hell, I didn't see a damn thing. A shark could have come along and bitten off both my legs and I wouldn't have seen him coming or going. I wouldn't have even known my legs were gone, because they went numb before I left the escape hatch."

Bosun's Mate Halloran, grinned at me with butter yellow teeth.

"Naw, no shark will get you here in the Sound. The water's too cold and dirty. A shark ain't that stupid. They'll be waiting for you in the warm blue South Pacific. An old discarded tire is the only thing that'll get you in the Sound."

Another man broke the water's surface coughing and sputtering. His lung had run out of oxygen when he was still twenty-five feet down. Halloran pulled the man out of the Sound. I gave him my blanket.

"Damn the water's cold down there. Seemed to me that bell went off as soon as I left the hatch," he said.

He'd done what I'd only thought about doing, making a break for the surface without knowing how deep he was. Fortunately, he was close enough that the pressure differential didn't get him. He'd paused enough to bleed the nitrogen off. Later in the day, two other guys weren't so lucky. I heard from my new buddy Halloran that they'd panicked in the dark and let the pressure bring them up too fast. They experienced the bends and had to spend several hours in the decompression chamber. Halloran was amused by this turn of events. "Rookies!" he'd snorted. I, however, had clearly passed the test. He'd decided he liked me. I wasn't sure this was a good thing.

"Jimmy Halloran, you're not a good influence."

"Never been a good influence on anyone before, Davis. Don't see why I should start now. Besides I have other noble qualities."

"Name one."

"I know New York like the back of my hand and I know all the New York women who drink like fish. That's two."

"Grew up here, didn't you?"

"Yep, the Bronx, two blocks from the New York Botanical Gardens. Had our own house too. Didn't have to grow up in a lower Eastside tenement like the other shanty Irish."

I didn't tell him I wouldn't have known the difference between the Lower East Side and Central Park West. He should have told me he was from North Dallas if he wanted to impress me. My job was to extricate him from fights when he'd had too much to drink.

"Good bar. Lots of people getting plastered," Halloran said. "Jimmy, try not to behave like a shit heel."

"You have a problem with me getting drunk and pinching women on the ass?"

"Yes, you have a talent for pinching the wives of big mean marines."

"True, those mothers can hit. I've got to pick on uglier women."

"I've kept you out of jail three different times. Thing is, I don't know why."

Halloran raised his hand. "Barkeep, another round here!"

"Where the hell are we, Davis?"

"The Blue Beach Comber."

"We found a place called the Blue Beach Comber in New York City?"

"Yeah and we're wearing out our welcome. You just upchucked on the nice blue tile floor. The bartender is pissed."

The bartender strode up and said, "If I never see another drunk squid, it'll be too soon."

"Really sorry about my buddy making a mess on your floor. If you've got a mop and a bucket, I'll clean the mess up," I said.

"Damn straight you will! You goddamn squids come in here three sheets to the wind on someone else's booze and fuck up the joint. Once the mess is cleaned up, get the hell out."

A feathery voice spoke close over my right shoulder. "I'm sure this young seaman didn't bring his buddy in here to have him get sick all over the floor. Am I wrong? Did you intend to let him puke in my bar?" The tone was definitely one of wry amusement.

I glanced back to see who was cutting us some slack.

She was wearing a pale yellow silk evening dress. Her eyes were fiery ice under a mane of dark black hair. She had a cigarette holder in one hand and a martini in the other.

"No ma'am. I'm sorry. Sometimes, Jimmy doesn't know his own limits. I'll be happy to clean everything up before we go."

The woman stared at us and said, "I expect that Jimmy hasn't known his limits for several years and that you, my young friend, are the latest in a long line of unfortunate if well-meaning caretakers."

She downed her drink and said, "Eddie, get Bert and Freddie in here to clean up this stink. We'll lose business if we don't hustle."

"Damn, Brett! The squids did the puking. Why should Bert and Freddie …"

"Only one squid did the puking, this one watched. In any event, Eddie, am I paying you to think for me or to pour quality liquor for thirsty customers?"

"Alright, Brett, Jeez, I didn't mean anything by it."

"Good, I'm glad. You're a fine bar man. The till is never short. The inventory is always dead on, and you stay sober. I'd hate to lose you. Go find Bert and Freddie. I'll keep an eye on things."

Once behind the bar, she announced, "we apologize for the temporary inconvenience our sick friend has caused. Starting at midnight, cocktails will be on the house for 15 minutes. Thank you for being loyal patrons."

Bert and Freddie showed up with a mop and a pail and the mess was quickly eliminated.

"Do you like my place?"

I jumped off my barstool. Brett was standing opposite me across the bar.

"Yes, I do like it, your place?"

"Yes, my dad built the Comber. He's gone but the bar remains. Building this was his dream."

Ma'am, this is a great bar. Never seen a floor like that."

"The tile is lapis lazuli and the bar is polished mahogany and teak. The diffuse lighting makes the joint look more elegant than it appears when the sun shines in through the window."

"On the contrary, the bar is like the bars' owner, elegant in any light."

She laughed softly. Actually, the sound she made was more like a chuckle or even a mellifluous growl.

"Ah, smooth, brave too."

I changed the subject. "Tell me about your dad. He must've been an interesting man."

"He was a lovely man. Gentle, you know? That was his most surprising quality because he was in the Merchant Marine. He left the sea for the final time in 1923 or 1924. He acquired the bar in 1925 and renovated it to resemble a bar he frequented in Tangiers. He met my mother in Tangiers too."

"Ah, so I was right. The exotic nature of the bar is truly a reflection of the proprietor."

Brett cut several limes into wedges.

"May I ask you two questions young sailor?"

"Sure."

"What is your name?"

"That's easy enough, I'm Wilson Davis."

"Wilson, I am Brett Andrews."

"Pleased to make your acquaintance, Brett."

"And I am pleased to make yours, Wilson. Have you ever played baseball?"

"Quite a lot but not in the last four months."

"Can you throw fairly hard and with accuracy?"

"Brett, if I had to, I could knock a fly off a tin can from 30 feet away and not move the can so much as an inch."

She smiled broadly at me. Her teeth were perfect. She was stunning. Yet, her manners drew no attention to her beauty. She moved through people with a cloak on.

"Wilson that much accuracy won't be necessary for what I have in mind."

"What, exactly, do you have in mind?"

"Would you like to come with me and find out?"

"Yes, but Jimmy's over there."

"Jimmy will not be a problem."

"Eddie, would you ring up Fritz at the Dorian on West 54th and procure a room for this sailor who is - sleeping with us at the moment?"

"Sure Brett, if you say so."

"Tell Fritz we'll be by in a cab in about twenty minutes."

"Easy does it Jimbo," I said, as I heaved him into the back seat and got in after him. Brett jumped in behind me, shutting the cab's door.

"Our final stop will be at the Dandridge on the park's west side, but we have two stops first," Brett said. "Please go to Florio's market on Fourth first. I need to make a couple of purchases and then we need to drop the young man, who is asleep back here, at the Dorian on West 54th."

"Sure lady, it's your dime. That guy looks like he got his nap out of a bottle."

"If you stay quiet the rest of the trip, I'll add five dollars to your final fare."

The cabbie shrugged. He didn't even speak to me while we waited for Brett.

She came out with a five - pound sack of oranges. She got back in the cab and said, "They're Valencia's. Florio has the freshest produce in the city."

Seeing the city from a cab was different than staggering around on the sidewalks with Halloran. We pulled up in front of the hotel. The cab's headlights illuminated a tall man in a yellow vest and stiff white shirt standing on the curb.

"Thank you for helping me out on such short notice, Fritz."

"Brett, this is not a problem."

"Here's twenty bucks. Feed him and shower him off when he wakes up. Provide him fare back to New London. If twenty isn't enough, let me know and we'll settle later."

"He smells rather ripe, doesn't he?"

"True, you may, unfortunately, need to bathe him before he wakes up."

"Don't worry. I'll take care of him, Brett."

"I owe you, Fritz."

"Ciao dear, off with you now."

Jimmy never once woke up. Later all he would say is that the old guy in the yellow vest made one mean potato pancake and that the navy could learn a thing or two from him about making a cup of joe.

Once Brett was back in the car, she leaned over and said, "now we play."

I had no idea what I was in for.

The Dandridge was, as Bob Sullivan would have put it, a swank joint for swells but he would've still been off the mark. When the cab pulled in under the awning, the doorman opened the cab's door before it stopped moving and, then, paid the cabbie for Brett. Another liveried doorman opened the door for us. He touched the brim of his cap and said, "good evening, Miss Andrews."

My feet sank six inches into the plush red carpet.

"Apparently, bars in New York do well," I said.

"I like that, Wilson, not too shocked by the surroundings. I rarely mix my business life with my...social life. Too messy."

We entered a gilt-edged elevator with a mirrored ceiling and red velvet tufted benches.

"Hello, Albert," Brett said to the elevator man, who took us to the 30th floor.

We got off the elevator and were standing in an alcove with a polished wood parquet floor. I could see only three residential doors. Brett unlocked the one on the far right and swung it inward, slowly. As I entered the foyer, I noticed the door closed silently on its own momentum. The hinges made no sound. I turned away from the door and was immediately conscious of ...space.

The apartment was sparse but elegant. Hand-woven Persian rugs covered a wide expanse of wood floor. A huge painting dominated the wall to my left.

The painting depicted a subway platform with no one on it; a half-opened newspaper lay abandoned on a bench.

"Rothko created the work. What do you think?"

"Aren't you lonely when you see that as you walk in every day? Don't get me wrong. The picture is stunning. Radiates isolation though. Makes you feel like you're about a thousand miles away from everyone."

"How perceptive. Wilson, you've surprised me twice in less than five minutes. I have known some people five years who've not surprised me once."

"Brett, do you think that because I'm some guy you met in your bar, following a bad drunk around that I lack mental capacity?"

"No, but you'd be surprised by the number of people, who look at that painting, and say something like, "what the hell did you want to go and put a subway platform on your wall for?"

I looked around the room we were in for a second time. A single white lily in a vase rested on a black pedestal in the room's center.

"I'd never say that. The work fits the space."

"I'm pleased that you approve. Come, I want to show you another room." We entered a smaller room, dark because the blinds were drawn. As my eyes grew accustomed to the dark, I realized we were in the bedroom. The room was painted and carpeted in a muted shade of mauve. The bed was in the center of the oval room and sat on a built up stone dais. A cream–colored divan, a bust of the Greek goddess, Diana, on a pedestal, and some sketches in frames on the wall accented the space.

"Wilson I'm going into my bath for a moment. Back in the other room, my attendant has placed the oranges I purchased into a bowl for you."

"There's somebody else here?"

"We have complete privacy. She has already completed her assigned tasks and left."

"What am I supposed to do with the oranges?" Brett smiled at me.

"Don't worry, I'll show you in a moment."

She exited the bedroom through the right of two doors on the other side of the room. I went back to the room we had entered upon our arrival. The oranges were neatly stacked in a silver bowl. The bowl rested on a wooden serving caddy. I stared at the bowl of fruit trying to figure out what was going on. This was a strange woman. I'd underestimated her. I heard a noise and wheeled around. Brett was standing in the entryway, nude, except for a pair of red high heels and long white gloves.

"Nice gloves, didn't realize the occasion was formal," I said. I raised my hands and faked a look of despair. "I'm not dressed for a soiree."

"Will, I simply can't shock you into silence. Do you like me, darling?"

"You're a pure caution. I've never seen the like of you."

"I'm not sure what that means, but gauging from the sudden tension in your trousers, I'd guess that's a compliment."

"Your guess is a good one."

"Okay, stand over by the door sailor. I'm going over and stand against the far wall with my backside pointed at you. There are three dozen oranges in the bowl. Throw them at my ass. Throw them *hard,* Will. If you hit me on the butt with at least thirty of them, I'll give you a hundred dollars and a blowjob you'll never forget. If you miss more than six times, I'll toss you out on your ear. She broadened her stance so that nothing was left to the imagination.

"I'll make you a counter Brett."

"Ahhh, negotiations. I'm listening."

"If I hit you with all thirty-six oranges, I squeeze the juice onto you...then lick it off - and I get the subway painting, when I come back from the war. You can keep your money, Brett."

"The painting is expensive Will. What do I get if you lose?"

I tapped on the bar with my lighter. Brett watched me from the far wall—naked and expressionless.

"If I lose, put a dog collar and leash on me and walk me into your bar like I was your pet. I'll even get down on all fours."

She was silent, suddenly she strode towards me. When she was directly in front of me, she took my right index finger and inserted it into her vagina. I gasped at the pleasure of her aggressive sexual act and marveled at the perversity. She was hotter than a coal fired boiler.

"Don't make a mess in your skivvies, sailor."

She stroked herself with my finger for several seconds. When she finally removed it, she licked it off, then, brought her face close to mine.

"I'll take your wager Will. But, make no mistake. When you miss, I'll thoroughly humiliate you. I will hold you to this bet."

"Brett, I have no doubt on that score. Get ready, dear. Even an orange will smart from this distance."

We were no more than fifteen yards apart. We were in a damn big room, but the room still wasn't a baseball diamond. Besides, her butt was a nice target.

"You ready, Brett?"

She was bent over, propping herself against the wall with her left hand. She was rubbing herself off with her right.

"Go ahead Will, hit me hard."

I faked a throw. She moved her fanny slightly to the left.

"That's a miss," she yelled.

214

"Afraid not, dear. I haven't let one go yet. I just wanted to see what tactics you'd use to mess me up."

"You sneaky little cretin."

I snapped off a curve to compensate for her movement. The orange started out looking like it was going wide right, then it smacked her hard–dead center.

She let out her breath.

"Again, Will, again."

This game went on for about ten minutes and her fanny was turning cherry red. Oranges were spread all around her feet. One was left. Brett had stopped trying to move after the sixth or seventh pitch. She was arching her back. I let go with everything I had. I hit her a little high with this one. The throw still counted but the force drove her into the wall just a bit.

"Is that all of them?"

"Every last one Brett."

"I'll hold the painting for you. I won't forget."

"I know you won't."

"Do you want your juice now...or later?"

She turned around. She was flushed and her nipples were erect.

I thought. I'll kick myself later.

"Thanks, Brett. I'll take a rain check on that part of the bet, if you don't mind. I'll get your mailing address from the doorman on my way out. See you around, kid."

I let myself out before she could say a word. I knew that no one had ever won a bet from her before. Several weeks later I received a package in the mail with no return address. The provost's office had unwrapped the box for security reasons and, upon seeing the contents, became confused. I came over from the barge we were living on, walked in to the provost's office and saw a glass of orange juice sitting on the provost marshal's desk.

"Davis, what the hell is this, some kind of prank? We opened this package and a damn glass of juice was sealed up in there. Packed in dry ice, like whoever mailed the package actually expected you to drink the stuff."

I opened the note.

Dear Will:

A bet is a bet. I bathed in a whole tub of orange juice. The enclosed glass is a sample taken from my bath, don't worry, I didn't use soap. I considered sending a package large enough to hold the entire tubfull, but I finally decided this was impractical. Also enclosed, is a receipt for the Rothko. A detailed description of the work is enclosed along with a sworn affidavit transferring ownership to you. I will wait for your instructions as to where to ship it, etc. Keep me informed as to your well being and whereabouts to the extent you are allowed to do so. Try hard not to get yourself killed. Life would be less interesting with you gone. If we do manage to get together again, I won't wear anything so...formal. We'll stick to dinner and stay away from all sporting events. I don't care to lose any more paintings.

Regards,
Brett R. Andrews

I drank the juice, which was still cold and had a distinct tang to it. The provost staff watched me with curiosity, like I'd done something obscene.

I raised my glass in mock salute. "Florio knows his oranges," I said. "The juice was excellent. You all should drink this stuff, its good for you."

Chapter 29
School is out

"Ladies, when you entered this nursing program nearly a year ago, I said that war would demand service worlds away from these ivy covered halls. Today, that prophecy is bearing fruit. Even though you are nowhere near the end of your educational program here, the demand for nurses has reached a crisis point. We've been asked by the Army Department to put together a volunteer nursing contingent to staff a field hospital in New Caledonia, which I believe is in the southwestern Pacific Ocean, north of New Zealand and west of Australia."

The Dean of Nurses paused to let the buzz settle in the auditorium.

"Although the Army is conservative and–intensely male, we have insisted that no woman here will receive a faculty recommendation unless the Army commissions the recommended women in our contingent at a grade no lower than First Lieutenant," the dean smiled. "The Army has, finally, agreed to this demand in writing."

"This provides each of you with official authority and status." The Dean paused to consult some notes on the rostrum.

"Further, eligibility to volunteer with a faculty endorsement is determined by the following. You must be carrying at least a 'B' average in biology and anatomy, and a 'C' in organic chemistry. If you have doubts about your eligibility, consult with me in private. A final list of eligible volunteers will be given to the Army by 30 April. I won't kid you ladies. Even if you're not eligible for the official Penn contingent, any Armed Service recruiter in the area will take you immediately for service elsewhere. I urge each of you to be prudent in your decision."

The Dean walked around the front of the podium, indicating she had something important to say.

"Now, let me share some personal thoughts with you. We're standing on the cusp of history. What we do in the coming months may determine our fate, those of our children, and even grandchildren. You, like many of our young men, are being asked to go in harms way. As I speak to you today, we all know that the Japanese have destroyed resistance in the Philippines. The Philippines will fall soon, despite our boys' heroic resistance. I don't know how far the Japanese will advance before they are stopped. Each one of you must consider the potential consequences of being wounded, captured, or killed. Make your decision with God resting on your shoulder. I shall miss all who decide to leave us, and pray for your success and safe return."

When the Dean had left the auditorium, a girl named Gloria spoke, "the way she talked you'd think we were six years old."

I retorted, "after we get to where the Army is sending us," I said. "We'll probably wish we were six years old again."

"So, we're going?" Asked Linda Huckaby.

"Sure, we're going!" Gloria said. "Who wants to hang around this fusty old place when all those muscle-bound men are sailing around the Pacific, lonesome, needing our attention."

"Gloria this is a shooting war not a picnic, or, a roman orgy."

"Why, thank you, Mindy. If you're as sharp with a bedpan as you are with that tongue, you'll be promoted in no time. I, on the other hand, intend to wrap these mitts around one of those fly-boys."

"That won't be all you wrap those fingers around if your track record holds," Donna Padget said.

Everyone laughed, even Gloria. "Alright, I've been sunk," she said. "I'm retreating to my room to try out some new hand lotion." She waggled her fingers at us as she headed for the auditorium exit.

"The Army and the Navy is going to love her," Linda said.

"Don't forget the Marines," Mindy said. "They'll get their chance too."

"I've never been out of Pennsylvania before," Linda said. "New Caledonia sounds like it's a long way off."

"It is," I replied. "Are you having second thoughts?"

"I'm not. My mother is. She heard a rumor at bridge that the Army was going to send out a call for nurses two weeks ago. She's been riding me since to stay here."

"Are you going to let your mother decide for you?" I asked.

"Hey, lay off her Mindy. At least she still talks to her mom," Donna said.

"Touché' Donna. Sorry Linda, I was out of line."

"That's okay Mindy. I didn't mean to sound like a big baby. The announcement has thrown me for a loop, that's all."

"Fair enough, my mind is spinning too. Besides, wait till I tell my aunt about this, she may lock me in a broom closet."

"I don't know if I feel up to *My Gal Sal* tonight, Aunt Shannon."

"First thing, quit with the Aunt title, I feel seventy every time you say the word. Second thing, I don't really give two flicks of a rat's tail about your feelings. I want to sneer at Rita and salivate over Victor. Here, rub this *Lucien LeLong* inside your thighs before you fasten your garters. The boys will try hard not to follow you around, but they will anyway."

I rolled my eyes.

"Why do you still care about men, when you've been treated vilely by so many of them?"

"Darling, all men are not worthless. Notice I said *all*. If you get the right one…besides, based upon what you've told me about Will Davis, haven't you figured out that the occasional male does find his way out of the primordial soup?"

"Hmmm, Will rising out of a bowl of split pea soup. Sounds fun."

"If he's been swimming around Long Island Sound, he'd be better off in split pea."

"I don't remember saying anything to you about his training. Have you been reading my mail?" I crossed over to button up the back of her dress so that she couldn't ignore me.

She looked back at me via the reflection in her vanity mirror.

"Only the one letter, the one you left in the breakfast nook the other morning."

"Auntie, you're a nosy Parker."

Shannon shrugged. "I admit it. I'm interested in what he's up to." She blotted her lips on a tissue. "I suspect there are lots of girls flashing him some leg up there in those off Broadway taverns."

"Twist the dagger Auntie. Will probably has been waxing his wick, as they say over at Penn. I refuse to moon over him or the situation. We may not see each other again until after the war, if then. He's consumed by his work as I'm consumed by mine. I hope girls are strutting their stuff in front of him. Soon, he'll be at sea."

"I've grown to like you Mindy. Figures, I grow used to having you around; so, you decide to run off and play nurse in the South Pacific. I trust you'll send me some pictures of yourself running naked on the beach with a bronzed sailor or two."

"Sure, I'll be the ghost running along under the ten coats of zinc oxide I'd have to wear to protect this pasty white skin from the Pacific sun. Living in Philly has done nothing for my tan."

"Serves you right. If you're going to live in a Yankee town, you ought to at least have the manners to look the part."

"Come on, Auntie. If we have to see Victor Mature ogle Rita Hayworth, I at least want popcorn and *Neccos* out of you."

"Those things stick to your teeth."

"That's why I like them so much."

"Let's get a move on then," Shannon said. "I want to sit close enough to see Victor's overbite."

"Right behind you, Auntie."

"Quit calling me that," Shannon said.

"Sure thing, Auntie. I want extra butter on my popcorn."

Chapter 30
Down Under

"Excuse me, Mr. Whitherspoon; I don't think I heard you correctly."

"Yes, you did Bob," his boss said. "Your services are required by this company and by the Navy Department in Australia."

"If you don't mind my asking, sir, what the hell is going on?"

Doug Whitherspoon was facing away from Bob Sullivan, so he smiled. Bob didn't waste time or mince words.

"Strange world, Bob," Doug answered, "getting stranger by the moment too." What were the odds? He thought. An Irishman from Texas shows up on his company's doorstep and turns out to be a mechanical genius. Irony was that Bob wasn't aware of his own talent.

Doug turned around and put his hands on his desk. He said softly, "Bob, a war is going on, and you, my friend have come to the attention of the United States Navy."

Bob rose and paced on the green carpet. He still loved the way his feet sank into the cushioned texture. He'd come a way long since he'd first walked onto this carpet seven months ago. A stranger observing them for the first time wouldn't immediately know which man was the boss. The two men wore identical suits. Bob remembered what he'd learned about clothing from Mr. Cheney. He only owned three suits, but they were wool blends. His shirts were starched and his ties were silk. Bob was amazed by the power of clothing, especially at swank restaurants. He could slick his hair back, put on a jacket and tie, flash a couple of ten spots and a whole army of waiters and maitre D's would line up to kiss his butt.

"Damn it Doug, you said that what I did here was critical to national defense."

"Absolutely, Bob," Doug said. "So critical that the Navy wants us to take a look at the team they've set up in Australia. They asked me who was responsible for our breakthrough. I said you and Fred Thornhill–a half-truth. I suggested they take Fred and leave you here. They talked to the work group. Thornhill stays. You go."

Bob sighed and looked down at his wingtips. He could see his reflection. Just when you think life is a sunny garden, someone dumps manure on you.

"Betty is expecting in two months. Will I still be here in two months?"

"If I said yes, I'd be lying."

"Are they going to draft me, or what?"

"You're on the team as a civilian contractor with the status of a Lt. Commander. They need you, so they're giving you a compartmentalized security clearance," Doug paused. He poured himself a drink of water out of a carafe that sat on his credenza.

"Something else, Doug?"

"Technodyne remains liable for your good conduct."

"My reputation precedes me," Bob said, as he poured himself some water too. "So, if I screw up they cut the company out of the pork?"

"You don't have to wear red, white, and blue and sing *Yankee Doodle Dandy*. Let's just say they'd prefer you stay sober and out of barroom brawls."

"Jesus, what is this about me and brawls? Has my conduct ever caused you concern since I've been here Doug?"

Doug Whitherspoon walked around the desk and sat down next to him.

"You're the best damn employee in this company, but that doesn't mean you haven't been checked out. Consider who we're dealing with here."

"Ran a background check on me, did they?"

"Yes," Doug said, "they did. They want you but they don't want the baggage you carry." Doug got back up and went over to the window. "Frankly," he said, with his back to Bob, "when Thornhill first asked you if you could figure the damn thing out, I wish you'd told him to piss up a rope and, then, come and told me what he wanted."

"You're right boss," Bob said. "Unfortunately, you can't turn bacon back into a prize hog. Fred acted like what he was asking was no big deal. Acted like he was doing me a favor by letting me look at the thing. Who knew?"

"Indeed," Doug said. "Did you consider the security breach he created by bringing you in without authorization?"

"Never crossed my mind," Bob said. He got up and stood next to his boss at the window. "The machine was just another gadget. Good thing I never took it home to tinker with in the evenings."

"Bob, I lay awake at night thinking about that. Care for a real drink before you head to the house and deliver the news?"

"I'd love one, Doug, but I'm going to pass. Betty is going to throw a gasket over this, and I don't want to have alcohol on my breath."

"Treat the Navy like you treat Bet, and we'll come out smelling like a rose. Before you go, here's a little sugar to go with the medicine. The Navy is paying me for your services under a lucrative, highly-classified, contract. Effective immediately, you make $1,600. per month."

"Know what, Doug?"

"What?"

"My dad never made that much in a year."

"Welcome to the war. I don't care to profit at the expense of men's lives, but if we pull this off, Bob we'll make serious money. The Navy agreed to a clause allowing Technodyne to keep the proprietary rights to your so-called gadget. You'll get a huge slice of the pie. I've set up a stock account in your name, Alice has the paperwork."

"Doug, why are you being so damn nice to me? Do I have to start watching my back around you?"

"No hidden agendas here. I'm taking care of you because I want you back. If other folks come snooping around, making you offers, please let me know."

"I'll never forget what you've done for me here, Doug - even if you are letting the squids haul me half way around the world."

"Like I said, Bob, I've no damn choice. Promise me one more thing."

"What?"

"Don't volunteer to field test the gadget in a combat setting. The Navy could end up killing you off on one of those leaky subs. Come home in one piece, and I, by God, will make you a rich man, Bob."

"Maybe I will have that drink."

"Straight up, or on the rocks?"

"Rocks, with a splash of soda."

"What shall we drink to?"

"Getting home in one piece."

Chapter 31
Resident Genius

"Bobby is this for real?"

"I am as serious as I have ever been Bets," Bob said. "You'll be okay. I've arranged for you to get my check every month. I'll live on a quarters stipend while I'm there."

"Why you Bobby? You're a smart guy, but all those college guys working there keep reminding you that you're nothing but a glorified wire monkey. Why can't they send those smart asses packing?"

Bobby shifted Bets weight on his lap. She was seven months pregnant and she still got him hot. She was rubbing her bottom against his lap, giving him an erection - she knew it too. She started petting him through his trousers.

"I suppose you'll look for some skinny blonde down there in Australia to do you - first chance you get."

She freed him from his trousers and immediately dropped onto on her knees. She licked him like he was a piece of hard candy.

"Bet," he said, as he groaned and tried to pull himself out of her mouth. She wouldn't let him. When he was spent, she went to the bathroom for a moment. While she was gone, he tucked himself back into his pants. The fit was tight because he was still hard as a rock.

She opened the bathroom door and said, "take off your clothes and get on the bed. Play with me while Conor is still asleep."

"Bet, I'm always happy to oblige, but aren't we going to finish this conversation?"

She stood naked in the doorway separating their bedroom from the bath. "I love the master bath," she said. "Never in a million years did I dream I'd be here–my own house - in San Juan Capistrano, California."

"Bets," Bob said. "I know you're upset."

His wife's nude body was bathed only in light as she leaned against the doorjamb. Angels wore no clothing other than light, thought Bob.

"Upset and selfish," she said.

She walked over to the bed and lay down.

"Remember that when you're in Australia and some horny, man-starved, bitch wants to ride you. This war hasn't even started and I'm already pissed."

"I know baby, I know, but Doug told me I've got no choice. I either go as a contractor, or they draft me and I go as a squid."

She climbed on the bed and pressed her bottom against his right hand.

"Hmmmm...good Bobby. Stick all four fingers right...there! These are the same jerks that wanted Doug to fire you three months ago because they griped about you being a potential security risk, right?"

"That was before..."

"I know," Betty interrupted. "That was before they figured out that you were the resident genius. Oh yes, keep doing that. Now, put your other hand there and ... oh God yes! I will hurt you bad, Bobby, if you don't come back."

"I will, baby, I'll always come back."

Bob was sitting at the table in his breakfast nook next morning.

He could see the ocean from his chair. The nook window faced south. He smiled slightly. No one but Bet, who knew his every mood could have guessed that he was incredibly, almost insanely happy. Conor was sitting on his right knee eating a banana. Well, actually he was smearing most of it on himself and on Bob's new chinos.

He looked up and caught Bet watching from the kitchen. He didn't recognize the look at first, and then it hit him right between the eyes. The look was one of pure love. He listened to the ocean roaring in the distance.

"Will your mom come out?"

"Nana splurg," Conor squashed the last quarter piece of banana into the table and spit out the remainder in his mouth at the same time.

"Bet, bring me a wet dish rag. Our son's table manners are remarkably similar to his old man's."

Bet came around the corner of the bar separating the kitchen from the nook and wiped the banana off the table and then gave Conor's face the once over too.

"Mama, noooooo!" Conor yelled.

"Conor, you're headed for the bathtub in two shakes." She went in to the bath located off the hall. Bob heard her turning the taps.

"Bob, do you mind giving him his bath?" She asked. "I'm having a tough time getting up once I'm down on the bathroom floor."

"Come on, you monkey," Bob said. "Let's go talk about your mother behind her back."

"I hope she'll come, Bobby. She'd be a godsend."

"I have no problems with Melrose. Your old man is a whole different kettle of fish. He'll screw with us Bet - don't bother to defend him, I know he will."

"My daddy is a pain in the butt and I know that better than you, Bobby Sullivan! But if he wants to visit and see his grandson he'll be welcome in this house!"

As she spoke, Betty burst into tears.

Conor wailed in sympathy with his mother.

"Ah geez Louise, Bets I didn't mean anything by it. It's just he's all the time busting my balls."

"At least he speaks to you," Betty said. "I can't get him to say word one to me. Besides, you don't have a thing to worry about. He won't leave his savings & loan long enough to visit his slut daughter in California."

"Yeah, he talks to me alright. Remember when you told your mom about the swallows returning here each year?"

"Yes," Bet said. "I told her the ocean was gorgeous here and that the spectacle of the swallows was enchanting."

"And what did your dad say?"

Betty laughed. "He said, 'great, the big dope picks the one place in California to live where birds come to shit.'"

"That sums up his attitude towards me. Only reason his attitude doesn't make me too angry is because my own dad would say the same thing."

Bob grabbed a towel off the rack to dry Conor's head.

"Bet, I'm sorry, but he gets under my skin. You're his daughter, but I'm your husband now. I can't permit him to pop off like that."

"Oh great, Bobby and what are you going to do if he shows up while you're helping kick the Japs from the Pacific over in Australia?"

Bob hoisted Conor over his head, tossed him in the air, caught him and tossed him up again. Conor screeched with excitement.

"Nothing Bet won't be able to."

"That's right. You won't. You're going to have to trust me to handle him, this house, and everything else around here. Just like I'll trust you to stay the hell away from all those skinny Australian blondes."

"Strange you'd bring that up, Betts. Doug told me last night that the Australian Government assigned a blonde to my task group named Wendy to chauffeur me and the other guys around."

"Give me our son, Bobby Sullivan. Get hold of Doug and change those arrangements immediately."

Bob laughed. "Jesus Bets there ain't a Wendy on the team. I'm just pulling your leg."

"Pull my leg about something else. I've no sense of humor about Australian women."

"Truce, Bets. I'll leave the blondes alone, if you promise to change your dad into a human being before I come home."

"Okay Bobby, truce. But, try and remember that I have enough problems with my dad. I don't need to hear about him from you too."

"I know, I'm no cup of tea to be around either," Bob said ruefully. "We are lucky in one respect though."

"What respect is that, Bobby?"

"You'll have your parents to contend with while I'm away - not mine. I wouldn't want my old man, God save him from hellfire, within 100 miles of you or Conor."

The argument over, they dressed Conor. Betty wished she could ship her dad off to Australia in place of Bobby. As she slid Conor into a clean jumper, she whispered a silent prayer,

Dear Lord: Forgive me for thinking this thought now and at the hour of my death. Bring Bobby home, alive and whole. Let some other poor soul die in his place if you must. I am just a mother and don't pretend to understand why old men continually seek the blood of young men in battle. The young always get killed and the old remain, haunted by their memories. Please let this be a quick war. Let my own son be a peaceful man who is never near a war. Finally, I give solemn thanks that my son is much too young to get involved in this awful mess. Amen.

This was a grudging prayer of guilty thanks to God. She had thanked God for allowing this war to come at a time when it could only take her husband, not her son. Problem is God probably didn't give a shit about her concerns. He killed his own Son despite the protests of the Son's mother. His record for protecting sons was, therefore, definitely suspect.

They headed back to the living room where Bob sat on the floor with Conor. They started building a tower with a set of wooden blocks. Betty sat at the small desk in the entry hall and began writing to her mom.

Dear Mom:

No reason to beat around the bush - I need you to come to California for an extended visit at your earliest opportunity. Bobby is being sent overseas to work for the Navy. Bobby is leaving the first week of June - the baby is due in July.

I know you and Daddy don't approve of Bobby, so be it. He has worked hard and is a good provider. When I met him, I thought he was a man in a world of whiny boys. I still believe that. I won't ask you to come a second time. If I don't see or hear from you within the next two weeks, I'll take that as your answer, and make other arrangements.

I love you mom and I even still love daddy. But, I won't keep in touch if you and daddy can't realize that I'm not a little girl anymore. Bobby is going to war. I am a woman and the mother of his children. Help me or not, as you see fit. My life is here with Bobby and always will be.

Love,
Betty

When she finished the letter, she said, "Bobby, I'm going to post this, then walk down to City Hall and register for sugar."

"Sure you want to hoof it, Bets? You'll probably be standing in line there."

"The weather's nice out and if I get too tired while I'm waiting, I'll faint. They'll put me up front to get rid of me."

"Okay, but don't push it. If you feel sick or something, send someone and I'll come get you."

"Bobby?"

"Yeah, Bets?"

"You haven't been pretending all these months, have you?"

"Pretending what, dear?"

"About liking me. I know at first you liked my car better than me. But now, you really like me, don't you, Bobby?"

Bob sat still for a moment, finally figuring out that she *really* was loco about his going off to Australia. Odds were whatever he said would be wrong.

"Bets, if I, you, Dorothy Lamore, Greta Garbo, and Madeleine Carroll were in a lifeboat - and only me and one woman could stay in the boat and survive, those other dreamboats would be fish food. I don't even like thinking about how alone I was before I met you. You're the only woman in the world for me."

She started to cry again. When he rose to go to her, she said, "no, keep an eye on our son. I'm going to pick up a nice steak at the market and grill it for you when I get home." Then, she left.

Bob stood there eyeing the door, then, turned to his son, sitting on the floor chewing on a block.

"Son, you tell me. Was she happy or mad at me?"

Conor pointed at the front door and said, "mama go?"

"Yes son, mama go." He sat back down on the floor with his son and began stacking blocks. The last thing she talked about before leaving was cooking for him. Therefore, he figured, he must have said the right thing. Out loud he said, "doesn't matter, son. I'll get back on her bad side soon enough."

Conor giggled and said, "funny, daddy." Bob agreed. He was pretty hilarious.

Melrose sat silently while her husband read the letter. When he was done, he sat back in his chair, took off his reading glasses and tapped them on the armrest.

"I don't wish to upset you, Robert, but I intend to go immediately."

"Even if I forbid it?"

"Of course, don't be ridiculous. I've sat by and watched you alienate our daughter. Bob Sullivan has beaten us. Betty is merely spelling the obvious out. "

Robert Stevens bent forward to massage his temples.

"That little thug has more fortitude than I gave him credit for. If he'd stayed around here, Prather DeWitt would have sent him to prison." Robert slapped his hands against his knees.

"Are you out of your mind Robert? You sound disappointed. Your grandson's father lands on his feet in California and all you can do is regret the fact that he's not in jail?"

Robert Stevens tapped his reading glasses on the armrest and said, "Melrose, I know when I'm beaten. Go help Bets. Send me pictures of my grandchildren. Let me know when it's safe for me to visit."

"No tricks, Robert. I intend to make amends."

"Why pet, whatever are you talking about?"

"No hidden agendas. That's what and don't call me 'pet'." Melrose said. "I'm not the housecat. Leave Betty and her husband's family alone."

"I will Rose, of course, I will."

"If you don't, Robert, I will watch our Mr. Sullivan break you in two without batting an eye. And if you try to get between him and his family, he will you know."

"Yes, I believe he would."

His wife stared at him, waiting for elaboration. Convinced that she had won this skirmish, she left to supervise supper preparations.

Robert finished his last spoken thought by saying, "if he was around." He then took his favorite pipe out of the rack on the end table, lit up a plug, and puffed thoughtfully while thinking about his grandson.

Chapter 32
Left Full Rudder

"Davis, here's your cup of joe."

"Thanks, cookie." I sat down at the mess table. I was finally at sea. It was June 1942. Ace Henson and Wally 'squawk box' Jeffers sat down across from me. We were headed south toward the Panama Canal. We lurched sideways as the boat turned sharply to port, the command, "right full rudder" sounded over the box after the boat had already began the turn. We jumped up from the table, feeling a slight buck as the boat fired a stern shot. No return fire was felt or otherwise heard. I reported to my battle station in the control room, manning the stern planes.

"Periscope's been sighted to starboard of our base course," Chief Bunton said. "In the future, Davis, if we have a future, get your ass to your battle station in a bigger hurry."

"Aye, aye, Chief."

"Stand down and get your skinny ass to the forward engine room and check on the distillation plant. I heard you got a knack for how the damn thing works. See, if you can coax 1200 gallons a day out of it."

"Aye, aye, Chief," I said. My war had begun in earnest.

Five minutes later, a distant rumble was heard.

"That's our fish," Henson said, as he handed me a wrench.

"Doesn't sound like it hit anything," I said.

"Didn't hit nothing," Henson said. "Wonder if there really was a periscope scoping us."

"Can't get any torque on this bolt. It's covered with oil. Hand me a rag, Henson."

Ace Henson dropped a rag on my chest. "If a U-boat had the drop on us, they missed too," he said.

"No shit, Henson," I said. "We'd know if we were slammed into by a 3000 - pound torpedo. Here, take the wrench. I'll find the Chief. I've got some bad news for him."

"Chief, the distillation plant's a piece of junk. The unit won't put out more than a 1000 to 1100 a day." I said.

"Okay, when you get off duty on the planes, put out the word. Only the cooks bathe everyday. Everyone else bathes, every third day. Make up a roster, so no one gets confused," he said. "I run short on fresh water for the batteries; I'll have your ass, Davis."

"My ass, Chief?"

"Affirmative. You're now in charge of crew hygiene. Anyone smells better than me goes on report, and so do you."

"Want me to give the word in officer land as well?"

"Negative. I'll tell the old man myself."

"The asshole isn't acknowledging the recognition signal." The intercom squawked.

"Sounds like the Exec," I said.

"Crap in a bucket and call it lunch," Chief Bunton said. "Now what."

"Recognition signal usually means a plane, doesn't it?" I said.

"Belay the squawking about planes and mind the bubble, Davis."

"Aye, Chief."

"We have a confused friendly, Captain," Lieutenant Dave Gunderschmidt said. "The aircraft is a Navy Catalina." "Fire the recognition flares, Dave." The old man, Lieutenant Commander Cromwell, ordered.

"Fire flares," Lt. Gunderschmidt said. The flares fired. The plane circled and opened its bay doors.

"Damn," The old man said. "The fucking moron hasn't updated his codes!"

A green flare lit the sky to our port side - our escort vessel had signaled as well. The plane veered off. Chief Bunton was still standing next to me at the stern planes on the wet or port side of the control room. We heard rather than saw the exchange topside. "Wouldn't that have been icing on the cake, attacked by one of our own bombers," Dave Gunderschmidt said.

"Dave, after we tie up at Coco Solo, find that SOB and bring him on board."

"Aye, Captain. I'd like to meet him too."

"Don't forget the lectures either," the Captain said.

"You want me to give the crew both?"

"Panama rates both Dave," the Captain replied. "Torpedo alcohol, bad local hooch, and venereal disease can disable half of a boat's crew. We can't afford that much down time."

"Aye, Captain."

When we put in at Coco Solo and the Boat was securely berthed, Gunny gave us the VD and alcohol lecture. He gathered the off duty crew together for the lecture, even though the old man ordered us to stay away from the local establishments until we were through the locks and on the Pacific side of the canal.

"Alright men, listen up," Gunny said. "The Captain has standing orders from fleet headquarters to court-martial any man rendered unfit for duty by drunkenness or venereal disease. Keep this in mind when you leave the boat. Every boat passing through the locks is losing crewmen to VD or torpedo juice. Now, I have some pictures I want to show you." The Lieutenant reached behind him for some panels. He lifted the first panel above his head. Groans erupted from the crew.

"Is that what I think it is, sir?" Ace said.

"Yes, Ace, this is a picture of a diseased male member."

"Sir," Ace said. "I was wondering. If I had a loaf of that bread you was talking about and I got it sopping wet with torpedo juice?"

"Yes, Ace?"

"Alcohol is a disinfectant isn't it?"

"Yes, Ace."

"Sir, what if I stuck my dick into that loaf of bread and got it all damp from that torpedo juice; that'd kill any of the cooties I pick up from these street sluts you're talking about wouldn't it?"

Several emotions crossed Lt Gunderschmidt's face before he replied, "yes, Ace, except for the really fast cooties. The ones that make the journey up your urethra before the alcohol is applied," he said. "The alcohol won't kill whatever might be crawling around on your insides. Also, this advice, if you disobey all else, I suggest inserting your penis into the loaf only after you have finished using the bread as a filter."

The entire crew rolled on the deck. Ace's new nickname was *doughboy.*

The following day, we had mail call. Ralph wrote me. I stashed the letter in my tunic. When we got over to Coconut Grove and my shipmates were out, using Lt Gunny's condoms, I wandered off by myself, in violation of orders and got lost. A flashing blue neon light, blinking the word, 'cervesa' caught my eye. I decided to go in and ask for directions back to the docks. The bar's ramshackle wood frame was white with weathering and the floor gave six inches when I stepped inside. A beat up phonograph in the far corner played something that sounded like the Dailey Paskman minstrels.

"Jesus," I murmured. "Thought my grandma was the only person who listened to Paskman." Some men at the bar were staring at me. I sat at an empty table as far away from them as I could get.

A waitress, wearing a bright green skirt and an orange blouse came up to my table and lifted her skirt. As she placed one heeled shoe on the table, she looked me over and said, "pussy and tequila–4 dollars. Pussy and beer–3 dollars. Tequila only–2 dollars. Beer only–1 dollar."

"One beer, two tequilas," I said. "The second tequila is for you."

"I like you," she said. "Maybe I screw you later–for free." She turned and headed back to the bar. Will wondered how he was going to turn her down, without causing a scene. He pulled the letter from Ralph out of his uniform tunic, smoothed it out on the table and began to read.

Dear Will:

I hope this catches up with you before you are out in the ocean somewheres. Mom has a blue service star up in the window. Mr. Chaney comes by often. It's okay. I'm glad Mom has someone paying her some attention. I guess I shouldn't feel sorry for myself...

SLAM! The waitress put a glass of beer down that must have held a quart and two chipped shot glasses filled to their tired looking brims with a light brown shimmering liquid. The waitress picked up the one shot glass and downed the liquor in one smooth motion. She placed the glass back on the table upside down. She then opened her blouse and freed her breasts to the world. Her nipples were very dark. She picked up the other shot glass looked me over from head to toe and said; "now you drink." She placed my mouth under her right nipple and with surprising languor poured the tequila over her nipple and by degree into my mouth.

The tequila was like molten lead as it traveled down my throat. When the shot glass was empty, she placed her nipple in my mouth and said, "suck." I did. After two or three minutes of this she lifted her skirt so that it billowed around her. She settled into my lap. I could feel the heat radiating from her.

"Aren't we going to…?"

She put her right index finger to my lips.

"Talk ruins sex. Americans never understand this."

I said something that sounded like condom.

"Don't worry, sailor with blue eyes. I do not have the clap." She rocked in my lap until my cock found its destination. She was wet and hot. After we finished, she looked at me in the eye and said, "I'm worth five dollars but, I'm free for you because I like your eyes."

Three or four other patrons had wandered in while we were screwing. They nodded in my direction. I took a huge gulp of beer and stared at the flickering blue neon light. When I finally decided no one was interested in me, or the fact I'd just had public sex with the waitress, I picked up the letter and read.

but I feel like someone pulled a rug out from under me, and I bumped my head when I fell. I miss you and daddy too, Will. You probably don't want to hear this now that you're getting ready to go fight Japs, but I got no one else to talk to. Mom won't talk to me about daddy. She just shrugs and turns away whenever I bring him up. I ain't whining, Will. But, I'm angry. Someone's going to pay for daddy's death. I pissed in the gas tank of Chester Harris' car and then threw a brick with a bag of dog shit tied to it through the front window of his house. I'm not stupid. I hear the whispers. Lots of people think Harris had daddy killed over a gambling dispute down there in Mexico. Now I have no dad.

I keep thinking on how he'd tussle my hair every night while he listened to Amos n' Andy or Winchell and smoked his pipe. We don't listen to the radio anymore.

Sorry big brother, I am real sad and can't get around it.
Be careful out there. I need you back. So does mom.

Love,
Your Brother Ralph

I figured a whorehouse district bar was no place for a crying man but the whole damn world was too fucked up. I sipped my beer as tears ran down my cheeks.

"So much sadness. I have screwed you blue eyes— so, now, you cry."

"It isn't that."

"I know I saw the letter. A girlfriend in search of another perhaps? This is very sad but it happens, no?"

"I wish my situation was that simple. By the way, now that we've...you know. I 'd like to know your name."

She stared at me. I didn't think she was going to answer at all. Then, she said, "you're the first of your kind who's ever asked. I'm called Elena."

"Elena, I'm Wilson, and I was crying because my brother reminded me in his letter that certain things, once lost, can't be found again - ever."

Elena sat, resting her chin on her fingers.

"I was right to do you while I had the chance. You are a sensitive boy, especially for an American."

She raised her left hand and snapped her fingers. A man in a yellow flowered shirt walked briskly over to the table.

"Lancasta, bring us a bottle of the good tequila from the stockroom."

"Yes Senora, of course."

Elena saw my look of surprise and smiled. "Yes, Wilson, appearance is reality," she said. "I am the owner here. I have public sex only with my most handsome patrons."

I thought, what is going on with me and women who own bars?

"Strange," I said. "You're the second woman I've met in the past three months in the bar business."

Lancasta brought the 'good' tequila back with two crystal shot glasses.

"Shall we drink to women barkeeps or, better yet, your continued health perhaps? I understand being onboard a submarine is risky."

"No, Elena. Let's drink to our fathers, be they good or bad, bastards or saviors…let's drink to them."

"This is good, Wilson. These times are not easy for fathers."

She lifted her glass and said, "to our papas."

I hoisted my shot glass. "To our papas."

We drank the liquor down.

Much later, I woke up with a raging headache, completely disoriented. I was in a rather comfortable bed; naked as the day I was born. I had no idea where my clothes were or, more importantly, where my wallet was. Dim sunlight filtered through French doors to my right. The sun was coming up. I was up to my neck in bilge water. My liberty had run at midnight.

"Do not worry, sailor Davis."

I fell out of the bed, which was five feet off the floor. I slowly picked myself up off of the woven carpet. Good thing the rug was there to cushion me, the floor was polished stone. I peeked over the top of the bed. Elena was watching me, propped up on her right elbow.

"Did you hurt yourself, sailor Davis?"

She was stunning. She had blue-black bobbed hair that glowed in the morning light. Her eyes were polished emeralds set in the bottom of a shallow pool of clear rainwater.

"Yes, young Davis, I am real," she said. "I am no more the hag now than I was last night when you were licking my-"

"Thanks Elena," I said. "I remember that well enough."

"How do you Americans say it? You have the devils' own luck. You really had no business being in this quarter without an escort. I could have cut your throat twice."

She sat up and faced me. She spread her legs, so that I was, again, facing her from the top of a vee formed by the polished, honed teak boughs she had for legs.

"Instead of killing you," she said. "I instructed Lancasta to wash your sailor suit, contact your ship via a formal deputation, and inform your navy that you were unfortunately indisposed." She lifted her legs straight up into the air and whipped her feet at the ceiling. "Then, I fucked you senseless for the second time in less than a day."

She rubbed her feet against my cheeks and let out a sigh.

"Your submarine is leaving today. This is good. If you were in Balboa for much longer, I would get nothing done. Your penis is a distraction. Be off, sailor Davis. Your suit is hanging in the wardrobe. We must quit this lovely nonsense for now. Your navy will tolerate no further excuses. Lancasta will escort you back to your naval base. Oh, by the way, there is a small package sewn inside your uniform tunic. Upon your return, a man will be waiting at your ship to retrieve it."

I walked over to the wardrobe. Elena, nude, on the bed had once again made me hard. My curiosity was slightly more compelling though. I pulled my tunic and pants out of the wardrobe. You could have cut meat with the creases pressed into my uniform pants. Sure enough, there was a package about the size of a cigarette pack, neatly wrapped, sewn into my tunic. I looked at Elena, still stretched out on the bed.

"Is this why you didn't?"

"Why didn't I what, darling sailor?"

"Cut my throat twice."

She walked over to me cupping my face in her hands. She kissed me deeply.

"No, the two things are unrelated," she said. "My affection for you is real, not contrived - you remind me of someone. I, too, have suffered irretrievable loss. Now go. Lancasta is waiting for you through the doors in the arbor. If you survive the war, come back and we'll speak of many things." She produced a second box from the bureau behind her. She pressed it into my hand. "This box is for you. Tell no one where you obtained it. If you wish to contact me in the future, show what's in the box to whoever is tending the downstairs bar. Wait three days and return. If you do not hear from me it is because I'm dead or because it's not safe to meet. Now go!"

I left and didn't look back. "Strange words for a woman who owns a dive in Coconut Grove," I said to myself. The larger of the two packages I was carrying made a slight bulge in my tunic. The bulge wasn't noticeable in the early light. Lancasta was as silent as he'd been the night before. I noticed that his solemn face was severely scarred. We headed down a cobbled street that gradually widened as we moved from wood frame shacks to homes made of stucco.

"What is that smell in the air?"

"Is the copra. We are near a drying pad. You must first dry the coconut meat before extracting the oil."

"I don't suppose you know what's in either of these packages I'm carrying."

Lancasta started, then, looked quickly around.

"Senor, with respect, speak not of these things to me. I have no idea what you are talking about."

"Sorry, my mistake."

We walked in silence to the security checkpoint. I watched Lancasta present a letter to the Army MP at the guard shack. We were waved through.

When we reached the boat, Lancasta faded into the crowd on the docks without a backward glance. I was immediately mustered in to the old man's presence in the control room.

"Machinist's Mate Davis reporting," I said, as I saluted. I noticed a Commander, dressed in formal blues standing with the Captain. I'd never seen this officer before.

"Very well, Will," the Captain said. "Let's move to the wardroom."

I knew the strange Commander wasn't a submariner because of the way he moved along the centerline gangway. He was graceful but cautious, clearly not used to being on a sub. Once in the wardroom, the Captain took the unusual step of clearing the entire forward battery compartment.

When we were seated at the officers' mess table, the mystery man said, "you have a package for me."

I looked at the Captain, who nodded and said, "He has a need to know Will. Give him what you have and tell him how you came by it."

"Give me a minute," I said. "The package is sewn to the inside of my tunic." I shrugged off my uniform tunic and turned it inside out. The package was wrapped in bright green paper with a pink bow.

The old man clipped the threads holding the package loose with a pocketknife, then handed the box over to the mystery man, who secreted the package away in an inside coat pocket. He was wearing a shoulder holster and a big knife pressed in between the waistband of his pants and his shirt.

"That a Bowie knife?" I asked.

He grinned like a wolf that had stumbled on a herd of unprotected sheep.

"Panama is a dangerous place, my young friend," he said.

"Yes sir. So I've been told."

He turned to go, then, stopped. He turned back toward Captain Cromwell and me.

"Curiosity is not a virtue in my business," he said. "But, I'm curious about her. What was she like?"

"Who, sir?"

"Come on, seaman. How many women did you encounter?"

"Are you asking about Elena, the bar owner?"

The commander's laughter had a raw nasal quality to it, like someone scraping their fingernails across a chalkboard.

"Amazing, that might be her real first name."

"You know her?" I asked.

"I know *of her*. No one I do business with has ever seen her in person–and lived. Her work is usually accomplished through the use of drops or intermediaries. When we received her signal, telling us this package was coming via a courier, we had no idea what to expect."

"Commander," Captain Cromwell said. "Is revealing the identity of foreign agents to people not in your chain of command customary in your business? We cooperated in this instance because we had no choice. Hasn't your business here ended?"

"Fair enough, Captain, fair enough," he said. "However, we don't get an opportunity everyday to obtain information on a foreign operative who is deemed to be the deadliest assassin, and most elusive spy in the Americas."

I felt like I'd been punched in the stomach. I struggled to breathe in.

"If her brother hadn't been tortured and killed by Nazi agents in Peru, she wouldn't have hesitated to work both sides of the fence. Have a good war." He was gone.

"Sir, I'm sorry as I can be. I went out for a beer last night and this, this woman, is on me like white on rice."

"Will, last night never happened. The crew log reflects you stood the midnight watch. Before retiring, you were seen playing dice in the crew mess. You never left the boat. If you say otherwise to anyone outside this wardroom, you will be sent back to Washington when we reach Pearl. The only reason you aren't going now is because they decided separating you from the boat here would attract too much attention." Before I could say anything, the Captain grinned and said, "no, you may not ask who 'they' is. This incident is closed."

As I came to attention to request permission to depart, the old man waved me back into my chair.

"Will, I, like the Commander, am curious. We'll never discuss this again, but I'm going to allow myself one question - when you met this woman and spent...time with her, did she give you any clue as to who...or what, she was?"

"Sir, she was sensual and erotic and beautiful. If she's killed people, they must have died happy. I left her thinking I might come back to take her away from all this. Pretty stupid, huh?"

"Pretty lucky I'd say. Did she give you any clue as to why she picked you?"

"At one point, she did say that I reminded her of someone she'd lost."

"Very interesting," the Captain said, as he leaned back. "I remind you again. You're under standing orders to speak to *no one* of this incident, unless and until ordered otherwise by competent authority. You will deny, forever, to everyone, including members of your immediate family, any knowledge of this incident for the duration of your life, unless relieved of the obligation sooner by written order."

"Take what I've said seriously, Will," the Captain said. "The malicious little prick who was in here wanted you to know who you were dealing with. He wanted you to carry this burden. Guard this secret carefully, for your own sake."

The Captain sat up. Ran his fingers through his hair and looked at me as if he hadn't seen me before. "Why are you standing in my wardroom? Get squared away and report to your duty station on the double. Don't you know enough to go through channels before wasting my time?"

"Aye, aye, sir," I said. "Excuse my impertinence. I'll speak to Chief Bunton about the laundry problem."

"Good, dismissed."

I rose, saluted, executed an about-face, and high-tailed my butt on out of officer country. "I'll be extremely happy when we get under way and leave Panama in our stern wake," I said, as I headed astern.

Crew's quarters was still empty when I reached the claustrophobic bunk area. I unwrapped the other package Elena had given me. This package was wrapped in plain brown butcher paper. Under the paper, a small white box, containing a smaller pale blue velvet box intrigued me. I opened the blue box. A gold ring rested on white satin. On the ring's face was an intricate pattern of interlocking chains. At each point where the chain loops joined, a blue stone was set. "Sapphires," I said. I held the ring above me to get a better view.

The ring was heavy, felt like a small rock in my hand. I had no idea why a woman, who had known me for less than a day, would give me something with such obvious value. There was an inscription engraved inside the band. I couldn't make the writing out. All I could tell was that the inscription wasn't in English. "Another mystery," I said. I heard voices drifting down the gangway. I secured the ring to my dog tags, and then slipped them back under my undershirt.

Chapter 33
Poetry amid Kunai Grass

"What the hell is he doing?"

"He is withdrawing, General."

"Does Admiral Ghormley concur in this withdrawal?"

"General Vandergrift, all I can tell you is that Admiral Fletcher has sent a dispatch to Admiral Ghormley indicating his intent to leave the area because of his reduced fighter capability. He's concerned about losing his carriers to Jap torpedo planes."

"Richmond, with all due respect to Admiral Fletcher, I cannot overstate my concern. If Mikawa sends a task force down the slot to attack our beachhead on Guadalcanal, we'll take a serious pounding. We're not equipped to fight off that kind of force."

Admiral Richmond Kelly Turner was sharp and knew the truth when he heard it.

"I know, General. Mikawa is already at sea. Unfortunately, we don't yet have any intelligence on his intentions. Fletcher's actions appear unwarranted to me too. Let's pray Mikawa is projecting force elsewhere–for the moment."

Unfortunately for Admiral Turner and the allied force attempting to take and hold Guadalcanal, the Japanese task force was coming right for them. The Navy would take a horrible beating during the battle of Savo Island, but, the Marines and the Army would take and hold Guadalcanal against the onslaught.

Dud stood in the sea spray being churned up by the transport. The spray felt good even if it was briny.

He turned his back to the sea and looked at his squad of riflemen. They were called paratroopers but most of them had never made a combat jump.

"The Solomon's are nothing but one stinking hot island after another," Louwicky said.

"Guadalcanal isn't going to be an improvement, Lou," Danny Ludlow said. "Scuttlebutt is that the Japs have a runway there that we have to take and hold against whatever the little yellow people throw against us. One thing is certain, a push is on and lots of folks back home are going to get War Department letters."

"Damn, Dud, don't say that shit out loud."

Dud shrugged and said, "I'm way past superstition, Lou. Better to look at the situation head on. Be damn sure the men are ready when push comes to shove. That's really all we have control over."

He heard one of his men talking behind him.

"I'm telling you what ladies, I bet the Japs retreat at just the sight of us," Bunny Howard said. "I don't know why the General even bothered to bring us over from Tulagi."

"You doggies better not start lighting victory smokes yet," Dud said over his shoulder. "We were lucky at Tasimboko. The scuttlebutt is that we're going to baby sit a runway–a runway that the Japs want back. They will come for their runway, and when they do we won't be having tea and cake on the back lawn when we meet up, ladies."

"Jesus, Sarge, don't go getting all philosophical on my ass. I didn't mean nothing."

"Jesus, listen to Bunny, will ya, boys. A Harvard boy talking like he was from New Jersey."

Dud grinned as he spoke. "O'Halleran, shut your pie hole. Bunny here sounds smarter than you, even when he's pretending he isn't."

Several guffaws and Bronx cheers came from the assembled company. Butch O' Halleran and Bunny Howard were both well-liked members of the Company.

Dud knelt down in front of his men.

"I know you meant no harm, Bunny. Still, I want us to stay hard. I want everyone's eyes open and butt low when we hit the beach. No one takes a round in the face or in the guts on my watch. The lieutenant has not given me the authority to lose one damn marine on this island. If you get shot dead while I'm in charge, you won't like the consequences. I won't say nice things about you to your mothers. I won't cry over your sorry dead asses. I will be pissed. Do you read me, marines!"

"Aye, aye, sergeant. We read you four-by-four!"

"Good, now make sure those dick covers are secure over those bores. We won't kill our enemies with rusty weapons."

"Sarge?"

"Yes, Bunny?"

"I went to Brown not Harvard."

"You know what, Bunny?"

"What, Sarge?"

"A year and a half ago, I was a Leaping Leopard in Gainesville, Texas, near the bottom of my class in a public high school. Truth is, we're both too damn far from home, and the little yellow guys waiting for us don't give a fart in the wind. They'll kill us both, given half a chance."

Someone tapped Dud on his shoulder. The Captain's aide was standing there.

"The Captain is getting briefed on the tactical situation by Colonel Edson. He wants you to deploy in a skirmish line somewhat to the South of Henderson Field once we hit the beach. He'll brief you squad leaders on any changes at 1745 this afternoon."

"Got it. Are we getting into a hot one here, or just trying to avoid malaria?"

The aide looked around, and then pulled Dud over to the transport's side.

'Word is that this'll be a real barn dance. The little yellow guys want their runway back and the brass is worried because we ain't got enough marines, airplanes, bullets and things that go boom-boom to make sure they don't get their way."

"Hell," Dud said. "If we run out of bullets, we can always throw our C-rations at them. If that doesn't kill 'em quick, nothing will."

"I have a confession to make," the aide said.

"What?" Dud said. "You found a coconut on Tavu point this morning that looks like Jesus?"

"Worse than that Marine," the aide said. "I like those C-ration meatballs."

"Don't tell anyone else," Dud said. "If the brass finds out, they'll identify you as officer material and hand you a battlefield commission."

"Roger that," the aide said. "My lips are sealed. Carry on Marine and don't miss the briefing."

"I'm a Sergeant now," Dud said. "I wouldn't place my career in this Corps in such jeopardy."

"You speak the truth," the aide said, as he turned to leave. "I hear the truth. See you on the beach."

"Aye, aye."

"What do you see when you really look hard, Sergeant?"

"You mean other than a godforsaken swamp covered by kunai grass, a jungle that smells like a garbage dump, and mosquitoes bigger than Texas hummingbirds, Captain?"

Captain Sweeney sighed. "Have you ever gone frog gigging in the bayou country?"

"Can't say that I have, sir."

"If you had, you'd understand our good luck. I once ran into a swarm of mosquitoes that looked like crows. Look again and tell me what you see."

Dud studied the ground surrounding them. "If we dig in here, we control the high ground. The little yellow guys will have to attack across the open ground. If we establish a field of fire from our nine o' clock to our three o' clock, we can hold this dirt with adequate artillery support."

"Glad to hear you say that, Sergeant, because your men will be at the center of the perimeter the Colonel has ordered us to establish. The attack won't be like Pickett's at Gettysburg. The enemy won't come marching in shoulder- to - shoulder in broad daylight."

"Maybe not, sir. Maybe it'll be like the Ardennes Forest. Maybe we'll kill them all and leave them for the buzzards and bugs."

"Ahh, Sergeant, you know military history."

Dud jammed a stick of Black Jack into his mouth. He offered one to the Captain.

"No thanks. Keep it for later, my teeth are bad."

"Listened to my best friend's daddy. He was a military history buff," Dud laughed. "He warned me against thinking that war was an adventure. Unlike General Pickett, I understand our situation. This is going to be a killing ground and I'm going to kill my fair share."

The Captain stared a second and then said, "sorry if I sounded patronizing Sergeant, but I don't think I ever heard such introspection out of a noncom before."

"That's okay sir. I'm done philosophizing. We both know war is fucking insanity with the lights turned off and the volume turned up. You've got a right to know if I'm going to crumble when the shit hits the fan. I ain't going nowhere. Besides, there ain't nowhere to go. We will hold our position."

"Aye, aye, Sergeant. I'll be on your immediate right flank. If we lose communications, I'll send up flares. Green will be the signal to drop back and rally at the knoll's highest point. If you see green, move on the double. Green'll mean we're getting ready to bombard our own perimeter."

"Got it. Anything else, sir?"

"Stay alive, Sergeant, and keep your men alive."

"Aye, aye, sir. I intend to."

Dud took one step back and walked away - he didn't salute; to do that would identify the Captain as an officer to any sniper sitting out in the bush.

Dud ordered his squad to dig in. He heard Howard talking to himself as he began to dig. "Bunny, what in the hell are you mumbling about?"

"Sorry, Sarge," Bunny said. "I didn't realize I was talking out loud."

"Bunny, I'm worried about you son. The yellow guys are crawling all over and you're in your hole mumbling."

"Sorry again, Sarge," Bunny said. "I didn't mean to aggravate you."

"I'm not aggravated. I'm antsy, the enemy is close. I want you focused, so that you stay alive. What the hell were you mumbling anyway?"

Dud shifted his position in the hole. His left leg was cramping up, not good. He popped a salt pill with a swig of water.

"They're sure making a lot of noise," Bunny said.

Dud listened to the racket - the little yellow guys were screaming and pounding on stuff several hundred yards in front of their position.

"Bunny," he said, "this little soiree is going to get interesting."

"When will they attack, Sarge?"

"When they're damn good and ready," Dud said. "Forget them for a moment and tell me what you were mumbling. Last time it was the mating habits of penguins, before that it was your girlfriends' thesis on the relationship between algebra and metered verse. What is it now?"

"Holy smoke Sarge you remember our talk on mathematical constants in metered verse?"

Dud broke his weapon down and wiped off the individual parts. "Sure, didn't understand a word but I remember. Clean your weapon while we have some time."

Bunny broke his weapon down. "You were rolling around on the floor of the head–puking and cussing out your old man. I was talking to keep you from running out of the hooch in your skivvies."

Calcium flares lit up the sky over the jungle. Rockets, red vapor trails flaring out behind, whizzed over their heads seeking the American artillery positions.

"Fuck! Here we go," Dud said. "Get your weapon reassembled on the double, Bunny."

KAAWRUUMMP KAAWRUUMMP Mortar shells landed around them, pieces of shrapnel sounded like angry bees as the metal fragments missed Dud's head by inches.

"Alright marines, get ready," Dud yelled. "Those mortars mean the little yellow guys are coming! Stay down, lock and load!"

"Jesus, the little yellow buggers sure know how to throw a party."

"Fuck'em straight into Buddhist Hell," Halleran said.

"I don't think Buddhism recognizes Hell as valid," Bunny yelled.

"Jesus, Mary, and Joseph listen to Bunny will ya?" Halleran said. "Catholic hell then, they can spend eternity getting stuck up the ass by Satan's pointy pitchfork."

"Can it!" Dud yelled. "Here they come. Steady…steady…fire…fire-at-will!"

Dud heard the Captain from behind and to his left "Battalion! Battalion this is Sweeney. I want that covering fire now. We are under an all out assault. Christ! Where the hell are they all coming from."

"Fix bayonets men!" Dud screamed.

"BAAANZI! Die Marine Die!"

"Looks like bad vaudeville," Dud said, under his breath. We'd look comical to spectators, he thought. Like sex, killing is deceptive. The ridiculous appearance belies the horrid consequence. He fired his weapon, the brains of a Japanese infantryman exited through the back of his head. He was still too slow, because he'd slipped on the dead Jap he'd just knifed with his left hand.

The troublesome yellow guy, now brainless and mostly head-less had jumped into Bunny's hole, and bayoneted Bunny, even as his blood sprayed into the air where his head had been seconds earlier. Bunny had blocked the yellow guy's initial thrust; the Jap had deftly slipped the second thrust under the block and sunk his bayonet into Bunny's midsection just as Dud sent him into eternity.

The hand-to-hand combat went on for hours. The yellow guys and the marines slipped and slid around in the dark, in the mud, in the blood. There was swearing, praying, groaning, crying. Lots of grown men wept for mothers–mothers they'd never see again.

The Japanese kept coming and they kept dying. They'd later admit bewilderment. "Who would have thought that Americans were formidable warriors - amazing."

Dud came back to consciousness sitting in a blood filled depression. Bunny Howard was propped up against the side of a sand bag berm. He and Bunny were both covered in blood spatter and mud. Litter bearers were carrying bodies towards the beach. The ground was churned up all around them. The ground smelled even worse than it looked.

Dud stood up, winced as he touched a crusted over slash above his left eye, and crouched next to

Bunny. Dud smoothed Bunny's hair back off of his forehead. Bunny was cool to the touch. Dud tried not to look at the blood-soaked gauze covering Bunny's midsection. The medics had worked on him while the fighting raged around them. If they hadn't, Bunny would have already been bagged and tagged.

"Thank God for morphine," Dud thought. Bunny was in no pain. The boy's eyelids fluttered. He looked up and finally focused on Dud's face.

"Don't worry, boy," Dud said. "You're out of here. They'll fix you up pronto."

"Sarge, still want to know what I was mumbling about last night?"

"Maybe you ought to save your strength."

Bunny smiled and said,

"Out–out are the lights–out all!
And, over each quivering form,
The curtain, a funeral pall,
Comes down with the rush of a storm,
While the angels, all pallid and wan,
Uprising, unveiling affirm
That the play is the tragedy, "Man"
And its hero the Conqueror Worm."

When Bunny coughed, blood spurted from his mouth. Dud wiped the blood off the boy's face with his sleeve.

"Sarge, I always thought Poe was morbid. Now though…I'm … not … sure."

Dud Ludlow, age nineteen, suddenly felt old. He closed Bunny's eyes. He took a wash cloth he always carried with him out of his back pocket, wet it with the remaining water in his canteen and wiped off the dead boy's face. He then pounded Bunny's rifle into the ground and placed his helmet onto the butt end. Dud yelled for the morgue detail.

"Yeah, Sarge?"

"I have one for the morgue unit here."

"We'll get to him, Sarge, we'll get to him."

Dud grabbed the corporal by his fatigues. "Yes, you're right. You're going to take him off the beach *right now* or I will personally ram my right arm up your ass, grab your beating heart, pull it out and eat it. Now, snap to it."

Dud waited. If the morgue guy fucked with him, he'd be joining his clients to play toe tag footsie.

"Alright, Sarge, alright. Take it easy. Bentsen, get over here! We got one that needs transport *on the double.*"

As they carried Bunny off, Dud headed off to find the Captain. He was probably late for the debriefing.

Chapter 34
Bedpan Slow Dance

The capital city of New Caledonia, Noumea, looked festive when seen from the harbor. The gabled roofs and painted tiles hid the fact that it was a rough and tumble sea port where supplies and men were being either on-loaded or off-loaded at all hours.

Nurses on the dock caused riotous celebration. Gaudily dressed vendors held coconuts, unsavory pastries, and green bananas out for inspection. The vendors competed with soldiers and sailors who also surrounded the nurses. Amid the catcalls and whistles, several of Mindy's colleagues yelled out in surprise as their bottoms were pinched. Mindy stomped on the foot of a grinning sailor who squeezed her left tit and said, "let me guess doll, - 34C."

After Mindy stomped his foot, she said, "that's *Lieutenant* Doll, to you."

About this time, an air horn let out a series of short, but loud bursts. An Army Major stood on a small mountain of crates silencing the crowd. He then jumped down onto the hood of his jeep. Gesturing to a big green truck with camouflage net stretched out over the back, he said, "I want this pier cleared of all military personnel not on official business here. If you're a member of the new nursing contingent, please get in the truck. Welcome to New Caledonia. Drop your gear at the vehicle's tailgate before mounting up. We'll transport your grip separately. Double time ladies, we haven't got all day. Last time I checked, the war was still raging."

"Ah, Mindy, doesn't he think he's the clever one now," Julie Shaunessy whispered, as she rubbed a spot on her bottom where she'd been pinched.

"Nessy," I said. "I don't see, hear, or smell clever here. All I smell is coconut oil mixed with testosterone."

"Men and their dicks," Nessy said. "How do they ever get anything done? We're in a war zone, thousands of miles from home and the men are still swaggering around looking for tail."

As they climbed into the rear of the truck, Mindy looked at her and snickered, "could be worse, you know."

Nessy snickered back. "Yeah, I mean, Jesus, we could be stuck out here with no men at all."

"Right," Mindy said, "and we both know that the only thing worse than too many men is - no men at all!"

The truck lurched up the hill toward the naval mobile hospital.

"Have you finished mopping the convalescent ward?"

"Yes ma'am," Mindy said. "I've also finished autoclaving the instrument packs."

"What about-?"

"Captain, the sanitary napkin cabinet is secure. The nursing staff is aware that anyone caught hoarding pads will be put on report."

Captain Myrtle Carouthers a.k.a. 'Myrt' or the 'Wicked Witch' turned red.

"My rules sound unreasonable to you, Lieutenant?"

"Sorry ma'am," Mindy said. "I meant no disrespect. I assumed your next question was going to be about the napkin inventory."

"Napkins aren't army issue items," Myrt said. "We run out, we're all dependent on whatever we manage to scrounge."

"Yes ma'am," Mindy said. "Of course, if nurses keep getting pregnant, we won't have a need for sanitary pads–because we'll all be gravid."

Captain Carouthers locked the narcotics cabinet and looked both ways outside the meds room before answering. "Lieutenant Hulen, our pregnancy rate is running at 35%," she said. "Yet, when I suggested nurses be forbidden to date or socialize - even other officers, I was nearly shipped home."

"That's the Navy for you," Mindy said. "The Navy expects nurses to service their male officers. I've heard the going rate is a dinner for a hand job."

Myrt laughed. "What happens if wine is served with dinner?"

Mindy puckered her lips suggestively.

"Lieutenant Hulen, that's really sick."

"Maybe so, ma'am," Mindy said. "But, I think we're fighting a losing battle against Mother Nature. Someone needs to come up with effective birth control—which women can access."

"That'll be the day," Myrt said, as she locked the door to the meds room and the women walked down the hall. "I'm tired of us being treated as glorified hookers when we're off-duty."

"Face it ma'am," Mindy said. "We're Army nurses working in a naval hospital. The Navy opposed giving women nurses rank at all."

"What time is it? My watch has stopped."

"It's 1517."

"Damn, nearly 4 hours left. Heard anything about incoming?"

"Guadalcanal," Mindy said. "We may have a massive push from that battle."

"Let's make good use of our down time," Myrt said. "Get the word out that we'll have an in service on treating gas gangrene induced by bullet wounds the day after tomorrow."

A few nights later, the push still hadn't come. Mindy was autoclaving instrument packs again because the ward was slow. The town clock chimed midnight and a cool breeze was wafting through the mosquito netting. Titsi flies buzzed around the window, looking for openings in the netting. Captain Carouthers wandered in. "Good evening, Lieutenant."

"Good evening, ma'am."

"Call me Myrt when we're alone," She said. "That's what my brothers call me. I really miss them, you know? I grew up being constantly teased, cajoled, and occasionally coddled by them." She picked up two instrument packs and placed them in the autoclave. "Is this batch ready?"

"Yes, ma'am."

I used to dream about what it would be like to be away from them," she said. "Now I know."

She stared out the window into the tropic darkness.

"We … I … didn't mean anything by the wicked witch business. When you aren't at the butt end, the taunt never seems as mean as when you are."

She waved her hand at Mindy. "Forget it. If you want to see mean, try getting through Army Officer Candidate School as a woman. My husband left me two weeks after I began because he was furious with me for joining the Army."

She dogged the autoclave shut and Mindy turned it on.

"I thought we were friends though," she said. "I admit it hurt a little to discover it was you who coined the phrase, *Mad Myrt, Pad Pirate.*"

Mindy could feel her skin heat up as she went beet red.

"Really, Mindy," she said. "Couldn't you have thought up something a little more...original?"

"Myrt, I was out of line," Mindy said. "This is no excuse, but I was frustrated about the sanitary pads being kept under lock and key. I vented."

"Understandable," Myrt said. "Cotton is scarce. When the wounded come, those pads will be the first item the triage medics go for if they're left out, because they're superior to the kit bandages."

As we walked the ward, Mindy changed the subject. "Where are your brothers now?"

A strange look came over her face. Finally, she said, "my younger brother, Paul, is resting on the bottom of Pearl Harbor. He was on the Arizona when it was attacked. I got word today that my twin brother, Benny, is missing in action, presumed dead. He's a dive-bomber pilot assigned to the Enterprise. He never returned after a bombing run against a Jap carrier. The wire I got said he ignored intense enemy fire to drop his bombs on a ship called the *Akagi.* They're sending me his Navy Cross. Luckily, my oldest brother George is okay. He's a doctor, who's been assigned out here. I can't wait to see him."

As she held the telegram out for me to see, she began to sink to the floor. Mindy caught her before she hit, and sat her on a campstool in the corner.

"Dear God Myrt," Mindy said. "I'm so sorry. I had no idea. Do your parents know?"

"They do now. Both were killed last year in a wreck - drunk driver ran a stop sign and broad - sided them. My brother George and I are the next of kin and the last of kin." Tears ran down her face.

Mindy went to a cupboard and reached behind some folded sheets for the bottle located there. Mindy poured two shots of whiskey.

Mindy handed Myrt her paper cup and said, "whatever happens from here on out, I'm your sister… and you're mine. Come to me with anything. You're not alone."

Mindy gulped down her whiskey. Myrt sipped hers. Mindy sat next to her on the floor and held her hand while they wept for Benny, Paul, and the rest of the lost brothers.   Captain Myrtle Carouthers was only twenty-four.   Mindy had just turned twenty, and both women were feeling very alone.   Out on the ward, Mindy heard a voice calling, "nurse, nurse could I get a bedpan here. My teeth are floating!"

Mindy got up. "Are you going to be alright, Myrt?"

"Do I have a choice, Mindy?"

"Nope.   Stop by my shack later.   I have something to show you."

On that note, Mindy grabbed a clean bedpan and headed onto the ward.   Myrt finished her whiskey and tossed the crumpled cup into the wastebasket.

"Bye, Benny," she said quietly.   Then, she stood up, straightened her uniform, and headed onto the ward to check meds.

Chapter 35
The Rain in Spain

"You're telling me the sequence is completely random?"

"Yes, Commander, completely."

The Commander leaned back in his chair and clasped his hands behind his head, then hurriedly wrote something down on a scrap of paper before speaking. "Mr. Sullivan, this sounds as far-fetched as the bat idea that came through here right after Pearl. We got the scuttle-butt that we were going to be responsible for developing a method of dropping several thousand bats on the Japs because they're supposedly terrified of the little winged rodents."

Bob shrugged his shoulders. "I don't much care for bats myself, Commander. But, I can tell you this–if you don't have the cipher sequence pad you can't break the code because there is no code."

"If I understand correctly, the character sequence changes every time you put a disc into that slot and push down on that lever?"

"Correct," Bob said. "Even if you have the pad, you've got to enter the proper decrypt sequence or the machine won't 'plain it' out."

The Commander leaned forward now. "You're telling me that I can send an encrypted message that says ∧gji (*tr), and when decrypted, means '22 submarines on patrol.' But, if I change discs and push down on the lever here and type ∧gji (*tr) again, the sequence might mean '4 tanks destroyed.'"

"That's right," Bob said. "The machine doesn't rely on a sequential use of any sort of numbers, letters, or symbols. The mechanism randomly selects these each time a disc is inserted and the lever is pushed."

Bob got up and leaned on the Commander's desk, to emphasize his next point. "Your best code breaker could look at sequence after sequence after sequence. His input wouldn't matter. There's no pattern, no cycle, no obvious logic."

"Good God," the Commander said. "If you're right, this machine makes the enigma device look like a child's toy."

"The enigma device is the Kraut code system, isn't it?"

The Commander said nothing. He continued to examine Bob's creation. Bob had heard the rumor that the British had cracked the German code system. Bob didn't ask the question again. By merely mentioning enigma, the Commander had leaked secure, container-ized information.

"You designed and built this device?"

"Yes," Bob said, "wasn't that difficult, once I un-derstood what we needed."

The intercom on the desk buzzed. "Would you excuse me for a moment, Bob? I need to confer with Captain Bates."

"Certainly, I'll retire to the anteroom," Bob said. "Stick your head out the door and yell when you're ready to continue."

The Commander waited for Bob to leave. He then stood up, turned on the portable radio in the room and opened a door that was hidden behind heavy velour curtains. Captain Bates sat down and said, "Was it prudent to mention enigma?"

"We're going to have to trust that Bob isn't a loose cannon. He's become very important, very fast."

Captain Bates got up and pushed a button on the side of the desk. A secretary, who disappeared as quickly as she had appeared, returned Bob to the office.

Bob eyed both men and said, "what gives?"

The Commander grinned and said, "sorry, Bob, we're accustomed to gathering information–not giving it out. We're with O.N.I. counterintelligence. Our chief concern is keeping your ... gizmo secure."

"I hope you don't blurt out the existence of my device as casually as you mentioned enigma a moment ago," Bob said. The men grinned. "That leak wasn't casual," the Commander said. "The President himself authorized the disclosure. He has asked for a clandestine brief on your device and wanted to provide you with an opportunity to examine enigma's mechanics, so that you could compare and contrast the workings of the two devices."

"Your reaction to enigma being mentioned is appropriate," Captain Bates said. "What's disturbing is that you knew enough about enigma to react. Is there a leak in your company?"

"Gentlemen," Bob said. "I've spent the last year working with guys who eat, breathe, and shit this stuff. Thornhill, in California, is the person who mentioned enigma, around 2 a.m. one morning, as we worked on the gizmo's internal wiring. He said something like *we'll just see how smart those limeys are. They'll never break this machine's inner workings. This jewel will make enigma look like clay tablet crap. If Hitler got on his knees and begged, the krauts couldn't come up with this.*

"Have you mentioned this to anyone else?" Captain Bates asked. "Your wife, perhaps?"

"No way," Bob said. "I don't want my wife involved in this crap. Hell, I don't even want to be involved."

The Commander and Captain Bates both laughed out loud.

"Mr. Sullivan," the Commander said. "You have a future in stand-up comedy. Hate to break the bad news to you, but, you're involved up to your eyeballs." He slapped his hands on his knees to emphasize the point. The creases in his pants were so sharp Bob thought he'd cut his hands.

Captain Bates went to a recessed shelf off to the right and said, "care for a snort Bob?"

"Is the drinking lamp lit, gentlemen?"

The Commander stood up and said, "the lamp is indeed lit Bob. I'd say a round or two is called for."

Once all three men were holding their drinks, the Commander said, "what shall we drink to, boys?"

"To keeping loose cannons lashed down, gentlemen," Bob said.

"Here, here," said the other two, draining their glasses.

Afterwards, the Commander looked at Bob and said, "guess you need to go pack, son."

"I just got here - and the trip was a bitch, even if I say so myself."

"Yes and the one back will be even longer … or shorter, depending on your perspective. One week from today, you're to brief the President on your gizmo."

The room went sideways and Bob had to grab the bar to keep from falling.

"Say again?"

"Son, you're unpolished and a little foul-mouthed, but you've come up with an encryption machine that's the biggest thing since the Wright brothers flew at Kitty Hawk. So you get an all-expense paid trip to Washington to tell him yourself."

"Just one thing," said Bob.

"Yes?"

"Hit me with another shot of that smooth tasting firewater."

The Commander filled his glass. "If this pans out, Bob, I'll see to it that you get a case of this stuff."

After Bob left to pack, Captain Bates and the Commander stayed behind.

"The kid called us loose cannons," Captain Bates said.

"He sure did." The Commander agreed. "Good for him, he's right you know. I felt like shit letting that information out into the open. Contact the FBI. I am pained in the extreme having to involve Hoover, but I want Thornhill tailed. Make sure the leak on enigma is sealed."

"You're not jacking around on this, are you?"

"No, Bates, I'm not. Mr. Sullivan has designed a random pad encryption device–without even trying. I'm considering asking the President for permission to send Bob and this machine to Bletchley Park."

"Jesus, you think the President will let the Brits - Turing - have a crack at this?"

"Don't know," the Commander said. "Not my job to worry about that. My impression is that our gizmo is something new - something more complex than enigma. I'm not smart enough to judge that for myself though.

Protect him Bates. Nothing obvious but solid just the same. I want him guarded round the clock. Put a security net round his family as well. If we have to we'll relocate the whole lot."

"You'll owe Hoover forever on this one, the little Nazi," Bates said.

"I know. Nothing I can do though. I need his resources. Remember to wear mufti to the White House," the Commander said. "Separate from Bob before entering. I don't want any pictures shot of you two together. We'll operate on the assumption that you'll be photographed entering and leaving. Make Bob look as unimportant as possible."

"I've never seen you this nervous before sir."

"Don't call me sir," the Commander said. "Remember that when we're in uniform, you're the Captain and I'm the Commander. If you slip up at the wrong time, you compromise us."

"Sorry, no excuse for that."

"I'm sorry for being so short, Martin. This one has me on edge. Do you comprehend the stakes?"

"This could change the course of the war."

The Commander swallowed deeply from his drink. He twirled the remaining bourbon in his glass.

"Martin, the Japs, notwithstanding the fact that they are currently kicking the shit out of us in Burma, have already lost. Possibly, Yamamoto comprehends the end game has started. The Imperial staff doesn't," the Commander said, as he finished his bourbon. "The real game is just now beginning. This war is merely a chapter. Bob Sullivan has shown a potential flair for long-term play, his work bears serious attention."

"He could also be a flash in the pan - an idiot savant," Bates said.

"Just so, Martin," conceded the Commander. "Time will tell. Now, go pack. Monitor his time with the President carefully. I'll be most interested in hearing your debrief of the trip."

Chapter 36
Pig Boat Latin

"The inscription is Latin," Father Hanlon said. "*De Profundis clamo ad te Domine,* means 'Out of the depths I cry to you O' Lord!' The opening verse of Psalm 130, a prayer of supplication for the souls of departed believers."

The Catholic Chaplain tapped his glasses on his desk. He looked at Will with curiosity and suspicion. He stood and walked over to his window. The Chaplain's office was located in the Carlton on Albert Street. The Army knows how to treat its senior cleric, thought Will.

"Did you know the ring is a significant religious relic?"

"No, but that doesn't surprise me sir," Will said.

"These interlocking rings that look like woven palm fronds are fish when viewed from a different angle," the Chaplain said. "The eyes of the fish are sapphires–remarkable craftsmanship. How did you come by this artifact, Mr. Davis?"

The chaplain handed the ring back with visible reluctance.

"Father, I can't say."

"Fair enough, I confess that my curiosity is piqued. I don't get requests from O.N.I. every day to examine religious artifacts in the possession of a submariner. Guard this artifact well. The ring is several hundred years old–maybe older. Unfortunately, there are people out there who'd harm you to possess it my son - and not think twice."

"Thank you, Father, I'll keep it safe."

The Colonel opened the door for him, patted him on the back, and said, "Go with God, my son."

Will wondered what had just happened. The senior Army Catholic priest in Australia had met with him and he'd been allowed to keep the ring. The priest had been ordered to examine the ring and, clearly, he'd wanted to keep it; yet, he hadn't raised a finger to stop Will from taking the ring back. Will was certain that he was being watched. He couldn't take the ring back out on combat patrol. Thievery wasn't his concern. Being sunk on patrol was. The ring was not his to lose or to take with him if he went on eternal patrol. He found himself in front of a Commonwealth Bank. He went in and inquired about safe deposit boxes. He filled out the requisite forms, paid for the box for a year in advance, the longest time available. Will examined the ring one last time before placing it in both of its boxes and, in turn, in the deposit box. Once the clerk secured the box and provided Will with the key, Will sat down and wrote Mr. Chaney a long letter detailing the existence, if not the contents, of the box. He then wrote the bank a letter authorizing Mr. Chaney to act as his attorney-in-fact for purposes of renewing the box and retrieving the contents of the box. Will left with the distinct impression that he was neither the first person nor would he be the last person who frequented the bank to make this kind of arrangement. The bank officials had looked bored throughout the entire transaction.

As he walked along the Brisbane Mall, he wondered if he'd ever return to reclaim his property. If I were in a card game, he thought, I wouldn't like my odds. On this note, he returned to the quay where the Starkfish was docked. All resupply, maintenance, and training sessions were completed. Will prayed he wasn't leaving Moreton Bay for the last time. As he boarded the boat at New Farm wharf, he realized his life in Gainesville was ancient history. He thought about Dud, Mindy, and Bob as he boarded the Starkfish and saluted the OD. His war had begun in earnest.

Chapter 37
On the Home Front

"Mom, I'm not working as a B-girl in a speakeasy for tips and drinks. This is a good job we're talking about."

"I tell you," Melrose Stevens said. "This war is changing everything and not for the better. Your father wouldn't stand for this. Two babies in this house and you want to work in a factory. "

Betty threw her dishtowel down on the counter.

"Mother, get a grip," Betty said. "Conor and baby Megan are doing fine. You, Louiza, and I are getting in each other's way. This is a great opportunity for me, can't you see that?"

"No, I don't understand why you're so determined to do this. Bob is sending money every month isn't he? Why can't you relax and be happy with what you have?"

Betty crossed the kitchen to the coffeepot and poured herself a cup of coffee.

"Truth is, mom, what I have isn't enough. The world is changing and I want to be part of the change."

Betty leaned on the counter and sipped her coffee. She didn't know how she'd get by when rationing started on November 28th. At least they waited until after Thanksgiving, she thought. Rationing gasoline was one thing; rationing coffee was something else entirely. One pot represented a fourth of her monthly allotment.

"Get yourself a cup of this, mom, or I'll drink it all myself."

Melrose regarded her daughter for a moment and then crossed the kitchen to the pot. She's so self-assured, Melrose thought. She realized Betty reminded her of

Robert.   The thought almost caused her to drop her coffee cup.

She sat down at the kitchen table and sipped her coffee.   "What will you be doing at this Long Beach factory?"

I'll be working in either gear assembly or sheet metal riveting.   If you show initiative, you can make more by learning how to do mill or lathe work."

"So, you're going off to Long Beach to rivet, and leaving me home to watch the Mexican maid and the babies."

"Mom, do you have to be difficult?   Louiza Rojas has been a godsend.   Besides, Louiza's family was landed gentry in this country when our ancestors were still indentured servants in England.   Don't take my word for it.   Go check the records down to the courthouse."

The women eyed each other over their coffee cups.

"What does riveting or gear making pay these days?"

"It starts at $1.10 an hour.   I get time and a half over forty and double time for any shift work on Sundays."

"Whatever will you do with that much money, child?"

"I'll bank it. After the war, I'm going to start a vineyard."

Melrose eyes grew wide.   "Run your own business?   Does Bob know about this?"

"Bobby's hands are full right now.   Something big is happening to him.   He called me the other day, but couldn't tell me where he was exactly. He was stateside though - the connection was good.   His letters are more interesting for what they don't say than for what they do. This vineyard idea is mine.   We'll talk about viticulture when the time is right."

"I thought Bob was in Australia."

"He was mom. They brought him home because he's working on something big. His work is real hush-hush - he *can't* talk about it."

"Lordy Bett, is your man a spy or something?"

"I hope its 'or something,' mom. What's clear is that Bobby doesn't need me yapping at him about vineyards or anything else–not while he has a war to fight."

Melrose finished her cup of coffee. "I'll help you, Bett," she said. "The world is changing and your idea is exciting. But, your daddy is old school. You riveting is going to cause him fits. I'd like to charge admission to see his face when he hears all of this."

"He can grumble all he wants, his disapproval won't stop me."

"No, I'm sure it won't. When you get old though, you don't want change, especially in your kids. You mumble a little, drool a little, and then you plop face first into your gruel and die."

"Oh mother, please. I don't see a bit of drool on you–yet."

The women laughed and a comfortable silence ensued as they enjoyed the ocean view from the kitchen window.

There was a knock at the kitchen door. Louiza had arrived with Conor and Megan. Betty took Megan from Louiza and kissed Conor's forehead. Betty urged Louiza to sit in the chair she had vacated. Betty retrieved her the final cup of coffee from the pot. The women didn't notice the ordinary looking man in the black sedan smoking a pipe and reading the paper while he watched them from across the street. Ten minutes after Louiza's return home, the man pulled away and drove off into the dusk.

"Gott in Himmel, my boy!" Mr. Chaney said. "This goyim country is going to train you to fly?"

Wat Eakins was grinning from ear to ear.

"Yes sir," Wat said. "I got my letter from the Army Air Corps today. I'm reporting to Tuskegee, in Alabama, on January 5th. "Wanted to thank you. Showing them the grade transcripts from my college correspondence work did the trick."

"You did the work, Wat."

Still, I'd never have signed up if you hadn't pushed me. I'm gonna be somebody, Mr. Chaney."

"Young Mr. Eakins, I don't doubt this for an instant. You have filled Mr. Davis' shoes well. Once again, I'm left looking for competent help. But - this is of no consequence to you, young man. Your job is now to learn how to defy gravity - learn how to land first thing, this is my advice to you."

"You know something?" Wat mused, as he waved his arm north, towards Oklahoma, if you don't count crossing the Red over to the Oklahoma side, I haven't been out of the county more than three times. Now I'm headed way over to Alabama."

Wat motioned Mr. Chaney closer to the stockroom entrance. "I hear they like black folks even less in Alabama than here in Texas. Think that's possible, Mr. Chaney?"

"Mr. Eakins, never underestimate the capacity of humankind to hate. I fear this is possible."

"Damn," Wat said. "That's a scary thought. We're downright unpopular here. I don't rightly see how a Negro could be hated worse than here."

"I hope I'm wrong," Mr. Chaney said. "But, my instincts tell me what you've heard is probably correct. Like Texas, Alabama is, I suspect, no haven for enlightened thought on racial equality."

"Short of killing me, they can't stop me," Wat said. "I *will* be an aviator. *I will fly.* This is my shot, Mr. Chaney. By all that's holy I thank God for this war. If Hitler hadn't come along, I'd be shoveling tiger shit at the circus till Jesus returns, or I die. The only reason I caught on here is because Will went off to the war. Ain't that one hell of a note? Set free by a crazy-ass Kraut dictator."

Mr. Chaney chuckled. "Perhaps you should write Herr Hitler a thank you note."

"Maybe I'll just strafe his ass and yell 'thanks' out of the cockpit."

"Yes, well, strafe tomorrow. Balance the account ledger today."

"Yes sir, no problem," Wat said. "Almost forgot, our woolens aren't coming. The War Department is procuring all the wool rolling stock for the war effort."

"Yes, I saw the memo. They give us nothing and, then, they tell us we're not permitted to raise prices on what little we have left to help cut our losses. Why am I in business?" Mr. Chaney shrugged his shoulders. "I've no idea. Mr. Eakins, let's put up the 'Closed' sign. If you are old enough to fly for the Army, you're old enough to have peppermint schnapps with me."

Mr. Chaney and Wat Eakins sat in the office and they had not one, but two schnapps each. The books never got balanced that evening.

Chapter 38
Deviled Eggs and Beer

"Chester, quit lying to me!"

"Eunice, I haven't said a damn thing. I'm looking at the damage."

"I can see that. You know what's going on. If you didn't, you wouldn't be so calm. Someone has heaved a brick through our front window three times now. This one had a note tied to it calling you a murderer."

Chester Harris ran his hands through his thinning hair. Eunice continued standing in the entry hall, her curlers quivering, waiting for his response.

She could wait till Lucifer handed out ice skates in hell, Chester thought. He had nothing to say. That little bastard Ralph Davis was of course the perpetrator. Ralph Davis believed Chester had arranged his dad's murder. Chester admitted to himself that his conscience was bothering him. Strange, he didn't know he even had a conscience until after Mason was killed. He broke off this chain of thought. Time to placate the ball and chain. "Nothing is going on, Eunice," he said. "Go back to bed. Chief Becker and Sheriff Williams are both on the way. Go on back to bed."

Eunice eyeballed him for another fifteen seconds. Then, deciding the argument would keep, headed upstairs after fixing herself a hot toddy in a large water tumbler. Chester fervently wished he could trade places with her.

He heard tires crunching on the gravel in his driveway. He went to the door. Sheriff Don Williams was on the porch holding his hat in his hand. His facial expression was glacial. "Chester, I'm getting too old for this."

"I'm not a spring chicken myself, Don."

"This is the last time I'm coming out on one of these calls. Are you going to press charges?"

"Sheriff, how can I press charges when I don't know who's doing it. Some drunken Negro is probably having a little fun at my expense, but I've no proof."

Sheriff Williams squatted next to the wreckage. "Chester, remember our junior year in high school?"

"That was a long time ago, Don," Chester lied; he knew where the Sheriff was going with this.

"We were studying that Shakespeare fella and you called me an undershirt."

"An *underling*," Chester said. "You dunked my head in the toilet in retaliation."

"Chester, I regret doing that, but, I don't appreciate being called stupid now anymore than I did then. Catch my drift?"

"I believe I do, Sheriff."

"We both know Ralph Davis is chunking bricks at your house and leaving shit-grams in your mailbox. He has a hard-on for you. Why?"

"I don't know, Sheriff."

"Right," the Sheriff said, as he stood up, "and I never dream about sucking Veronica Lake's tits either. Maybe I can help you out, Chester. I got another telegram from the FBI today. Want to guess what it was about?"

Chester thought he might pee himself on the spot. "Sorry Sheriff, you've lost me."

Chief Becker appeared in the doorway wearing one white sock and one green sock.

"Chester, plate glass is real expensive, even for a bank president, ain't it?" He looked at Sheriff Williams, as he hitched up his Sam Browne.

"Think it's the Davis boy again, Donnie?"

"Yeah, but Chester thinks differently. He believes phantom Negroes are coming across town to bust his window."

"Chester, we do have some dumb niggers around these parts, but none that contrary."

"I was telling Chester about the FBI telegram I received today. You want to tell him what the message said?"

"Nah, you tell him."

"Gentlemen," Chester said. "I've been a poor host, would ya'll care to come inside?"

Chief Becker grinned. "Don't mind if I do, Mr. Harris."

The Sheriff followed the other two men into the front parlor.

"Mind the broken glass, gentlemen. What can I get you to drink?"

Chief Becker had a beer. Sheriff Williams settled for a soda pop.

When they'd settled in the study, Sheriff Williams continued his story about the FBI letter.

"The Federales sent a police report to the FBI via their embassy in Washington indicating they had two men in custody claiming to have information about a murder-for-hire. This was of no interest to the Mexican authorities until these mutts mentioned they'd rubbed out an American gringo."

"Must be the hour, Sheriff," Chester said. "I've got a busted window, and now we're discussing dogs in Mexico?"

"Not dogs, Chester, suspects in Mason Davis' murder. These two have been smuggling arms. You know, the odd gun or two or three. What isn't clear *yet* is how good their information is. They're holding onto their information in exchange for a deal on the smuggling collar."

"Sounds like a damn dime store novel, don't it, Chester?" Chief Becker said, as he belched, and stood up. "Boys, this has been fun, but I gotta be at work later this morning. Donnie, keep me posted on what develops. I'd surely like to collar Mason's killers. Hell, the city council might even vote me a pay raise, if I got some credit for the bust. But, this is yours all the way Donnie. I ain't trying to step on your toes here. I only want to stand behind you on the podium if something gives." With this, he headed out the door.

"Know what, Chester?"

"What, Sheriff?"

"When I first read the FBI report, I was dumbfounded. I couldn't fathom who'd want Mason dead. The story made no sense. But, now that I've been thinking on this some, I can't shake my memories of last Christmas Eve. You remember last Christmas Eve, don't you, Chester?"

"Sheriff, say what's on your mind."

The Sheriff went silent and stared at the broken window for a moment.

"Do me a favor, Chester. Don't plan any sudden trips out of the county until I convince myself that Mason wasn't murdered over a $45 grudge."

The Sheriff stood.

"If you change your mind and want to file on the window, you know where to find me."

"Yes, of course. I'll keep in touch."

"I'll let myself out. Thanks for the drink."

Chester Harris sat at his desk for half an hour after the Sheriff left. Finally, he sighed and took some stationary out of his desk and wrote out a long note. When he was done, he blotted the page and placed it in an envelope. He then went to his wall safe and spun the dial until the tumblers clicked into place. Once he had the safe open, he examined the contents of a manila folder. Satisfied the contents were in order; he placed the manila folder and the envelope containing the note in the safe. He propped both the folder and the envelope up against the $15,000.00 he had stacked neatly in the safe— so that no one would miss either item when they opened the wall safe later. He closed the safe and went into the bathroom adjacent to his study and stared at himself in the vanity mirror, saying, "you were duped and now amends must be made."

Chester then went to the kitchen and got a couple of deviled eggs and a bottle of beer out of the refrigerator to take back to the study. He wrote a second note and put this note in an envelope too. He left this note on the front corner of his desk.

"This batch of deviled eggs is Eunice's best," he said. After he'd finished both eggs and the beer, he wiped his mouth on his sleeve and dialed the phone. Someone picked up on the second ring. "This had better be good," The irate voice rasped. "It's two o'clock in the morning."

"This is good alright, asshole. The Sheriff knows, and I'm not hanging around to take the fall for you. I've been listening to you all my life and now I see what a moron I've been. I hope you rot in hell. See you there!" Chester slammed down the phone.

The phone promptly rang back. Chester took the receiver off it's' hook and reached into the bottom left drawer of his desk for his .38 revolver. He placed the barrel under his chin and cocked the weapon. Just before he pulled the trigger, he said, "I am truly sorry about the mess, Eunice, but now you'll have a reason to replace the wallpaper."

The weapon going off woke Eunice from a sound sleep. She tromped downstairs to see what had happened. She screamed hysterically for five minutes before the Whitehursts came from across the street to see what the ruckus was about.

The Sheriff, the Chief of Police, the local J.P., and the doctor were all called to the house. Mrs. Whitehurst volunteered to stay with Mrs. Harris until the sedative she was given wore off.

Chief Becker stared at Chester Harris' remains and, then, looked at Sheriff Williams dourly. "Donnie, I don't know about you, but I ain't ever seen a man get so worked up about a busted picture window before."

Sheriff Williams saw the envelope on the desk's corner.

"Put on some gloves and bag that envelope. Might be evidence," he said to one of his men.

He turned to the Chief and said, "I agree. This mess isn't about a busted window. Maybe the coroner's inquiry will help us with this one."

"Well," observed Chief Becker, "This'll take everyone's mind off of the war for a few days, won't it?"

The Chief hitched up his pants and headed to the kitchen, saying "I guess Chester won't care if I have another beer out of his fridge - will he?"

Sheriff Williams shrugged and turned back to the crime scene. "Make sure you don't miss any bullet fragments that may have hit the plaster," he said.

The Chief opened the fridge, grabbed a beer, and let out a small yelp of delight. Two of Eunice's deviled eggs were left. He loved those things. He sat down at the kitchen table and ate the eggs between swallows of beer. He started on his preliminary report after he'd finished the eggs while the evening's events were still fresh in his mind. Hot damn, he thought while he wrote. Rich folks ain't one damn bit happier than most poor folks. "Poor old Chester," the Chief muttered. "All your money isn't good for a darn thing now–except a casket."

Chapter 39
Hail to the Chief

"Sorry about the wait gentlemen. Traffic is murder. Too many people, too little space."

The driver hefted Bob's luggage into the trunk with one hand and threw Martin Bates' case into the back seat with the other. Bob tried hard not to look like a country hick when they stepped off the train at Union Station. He refused to lift his head and gawk at the gilt and marble in the central terminal.

"You guys flew into Philly?"

"Air traffic was completely snarled," Martin replied.

"Been that way since they closed the old airport, Hoover field, so they could build that military office building. Thing's huge, everyone in town calls it the Pentagon. National Airport just opened. The bugs aren't all worked out yet."

Bob wondered how big the thing could be. Union Station was easily the largest building Bob had ever been in. Washington was like another universe–a waking dream. On the train, he'd gone to the head several times to look in the mirror and make sure he was still Bob Sullivan. Bob Sullivan, master cipher expert and advisor to the President, was dropping by the White House for a visit with FDR.

"Gentlemen, you're both booked at the Mayflower. Took a call from the White House to get you in. A three-day rule now exists on hotel rooms. You can't stay in any hotel in this town for more than three days." Their driver rubbed the back of his neck.

"I remember when you had to dodge livestock on these streets. The war has sure changed all that."

Bob and Martin Bates offered no conversation in response. They were tired and had been ordered to say nothing about where they'd come from, where they were going, or why they were there. On the long ride from San Francisco, Bates had told Bob that Washington was rife with foreign agents, most looking more American than most Americans. Bates had relented on one thing. He'd allowed Bob a phone call home before they'd gotten into the cab. It'd been pure heaven to listen to his boy chortle over the phone. The rest of the call had been less satisfactory. His mother-in-law had answered the phone.

"Your mother is answering our phone now?"

"Oh Bobby, quit wasting time worrying about mom. You okay?"

"Yeah, Betts, I don't want to blow hot air up your skirt here, but I'm doing great. Still not allowed to say anything over the phone about what's going on though."

Betty lowered her voice. "That's okay, Bobby. I'm real glad that you could call. Good to hear your voice…I wish you were here blowing air up my skirt."

"Don't get me going, Bett. If I get to thinking about you…I won't be able to sleep."

"Well, just one more thing. Hang on." Betty peeked around the corner to make sure her mom wasn't listening on the extension.

"I'm wearing a white and blue cotton sundress, and Bobby?"

"Yeah, Bett?"

"I'm naked underneath it."

"Jesus Betty, put Conor on before I go nuts."

"I'm crazy about you, Bobby. I miss you so bad."

"I know, baby. I know. This war won't last for-ever."

Even while he was talking to his son and listening to his baby daughter gurgle, his mind's eye pictured Betty in nothing but her thin cotton dress. He was about to see the President, and all he could think about was his beautiful, sex-crazed wife.

"Ain't this place the damnedest mess you ever saw?" The driver laughed. "The whole town is worthless - like our baseball team!"

"Perhaps," said Bob. "But, the bureaucrats and the Congress think highly of themselves. Didn't they try to hog all the X cards when gas rationing took effect?"

"You got that right. They also jumped on the press for ratting on them. Jesus, look at my job. I drive for the government, right? The morons at the Office of Petroleum Administration wanted us to make do with B books so the cabbies union would accept B books too. This is going on while all the Hill types are driving around burning gas like there is no tomorrow with X books in their pockets."

As the car pulled in front of the Mayflower, he said, "Hey Mac, if I catch you two on the return trip, we'll talk tires. Gas is nothing compared to finding usable tires."

Captain Bates and Bob stood on the sidewalk in front of the hotel before entering the lobby, Captain Bates looked at Bob and said, "Bob, I have some advice."

"Shoot, Marty."

"Politics is the wheat this town grinds to make bread. Everyone has an opinion on everything. Tomorrow you're getting fifteen minutes with the man whose opinions always matter. Be careful. The President has survived a long time by saying one thing and doing another."

The liveried porter came up to them. "Gentlemen, are you registered here?"

Captain Bates handed the man three dollars and said, "Yes, we are. Please see to our bags. The rooms are registered under my name, Captain Martin Bates."

"Yes sir, Captain, I'll tend to these right away."

"What's eating you, Marty? Afraid I might drop my drawers in front of the old boy?"

"No, but, you strike me as a man who loves fire. Fire will burn - even if you love it."

"Thanks, Marty, I'll keep that in mind. Let's grab a snort at the hoity-toity bar in this hotel. We'll call it a fire drill."

"What the hell," Martin said. "If we can find a table in a dark corner - away from the bar."

Their driver stopped at a pay phone two blocks down Connecticut Avenue from the Mayflower.

"Yes," he said. "I picked them up on schedule and dropped them at the Mayflower five minutes ago. No, they didn't say a thing. Right, okay. Starting at eleven, I'll cover the delivery dock."

Bob's room was small but was, easily, the fanciest room Bob had ever slept in. Bob tested the four-poster job. The mattress was a good one. He took his shoes off and wiggled them in the deep pile carpet. He flipped the radio on to hear Glenn Miller playing, *In the Mood*.

Someone tapped at his door. He opened it. Martin Bates was standing in the hall with his pipe in his hand.

"Marty, I know you like me, but you do have your own room."

He surprised Bob by quipping back. "I heard the Glenn Miller on the radio and thought that we could dance."

Bob guffawed. "Got me Marty, what do you really want?"

Martin brushed past Bob to the radio and turned it up. Then, came back and stood face-to-face with Bob.

"Jesus, you've got to be kidding," Bob said.

"Don't worry, besides, I don't dance all that well. I'm being careful. The room may be bugged."

"Should we go outside?"

"No. Just came by to discuss our itinerary. A car will be waiting for us out front at 0900. You'll ride in the front, as if you were an aide. We'll head over to G Street to pick up a package at the Saltz clothing store. When we get to the White House, I'll go in the front entrance; you'll carry the package around to the east portico. When you get to the portico entrance, tell the guards, "Captain Bates wants to make sure Mr. Early gets this package. It's his new army uniform."

"What's really in the package?"

"Exactly what I said. Steve Early is the President's press secretary. We did him a favor and picked up his uniform."

"Why am I the errand boy on this, Marty? Trying to remind me who's in charge?"

"Be sure and smile when you get out of the car."

"Have you lost your mind?"

"Don't you always smile when your picture is being taken, Bob? Although with your mug, I'm not sure smiling helps."

"My picture? Oh, shit! You think we're being watched that closely?"

"Don't take it personally. Everyone frequenting the White House these days is getting some attention. Simple precautions create confusion. Someone carrying cleaning creates little interest–at least that's our hope."

"Got it. Anything else?"

"Yes, this is an off the book meeting with the President. We will meet in the library, not the Oval Office. The official records will not show we were ever in the building. This means that you may see the President in his wheel chair. Don't mention the chair or comment on his health. Do not speak to the President unless spoken to. These rules are serious. Everything said in the President's presence has potential consequences. Any questions?"

"Guess farting or belching is out of the question then."

"Bob, this is no game. This crippled old man can kill our entire budget with the swipe of a pen. He currently tolerates us because he's intrigued by cloak and dagger mystery. This is what we offer him. If we piss him off, he won't give us a clue. I've known men, who thought he loved them, end their careers taking weather readings in Alaska."

"Marty, you're afraid of him."

"Hell yes, I'm afraid. You're new to the game. If you're smart, you'll be afraid too. When you're asked something, answer only the question asked, then button up."

The radio began to play '*At Long Last Love*'.

"Does the President love you, Marty? Are you afraid I'm going to screw your career progression up and run the ball the wrong way for you and your boss?"

"Nothing like that." Martin parted the curtains enough to check the late-night traffic.

"Don't bullshit a bull-shitter, Marty. I know the Commander, if that's what he really is, is on pins because a hick out of the back woods invented this gadget. Your problem is that you can't relax, even before someone takes a bite out of your ass."

"Forgive me if I'm a little tense. Every damn code freak in the world is working on this issue and you …what were you at that place anyway?"

"An electrician, Marty."

"Yeah, an electrician. You fiddle with the thing; work on it in your spare time, then come up with this improbably complex machine."

"Yep, Marty my boy, that's the long and short of it. Guess I have your immediate future by the short hairs. Let's think about this, one slip-up on my part, and you go to the Aleutians."

Martin headed for the door. "Just don't tug too hard on my hair, Bob. The tables can always turn, you know."

"I know all about tables and how they turn."

After Bates left, Bob poured himself a drink from a small silver flask the barkeep had filled downstairs. He turned out the lights and stared out the window. He rang up room service. Even though it was late, the kitchen said it could still bring him some cream of potato soup and a garden salad. That was fine with Bob.

When the food arrived, the colored waiter, a man of indeterminate age, set the table. When everything was in order, he asked Bob if that would be all. "Yes," Bob said. "But, I want to ask you something."

The waiter regarded Bob with a studied wariness.

"Yes, sir?" His tone indicated he would rather sit on nails.

Bob sat on the bedstead's corner and bounced up and down a couple of times.

"Will you boys fight if you get the chance?"

The waiter looked back at Bob and snorted. "By us *boys* I take it, sir that you're referring to all the male adult Negroes in the country?" The waiter made a 360° circle with his hands.

"Didn't mean to insult you," Bob said. "Really want to know what you think."

"You white boys are even more insulting when you are trying not to be. Do you know what all the crackers in Alabama are going to do if war comes?"

"Nope, not a clue."

"Why, then, do you assume that I know what all the blacks are going to do?"

Bob stood and said, "damn if you ain't right, old son. Will you have a drink with me or do the rules forbid it?"

"The rules do forbid it, but if you're pouring, I'm not turning one down."

"I am pouring."

"That's mighty black of you, if you don't mind my saying so."

Bob laughed.

"Doesn't matter anyway. I enlisted this morning, then, came into work and gave notice."

Bob handed the man his drink. "Where are you headed?"

"London. I am a rare breed of Negro - I speak and write fluent French, German, and Italian. I pick up languages like a sponge adsorbs water."

The man took a deep swallow of the bourbon.

"The Army is generously overlooking my skin color, since I have something they need. They even made me an officer. You're looking at 2d Lieutenant Abraham Moss."

Bob tapped his glass against the one Moss's held and said, "hell, I'll drink to that." He downed his whiskey in one swallow. He pointed to the soup on the table. "How's the soup?"

"The soup is white, sir, very white."

Bob agreed and poured himself and the waiter/Lieutenant another drink. When the radio began to play a Christmas tune, Bob realized how close to December it was. A little over a year ago, he was a glorified bum, a bum who had been forced to leave town. Now, he was drinking with a Negro in Washington D.C., while waiting to trot over to the White House and have a comfy talk with the President.

The soup was excellent, even if it was white.

Bob tried not to tug at his tie. The tie in question was dark blue watered silk with tiny white polka dots on it. The shirt he had on was so stiff that he felt like he was a wearing a board. His I.D. was carefully checked, then, he was provided a wing chair in the hall and told not to move.

His first impression of the White House was surprise–the place was small. He fidgeted, wondering where Marty was. Probably warning the staff that someone who hadn't finished public school was preparing to speak to the President, he thought glumly.

His head ached. Lieutenant Moss was younger than he and could hold his liquor. He grinned inwardly. Will Davis sure would be shocked if he knew I spent the evening drinking with a black man in a hotel for swells. He wouldn't recognize me now either, dressed to the nines and acting the top dog. Then reality hit him. He was a top dog. He'd never revert to what he was before the war - ever.

"Mr. Sullivan, Mr. Sullivan?"
Bob looked up. An attendant in a white coat was staring down at him. "I'm sorry," Bob said. "You caught me wool gathering."
"Sir, the President will see you now. Please follow me."
Bob followed the man down the hall, noticing, as he walked, that the red runner was worn and frayed at the edges. Two men stood outside of the room where the President was presumably waiting. The men frowned at Bob as he came to the threshold. The attendant had already entered the room ahead of him, announcing, "Mr. President, your appointment is here."
Bob heard a familiar voice boom out. "Good, good. Show the young man in!"
The attendant motioned for Bob to enter.

The President was sitting in a straight back chair next to a reading table. A bright red throw was tucked around his legs. Martin Bates was not in the room. A balding man with glasses was sitting next to the President. He stood and extended his hand to Bob. "No need to be nervous Mr. Sullivan," the President said. "This is the Secretary of War, Henry Stimson. He wouldn't sit still until I promised him he could attend this meeting."

Bob shook hands with Secretary Stimson.

"Do you stand while speaking, Bob, or would you feel more comfortable sitting?" The President gestured towards a chair situated next to his own. Bob sat. "Forgive me for being somewhat tongue-tied Mr. President," Bob said. "My Navy liaison isn't here and I'm not quite sure where to start."

The President tilted back his head and chuckled at the ceiling. "I can imagine how desperately Martin wanted to be here. He's afraid of me, you know, a perfectly competent man - but he shakes like a poodle every time I look at him." The light glinted off the President's spectacles as he patted Bob on the knee.

"On the other hand, Bob, you're not shaking at all. Henry, get Bob a drink before we start our visit about code machines."

As if on cue, two men in white coats brought in a bucket of ice, several tumblers, and assorted bottles of liquor.

"What's your pleasure, Mr. Sullivan?"

"Bourbon on the rocks, Mr. Secretary."

"Henry, I'll have a club soda."

"Of course Mr. President. I'll follow Mr. Sullivan's lead and have bourbon."

The stewards' left after all three men had their drinks. The President looked at Bob and said, "I am intrigued by what I've heard about your code device. Tell me about it."

At some point during the conversation, Bob took out a pen and began drawing pictures. Secretary Stimson drew closer to see. This session lasted well over an hour, even with discreet coughs and signals from the White House staff, reminding the President that several other appointments were waiting.

Bob didn't notice the signals. He was completely focused. He'd never seen a President before, so, the time he was being given with the President didn't strike him as unusual; nor did the fact that he had the President's undivided attention for the entire session. When they were done, Secretary Stimson said, "I'll have to keep your drawings here Mr. Sullivan. They're now classified, as is everything that was discussed here today."

"I understand, Mr. Secretary. Am I authorized to speak to Captain Bates or the Commander about this meeting?"

"Of course, Bob," The President said. "Just don't talk to your friends or loved ones about being here…or how ugly your Commander-in-Chief is in the flesh. My boy, your invention is extraordinary. You've been of great service to your country."

"Thank you, Mr. President. This has been a great honor. I'm pleased to have been of service to you and to the country."

"Come Mr. Sullivan," Secretary Stimson said. "I'll walk you out. Captain Bates is waiting."

The President was surrounded now by staff Bob noticed. Bob and the Secretary walked back out to the East Wing portico.

Captain Bates was waiting in the same chair Bob had waited in. When he saw the Secretary of War and Bob approach, he leapt to his feet.

"Good afternoon, Mr. Secretary. I apologize for missing the meeting. I was ordered over to the Navy yard."

"I know, Martin. I arranged that at the President's request. The President was eager to see Mr. Sullivan without his handler." The Secretary put his arm around Martin's shoulders and said, "Don't fret, Martin. The President was impressed. So was I. We'll be in touch. We'll also want a field test at the earliest possible opportunity."

The Secretary handed Bates a piece of paper with one word on it. Bates looked, and then handed the paper back to Secretary Stimson. The Secretary showed the word to Bob. 'Lamplight' was the word scrawled across the page. Bob handed the paper back to Secretary Stimson, who lit the paper with a match, then, dropped the flaming scrap into an ashtray. When the fire went out, he used his pen to grind what remained to fine ash. Without another word, the Secretary headed back down the hall toward the west wing.

"What the hell was that about?" asked Bob.

"Once we leave the building, we won't speak of this, but, suffice it to say, you didn't screw up. Lamplight is our project name. The President is giving your machine priority in his next war production submission to Congress."

"Just like that Marty?"

"Yep."

The two men made their way by separate exits onto Pennsylvania Avenue. They walked casually up to each other as if they'd met by accident in front of the Hay Adams Hotel. "I've already checked us out. We head back for Australia tomorrow, but, tonight we have a meeting in New York."

"Damn Marty, you'd think there was a war on or something."

Martin Bates smiled momentarily. "Yes, and you single handedly advanced us right into the thick of the big dance," Martin said. "I owe you one. The thought of you all alone with the President and Stimson scared me shitless. You pulled it off though. Whatever you told them blew their socks off. Stimson didn't even pretend disinterest."

"Why would he?"

"Because he correctly perceives that a separate intelligence service usurps power from the War Department. He has a political stake in seeing us fail."

"Marty the meet wasn't all that bad. They were nice the whole time. Once when I was explaining something, we actually bumped heads since we were all hunched up together."

"You bumped heads with the President?"

"I did."

"Wonders never cease."

They hailed a cab and headed for the train station.

Chapter 40
Begging Pardon

The 0400 watch was difficult, the sky and ocean blended into seamless gray, no horizon was visible as the sub coursed through Vitiaz Strait separating New Britain from New Guinea. "I should enjoy the peace and quiet while it exists." I said to myself. Ace Henson appeared on the bridge to relieve me. "The old man just announced that we're headed for Saint George's channel between New Britain and New Ireland to patrol for Japanese shipping," he said.

"Hope we get us a carrier."

"Aren't many places to hide from depth charges in a channel," Ace said.

"Change the subject," I said. "I don't want to be anymore depressed than I already am."

"Okay, here's a positive thought for you, Davis. Think all the kinks have been worked out of the detonator for the new MK-14 fish?"

"That's what the brass said. I'm sure they wouldn't feed us a line," I said. Ace frowned and his eyebrows arched. "What, like we have a choice? Are we going to refuse to go on patrol because the torpedoes don't detonate?"

I shrugged and headed down the hatch.

"By the way Davis, why are you always pulling the midnight watch?"

"My acute night vision."

"What about your night vision?"

"Bunton sent me into the battery compartment to fix a gauge tube leak after we'd been depth-charged with no flashlight. Claimed a flashlight could spark a fire. I managed to fix the gauge in the dark."

"Bunton must love you."

"He hid his disappointment really well when I didn't choke and die on the chlorine gas in the battery compartments."

The seas had risen and were beginning to pitch the sub around. "Davis, toggle the mike and tell the Captain that I see a wake about 15 degrees off the starboard bow. Whatever it is, it's heading east."

The Captain came onto the bridge and studied the horizon for a moment, then said, "got it."

He toggled the mike and said, "Mr. Gunderschmidt, dive to periscope depth."

I dogged down the hatch from the bridge to the tower as the second dive bell sounded, the Captain already had the periscope trained on the potential targets. He stated, "I hold the conn."

"Aye, the Captain has the conn." Replied the Exec.

"We are trimmed off at periscope depth."

"Mind the swells Ralph, I don't want to broach in this crap."

"Aye, Captain."

"Battle stations if you please Dave. Seamen Henson and Davis have found us a convoy."

I dropped down the hatch between the tower and the control room to my battle station at the stern planes just as the klaxon sounded and we went to red light.

No one spoke, as we stood in the eerie red of the battle lamps and sweated. Finally, the Captain slid down the ladder into the control room and squawked a message to the crew. "Ladies, we're 7,000 yards out from a Shokaku class carrier. She's zigzagging on six-minute legs approximately 30 degrees off of her base course at about 18 knots. We're going to come around inside her destroyer screen on the surface, dive, and, then, blow her the hell out of the water. Get ready for some rough sledding. Those destroyers are gonna go ape on us - out."

"The old man has traded in his big brass balls for gold ones," Chief Bunton said.

"Chief," I said. "Have you ever made a surface run at a carrier task force before?"

"Never made a run at anything on the surface before–not even in my worst nightmare. We could be shark bait soon, but we'll take a lot of Japs with us if this works." The dive officer, Mr. Evans, who was stripped down to his skivvies and wheel cap, grinned. "I agree Chief. We're going to definitely ruin their karma."

"Dave," the Captain said. "Take us up and give me full power out of the girl."

"Aye, Captain," Lt Gunderschmidt responded. "Surface and full power."

We ran on the surface for another ten minutes, then, the dive command came over the blower. We went down to periscope depth. Minutes passed into what seemed like hours. Finally, the old man fired a spread of four fish from 2000 yards out. The ship bucked as the torpedoes left the forward tubes.

"Hard to port, Dave. Ralph, pull the plug. I want us at 400 feet pronto. Those Terutsuki class destroyers are loaded for bear and they aren't coming to play tiddly-winks."

"Aye Captain, four hundred feet down bubble."

"Time to target?"

"Forty-eight seconds, Captain."

We heard and then felt three distinct concussions as the fish contacted something. We found out later that we had hit the carrier with three of our four fish. We weren't celebrating.

"Four hundred feet is a fair amount of pressure Captain."

The Captain laughed. "No shit, Chief. If I stove us in, I reckon we'll all be dead in about five seconds."

"Sir, with respect," Chief Bunton replied. "I'd say six."

Suddenly, there was a hand on my left shoulder. The old man was at my side.

"Will, you're relieved here. I want you eyeballing that water gauge line. If we begin to take any water, I want to know in a hurry. Six it is Chief."

"Aye Captain."

Chief Bunton stopped me on my way out of the control room to the after battery.

He whispered, "Davis, if you fucked up the gauge line repair job, I'll boil you in torpedo grease."

"Chief, if I fucked up that repair job up, I'll be happy to live long enough to be boiled."

I headed aft.

The gauge line was okay. By the time I got back to where I needed to be to check it though, all hell broke loose. We had gotten deep enough so that the first charges seemed harmless, then the Japs got serious. Over the blower came, "damage control party to the aft torpedo room."

I crawled out of the battery storage compartment and ran for the aft torpedo room. The charge had opened various valves. I manned a couple of handles and cranked several valves shut.

People were swirling around me in the spraying water closing valves and saying prayers. I figured we were about two shakes and a jigger from heading right to the bottom. The water spewing through the aft torpedo room slowed to a fast trickle.

"Well, that's that," I said. "Maybe we won't be holding our breaths and making funny faces till we turn purple today."

"Hey Smitty," Ace Henson drawled. "Davis here thinks we might all live to see another day. Tell him what else we got going for ourselves."

Smitty was the noncom in charge of the aft torpedo room. He had a big, bald head and a maniacal laugh. He was splashing in the seawater on the deck. His head was jerking in all different directions, like a vulture after eating some bad road-kill.

"One little problem, Wee Willie."

"Quit calling me that, Smitty, or I'll fire you out of one of the stern tubes."

"We may all be fired out of here. We have a live fish in four. That last depth charge tripped the lever."

"Holy shit!"

"I agree." He got on the intercom, "Captain, could either you or the torpedo officer come aft. We have an armed fish stuck in the number four tube."

The Captain showed up before anyone had time to blink. He then tried to light a damp cigarette three or four times. He couldn't do it. Smitty took out his lighter and held it under the old man's cigarette until it lit. The old man took a deep drag, and then sloshed over to the mike. No one said a thing for about fifteen seconds.

The Captain toggled the mike.

"Dave, is the outer door open on aft number four?"

"Board says yes Captain."

"How's our trim?"

"We're okay. I pumped all the water out of the aft ballast tanks to hold us level."

"So...the stern is behaving as if we have flooded at least one stern tube?"

"I agree Captain. The boat's behaving consistent with that assessment."

The Captain took another drag on his cigarette.

"Alright Dave, I'm clearing the aft torpedo room of everyone except myself and the chief. Rig the boat for collision."

"Ah sir, we already are rigged for collision."

"Then tell everyone to double-check all valves and hatches."

"Aye, Captain…may I ask what you intend to do?"

"Build the air pressure in four to about six hundred pounds after bringing the boat to full power and use the pressure to blow the fish clear."

"Sir, are we sure the fish is live?"

The Captain looked at Smitty.

"Captain," Smitty said. "The damn thing smoked the torpedo room up and battered the hell out of the outer door. Getting the outer door to crank open manually was a minor dang miracle after the beating the fish gave it."

"How do you know the door actually opened?"

"Sir, you heard the exec. The light is green and we had to torque the crank hard to rotate it. I believe the outer door is open."

"Bet your life on it?"

"All of our lives on it - Chief?" Ace said.

"Blow it out your ass, Ace," The Chief said. "Begging the Captain's pardon."

The Captain rolled his eyes and keyed the mike.

"Dave, we're going to blow the fish."

"Men," the Chief ordered, "clear the torpedo room."

I raised my hand.

"Yes, Davis?"

"Captain, with your permission, I'd like to stay. If this doesn't work I'd like to go quickly."

The Captain laughed. "Fair enough. Find something to hold onto. Even if this works, the pressure'll kick the boat like a Missouri mule."

"Dave, any destroyers still hovering nearby?"

"Negative, Captain. The closest ping we're getting is about 12,000 yards now."

"Alright, full speed ahead. I'm commencing pressure build up in the number four aft tube. Let me know when we've achieved 9 knots."

"Aye Captain, break a leg."

So, there we stood; the Chief, the old man, and I watching each other drip sweat onto the already wet deck. I found myself suddenly needing to pee badly. I thought with great clarity that this really could be the end of everything.

"Got to pee, Will?"

"Sorry sir, but yes I do."

"So do I."

"How about you Chief?"

"Captain I pissed my pants 10 minutes ago when I heard that fish banging around in the tube. My bladder is empty."

"Lucky you Chief. Alright, on my mark hit the key–and Chief?"

"Yes sir?"

"Think gentle thoughts."

"Aye skipper, gentle thoughts for all of us."

"Mark!"

The Chief hit the key. I counted to three.

WHAAAAM!

At first, I thought that we'd blown the stern off because so much water hit me in the face. A hand pulled me off the deck. The stern was still intact! The force of the torpedo exiting had cracked the bronze tube door. The Captain and the Chief, with a bloody gash on his forehead, were cranking like madmen to close the outer door to shunt the leak. I slogged over to help them. On pure adrenaline, we shut the door. For the moment, we had survived the near detonation of one of our own fish.

The Captain got on the mike and said, "Dave, surface us now even if a destroyer is sitting on us."

"Aye, surface order is acknowledged. Glad you're still with us, Skipper."

"So am I. That was one helluva blast."

"Yes sir, I figure the warhead detonated approximately 50 yards off of our stern."

I headed for the hatch. I was soaked to the skin, but I was alive. I once again felt a hand on my shoulder.

"Thank you, Will."

"For what, Captain? I didn't do a thing. I was in the way."

"Will, you stayed when you could have left. Took courage to do that."

"Thank you, sir."

"Get into some dry clothes and then come forward to my cabin if you please."

"Aye Captain," I saluted and headed for my bunk. Another day of sparring with problems at the office. If only Mom could see me now.

Chapter 41

Cranberry Sauce and Brine

"Mr. Davis you have potential. I'm recommending you for stateside schooling at Navy expense. You could earn a commission. Are you up to the challenge?"

"Sir, if you think I can handle the responsibility, I'll give it my best shot."

"Great, read these two books to start." He handed me two well-thumbed books. "The one with the blue cover is by Alfred Mahan. The second is by Carl Von Clausewitz. Read these guys and you'll be miles ahead of the game in terms of understanding how most of the brass thinks."

I tried to look interested.

The Captain took one look at my face and snorted.

"Will, this reading assignment isn't a death sentence. Mahan is a little dated and pompous but the Navy still respects his work. Clausewitz's perception on why war is fought is very interesting."

"I'll read them, sir."

"Good, the Navy needs young men like you. Carry on."

I saluted as I backed my way out of the Captain's small stateroom and literally bumped into Chief Bunton in the gangway.

He noticed the books.

"So, the skipper's giving books to the teacher's pet now."

"Believe me, Chief; this isn't my idea of a good time."

"Good, because you're butt is now mine. Get to work on the distillation plant and in case you forgot while you were having tea and crumpets with the old man, the batteries need watering."

"I haven't forgotten. By the way, does your mother know what a mean little shit you've become. War really doesn't agree with you one bit Chief."

"Dear old mom hit me with a waffle iron once a day to punish me for whatever I'd done that she didn't know about. I've grown soft on this here boat. Move out before you really piss me off."

I headed aft. "The Chief and I are not going to be buddies after the war...if we survive," I said to myself. I stowed the books the Captain had given me in my footlocker. Everyone in the berthing compartment was asleep. So, no one razzed me about my reading material.

I eyed the distillation plant, my old nemesis. The distillation plant was not complicated or glamorous; really the contraption was nothing but a glorified pressure cooker that heated seawater to vapor. The brine condensed out, leaving the crew, hopefully, with enough fresh water to drink and to water the batteries with. The batteries used 60 to 100 gallons a day depending upon our operational status. The crew used roughly 400 gallons a day for drinking. Do the math.

The distillation plant was constantly used and was constantly breaking down due to brine clogs. Cleaning the mechanism was a nasty job. I made the mistake of showing the aptitude for being able to keep it and the diesel fuel filter, another vital pain-in-the-butt piece of equipment, running smoothly. So, whenever we had really dirty fuel, I'd be tasked to work on the fuel filter, which worked on the same principle as a centrifuge. If our water demands were great, I'd be tasked to work on the distillation plant. Chief Bunton kept himself happy by keeping me soaked in diesel or coated in brine.

On Christmas morning, 1943, we were patrolling approximately 100 nautical miles north, northwest of New Ireland. I was tightening the bolts on the distillation plant. I heard a sound and looked over. A pair of brogans, and dungarees was standing next to me on the cork deck matting.

"Hello, Chief," I said.

"Glad you're making yourself useful for a change, Davis. I expected to find you and Ace goldbricking in the mess."

"Thank you, Chief. So what's your excuse? How do you pull your weight around here?"

"Get cleaned up. The old man wants to see you. Since you're a regular wizard with the distillation plant, I assume you'll have enough water to bathe. Oh, by the way, I brought you your lunch."

He dropped a plate on my chest that was loaded down with cranberry sauce. The sauce covered a big lump of Spam.

"Thanks Chief, I appreciate the consideration."

Walking away, he said, "don't mention it, Davis. I didn't want you forgotten on this special day."

I crawled out from under the plant. Nate Wiesniewski was on duty in the forward engine room.

"Nate!" I yelled over the sound of the engines.

"Yeah, Will?"

"Can you get someone to check the bolts on the distillation plant? I think they're okay, but the Chief interrupted me before I could torque them all a second time."

"Sure Will, no sweat. You going to play cards with us tonight?"

"I don't know. Do you boys have any money left for me to take?"

"Sure, besides, Ace has told everyone he's figured out your system."

"Oh really?"

"Says you cheat like a banker running a farm foreclosure. Says we're playing with his cards tonight."

"Believe me; I hate bankers worse than anyone. Tell Ace to bring all his money tonight. I'm taking every cent he owns–with his cards, no less."

"See you tonight, Will–Oh Will?"

"Yeah, Nate?"

"You have sticky red stuff all over your shirt. Is that shit off the distillation plant?"

"No, that red stuff is my lunch. Courtesy of Chief Bunton, he likes me so much; he brought lunch to me while I was working. I'm just a messy eater."

"Okay man, see you tonight. Don't worry about the plant."

"Thanks, Nate."

On my way to the shower, I ran my finger over the front of my shirt and then licked it. Not to bad, I thought. I'd always liked cranberry sauce.

Chapter 42
Card Sharks and Torpedoes

The hot shower was a treat. I don't think I'll ever take cleanliness for granted again. My mind began dwelling on Mindy, and then Brett and those oranges, and then the nurses on the train. I had a huge boner. I took a risk that no one would walk in on me - and jacked off. I hadn't relieved myself in so long that the whole business only took thirty seconds. No sooner had I finished and sprayed myself off than Bunton was yelling, "Davis, I told you to rinse off, not use the crew's fresh water allotment for a month!"

"Aye Chief, I'm done."

"I sure as hell hope so!"

I pulled on some fresh dungarees and headed for officer territory. We were running on the surface. The thermometer on the bulkhead in the crew mess indicated that the ambient air temperature was a pleasant 77°F. As I headed forward, I could smell the clean air running through the boat. The condensation had evaporated off all of the bulkhead surfaces. I felt like I might survive after all. At the Captain's stateroom, I knocked.

"Enter."

I saluted. "Machinist's mate Davis reporting as ordered, sir."

"Will, Chief Bunton grumbles about you a lot. Any particular reason?"

"True sir, Chief Bunton and I have our disagreements. He doesn't appreciate my keen sense of humor or my boyish charm. With all due respect, he lacks both."

The Captain put the pen that he'd been writing with down on his desk, and said, "ah yes."

"I'll try to do a better job of staying in the Chief's good graces, has he put me on report?"

"No, he grudgingly admits that you're the sailor responsible for keeping our fuel filter and distillation plant running smoothly."

"My compliments to the Chief for speaking the truth."

"How's your reading coming?" The Captain asked as he turned to review a file on his desk. "Slowly, sir. Von Clausewitz could be writing about current events, rather than the 18th century, when he talks about war being the employment of organized violence to achieve political ends."

"Good, Will. You've correctly postulated one of Von Clausewitz's key tenets right off the bat. I wish we had more time to talk about this. Neither Chief Bunton nor Von Clausewitz, however, is why I asked you to report. We've been ordered off patrol to deliver Bob Crenshaw to Brisbane. At the same time, we're picking up our mystery Commander. You remember - our friend from Panama? He's bringing a navy contractor named Bob Sullivan with him."

My eyes got big. My eyebrows arched. The Captain stared at me.

"What! It can't be," I said.

"I was told you might have that reaction. This is all classified of course. Officially, their visit won't be noted in the log."

"I know a Bob Sullivan, but this can't be the same guy. The Bob Sullivan I know is a big thug who ran off with a blonde bombshell from a rich family in my hometown. He's got to be dead or in prison."

"Apparently not. Our friend the Commander remembered this boat from Panama. He was looking at our muster list, trying to determine if this boat would be a good candidate for a gadget they've designed. Sullivan apparently recognized your name and said, 'that's our boat.'"

The Captain tapped the folder on his writing table.

"The Commander remembered you too. He was astounded to learn that his ace inventor knew the seaman who got mixed up with the Panama assassin."

"I'm amazed too," I said. "Bob invented something? My brother Ralph told me that Bob had gone to California, but I didn't believe it. Ralph also told me that Bob had gotten work as a janitor, or something."

"'Or something' is the winner," the Captain said. "My message indicates that he's cleared for this project at the highest levels of government and is to receive all courtesy due an officer with the rank of lieutenant commander."

"All I can say is paint me green and call me grass," I said. "Real life is stranger than fiction after all."

"Be ready for anything and, as always, don't speak of this outside this cabin. I doubt that you're going to stay attached to my command after we dock. My educated guess is that this Intel commander, having run into you twice under strange circumstances, will haul you off with him when this project, whatever it is, is complete."

"Great, just great. First the Japs and Chief Bunton. Now, Bob Sullivan and the spook."

"Look at the strange turn of events this way, Will. Whatever happens, you'll probably be drier and cleaner than you are right now."

That night, I said nothing about these events to my fellow boat mates around the card table. Keeping my personal business out of the scuttlebutt network was becoming difficult. Living with over sixty men on a sub that was scarcely longer than a football field and only ten yards wide was not a recipe for privacy.

"Saw you in the Captain's cabin today, Tex," Bob Crenshaw said.

Wally Jeffers looked up and said, "I heard about that too. What were you and the Captain doing today?" He grinned, then, said. "There are strict navy regulations against officers and enlisted men fraternizing, even on a submarine."

I threw a dollar into the pot, and said, "Jeffers, are you talking or farting? I can't tell the difference."

"Sorry that I offended you, oh king of the distillation plant."

"The Captain told me that an old friend of mine is coming aboard when we make port."

"Is that really it?" Ace said. "Or, are you the old man's cabana boy, Davis?"

I dropped two cards and signaled for two from the dealer.

"Blow it out your ass, Ace," I said.

"I couldn't be his boy even if I wanted to be," I said. "Word is he already gets high quality service from you."

"Yes, he does," Ace said. "I learned every trick in the book from your mom."

"Here's to mom," I said. "Hope she didn't give you the clap."

"I've got to get off this boat. You boys are the sickest I've ever run into," Crenshaw said. "Besides, I can't take the rank stench anymore. Does this tin tube always smell this bad?"

"Yeah, most of the time," I said. "If I survive, I'm sure I'll always long for the smell of this here boat."

"Nothing better than the smell of diesel fuel, sweat, and cigarette smoke all mixed together," Crenshaw said. "Disturbs me to think the possibility exists that the last thing I'd smell if a depth charge with our names on it arrives, is you and Ace farting in this oily, greasy metal tube."

"Bob, I'll take no offense," I said. "You got dumped in this billet on short notice, but you're not exactly the sharpest knife in the drawer. If the Starkfish's pressure hull gives, you won't have time to think about farting or anything else."

"Wally has a ten showing, Davis has a jack up, and Crenshaw is sporting a queen," Ace said.

"In my wildest dreams," I said. "Never thought I'd be sealed up in a tube in the Bismarck Archipelago while 4 *Asashio - class* Japanese destroyers stalked my ass. The last eight hours have been hairy."

"Not just your ass," Ace said. "There are several other souls on this boat too."

"Surprised to hear you have a soul, Ace. A couple of weeks ago, you hauled your soul out of the aft torpedo room pretty quickly when the old man said he was going to blow out that live fish under pressure."

"I didn't fall off the turnip truck yesterday, Davis. I don't have a death wish, like some people around here."

Ace always whined when he was losing at cards. He was losing again, mainly to me. I looked over at Crenshaw as I shuffled the deck.

"Ace, do you think you'd have been luckier in the bow than the stern if that torpedo had detonated in the aft tube?"

Ace didn't say anything for a minute. Suddenly, he threw his cards on the table. "This game stinks. So does the company." He got up and left.

Crenshaw shrugged and said, "what's eating him?"

He's losing," I said. "And, he's a long way from Omaha. Are you calling, raising, or folding?"

He raised. "Crenshaw," I said, "you're a smart boy, but you put too much faith in two pair." I scooped all the chips out of the pot to my side of the table.

"Davis, you just separated me from three months pay."

"You still didn't lose as much as Ace though," I said.

"That's a comfort, is there anyone on this sub you wouldn't play poker with?"

"The Skipper," I said. "Chief Bunton was right for a change when he said the old man has gold ones, not just brass ones. He was cold as ice when he blew that armed fish out of the tube. His facial expression never changed, looked like he was playing golf."

The card game broke up. I never played with Bob Crenshaw again. He was aboard the USS Indianapolis when she was torpedoed in the Philippine Sea 16 days before the war ended. He didn't survive long enough to be rescued. Someone who'd been on the Indianapolis mentioned that Crenshaw had saved him from a shark but had then been attacked himself. This was at a veteran's reunion in the seventies. Anyway, the last time I saw him alive was on the Brisbane docks in the winter of '43.

After the card game, I hit the rack for about ten minutes when the battle stations klaxon sounded. This was the story of my life on the sub - there were periods on that sub when I'd go thirty hours without shuteye. I groaned, put my dogs back on the deck, and headed to my station on the stern planes. Two guys were plotting intercept vectors in the control room. One looked up and said, "convoy," then, continued plotting. My watch said 0322. The Captain had us closing in on the targets using a radar surface approach. I heard the OD say, "3400 yards, Captain."

Since we were engaged in a surface approach, the Captain was on the bridge entering tracking data into the Torpedo Data Computer, or TDC. The TDC set the gyro angles for the torpedoes based upon data input by the Captain and the boat's gyro. Positioning data and gyro angle data was entered via dials on the TDC face. This

314

data was sent to the fish in whichever forward or aft tubes had been prepped to fire.

"Captain, we have firing solutions for both transports," the OD said. "Their relative course headings and speed?" The Captain asked.

"Base course for both vessels is to the North, 14 knots. The second transport is trailing the first by 1800 yards," the OD said.

"Very well, Dave," the Captain said. "Fire two separate spreads of fish. Fire the second spread one minute after the first. Submerge the boat immediately after firing the second spread.

The Starkfish bucked as the first salvo of three torpedoes left the tubes. One minute after the first spread had been fired; the second spread was fired as ordered. As the last torpedo left the boat, the dive gong sounded. The switch from diesel to electrical power went smoothly and the boat changed headings in order to evade escort pursuit.

"Put some muscle into the dive plane wheel, Will," the OD said.

"Aye, muscle it is, sir."

The concussion of several explosions bounced off the sub's hull.

"Captain, sonar reports four of the six torpedoes hit their targets and exploded properly."

"Hold us at periscope depth, Dave."

"Aye, periscope depth, Captain," Dave Gunderschmidt said.

"The two torpedoes that failed had nothing to hit," the Captain said, as he looked through the scope. "The bows of both ships were lifted out of the water by the impact of the initial torpedoes fired. That's our story and we're sticking to it."

Our morale skyrocketed. We had taken on a carrier task force by ourselves, survived a live fish banging around in one of our aft tubes, sank two transports and we were still alive. Even Chief Bunton looked at me later in the day and said, "why don't you get some sleep, Davis. You look like shit." This was as close as the Chief ever came to expressing concern for my well being. I hit the rack for several hours, a good feeling. We were in the northern quadrant of the Coral Sea heading for port at Brisbane. Life was good.

Chapter 43
The Pinch of a Clamp

"Jesus, I can't see! Irrigation please. I've got blood in both eyes!" Mindy said.

The second scrub nurse released a retractor, grabbed a saline bottle and squirted Mindy's face and eyes. Mindy dodged a fountain of blood squirting up out of the boy's abdomen.

"Doctor," Mindy said. "There's a nick in this kid's external iliac artery. He's going to bleed out in about 20 seconds."

"Clamp the damn thing and get some sutures in it," Doctor Scranton said. "I can't leave this liver - looks like Swiss cheese. If he's too far gone, wrap him up and move over to this table."

Mindy got a clamp on the bleeder, and then glanced at the bulkhead clock. She figured she had 3 minutes before she cost this kid use of his legs. She irrigated the nick and began the delicate process of suturing the artery.

"Nurse, what the bloody hell are you doing?"

Dr. Curry was standing over her right shoulder.

"Right now, I'm doing my best to save this boy's life and legs. Get out of my light."

"Hand me those instruments! You're practicing medicine without a license!"

"Jerry," General Scranton said, without looking up from the liver he was repairing, "she's working under my supervision. The girl has gifted hands and good judgment. We're up to our ass in alligators, and she won't hurt the patient any worse than the shrapnel already has. Leave her alone and get back to triage. That's where you're needed."

"General, with respect, I intend to report your actions. This is highly inappropriate and you know it."

"Fair enough, doctor. For now though, get your butt out there and triage."

Mindy glanced around the ship's OR. If any other doctors or nurses were concerned by the exchange, they didn't show it. The carnage created by the Tarawa landing had overwhelmed the ship's surgical resources.

Mindy released the clamp. The stitching held.

"Sir, I have the artery stitched and have released the clamp. Want me to pack him in gauze, or close him?"

"Did you get everything? He'll be dead in two days tops from sepsis if you didn't."

"I ran everything," Mindy said. "I'll run the bowel again if you want me to."

"No, time," Scranton said. "Close the musculature, leave the outer epidermal layer open, and pack him in gauze. Annotate on his post-op orders that I'm to be notified if he shows signs of internal bleeding or if his temperature spikes over 103."

"Yes sir."

As Mindy began closing the initial layer of musculature, she thought back on the events that had brought her to this table.

"This guy looks half dead," Mindy said.

"Honey, don't you worry your pretty little head about it," Dr. Curry said.

"Doctor, his pulse just went south. He's in arrest."

"Give me ten milligrams of adrenaline in a syringe, *now!*"

Mindy handed the syringe over and watched as Curry tried to administer the dose. Dr. Curry missed the sweet spot in the sternum that he needed to hit to inject the medicine into the heart muscle. He tried a second time and missed again. Mindy looked over at Myrt, who was watching from the entrance to the surgical suite. She gave Mindy an almost imperceptible nod.

"Excuse me, doctor, but I think if you hit him here…." Mindy put her finger on the slight depression on the patient's chest where the needle needed to be inserted.

"Gently," she said. "We want to save the patient."

"Nurse Hulen, one more word and I'll report you for insubordination."

"Doctor, one more botched attempt, and I'll be writing your state medical board."

Dr. Curry's head jerked up at the sound of a male voice.

"Allow me to introduce myself, Dr. Scranton at your service."

Dr. Curry didn't turn around, "I've heard of a Dr. George Scranton. He heads up thoracic surgery at Hopkins in Baltimore."

"One and the same; although I have a new, if temporary, title. For the moment, I'm Major General Scranton, head of the Pacific Theater's Army Medical Corps. Captain Carouthers is my sister."

I listened for a pulse and heard one, faint but steady.

"If you like, doctor, I'll keep an eye on the patient's vitals while you confer with Dr. Scranton."

"Very well, nurse. Call me at the slightest hint of a problem. Sir, if you will excuse me, I'd like to wash up."

"Certainly, Doctor."

Doctor Curry exited the room without another glance Mindy's way.

"Lieutenant Hulen, I'm here looking for volunteers to man a hospital ship off of the Solomon Islands. My task is to round up doctors but would you be interested in a transfer too? Sis here calls you gifted, and she doesn't hand out compliments lightly."

"If I can be of use and if your sister can spare me, certainly," Mindy said.

"There is one caveat, Lieutenant."

"What's that, sir?"

"You'll be seeing a lot of Dr. Curry. He doesn't know this yet, but he's coming too."

"Dr. Curry's alright once you get past his arrogance, ego, and unchecked horniness."

"Good, I'm glad there are no problems."

Mindy looked over at Myrt.

"I'll miss you dearly, Mindy, but my instincts tell me you'll be of great benefit to the wounded boys coming off that island."

"Mindy?" the general asked.

"Yes, sir?"

"Sis here also informs me you can tie square knots with two fingers using sutures. Is that correct?"

Mindy laughed. "It's true. I've won a lot of bets and drinks from the GI's around here by tying those little knots."

"That skill is going to be tested. See you later. Good luck with your patient."

"Thank you. I'm pleased to have met you, sir."

"I'm covered in blood," Mindy said, as her mind sling-shot itself back to the present.

"That's what standing in an OR for 18 hours will do to you," Marge Hilton said. Once the stream of seriously wounded patients had subsided, and the docs had caught up, Mindy had returned to merely assisting. Marge was a fellow scrub nurse.

"That kid you worked on, the one that screwed Dr. Curry into the bulkhead, still alive?"

"Still alive and doing as well as can be expected," Mindy said. "I'm getting out of here before I fall down. I'm so messed up that people are staring."

"You did well today. The Army isn't normally a place where you want to draw attention to yourself, especially if you're a woman," Marge said. "You might be the exception to the rule."

"What are you talking about?"

Marge shook her head. "Never mind. Do me a favor though, will you?"

"What's that?"

"Stay out of Dr. Curry's path."

Mindy felt a nudge. She opened her eyes and found herself staring across a dressing-strewn deck. Her head was resting on a pile of army blankets.

"Don't worry Lieutenant, those blankets are all clean." She looked up. General Scranton was standing over her.

"Come on Lieutenant; let's grab ourselves a cup of joe and a sandwich."

Mindy followed him up several deck levels and through several hatchways. When they got to the General's stateroom, he got on the intercom and ordered food from the steward. He grinned. "Rank has its' privileges."

"Sure does. I'd be lucky to find a rind of cheese on my own."

"How was your war today Lieutenant?"

"Bloody awful. You scared me witless when you left me with that nicked artery to work on that other boy's liver. May I speak frankly, sir?"

"By all means, Lieutenant."

"General, when Doctor Curry files a report regarding my actions in the OR today I'm not sure that even you, sir, have enough rank to withstand the storm this will generate. I'm toast for sure."

The general leaned back in his chair, pulling off his blood, spattered boots.

"Remind me never to operate in boots again. Doing so was agony."

He wiggled his toes and stretched. There was a knock at the bulkhead door.

"Come in, please."

A mess steward entered. He placed a pot of coffee, a tureen of vegetable soup and a tray of sandwiches on the general's small conference table. The smell emanating from the tureen was divine. The steward began to pour two cups of coffee, when the general said, "thank you, we'll serve ourselves."

After the steward left, the general said, "Mindy, what does the military fear most?"

"Casualties?"

"No, bureaucratic loose ends. Some action or event not accounted for by a paper trail. Coffee, Lieutenant?"

"I can get that, sir."

"Stay put, Lieutenant. I'll play mother today."

He ladled soup into two bowls, and then he placed sandwiches onto small plates next to the soup. Finally, he poured two cups of coffee and put three cubes of sugar into each. He smiled and said, "we need the glucose."

The food was good. Her sense of smell hadn't deceived her. Mindy and the General ate without talking. The general slurped up the last bit of soup in his bowl and signed some paperwork. Finally, he said, "nothing will happen because the paperwork is in order. Anyway, what might happen isn't the interesting question."

"Sorry, sir, but I'm beat," Mindy said. "I'm not following you."

"The paperwork reflects that I was the surgeon in charge of the patient you worked on. I signed off on the referenced paperwork. The official record doesn't even reflect you were there. Not one person working in that OR today will support Curry in contradicting the official record. Why should they? My patient is my problem–I'm the big dog on the block. If Curry tries to make this an issue, he'll find himself removing fecal impactions from elderly patients at Walter Reed."

"Rank has its privileges," Mindy said.

"Exactly. Now for the interesting question–how?" As he said this, he leaned forward and stared directly into Mindy's eyes.

"How what, sir?"

"Oh, for crying out loud, Mindy. How many nurses are there in this war that could do what you've done over the last two days?"

"What happened was irregular but I figured you were used to handing cases over when something more urgent came along."

"I've practiced medicine for 30 years and I've never handed a surgical case over to a scrub nurse."

"Then why today, and why me?"

"The case was yesterday. Don't you remember what happened in there?"

"Sir, with all due respect, I think I do. You changed gloves and said, "'next patient'."

The general rested his chin on his fingertips. "That's right, I did say that. Remember why?"

"The liver case came in."

"Not exactly. When I left that boy, he was gone. His injuries were so massive, and his organs so brutally traumatized that I reached the conclusion that he couldn't be saved. All of a sudden, you start yammering about how he's going to bleed out. To be honest, I had lost track of you until you yelled about the nicked artery."

"This makes no sense to me."

The general went to the bulkhead door and checked to make sure no one was waiting to see him.

"I thought you'd gone around the bend Mindy."

"What!"

"I was humoring you - a huge mistake on my part, but that doesn't explain what happened at that table. I let you continue because I thought that boy was already dead. I knew you couldn't hurt him any worse than the Japs had. Somehow, you saved him. Literally snatched him back from the jaws of death. Before I woke you, Doctor Curry and I examined that boy carefully."

The general leaned back in his chair and peered out his portal.

"And?"

"And what?"

"Oh, come on, sir. Now who's being coy?"

"Mindy, he's doing fine. He was sewn up tighter than a drum and his pressure is holding steady albeit after receiving eight units of blood. Looks like he'll live. Back to my question. How in the name of God did you do it?"

"I don't know."

"Try again. The work was flawless."

"You've had me reading Gray's anatomy since we left New Caledonia. I had a clear picture in my mind of what his abdominal cavity should look like and just kept sewing until his insides resembled the picture in my mind. I kept my sutures tight and close together because his tissue looked and felt like it wouldn't hold the stitching otherwise. I had some difficulty reattaching his small intestine to the posterior abdominal wall. The peritoneal membrane was severely lacerated by shrapnel. I was working on that when I nicked the artery and you told me to clamp it."

"You asked me about that artery 30 minutes after I had written the patient off as clinically dead. I'm curious, Lieutenant. You were never unsure of yourself or what you were attempting? You didn't feel inadequate or unprepared to work surgically on another human being?"

"I guess this sounds strange but...no. We were busy. You had moved on, so I just picked up the needle and forceps and went to work."

The general ran his hand through his thinning hair and paced around the stateroom in a small circle.

"Thirty years of medicine and I've never seen the likes of you. Mindy, I intend to arrange for your transfer stateside. Medical school at Johns Hopkins is in your future. At least, I want to have you evaluated by my colleagues on the faculty."

The room began to spin. "Sir? I have quite a bit of commitment left. I don't know if the nursing corps will go for this."

The general smiled and said, "what is the one lesson I have repeated several times during the course of this conversation?"

Mindy yawned and said, "rank has its privileges."

She then slumped down in the chair and fell asleep.

"Remarkable, just remarkable," the general said, covering the blood-spattered nurse with a blanket. He placed a 'do not disturb' sign on his stateroom door and went to find Doctor Curry. He and Jerry needed to talk.

Chapter 44
Perchance to Dream

"The little buggers ain't shooting' at us - yet." Butch O'Halleran said to the wide-eyed fucking new guys. "But, I've seen a whole bunch of what I thought was mockingbirds. But I say to myself, 'Butch', there ain't no fucking mockingbirds on this stinking island. I look again and sure as shit I'm looking at a herd of mosquitoes, biggest I've ever seen headed right for me while my pants are around my knees."

Dud sighed. O'Halleran would talk to a tornado if he thought the whirl of wind would listen. "Butch, leave the greenies alone and get some sleep."

"Yeah, L-T, like we're at the Ritz here, only difference is the hot and cold running scorpions. I also enjoy the room service. Christmas in the South Pacific, should have brought the wife and kids."

"Those skeeters get you, Butch?" Lester Pritchard, one of the newest replacements, asked. "No, but check this out, I was humping the swamps back on the canal..."

Lieutenant Danny, 'Dud' Ludlow looked at his watch. The time was 2234 on Christmas Day, 1943. "Butch was right," Dud said to himself, "New Britain is a real paradise. At least we didn't get our butts handed to us like the Second Marine Division at Tarawa."

"That's because we didn't get hung up on the reefs," Sgt. Louwicky said, as he dropped into the foxhole. "Spending Christmas Day wading through a god-awful swamp and watching guys drown in sinkholes, ain't a barrel of monkeys either though."

"I'm going to shoot you right between your beady eyes the next time you drop into the hole without the password," Dud said, as he twisted his socks to squeeze as much water out of them as he could.

"That's useless, but you knew that already, right?"

Dud drove his helmet into the squishy mud at the bottom of his hole and lit a wax-cardboard fire-starter in the base. He laid his socks over the top of the helmet. He watched to see if any discernable light or smoke was escaping his hole. "Think any smoke is visible?" He and Louwicky stared off towards a point at their two o' clock, where Hill 660 sat. 660 was their next offensive objective.

He heard something from behind him. In one move he drew his .45, cocked it, and crouched into firing position. He whispered, "Johnny." The response came.

"Weissmuller"

O'Halleran dropped into the hole beside him and Louwicky, nearly tipping Dud's drying socks over.

"Sorry L-T."

"What's the word?"

"The company is bedded down as best as it can be under the circumstances. I chewed everybody's ass about keeping their clips dry."

"How are the greenhorns?" Louwicky asked.

"Scared shitless."

"He told them his favorite mosquito story," Dud said.

"Good, scared is good," Louwicky said. "After all, this whole war is a shit sandwich…"

"And there ain't no bread," O' Halleran said, as he left the hole.

"Make sure…"

"Yeah, I know," Louwicky said. "I already told them that."

"You didn't let me finish."

"I told them to keep pecker covers on their bores because we're not killing the enemy with dirty weapons."

"Am I getting that predictable?"

"Only on the worrying part, L-T, only on keeping the babies alive till we can send them home to their mommies."

"You stay alive too, Lou. I'll plant one of my size ten Marine issue boon-dockers up your ass if you turn buzzard entrée on me."

"Aye L-T, why don't you catch some sleep? I'll worry about the babies for a few hours. If the little yellow men pay us a call, I'll wake up your officer ass pronto."

"Insubordination, Lou. All I catch is insubordination from you."

"Aye L-T, make me a sergeant and send me to some pacific hellhole. Go to sleep...sir."

Though the L-T and the Sergeant were barely speaking above a whisper, their voices carried to the men in the company. The give and take was their lullaby. In the muck, amidst the bugs and the falling wounded trees; Company B slept. There was no attack.

The next day Company B stayed put while the Navy and Army Liberators and Mitchell's hit Hill 660. When the sun went down on the 26th, the bomb craters on Hill 660 gave off an eerie light as the heated embers continued to burn.

"Lou, take a good look. We're still alive, but, standing at the gates of hell."

"L-T, in his wildest imagination Dante never conceived of anything that looked like this."

"Listen to you, Lou. That top-notch public school education is showing again."

"I wish P.S. 131 could claim credit. Bunny gave me his copy of *Inferno* to read when he was through with it. I was so bored, I actually read it."

"What'd you think?"

"Like I said, Dante never saw this place. If he had, he would have written about the smell of rotting, burning jungle and the stink of dying."

"No shit. Get down the line, Lou. Tell everyone I want those carbines locked and loaded. I want bayonets fixed. Tell the new babies to do everything the old guys are doing. No shooting unless something's clearly in their field of fire. I don't want our position given away by panic firing. Also I want one guy in each hole awake at all times. No one gets bayoneted in their sleep because we let our guard down."

"Aye L-T, I'm out of this hole."

"Stay low, Lou. We don't appear to be backlit, but if you stick that ugly mug up, a sniper could still nail you."

"No worries, L-T. I'll stay so low that I'll have to look up to see down."

After Lou left, the rain started and didn't stop, or let up. The sky opened up and poured.

"Hope the damn Japs are miserable too," Dud thought. The field phone clicked. "Ludlow, Company B."

"Anything going on, on your piece of the perimeter Danny?"

"No sir, but, my visibility is almost nil. The little yellow guys could be at the wire before we know it."

"Roger that. If our forward observation posts see or hear anything I'll be back to you pronto."

"Aye Colonel."

"Keep up the good work Danny. Hold your position and let me know if anything pops in your sector."

The phone went dead. There was no attack, only rain. Danny hadn't been dry in days.

Company B spent Christmas and New Year's day holed up in the rain. Then, the Japs attacked.

"You'd think the little bastards would learn that their signal flares back light them," Dud said.

"I'm glad they're slow studies myself, L-T."

Dud felt the two Jap sappers before he saw them.

Lou was quicker and got the first one in the head. The dead yellow guy fell on Dud. The second one screamed, while arming the fuse on his charge, and then he too tried to jump into the hole. Louwicky caught him in mid-air. The Jap caught hold of Lou's shirt and they both tumbled down the hill.

Dud heard someone screaming and realized that the scream was his. The charge went off. Twenty minutes later the Japanese charge was over, the Marine's concentrated fire having decimated them. Mounds of Japanese lay, like driftwood, just inside the Marine perimeter.

When dawn came and there was enough light, a detail went down the hill to search for Lou. When they came back they told Dud they'd found his tags. They didn't elaborate and Dud didn't press them. The blood-caked tags told the story.

Dud put Louwicky in for a Silver Star. The medal wasn't much, but the citation was the only gesture Dud could think of that might help Lou's family weather the grief.

"Lieutenant, I want you to try your hand at writing a letter home to Sergeant Louwicky's parents," the Colonel said. Dud paused; he wanted to say, "go eat shit without the shingle." Then, he saw the huge stack of drafts the Colonel had already written himself and said, "yes, sir, I'll write the draft."

This is what Dud wrote.

Dear Mrs. Louwicky:
Frank saved my life. He died in my place. We once had to stand guard duty naked during boot camp. I don't even remember why now. I just know that after we did we were fast friends.

I will never understand why certain men are so brave that they accomplish noble deeds without hesitation. Perhaps, because war, as horrid as it is, truly raises in some men the ability to care for their comrades in arms more than they care for themselves. Frank was one of these men.

I know you will grieve for Frank. I will too. Take some small measure of comfort in the fact that Frank was a brave and heroic man. He was fearless in the face of his enemies and loyal to his friends. He was and always will be a Marine.
God grant you serenity during your bereavement.
Respectfully,
Daniel Ludlow, 1ˢᵗ Lt, USMC

The Colonel read the letter and said, "I'm sending this one out as is. I'll send out my own letter later. By the way, tell your men to prepare to bug out. We've been relieved."

"Aye, sir."

"Good job on the letter, Danny. I know writing these is a tough chore. I appreciate the effort."

The Colonel sighed and ran his hand through his close-cropped hair.

"I write these letters in my dreams now Danny. I am living my life in a combat zone being followed around by ghosts. Sometimes I just run out of words."

"Sir, there are no words to describe any part of this. I mean, where do you begin?"

"I don't know," the Colonel said. "Perhaps, by honoring all the men and women who rise through everything to become better or greater than what they were before - men like you."

"I'm not a great man. I'm certainly no Frank Louwicky, sir."

"Thirty men or more are hoping and praying that you are great. Great enough to get them home alive. I'll worry about the ghosts. You're job is to watch over the Marines who're still with us on this piece of dirt."

"Aye, sir." Danny snapped off a salute and went to find his men.

The Colonel called in an orderly "Prepare the necessary paperwork and forward it to Division expediting Lieutenant Ludlow's promotion to Captain."

"Yes sir."

After the orderly left, the Colonel opened his desk and stared at all the dog tags lying in the drawer. Finally, he shut the drawer, and then placed the finished letters in a folio. He headed for the field mail depot to mail them himself. Posting these was too solemn a task to delegate.

Chapter 45
On Holiday

"I didn't realize we'd be spending our entire shore leave on a train crossing the Australian continent."

"Better than walking, Bob. Where we're going is far from the ocean. I don't want to see a drop of water for the next two weeks."

Bob snorted from across the aisle.

"Still a smart ass huh Will? Glad the war hasn't changed everything."

Bob lifted his hat brim from his eyes and said, "how about a stroll?"

Will got up and followed Bob to the door at the end of the compartment.

"Let's walk along the top of the train," Bob said. "Gets us away from all the prying eyes and ears."

"Lead on Commander, your wish is my command."

"Sarcasm really doesn't suit you, Will."

They walked onto the carriage platform and studied the pitch and yaw of the train as it wended its way through the Outback to Kalgoorlie. Will went first. Compared to the motion on a combat sub, walking along the top of the train was like walking in a park. When Will got on top, he walked along with his eyes closed and his arms outstretched like a tightrope walker. When he reached the end he turned around and came back in six or seven leaps across the spine of the car.

Bob sat Indian-style watching him.

"Damn show off. What's wrong with you?"

"I'm so glad to be away from water–and alive. Hard to believe most of the crew isn't even going to leave port on R&R."

"Speaking of crews, wonders never cease. Couldn't believe my eyes when I saw your name on that muster list. Now I think you've headed round the bend."

"Can you blame me?"

"No, not really," Bob said. "I get the creeps just thinking about being locked in a tube underwater with sixty other swinging dicks."

"Sorry you feel that way because you're going to get your chance," I said. "Hope you're not claustrophobic."

"I can handle a couple of days while we install and field test my gizmo," Bob said, as he tried to light a cigarette. He decided lighting anything was a waste of time in the air turbulence.

"Better enjoy your next patrol, orders are being cut to reassign you," Bob said.

"I'm okay with that," Will said. "On our last patrol, we nearly had a fish in one of the stern tubes detonate on us. I helped blow the damn thing out using air pressure. That was my eighth life. I only have one left. The Navy will take it too given the opportunity. I'll take my chances with the spooks."

"We'll see how you feel after you've been around them for awhile. In her last letter, Bett told me that she thinks some G-men types are following her." Bob suddenly pointed. "Damn, look at that."

Will's eyes followed Bob's finger. The sun was going down and its' rays were painting the outback a brilliant red-gold.

"That's stunning. Prettier than the Red River in the spring," Will said.

"Ain't it a pisser that the only reason we're getting to see the outback is because the fucking Japs can't behave."

"So, what's this about Betty being followed?"

"Normally, in Capistrano, there aren't many big black sedans with suits sitting in them reading newspapers. Lately though, wherever she happens to be, there's always a suit sitting in a black car."

"Have they said anything to her?"

"Nope, they just follow her."

"Have you spoken to your mysterious boss about this?"

"Hell no Will. Don't be a dope. I figure he's the one responsible. If I talk to him, he'll change the tail. At least we know where they are, even if we don't know why they're nosing around."

As the sun went down, the air grew cold. The men climbed back down onto the carriage platform.

"I'll say one thing in their favor," Bob said. "Bett says they've spooked my mother-in-law. She's staying on her best behavior lest the suits take her away."

Bob dropped with a thump beside Will onto the carriage platform.

"What about your father-in-law's behavior, Bob?"

Bob's eyes darkened, as he pursed his lips. "Robert Stevens gives me a hernia. The slimy little creep wants to come out and see his grandkids. What am I supposed to say?"

"No?" Will said.

"No is a great answer. I don't want him within a hundred miles of my wife and kids."

Bob successfully lit a cigarette on the platform; he took a deep drag, and then offered it to Will.

"Problem is, can't tell Bett to tell her old man to go piss up a rope in a high wind. Won't win that one."

"I'll be glad to piss on him for you, if I ever get the chance."

Bob draped his arm over my shoulders.

"Will, if that day ever comes, you'll be waiting your turn, behind me."

Kalgoorlie was a wild mining town in the southern outback, roughly 200 miles away from water - dry as a bone. I loved it. Bob made a good impression right away. He got drunker than a well digger on holiday and proceeded to urinate into the gutter on Hannan Street. When the Constables showed up while Bob was in the midst of relieving himself, they were in no mood to play around.

"Hey, what's this, you sotted Yank. No pissing here!"

"Piss off you underground limeys! Rousting me just because I'm American. I've seen at least ten Aussies pissing off the curb tonight."

The senior constable struck Bob's left knee with his billy.

As Bob fell on the walk, the Constable said, "here now, Yank, let's show a little courtesy. You wouldn't want us to come away with a bad impression of America, would you?"

His partner thought this remark was a riot and kicked Bob in the gut to show his amusement.

I'd missed everything to this point. I came around the corner just as Bob vomited what was still in his stomach onto the street.

"Look here Yank, we ask you not to piss on our streets. So, what do you go and do? You chuckie. We don't much care for that either."

"Gentlemen?" Both constables turned to stare at me. The younger one said, "you this Yank's mate?"

"Yes, and while I understand he isn't the most polite Yank in town, he's had enough."

Bob tried to get up. The Sergeant, without taking his eyes off me, slammed his right boot into Bob's chest. "Stay put for a moment, mate, until we decide what's up with your bugger-eyed friend here."

I took a piece of paper out of my pocket and held it up in the air so the constables could see it.

"Could one of you call this number? I won't move, and neither will Bob."

By now a crowd had gathered. I heard several people shout, "yeah, we won't move either."

The Sergeant took the number from me. He squinted at it and said, "this is a Sydney number."

"Yes, it is, Sergeant."

The constable told his partner to stay next to Bob and then he looked at me and said, "don't you go anywhere either. If this is some dance hall full of skimpies, I'll bust your head when I get back."

"Like I said Sergeant, I'm not going anywhere."

We stood around and stared at each other for ten minutes. A couple of people shouted, "you Yanks act like you own the place." Some others shouted, "got your balls in a crank now."

The Sergeant finally came back, looked at his partner, and said, "get him up." Once Bob was on his feet, the Sergeant said, "okay, let's move. We're headed to the Gibson."

His partner said, "Brian, have you lost your mind? This Yank is headed for lock-up."

The Sergeant turned red and said, "Officer Kenna, do not call me by my Christian name while we're on duty. Get the muck out and hear me. We're for the Gibson, now move out. He looked at me and said, "stay where I can see you, boy."

When we got to the hotel, just up the street, the constables dumped Bob on a couch in the lobby. The Sergeant came up to me and said, "that number was the private line for the Chief of Constabulary."

I shrugged but didn't say how I'd gotten the number.

He sighed. "I'm not denying that we need you Yanks. Would be nice, though, if the lot of you could behave like you weren't born in a sty. We're rough out here, boy, but we don't like being insulted. Your mate there was right. We do look the other way when some of our boys piss in the street." He straightened his tie. "After all, the street's ours, not yours."

He proceeded to brush the dust off his boots with one of Bob's pant legs. Bob was snoring and could have cared less. His partner sneered at me. I forced myself to be calm.

"If I run into you two again. Even if you're only thinking about spitting, much less pissing in public I'll lock you both down no matter how important you are to the bullock's war effort."

With that he turned on his heel and said, "come along, Kenna. I've had quite enough of this lot."

"Indeed," Kenna said. Then, he trotted out of the lobby after the Sergeant.

"Damn, that was one mean cop." Bob was staring at the gilt ceiling from the couch.

"Damn it, Bob, when are you going to get the clue? Tonight looked like your same old shit, only on a different continent."

Bob sat up slowly and said, "when you're right, you're right. I shouldn't have taken those guys on drunk."

"That wasn't my point at all."

"I know I was pulling your chain."

"Well stop yanking. This isn't Gainesville, and we aren't quarreling over smokes. When are you going to grow up? You're always talking about your family and how you miss them, then, you pull crap like this. I don't want to be a bit player anymore in your vaudeville act. You'll end up getting us either hurt or killed."

"Know what I liked most about California Street, Will?"

I sat down next to him. "I thought Betty was the only thing you liked on California Street ... or anywhere else, for that matter."

"Guess when the sum is toted up, I'm in way over my head. I can't explain what I mean, I'm not allowed to. Let's just say, I'm a little shaky right now. Events are moving too fast."

Bob peered around the deserted lobby. We were the only people there along with the potted palms, the gilt ceiling, and the fans - squeaking like they hadn't been oiled in a century.

"I saw your name on that sub muster, and I nearly jumped out of my shorts. I mean Jesus, someone I knew. Sounds dumb, but I was happy tonight. Getting drunk, and then getting beat on–tonight felt like old times."

Bob rubbed his hands through his hair and slowly stood.

"I know we can't go back, Will. I give you a hard time, but I've always liked you because you're smart. The last thing I want is to get you, or anyone else, killed. I'm just trying to escape the feeling that I'm a boxer at a poodle show."

"A boxer at a poodle show, Bob? That Sergeant kicked you harder than I thought. Come on I'll buy you a drink."

"Are you kidding? If we get tossed, Sergeant Hardballs and Officer Hairball will be back on us."

"Won't get tossed from here, Bob. We own the joint. I plunked twenty thousand American on the desk, and the Commander wired me twenty more from Sydney. He told me to tell you that you probably won't get paid for the rest of the war. The twenty grand is coming out of your pay."

"How the hell did you reach him?"

"I didn't, the Constabulary in Sydney did."

"Huh?"

"My sub skipper passed a number and a code word along to me. He told me to use it if I had any foreign agent contacts. When I saw that you were in trouble with the local law enforcement folks, I figured that qualified as a foreign agent contact. I asked the Constabulary to patch me through to the number and when they did, I mouthed the code word. The Commander and the Chief Constable had some words and, then hocus pocus; you're in a hotel rather than jail."

"Well, I'll be dipped in manure and hung up to dry."

"You're under house arrest, by the way. You can't leave this hotel until we board our train back in four days."

"Is the bar well-stocked?"

"Yep."

"Guess there are worse things than house arrest. Last one to the bar is a Japanese cave dweller with no ammo."

"Bob, if we live through this, I'm going to find a poodle show somewhere and make you go."

"Hell, if we live through this, I'll buy myself a poodle–to feed to my boxer."

"I thought you discarded the Jack, mate. Bloody hell."

Sergeant Brian Maitland gave Officer Jimmy Kenna a fish eye.

"Officer Kenna, he sloughed the queen. You have the memory of a baboon in heat. I'm out too."

The two constables had shown up the next day to check up on us and had been persuaded to stay for a friendly game of cards. The cards had not been kind to them.

I raked the pot in and asked, "Sergeant allow me a nosy question and I'll return the money you just lost in this pot to your side of the table."

Brian Maitland lit his pipe, blew a cloud of blue smoke my way, then said, "Ask, but if I don't like the question, I'm closing your bar and impounding the liquor."

"What does an Australian constable make in a month?"

Sergeant Maitland considered.

"I make about two fifty a month, American."

I pushed twenty dollars in chips back across the table.

"Have you ever considered the hotel business?"

"Can't say that I have."

"Here's the deal. Bob and I are leaving soon."

"More's the pity," Jimmy Kenna said.

"Shut up Jimmy. The lad here is talking."

"The previous owner has been bought out by my employer, Uncle Sam, and me. We're joint owners of this fine establishment. Once we're gone, we have no further use for a hotel in Kalgoorlie. Thought you and Officer Jimmy here might."

Sergeant Maitland pulled on his pipe for a moment and said, "are you daft? I don't know what you put up but I couldn't come near to matching whatever the amount was."

"Put your twenty dollars back in the pot."

I placed the deck of cards in front of Jimmy Kenna and said, "shuffle Jimmy." We all sat silently as Jimmy shuffled. He offered me the cut. I tapped the top of the deck and asked, "first or second draw, Sergeant?"

"Brian Maitland stared and said; "again, I ask are you completely daft? This place is worth $30,000 American if it's worth a shilling. Are we cutting for the Gibson?"

"We are. First or second draw?"

"Second, if you please."

I drew a card off the top of the deck, a jack, and turned it over on the felt.

"Bloody Hell, you're trying to give this place away, and you draw a jack."

The Sergeant drew his card and without looking at it, slammed it down on the felt.

"Law enforcement is going to miss you, Sergeant. The paperwork and linens alone will keep you too busy for the Constabulary. The office paperwork is stacked behind the bar. Before we leave tomorrow, we'll go to the bank together to confirm the transfer."

Maitland sat, staring wide-eyed at the queen he'd slapped on the table.

"Gentlemen," I said. "I'd say this turn of events calls for drinks all around."

Bob headed for the bar, returning with a bottle of Bush Mills and four shot glasses. The Sergeant poured, and then lifted his glass to propose a toast, "To the President of the United States," we all responded, "To the President."

I took the bottle and proposed a second toast, "To the Honorable Prime Minister, Pig Iron Bob." All responded, "To Pig Iron Bob."

The deal was done. I'd owned an Australian hotel for two days, and then given the establishment away. The next morning as we were leaving the bank, the soon-to-be former Sergeant Maitland smiled at Bob and said, "go ahead, piss on the street. If you're of a mind to."

Bob laughed, "thanks Sergeant, but this isn't my street to piss on. I'm a visitor here."

As we turned to leave for the train station, Sergeant Maitland said, "stay alive, Yank. Losing such a good card cheat would be a damn shame."

"Without turning around, I said, "you saw that, huh?"

"As deft as I've seen, lad. I'd have drawn a sixer otherwise."

As I walked away, I said, "yes, but then I'd have been stuck with a hotel in the Outback, mate."

The last thing I heard was Brian Maitland's hoarse laugh as I headed out. Bob was waiting for me on the platform.

"Does he know you cheated?"

"Damn, am I losing my touch here or what?"

"I didn't see the play. However, I've never known you to lose a draw on a face card."

"I didn't tell him, but he let me know he was onto me. Sure wouldn't want to be someone who pisses Brian Maitland off. He's meaner than you and he misses nothing."

"Tell me about it," Bob replied. "Kicked the stuffing out of me, didn't even work up a sweat."

The train pulled out of the station in a whirl of smoke and blowing red dust. The date was January, 1944, and we were headed back to the war.

Chapter 46
Last Moment for a Hero

"Tango Delta one four, we have feathered engines two and four."

"Roger that, Delta Dawn," Wat Eakins said. "I confirm two and four are feathered."

"Black Bishop, I don't know if we're going to make it. Our oil pressure is down to eighty-six and our fuel load is down to 1200 pounds."

Wat grimaced. If Bobby Joe Wallace of Macon, Georgia was scared enough to squawk his call sign, he was truly scared.

"Jettison stuff, Tango. We got to get you over the cliffs. I'm not going to be the first red tail to lose a fortress."

The Messerschmitt contingent came out of nowhere. Four Me-109s looking for an easy kill. Wat was underneath the Flying Fortress looking for landing gear damage when he caught the glint of their wings in his peripheral vision. Wat glanced at his fuel. His P-51 had a British designed paper belly tank with about two hundred pounds of fuel sloshing around in it. His wing tanks were eighty-six - dry as the Sahara.

"That's why I get flight pay," Wat said to himself. "Wish swimming lessons were in the package too."

Wat rolled out and came up underneath the bogeys with his cannon blazing. One of the German bogeys exploded. Wat noticed that the B-47's nose and waist guns had opened up.

"Don't hit the good guy, Delta."

"Roger Bishop, watch your six."

"Roger Delta, head for the deck. I'll try to ruin their day."

"Godspeed and happy hunting, Bishop."

The only good thing about his fuel situation was his performance. He was light and, therefore, better able to maneuver. He pulled back on the stick and climbed steeply. Tracer rounds zipped by him. The Krauts pursued like a pack of dogs. Wat throttled back and nosed the plane over. He waggled his wings in an attempt to fake a death spin. The G-force began to pound him as his rate of descent increased. The German pilots were surprised by his dive maneuver. They hesitated. He killed one with a close range machine gun burst. The debris filled fireball slammed into him as he executed an aileron roll to his left to try and avoid the fatal collision. His flaming aircraft rolled out of the collision and clipped the third German bogey.

The pilot of this bogey ditched. Wat Eakins, however, was dead in the air over Western France, on his 10th combat mission. His dog tags and one badly charred flight boot were turned over to the Allies by the French underground. Nothing else was left of the man who could run with a football faster than the devil himself.

The fourth German fighter violated a cardinal rule by leaving his wingman. The Delta Dawn turned his left wing into Swiss cheese as he made a strafing pass over the Channel. The Kraut pilot decided the Fortress was not an easy kill after all. He limped home to Cherbourg wondering how his comrades had fared. The Fortress crew swore later that waves from the Channel slapped their wings as they fought a crippled plane and gravity to gain enough altitude to clear the cliffs at Dover.

Captain Bobby Joe Wallace filed his report detailing Black Bishop's heroics. He recommended that Lieutenant Eakins of Gainesville, Texas receive the

Distinguished Flying Cross. He recalled asking Eakins over an open mike on a previous mission 'whether niggers were liked any better in Texas then they were in Georgia.' Wat had responded, saying, "naw, Texas crackers are just as prejudiced as Georgia ones." Wallace recalled that Wat's voice hadn't even betrayed any anger, only resignation.

After Captain Wallace filed his report, he waited several hours in the tower, hoping to hear a radio squawk from Black Bishop. One never came. Wallace walked across the tarmac to a waiting crew jeep.

"Your crew told me to come back for you," the driver said. "They said you were going extra innings on the flight line."

"Yeah, we had our bacon saved today by one shit hot pilot," Wallace said. "Took on four Me - 109's, no problem. I know damn well that he didn't have any fuel left - he took them on anyway to buy us time."

"The word is he was from that nigger outfit," the driver said. "Glad to see one of them finally did something useful."

"Stop the jeep, Sergeant."

The driver stopped the vehicle.

The Captain came around to the driver's side and said, "get out. That's a direct order."

"Captain, I don't want any trouble here."

"Too late, Sergeant," Wallace said. "I'll give you the first punch. You have ten seconds. Then, I'm going to deck you."

The Sergeant took a roundhouse swing, which Captain Wallace blocked; Wallace then punched the Sergeant hard in the stomach. He straightened his hat and jacket, and then helped the Sergeant lean against the side of the jeep. He squatted in front of the gasping man.

"Sergeant, if you want to file specifications against me, I'll be at the provost Marshall's office at 0700 in the morning. I will not dispute any allegation you make. I, too, have called these black pilots *niggers* before, but I'll never use the word again. Nor do I care to hear the word again, especially in reference to the man who saved my entire crew."

The Captain and the Sergeant got back in the jeep. They drove back to officer crew quarters in silence. Captain Wallace waited thirty minutes at the provost Marshall's office the next morning.

The driver never showed.

Wallace went out to the flight line where maintenance crews were scurrying over his plane like an ant colony. He found the crew chief and said, "repaint the mascot. This aircraft is now 'Black Bishop.' I'll tell the CO myself."

"Anything you say, Captain."

The newly christened Black Bishop flew daylight raids over Berlin, repeat missions over the aircraft manufacturing plant at Regensburg, and bombed communications centers located in Dresden and Hamburg. The German counter air defenses were formidable. The Black Bishop came home from these missions without a mar on her paint. Captain Wallace and the crew never spoke about their good fortune, but whenever anyone asked them about their uncanny luck, all anyone said was, "luck? Screw luck. Wat was flying top cover for us."

Chapter 47
Home is Where the Heart is

February 27, 1944

Dear Wilson:

I have been remiss in writing you for awhile. I'm glad Ralph has written you occasionally. Frankly, I have no idea what exactly to write to a son at war. My daily activities haven't changed. The sewing, cooking, cleaning, pickling, canning, and gossiping is as banal now as when you were home. The only thing is that some people are crankier than before the war. They grow impatient with shortages. In the Paulsen Bakery the other day, Mrs. Patrick bought the last lemon pie. Mr. Paulsen announced he was closing for the month because he couldn't get anymore flour or sugar until the first of the month.

Further back in the line, Mrs. Pike said, "when is this damned war going to be over? Can't our boys do a better job against the lousy Germans?" Mrs. Patrick walked over and smashed her lemon pie in Mrs. Pike's face, saying, "here, take my pie." Mrs. Pike failed to remember that Mrs. Patrick's only son, Lyle, was blown to smithereens at Anzio.

This brings me to why I'm writing you. I have prayed hard about this. Ralph would have told you before now, but I wouldn't let him. George, that is, Mr. Chaney, told me you were a man and were entitled to know. So, here it is, Wat Eakins was killed over France. There is some big debate in Congress about whether he's entitled to some medal or other for saving the plane he was escorting. I personally can't see it makes a whisker of difference to his mama. Dead is dead. George, however, says, "Elizabeth, how Wat is treated makes all the difference in the world. If the poor boy doesn't get his medal, his family will have been dealt a grave injustice."

I'm troubled that George is a member of the race that persecuted our Lord, Jesus. As he reminds me though, Jesus was a Jew. I have thought on this and prayed on it. I am now convinced that our association is the Lord's will. So, I wanted to let you know that George and I are getting married two weeks from now in a civil ceremony.

I hope and pray that you'll accept this and not see the marriage as a slight to your father's memory. He was a scoundrel and a card player - but I did love him, as I love you.

Love,
Mom

I read this letter while sitting in the crew mess on the Starkfish. I was astonished. She hadn't been merely remiss–she'd never written me. "Good-bye Wat," I whispered. "You'll be missed."

Bob stormed in at this point and said, "know what my father-in-law is pulling?"

"I have no damn idea, Bob."

Bob squinted at me. "Hey, what's up? Someone piss in your coffee?"

"Got a letter from my mother."

"Yep," Bob said. "That'll fuck up your day every time."

"Shut up and uncork your ears for two shakes. This news should interest you too."

Bob waited.

"Wat Eakins was killed over France about three months ago. He was escorting a bomber and although my mom doesn't say what he did to save the bomber; a debate is raging in Congress over whether to award him a medal."

Bob dropped his head for a moment and said, "doesn't surprise me. Wat was a born leader and certainly no coward."

"What, Bob? You of all people complimenting Wat? He was black, after all."

"Bust my balls if you need to," Bob said. "I probably have it coming. Tact's never been my strong suit. Just because Wat was black doesn't mean I didn't see him for what he was. That day we played football together, I taunted him to distract him. If I hadn't, those boys would've killed us. I was surprised when you ended up hurt. I figured they'd come after me."

"They meant to come after you; I was in the wrong place at the wrong time."

"Well, there you go," Bob said. "I'd have saved you if I could have. You were too stubborn to admit you had no business lining up against Wat and Pancake."

"What about the Klan, Bob?"

"What about it?"

"Word was that you were big into the Klan."

Bob laughed. "I have to get back to the radio room, but let me educate you on a few things. I was practically dragged to a couple of Klan meetings. Certain upstanding members of Gainesville society, including my father-in-law, wanted me to be an enforcer. Wanted me to do their dirty work. They asked me, no that's too nice; they demanded that I burn George Chaney's store down. Apparently several merchants were furious that Chaney undercut their trade with the blacks. When I refused, I lost my job."

Bob lowered his voice and ran his fingers through his hair. "Stevens told people I was fired to get me away from his daughter," Bob said. "Wasn't that though. At a Klan rally, he told me that if I chased off the Jewish

350

nigger lover, I could screw his daughter until my balls turned blue. I wanted to kill him on the spot."

"Bob, I had no idea."

"You weren't supposed to - you were only a kid then." As he got up to leave he said, "now that same scum bucket wants to take my son back to Gainesville to raise, Bet has written me about his bullshit. He's shown up in California and started calling Bet and me incompetent parents."

With that, Bob headed back to continue his work on the gizmo installation. I had a date with a fouled-up oil filter. As Chief Bunton walked by, he heard me mumbling.

"What'd you say, Davis?"

"Nothing important, Chief," I said, "*people and their secrets* is all I was mumbling.'"

Chapter 48
Stateside

November 7, 1943

Dear Aunt Shannon:

Strange circumstance is now my bedfellow. I am being assigned to Walter Reed, but that is official pretense. Once here, orders will be cut assigning me to Johns Hopkins to complete medical training. Yes, that's right, an MD. Can you believe it? My mentor is convinced that I'll make a gifted surgeon. We'll see. I remain unconvinced that the powers that be will tolerate someone with no penis in their midst.

I haven't told my parents. I want to tell them in person about my entrance into such a 'manly profession'. My wartime experiences haven't been pleasant, but they have awakened something in me. I have a sense of purpose and worth beyond my years. I hope that doesn't change once I'm stateside again. See you soon. Hope this letter finds you well.

All My Love

Mindy

Chapter 49
Service Star

November 10, 1943

Dear Danny,

I'm glad to hear that you're doing so well with the Marines. Hearing that your good friend from training school was killed made me very sad. Even your daddy read your last letter. He ran out to tell all of his friends that he wasn't saluting you just because you were an officer now. You probably won't believe this, but your dad's so proud of you. He keeps telling people that his boy is going to single-handedly kick the Japs back to Tokyo. Before you joined up, he didn't even know where Tokyo was.

He would be mad knowing I told you this, but he checks the paper everyday for news about the war in the Pacific. He's even cut back on his drinking so he'll be sober enough to read the morning paper. He also makes sure the service star in the window is visible every morning; our milkman has heard that you are now a Marine Officer everyday for the last week.

Danny, I know your father has never done right by you and I haven't been such a good parent either. Still, you need to know that we are paying attention and we love you more than anything. Guess I feel sad that we chased you into a war before we could tell you that. What I am proudest of is that you have not let our failures become your failures.

Be careful, Danny. May God protect and shield you. Come home soon.

Love
Mama

Honorable Sam Rayburn
Speaker
United States House of Representatives
Washington, DC

Dear Mr. Speaker:

I am a constituent from Gainesville Texas. But, I am writing this letter on behalf of Will Davis, another constituent, whom you met at the train station in Dallas when he was on his way to Iowa. Mr. Johnson was with you at the time. Will asked me to write you because he doesn't believe a letter from him would make it through the censors.

Mr. Speaker, young Mr. Davis is concerned that a young black man from Gainesville, who was killed over France, will be deprived of justice even in death. I don't know if you are aware of the circumstances surrounding Airman Eakins' demise. His aircraft was destroyed while he was engaged in an air battle with four Messerschmitts. His actions saved the crewmembers in a severely damaged B-47. By saving the B-47, Airman Eakins upheld his unit's record, for not losing a single bomber to enemy fighter action. He was and always will be a Tuskegee Airman.

I have no idea whether you can assist in persuading your fellow members to overcome their fears to do what is appropriate. For his efforts, Airman Eakins is entitled to a Distinguished Flying Cross. Captain Wallace, who commanded the B-47 Wat Eakins saved, said to me and I quote, "Lt Eakins intentionally sacrificed himself and his aircraft to give me and my nine crew members a chance to make it back to our base in England. We made it, and he didn't. I have yet to witness a greater act of courage in this war."

Mr. Davis wanted me to pass along that Wat Eakins was not only a friend, but also an American who gave his devotion to men who, on the ground, detested *him. If this is not heroic behavior, what does 'heroic' mean, Mr. Speaker?*

Respectfully,
George Chaney

Sam Rayburn dropped the letter on his desk, and rubbed his temples.

"What are you going to do, Mr. Sam?"

"I don't know, Lyndon. The man is right, of course."

The Speaker of the House, arguably the most influential man in the government, next to President Roosevelt, got up to pour himself three fingers of bourbon. He held the bottle towards Mr. Johnson.

"No sir, I'm good for the moment."

Mr. Sam twirled the amber liquid in his glass, and then downed it in one quick swallow.

"How we treat colored people in this country has been a national disgrace since our beginning. Our track record on the issue of race relations in this country is a stain upon our Constitution, and, further, is an issue that won't go away."

The Speaker sat back down in his high-backed desk chair and picked the letter back up. "The ugly truth is that for every George Chaney and Will Davis out there, I have fifty God-fearing Christian constituents who'd hang me in effigy if I publicly supported Negro rights."

"True, Mr. Sam, true enough," Johnson swung his long leg over the chair's arm. Here though, you might get away with supporting this poor boy for a medal. He did kill three or four Nazi Huns before crashing his plane."

"Lyndon, are you suggesting that Wat Eakins got lucky before he managed to kill himself doing a white man's job?"

"Mr. Sam, I am suggesting that to gain support for what we need to do here, you simply let people think whatever they want."

The Speaker grinned widely. "I assume you want to get this dead aviator his medal."

"Precisely, Mr. Sam. My only regret is that he's not a Navy man like myself. May I have that refresher now?"

"Help yourself, Lyndon. I'm going to call some folks on this."

Chapter 50
Service of Process

"Daddy, I love you but if you don't get out of my house this very minute, I *will* pull this trigger. Bob taught me how to shoot before he left; he figured you'd pull a stunt like this."

Robert Stevens put down the suitcase filled with his grandson's clothes, then, leaned against the doorjamb. "If you do, you'll lose both your babies for sure."

"Maybe I will, daddy, but you won't be around to poison their minds. Now, get out and leave Conor's case right there."

"Honey, this is already over. The boy is already gone."

"What!" Without dropping the weapon, Bet motioned her father into the hall, where she peered into Conor's bedroom. Sure enough, he was gone.

Bet screamed, "mother!"

"Don't worry, Betty. The boy is perfectly safe. You can see him again when you come to your senses." When he turned to leave his sobbing daughter, he jumped in surprise. A man stood on the front porch. Wearing a dark suit and tie, the man stepped up and flashed a badge. "Are you Robert Stevens of Gainesville, Texas?"

Stevens nodded.

"May I come in please?"

"Suit yourself," Stevens squinted at the I.D. card, "Agent Park, I'm leaving."

Agent Park opened the screen door and came in.

"Careful Agent, my daughter is armed. I'll understand if you need to arrest her."

"Quite the contrary, Mr. Stevens, I have a federal warrant for *your* arrest. We have information that you have conspired to take a kidnap victim across state lines. Further, we understand that the State of Texas has requested your extradition on suspicion of murder."

Stevens's mouth dropped open. He didn't resist as the agent slapped cuffs on his wrists.

"Sounds like an interesting case," Agent Park said. "The Mexican government is interested in talking to you as well. They're claiming jurisdiction in the same murder case the Texas authorities want to talk to you about. Come along, Mr. Stevens."

As they proceeded out the door, Melrose Stevens came up the walk holding Conor.

"You betrayed me, Rose."

"Robert, you've become an evil, mean-spirited man. Your grandson will not be. Besides, I didn't have to go far. We wouldn't have gotten a block with this sweet baby. The FBI has been watching us for weeks now. What in hell is the murder accusation all about?"

"I haven't the slightest."

"Of course, dear."

"Watch your head, Stevens," Agent Park said, as he placed him into the back seat of his sedan.

Betty and her mother watched them drive off.

"Lawyer," Robert said out the back window, as they faded away.

Agent Park had left a number for them to call if they wanted to locate Robert later.

Betty turned and stared at her mother.

"You knew Daddy was planning to take my son, and said nothing?"

When Melrose handed Conor to Betty, he grabbed a handful of her hair.

Melrose then sat on the front porch and sighed, as she looked over the small front yard.

"Yes, but, I knew this house was under surveillance," she said. "I would never have allowed your father to step outside of this yard with my grandson. Your father hasn't been quite right for some time. He's the last person I'd trust with my grandbabies." She lowered her head into her hands and cried.

Betty sat beside her on the stoop. Conor took one look at his grandmother and also started to cry. Betty thought crying under the circumstances was a pretty good idea. So, she started in too. This is how Louiza Rojas found them five minutes later.

"This war needs to be over quickly," she said. "We are not doing so well here without our man."

Chapter 51
Reading the Mail

November 11, 1943
Brett Andrews
122 W. 57th
New York, New York

Dear Will:

Never mind how I got your address. I had a glass of orange juice (with a splash of icy vodka) for breakfast this morning...and thought of you. A group of us went down to Minton's Playhouse on 52nd Street last Monday night to hear Bird Parker and Dizzy Gillespie play–both on the same night! You too appreciate music...in addition to being a rather nice pitcher.

I don't know if I can get any bebop artists into my place - they're a tightly knit bunch who don't much care if white folks hear them or not. Still, the twelve - note arrangements these guys come up with are to die for. The arrangements we heard Monday night are coming out on the Decca label. I'm thinking of starting my own recording group. Les McShaun has offered to help get it off the ground if I decide to give it a go.

Wish you were here. I'd let you drink champers out of whichever one of my heels you wanted...left or right. Stay safe. I don't know why you haunt me so. I guess high fast ballers are just hard to come by...

Make sure you come back this way when the war gets tired of you, baby.

Love,
Brett

Will sighed as he read the letter. He'd had one episode of fairly strange sex with the woman, who did intrigue him - and she was offering to let him drink bubbly from her shoes. The country must be hurting for young able-bodied men for Brett Andrews to spend any time thinking about him, let alone writing him a love letter. Will marveled at the thought. A love letter from a gorgeous woman with a ton of money and looks to match. Wonders never cease, Will thought.

Gainesville seemed far away, even farther than 52nd Street in New York. He tried to picture what would happen if Brett and his mother ever met. He shuddered. His mother had thought Mindy was too racy for him. Will laughed out loud, which earned him a chorus of "shut the fuck up!" remarks from the other crewman in their bunks trying to get some rack time.

"Yeah, yeah ladies shut your pie holes," He said, with no rancor in his voice. They were right. He needed to shut up and get some sleep. He sniffed the letter again; the stationary had been soaked in an exotic perfume. He stuffed the missive in his dungaree shirt pocket and closed his eyes.

Chapter 52
Playing Doctor

Doctor Douglas Chamberlain tapped the introduction letter he'd just read on the blotter that was centered on his desk.

"Young lady, I greatly respect George Scranton's views, but, I must tell you your presence has raised a lot of eyebrows."

"Mine have raised several times already, sir," Mindy said.

Chamberlain quit tapping the letter and said, "you can't imagine how hard this will be on you. For starters, you'll have to take two years of leveling courses just to know enough to start our medical degree program. You don't have German, Latin, chemistry, or biology. If you fail *any* courses, I'll wash you out of here quicker than you can say 'doctor.'"

Mindy sat stock still as the man who held her immediate fate in his hands opened the window behind his desk. He turned back around to face her.

"Don't repeat this to anyone but these days I often think about my medical school experiences. One time, I'd gone 40 hours without any sleep. I was a fourth year at the time and interning at the school hospital. I had to sleep or die. No one cared at all. We were busy treating train wreck victims. Finally, I found a janitor's closet filled with mops, buckets, brooms, and tins of floor polish. I crawled to the very back of the closet and covered myself with painting drop cloths so that if anyone came by and casually peeked in they wouldn't see me."

Doctor Chamberlain rocked back and forth in his chair. "I slept for ten hours in that closet, the janitor discovered me the next morning. I got up, straightened out my jacket and worked for another six hours before I was relieved."

He leaned across the desk and looked into Mindy's eyes. "You'll have entire months, if not years that will be tougher than my forty hour stint without sleep. Walk away now. Don't waste my time or your own, if this isn't what you really want."

"I can handle this."

"Even when you're alone? Even when the contempt from your male classmates rises to a fever pitch?"

"Yes."

"Hopkins was the first medical school to admit women, but this won't make the program easier on you. This fact will make the curricula harder. If you do not measure up to the women who came before you, you'll be tossed."

"I am curious sir. Do you believe I am taking the slot away from a man or another woman, better qualified than I, who wants to be a doctor?"

"Sorry, but the answer is yes. I think you'll collapse under the pressure and that George's little social experiment will prove to be a complete waste. I don't think you're qualified."

"Thank you for not lying to me, Dean Chamberlain. You've just cinched my decision for me - I'm staying."

Without further comment, Dean Chamberlain hit the intercom button on his desk and said, "Miss Bizbee, please bring in Miss Hulen's books."

Miss Bizbee wheeled a stack of books in that looked six feet high.

"I suggest you get to work," Chamberlain said. "Miss Bizbee also has a course list. You're already behind. Normally, we don't allow new students in the spring term. Because of the special circumstances surrounding your arrival, the faculty has made an exception in your case. They will delay spring midterms for you for three additional weeks.

If you fail a mid-term, you will be disenrolled. In short, we're cramming two semesters work down your throat in one. Study the anatomy most carefully. The mid-term will be...problematic. Good luck, Miss Hulen. Welcome to Hopkins."

After the wide-eyed Miss Hulen and Miss Bizbee left, Chamberlain picked up the phone and said, "she's staying for now. I couldn't scare her. Hold on a moment." Chamberlain closed his window and checked the anteroom before picking up the phone again.

"Even some of the more progressive regents are steamed up over this. Yes, I agree. If she goes down the tubes, George is taking the heat. And who knows? She might make it to end of term. What? Slim to none. Like her though. She's got a spark. Yes, I'll keep you posted. Our press office is ready for questions."

Dean Chamberlain stood and watched Miss Hulen struggling to pull the book-laden dolly across the campus mall. No one helped her. "Get used to the lack of companionship, Miss Hulen," he whispered. "If you intend to succeed in this profession, you'll unfortunately be alone most of the time."

Her looks won't help her, he thought, she'd be better off if she were less attractive. Even with no make-up and her hair pulled back, she was easily the most attractive woman he'd seen in six months. If the pattern held true, the male students would hate her for being smart, then, hate her for refusing to date, and, finally, they'd hate her for graduating above them. This unbidden thought surprised him. "Damn," he said, "I think she's going to make it." He then shook his head as he turned back to the huge pile of administrative work stacked on his desk.

Several weeks later, Mindy was called back to Dean Chamberlain's office. She was jumpy. Living on four hours of sleep and 12 cups of coffee a day tended to fry your nerves.

Miss Bizbee, once again, ushered Mindy in to see the Dean. Thick shafts of light illuminated his desk.

"Sir, why am I here?" Mindy asked. "My lowest grade was the 87 I pulled in organic chemistry. What gives?"

"Ah, Lieutenant Hulen, even when sleep deprived and grumpy you begin and end every sentence with sir."

"I figured respect would work better than, 'go piss up a rope.'"

If Dean Chamberlain was shocked by her use of colorful language, he didn't show it via his reaction. He grinned widely.

"Only six weeks in Miss Hulen and already feeling the pinch. I wanted to congratulate you. Your initial grades reflect either intellect or sheer hard work or both. The 97 in anatomy surprised your professor. He reports that your manual dexterity in lab is impressive, but he wasn't prepared for you to–shall we say, 'smoke' his other students on the exam."

"Yeah, okay. I've proved I'm not stupid. May I go? I have Latin in 30 ticks of the clock, and I have a practical coming up."

"Yes, in a moment. I told your Latin instructor about our appointment. You aren't going to be dunned if you're late for Latin. Relax and bear with me for a few moments."

Dean Chamberlain came around the desk and said, "would you care for anything? Some hot tea perhaps?"

"Thank you, tea would be nice."

"After I read the critique you wrote on Joyce in your composition class, I thought you might be the right person to help me write my paper on communicable disease vectors in urban areas. My research assistant has already assembled much of the raw data from patient files here and at Sydenham Hospital. You would get three hours of research credit and a pass out of composition for the rest of the semester. I also pay a stipend of fifty dollars a month for incidental expenses associated with converting my notes and thoughts into a final paper."

Dean Chamberlain had rendered her speechless. As Mindy gathered her thoughts, the Dean helped Miss Bizbee pour tea.

"If you decide you want to have a go at the project, Miss Bizbee has the format requirements. I won't be upset if you decline. I' m concerned this may be asking too much from you too soon."

"Is this drudge work you can't convince anyone else to take on?"

"Hardly," the Dean said. "Most students consider an offer like this an honor."

"Why, me? Six weeks ago you were sewing me a death shroud," Mindy said, as she sipped her tea. The tea was thick with sugar and very fragrant.

"I had to be tough on you. See if you could cut the mustard. I had my doubts, but now freely admit you've exceeded my expectations. George Scranton was right."

The dean sipped some tea before he said. "To answer your question, my initial research into the transmission of viral particles and their mutation in living organisms is cutting edge."

"I'm the new kid on the block," Mindy said. "Again, why give me this opportunity?"

"More tea?"

"Yes, please. It's good."

The Dean poured them both another cup. "I don't know. Two months ago I didn't even know you existed. Then, Scranton sends me a letter about finding a *prodigy*, his word not mine, in the South Pacific."

The Dean laughed. "He was most anxious to get you out of that combat zone."

He held his teacup in both hands. Mindy noticed that his fingers matched the rest of him - long and slender.

"He told me he would regret his failure to transfer you for the rest of his life if you were killed before we could train your mind and focus your skill," the Dean said, "Frankly, I thought he was nuts."

"My parents would buy that. They think I'm a complete and utter disaster."

"You're a gifted student who has shown early promise as a healer. Further, your writing reflects insight and compassion. Take my word for it, that's a rare commodity in anyone."

"You believe I can work this paper without falling behind in my other studies?"

"I'll lay even money this work doesn't even slow you down."

"I'll do the project on one condition."

"Yes?"

"I reserve the right to back out if my course work begins to head south."

"I accept that. Please let me know if you are getting into academic difficulty."

"Okay, guess it's a deal."

The Dean glanced at his watch. "I've caused you to miss Latin. How about taking some time now to review my research, get your feet wet as it were?"

"Now's as good a time as any."

"Excellent!"

The Dean got up and went to a recessed wooden cabinet across from where they were seated. As he opened the cabinet, he began to explain his approach.

"Certain viral and bacteriological processes bear confusing similarities in part because routes of infection are often similar notwithstanding the research completed already that indicates viruses are inorganic in nature...."

They barely looked up from their conversation on the research an hour later when Miss Bizbee brought in sandwiches and a second pot of tea. As she returned to her desk, she thought, "well, he's thirty-eight and widowed. She's younger, but an army lieutenant. I guess if they want to pretend this is only research between two smart people that's okay. All I know is that he's completely taken by her."

Chapter 53
Reflections off the Water

"Beautiful isn't it?"

"Yes sir," Dud said. "Too bad we're in the big, bad middle of a shooting war. I'm glad to be leaving, hopefully south across the Coral Sea to Australia."

Lt. Col. Wyeth was silent for a moment. Some jobs stank worse than others. This one was a real stinker.

"Captain Ludlow, you're not bugging out with the 3rd."

Wyeth admired the younger man's composure - he didn't say a thing. Or, perhaps, he was merely exhausted.

"We anticipate the enemy will counterattack our airfield here in mass. The Army wants us to leave them a Marine reconnaissance platoon to scout out enemy jungle emplacements."

"And my men are it?"

Colonel Wyeth took a long drag on his butt. He'd hated cigarettes before the war. Now he always had one lit when they weren't under a complete blackout.

"Captain, I'm an Academy graduate, a pretty boy who rowed crew. Before the war, I had no use for men who came up through the ranks."

Still, Ludlow said nothing.

"But, I've seen you in action. You're the best killer and, more importantly, the best field officer I've ever seen. Chesty Puller might be better, but that's only because he's been stomping around battlefields longer than you have. The problem you have is that your reputation is beginning to precede you. The 145th Big Dog requested your two platoons by name."

Dud studied how the light reflected off Empress Augusta Bay. There was no way to describe the beauty of the tropics - you had to eyeball the scenery for yourself.

"Sir, if you lay the syrup on any thicker, I'll go crawl in a body bag right now. Praise always sounds like a eulogy to me."

"Guess I should save the balloon juice for the press."

Dud got down to business. "May I speak candidly, sir?"

"Please do, Captain."

"I'm not bothered that I'm not bugging out. What does bother me is that I don't think the Army is equipped to defend the perimeter if the 3rd leaves its defensive positions."

Dud squatted on the sand and drew a rough map of the island with his finger.

"Hill 700 is the key to holding the perimeter," Dud said. "The perimeter here and here along this two-mile long battle line is thin. If the Japanese attack in mass at these two points, while demonstrating along our flanks to keep us off balance, the perimeter can't be held. Hill 700 and the airport are vulnerable in the face of a well-coordinated attack."

Dud paused. "We can be pushed the hell off of Bougainville. Everything accomplished from November until now will be wasted. The entire 3rd should be left in place along the perimeter."

"What if your wrong, Captain, and we hold the 3rd here cooling its heels for no good reason?"

"Then, sir, the Corps can court-martial me, bust me down, and either shoot me or send me to a stateside prison where I'll be getting hot chow three times a day and lots of affection when I shower."

"No such luck, Marine. Cushy billets in stateside prisons are reserved for rapists and murderers not jar heads."

"Aye, aye, sir. I'll tell my company that we'll be having tea with our little yellow buddies."

"I don't have enough clout to stop the withdrawal of the 3rd, but, I agree with your analysis. The runway must be held, so must Hill 700. Carry on, Captain."

"Aye, aye, sir."

Dud wondered how many lives he had left. He was getting ready to be involved in another serious property dispute with armed representatives of the Empire of Japan. He hated the Japs but respected their prowess in combat. They just didn't give a shit. Like Pickett's Division at Gettysburg, they just kept coming until they prevailed or died.

Corporal Lance Washburn of Macon, Georgia was transfixed, a bright green scorpion, roughly the size of a lobster, was taking an afternoon stroll up his right forearm. If he made any noise, the twenty Japanese riflemen bivouacked about ten feet from him would get real upset. Exercising the patience of Job, the corporal removed his bayonet from its sheath and brought the tip of it up next to the unwanted arachnid. The corporal made his move just as the scorpion raised its stinger and flicked the scorpion off of his forearm...right onto the back of a Jap rifleman.

The scorpion steadied himself for a moment, and then struck. If Washburn hadn't been up to his eyeballs in serious shit, the chaos created by the scorpion would have been a riot. The Jap rifleman leaped straight into the air like he was shot out of a cannon. Two of his buddies leaped up and swung their rifles around thinking they were under attack, which of course they were - they just didn't know it yet. When one of the standing riflemen finally noticed the huge green scorpion standing triumphantly on his friend's head, he pointed and started laughing.

These boys aren't too concerned about enemy infiltration, Lance thought. The laughing rifleman brushed the scorpion off his friend's head into the underbrush. Lance saw the attack signal. He counted down from ten, waiting until the agreed upon time hack, sighted his carbine in and placed a round squarely between the eyes of the scorpion brusher. The entire Japanese patrol was killed in less than ten seconds. Washburn was worried though. In three months of combat, he'd never seen a Jap infantryman out in the open. Why today? They retreated silently back to their own lines.

"Cap'n, if I was a Jappo commander out there what do I rely on to get under the wire?"

Dud eyed the Staff Sergeant. The Army was different. No Marine sergeant would approach a captain directly, if he could avoid doing so. Always best to find a lieutenant to take the flak for you. Lieutenants were funny that way, most would take any damn fool idea to the next level, if they thought the idea would gain them some attention. Usually they got the attention, but the wrong sort. Dud considered the question.

"Darkness and rain. The little yellow guys love to attack on dark rainy nights, no moon to contend with."

"Precisely sir. You're pretty bright for a Captain, no offense sir."

"None taken. I haven't been a Captain all that long."

"Good, sir, because I have a lulu of an idea. What if we lit the perimeter up like a big candle once we know we're under attack."

"How would you do that, Sergeant?"

"We have thousands of gallons of fuel oil stock-piled. We could commandeer several hundred gallons, set the stuff along our perimeter in buckets, and light it off with phosphorus grenades wired to the buckets."

"Sergeant, that isn't half bad. Even if the oil doesn't work like you think it might, the oil and grenades will still scare the crap out of the enemy."

"There you go, sir."

"Start getting together what you think you'll need. I'll grease the slides with the quartermaster." The Sergeant tromped off toward the beach.

Dud thought, pitched hand-to-hand combat by candlelight - where's Bob Sullivan when you need him. Then, he thought, no, at this point in time Bob would probably require his assistance. Killing screaming Japanese soldiers was his niche, not Bob's.

He cleared his mind and yelled out, "No! I want those automatics set up to deliver a concentrated field of fire. Focus the fire lines on the perimeter there and there." A serious shooting war was on and Captain Daniel Ludlow was in the thick of the bloody mess.

Lieutenant Hideo Tanaka of the 23rd Infantry saw no sense in screaming epithets at the American enemy. He'd graduated from the University of California in 1940. He knew that phrases like "Chusuto!" and "San nen kire" meant nothing to the Yankees. The Americans spoke no language other than bastardized English.

Tanaka called for a Bangalore torpedo, then, thanked Buddha for the heavy rain that weakened his enemies aim. Just then, the man who had brought him the torpedo, Corporal Yashimi Noguchi, took a round in the head and collapsed next to him. Tanaka rammed the torpedo home and lit the fuse. He then jumped behind Noguchi's body to shield himself from the blast. "Pardon me, Noguchi san, for my appalling lack of manners," he said.

The torpedo blew a hole about two meters across the American wire. His screaming men poured into the breech. The Americans responded by lighting off a barrage of 60mm mortar fire on his position. Withering fire from their Browning automatics also poured down on his position. He allowed himself one quick thought for his two-year-old daughter, Tomicka, and his infant son, Namurasai, then, he was up and running. Several bullets ripped through his clothing. He felt a severe pain in his right shoulder, which he ignored. He unsheathed his sword with his left hand. His right arm would not obey his mental commands to move.

He came over a slight rise and tripped over one of his dead comrades, temporarily saving his life. A bullet fired from Captain Danny Ludlow's .45 whizzed over Tanaka's head as he stumbled. He blindly thrust upward with his sword and caught Dud in the right thigh.

Dud felt nothing at first, When he couldn't move; he realized the sword had torn through his leg. He fired a shot through the nose of the Jap officer who'd skewered him. Tanaka's brains flew out the back of his head.

Dud pulled out the sword in one swift, painful tug. His Sergeant came up behind him and tossed two hand grenades at the Japanese infantrymen who were ten yards from over-running their current position. Dud fired his weapon while being dragged into the nearest pillbox. Shrapnel from the Sergeant's own hand grenades whizzed by them as they fell into the box. Sergeant Arnie Wilkerson opened up with his Browning automatic. Dud grabbed a walkie-talkie and called in for 60 mm mortar rounds to be dropped right on their position.

The Army artillery guy said, "duck and cover. Life is going to get hairy."

Danny yelled, "if I duck, some damn Jap will stick me. Start dropping those rounds now, asshole!"

Dud dropped the walkie-talkie and pried another BAR out of the hands of a dead Army private and started firing out of the portal. An explosion knocked both men down. Several more blasts followed. The men could hear Japanese infantrymen screaming in agony all around them. They stayed low. Several rounds fired by the Japanese salient that had broken the line came through the portals and bounced around the box just above them. Three Japs appeared at the box hatch.

Wilkerson and Danny opened up on them - the first two dropped. The third one screamed and lobbed a grenade into the box. Wilkerson covered the bomb with his body, as Danny killed the Jap infantryman who'd tossed it. The force of the grenade blew Sergeant Wilkerson's guts all over Danny. He was covered in blood. He couldn't tell if the blood was all Wilkerson's or not.

Another Jap came flying through the hatch of the box, propelled by the force of a mortar round that had exploded literally next to the box. He tried to get up and bayonet Danny, all at the same time. He couldn't gain his footing on the blood - slicked floor. Danny noticed his right arm wouldn't function. Glancing, he saw that his arm had been badly mangled. He rolled slightly to shift his .45 to the left side of his lap where he could get his left hand on the weapon. The Jap had now taken off his bayonet and was crawling toward Dud with the long knife.

"You stupid shit!" Danny yelled. "Why didn't you just shoot me?"

He fired three rounds as the Jap lunged at him. The bayonet caught him in the gut, with the weight of the dead Jap behind the thrust; the weapon went nearly to the hilt into Danny's midsection. Danny managed to pull the knife out and push the dead Jap off to his side. The KAAWHUUMP of mortar shells continued to fall around his position.

Danny didn't have the strength to move. He tried screaming for help, but the effort hurt too much. He stopped trying. A shell landed directly on the bunker. Danny's last thought was, "at least the Army got the coordinates right." Everything went blank. The war was over for Captain Danny Ludlow, USMC.

Chapter 54
The Night Air

Bob and Will were the last to leave the boat after reaching port in San Francisco. Will had to finish paperwork pertaining to his security clearance. Bob waited on him. His new orders would be waiting for him at the Presidio when he returned from two weeks of leave.

Bob was chomping at the bit to get home. He couldn't tell Betty he was coming because, officially, he wasn't on the boat. Officially, he was still in Australia. Therefore, no one met the two men on the dock.

They dropped their respective duffels in the back of a deuce and a half that stopped in front of Pier 32 to give them a hitch to the security gate that now separated the Pier from the Embarcadero. Bob was entitled to wear officer rank, but said he felt too much like a swell. He wore a pea coat over dungarees, like Will.

"Headed home, Will?"

"You know, Bob, I should go home. Ralphie needs to see me."

Bob lit a cigarette and handed the butt over.

"Don't think I will though. I don't want people, even Ralph and my mom, giving me the once over about the war, or my dad, or anything else for that matter."

"I know what you mean. I can't wait to see Bet, but I don't give a rat's ass for all the questions I'll get that I can't answer."

The truck dropped them off at the main gate. Men were in a queue for taxis across the road from the gate.

Bob decided to take a taxi. Will sighed and said, "think I'll hang around here for a couple of days."

"Sure you don't want to come down the coast with me Will?"

"No way. You need time with your family, and besides, I'm sick of you."

Bob laughed. "Yeah, I'm sick of you too. Well, see you around, if you know what I mean." As he was walking away, he snapped his fingers and started fishing in his pants pockets. "Here, take this." Bob handed him a battered matchbook. "Our number is on the inside cover. If you need anything, call."

"Hug Betty and the babies for me. I promise I'll head your way if I don't go home."

Will headed up Second Street with no particular plan in mind, other than to escape the sound of water lapping against the docks. The only men he saw were dockhands or longshoremen huddled around fires lit in drums. The night was cold. Fog was rolling in off of the bay. A cab rolled by and slowed to a stop.

"Need a lift, buddy?"

"No, but I could use directions to a decent boarding house."

"Hop in. I know a couple of places up on Post."

The cabbie glanced back from where Will had come and said, "take my word for it, you need a lift."

Will looked back and for the first time saw three men, standing across the street watching him.

"They were trailing you," the cabbie said. "Sailors are known to come off the piers carrying cash. With the war on, the only men left down here ain't the kind you'd introduce to your momma."

Will climbed up into the cab right behind his duffel.

"Thanks for not leaving me to fend for myself."

"No problem. Could tell you were new in town." The cabbie looked back at Will. "I lost a boy at Pearl.

He's resting with the fishes on the Arizona. They tell me he was in the engine room on fire watch when the Japs hit. He was seventeen. We had to sign papers so he could enlist."

The cab turned left onto Market off of Second.

"He wanted to see the world, and then get his engineering degree at Stanford."

The cab turned north onto Stockton.

"He'd have done it too. He was a bright boy. You look like a bright boy too, even walking around late at night in the warehouse district. The longshoremen work hard, but they still remember the strike of 1934 like it was yesterday. They resent uniforms, and like I said, only the dregs are still around."

The cab pulled over at a sedate looking home that dominated the corner at Stockton and Pine Streets. The cab driver told Will, "this is Mrs. Borinski's place. Her boy was killed at Tarawa. She hates the Navy brass, but loves sailors and marines. You'll be okay here. The food is great and the rooms are top notch."

Will handed the cab driver his fare and said, "Thanks, you're the second cab driver who's helped me out of a jam."

"No problem. Tell Mrs. Borinski that Boris says, 'Tovarisch'." With that, he sped off into the thick fog.

Will half-carried, half dragged his duffel up the winding stone steps leading to the boarding house porch. Before he could reach the porch, lights came on and a tall, heavy-set woman stepped out the front door. Will's first thought was I'll wager no one raises any hell in this house.

"Hurry up, boy. The night air is rolling in off the bay. I don't care to catch my death out here."

"Yes ma'am. Sorry to wake you."

"Nonsense, I was having tea in the kitchen. From the looks of you, I suspect a cup of hot tea wouldn't hurt you either."

"No ma'am I expect not. A cup of tea would be fine."

"Oh my. Boris has brought me a young sailor with manners. Wonders never cease. Take those brogans off at the door. I've just waxed."

The hot tea was strong, with a hint of lemon. They drank the tea in companionable silence. Afterwards, Mrs. Borinski took him to a corner room on the second floor.

"Towels are in the pantry next to the landing. The shower is on the other side of the landing on the right. Breakfast is at 0800. Dinner is at 1800. You're on your own for lunch. The dining room is on the opposite side of the entry hall from the kitchen." She closed the door behind herself.

He listened to her footfalls on the hall runner that covered the center of the upper hall. He dropped his brogans on the floor and thought in passing about Dud and his brother Ralph at the football game against Denison so long ago. He drifted off to sleep.

He dreamed that he, Dud, and Ralph were at Leonard Park playing football in the rain. He threw Dud a long pass. Dud caught the pass, but was tackled by a big well-muscled guy that Will had never seen before. The stranger not only tackled Dud, he held Dud's head under water in a big puddle that had formed on the goal line. Will saw Dud struggling to get his head out of the water. The stranger didn't let him up though.

Will started screaming, "hey you big jerk, get off!"

The stranger turned and stared at Will. He smiled. "Ain't anything to worry about baby, this is just one more game we have to play."

Will started running towards them. Dud's struggling was getting weaker. Will kept slipping on the wet field. The stranger started laughing. "Don't trouble yourself, Will. The game's up."

Will screamed again. "Get off him, you freaking piece of crap."

Someone was shoving him. He sat straight up. Mrs. Borinski was staring at him with a mixture of concern and pity on her face. "Sorry to wake you, but you were screaming. My only other patron on this floor was concerned."

Will's tee shirt was soaked through.

"Ma'am, I'm the one who's sorry. Guess I had a nightmare. Do you want me to leave?"

"Don't be absurd, Mr. Davis. If I kicked out every serviceman who woke up screaming, I'd go out of business. Here, take this pill and don't worry. My physician prescribed them for this purpose." He accepted the pill and downed it with a glass of water. He lay back down and closed his eyes as Mrs. Borinski sat quietly rocking in the corner. When he stirred in the night, she rubbed his brow with a cold cloth.

Will woke the next morning feeling like someone had used his head for a croquet ball. He pawed around till he found his cigarettes. He fired one up and inhaled deeply. He wasn't a heavy smoker; half a pack a day was his usual limit. The nicotine, therefore, still caused almost immediate euphoria. He decided that Chesterfields had more zip than Lucky Strikes.

Dud was dead. He knew this. Didn't matter that he didn't know where Dud was. Dud was gone, and that was that.

"Hope they find a way to bring you home, buddy."

He sat on the worn but comfortable wing chair in his room. The early morning light filled his room with buttery slices of light. He'd heard that San Francisco's light was unique because it danced with the mist coming off of the bay.

He felt completely worn out, and this angered him. "What the hell have I done to be so tired?" He took another cigarette out of the pack, having smoked the previous butt down to his fingers. The room had no answers, he felt closed in - in a way he never had on the sub.

Chapter 55
Homecoming

"God Bet, I can't believe how big he's gotten. Would you look at the mitts on him?"

"They're into everything. You can't leave anything on the end tables, and you can't use table cloths because he pulls on them."

Bob tossed his son in the air as Conor screeched in delight.

"Like his old man. Can't be in a room for five minutes without busting something."

Conor chortled, "again, Da." Bob was more than happy to oblige.

"Bobby, are you going back to one of those awful submarines?"

Bob considered and said, "maybe for awhile. The work we're doing on the boat is nearly complete."

"Good, because from what little is said in the paper, the last place you want to be is on a sub."

"That's true enough. But the strange thing is that the old boys working those boats wouldn't have it any other way. They stay cool as ice under conditions you couldn't believe. I watched Will Davis eat a baloney sandwich while depth charges battered the crap out of us. Know what he said when I asked how he could eat at battle stations?"

"No, what?"

"He said, 'They may not have fried baloney sandwiches in hell. This is worse than hell, but the food is better. So I'll eat now and fry later.'"

"Will said that?"

Bob hung Conor by his heels and swung him like he was the pendulum to a clock.

"Now Bobby, watch out! If he hits his head on something, I'll brain you with a frying pan!"

"Yeah, Will said that."

"Sure doesn't sound like him."

"No, but then combat patrol on a sub ain't Sunday meeting at the pond."

Betty snatched Conor away from his dad. Conor had nap in his immediate future. Conor held out his arms for his dad and screamed.

"Don't worry, baby. Daddy will be here when you wake up. He can give you a concussion then."

Conor considered this and said, "okay, momma."

Bob laughed and said, "yep, like his old man - always looking for something to bang his head into."

Chapter 56
Navy Cross and a Shave

Dot felt her legs go numb. She fell to the stoop and lay there. Bert spoke to the uniformed men on the walk. After they left, Dot didn't move. Bert knelt beside her. He was smart enough not to touch her, if he had, Dot would've clawed his eyes out.

"Dot, there's a small bit of good news. The War Department is bringing him home. Normally they would bury him at sea. He held off almost an entire Jap platoon single-handed. They awarded him the Navy Cross and a Silver Star. Because he's a hero, he's coming home."

Dud's mother noted as he said this that tears were rolling down his cheeks.

"Now that he's gone and got himself killed, you've decided our poor dead son is worth something. Spare me please."

Bert sat there staring out onto the street. "Dot, I been a drunk and a thief long as I can remember. Fact is our son has always been worth something. I'm the one that ain't worth two roaches on a griddle. I can live with that. What scares me is that I can hardly remember what he looks like."

Bert put his face into his hands and sobbed.

Danny, even dead, was still in the Marines, until all paperwork was complete. The military representative had brought a flag that had been draped over her son's casket, along with the disposition paperwork. She didn't want Bert raining all over the standard, she grabbed the folded triangle, got up, and opened the door to go inside. She stopped on the threshold with her back to Bert.

"I'm going in to get dressed, and then we're going down to the Baptist church. Our boy will be acknowledged in church by this damn town, or there will be hell to pay. There will be a funeral. Our boy is somebody now and we're not going to let him down. Come shave - you're going too."

For the first time in his life, Bert Ludlow took 'lip' from his wife with no comment. He went in to shave off his stubble.

Dear Will:

Hope that I'm not the one to break this awful news to you. Danny is gone. He was killed in the battle of [censored]. Turns out, the battle was mainly an [censored] operation. We're not sure why Danny was even there. The funeral service will be the second week in April. Mom said to tell you that she understands this is an awful reason to come home. Still...it's Danny.

I don't know how to give you this news, so, I'll just tell you. Betty's dad, as you know, was arrested in California for conspiracy to commit murder–dads! He's out on bail and back here. The rumor is spreading that he's told his defense attorney that mom put him up to it. Mom's response is that 'Satan has one of the lower levels of hell reserved for scum like Stevens and his suicidal pal Chester Harris. Will, if it's possible, I really need you to come home.

> *Love,*
> *Ralph*

Will sat on a bench looking out at the water while he smoked. He lit the letter on fire with his cigarette and watched the charred remnants drift away. "Christ on a pogo stick," was the only response that came to mind.

"A Dear John letter, perhaps?"

Will leapt off the bench and assumed a crouch. The man who had wandered up behind him smiled and sat down. He was dressed in a drab blue coat and worn dungarees. He patted the spot on the bench where Will had been sitting.

"Don't worry son," he said. "Sit back down and relax. I've no use for your wallet."

"Wasn't worried. Thought I was alone."

"Just got here. Been out fishing and I'm too tired to make the trek up the hill yet. I usually stop here to clear my head."

"Yeah okay. What's that got to do with me?"

"Nothing, you on shore leave?"

"You don't look like my mother, are you shore patrol?"

The man laughed and said, "Martin Graber, at your service."

He held out his hand. Will studied the proffered hand for a second before shaking it, and saying, "Will Davis."

"I take from your accent that you don't originally hail from California?"

"Where do you think I hail from?"

The man stroked his chin for a moment and said, "either southern Oklahoma or northern Texas. The twang is slightly heavy on the vowels for an Okie. My guess is that I'm speaking to a native Texan."

Will chuckled. "Nice parlor trick, Mr. Graber. Bet the ladies eat that up."

"No trick really. When you run into as many people as I do your ears become acutely sensitive to accents and inflections. As to women, I no longer cultivate their company on a regular basis."

"You don't talk like a fisherman, Mr. Graber."

"You don't talk like a sailor. I haven't heard an expletive yet."

"Touché, Mr. Graber. My fine Christian upbring-ing rears its ugly head."

The man stretched and rose off the bench.

"Godspeed, Mr. Davis. I will pray to the God presumably looking after all of us that you survive this awful conflict."

Will looked back out at the bay. The wind had picked up. The water churned and frothed as if Neptune were stirring the bay water himself. When he glanced back, only an envelope remained on the park bench. Graber had vanished. Will opened the envelope. Inside was a note and another envelope. The note was addressed to him. So, Graber was a courier.

Dearest Will:

I regret having to involve you in my affairs a second time. But, my enemies carefully watch the people whom they suspect are my regular contacts. Please pass the enclosed message along to the people your Mr. Sullivan works for. Memorize the message and then destroy both this note and the message. It is short...but vital. Mention this to no one!

E.

Will groaned. The woman's nerve was immeasur-able. If the navy didn't get him killed, Elena would give it a go. He opened the second envelope.

'If the roses don't bloom in Manhattan very soon, it will not matter. The arbor in Baltimore is close to blooming. Water is the key and the gardener is dedicated.'

Will read the note till he'd memorized the words. He had no idea what the message meant and didn't want to know. He headed back to Mrs. Borinski's to pack his grip. He was headed to San Juan Capistrano, and, then home, he hoped.

Will's stay in Capistrano was short.

Bob called a number he'd been given for emergency purposes, indicating they had a message from a friend concerning best wishes for the upcoming Easter holidays. A car was at Bob's front door within an hour. Bob and Will were both trundled into the back seat. Bob didn't really need to hear Betty's thoughts. Her eyes said everything. The two spooks in the front said nothing after telling Bob and Will 'not to flap their pie holes at each other' for the duration of the trip.

The Commander was waiting for them at the Presidio. The Commander and Will ended up in a square, windowless room furnished with a gray table and two chairs. The Commander made Will repeat the message three times. The Commander wrote the words out each time Will said them to ensure Will didn't change either the words or the sequence of words.

Finally, the Commander pulled back from the table and said, "you're certain you repeated everything set forth in the message?"

"Yes sir, I am."

After The Commander had listened to the message for the third time, he said, "have any idea about what this message might mean?"

"No sir, I don't."

"Graber gave no indication of what was meant or intended?"

"Sir, Graber didn't even indicate that he was giving me a message. He was gone before I noticed the envelope lying on the bench. He's lucky I saw the envelope. I could have simply walked off."

The Commander smiled tightly and said, "I suspect if you had, you would have run into him elsewhere—or someone like him."

"Sir, may I get up and stretch for a bit?"

"Of course."

A second man came in the room and put the Commander's written notes into a bright red pouch. The red pouch was then sealed into a white and red striped pouch and the striped pouch was placed into a black folio. The black folio was then placed into a slender case handcuffed to the man's wrist. A third man came into the room, armed with both an automatic sidearm and a carbine. The Commander looked at this man and said, "Rounds chambered?" The man responded, "aye, sir."

"You have your instructions. Get to the plane now. If anyone and I mean *anyone* tries to open that case before you get to the White House, kill them. Destroy the case if you feel threatened or its' contents are in danger of being compromised."

After the men left, Will looked the Commander in the eye, and said, "am I going to be killed as well?"

The Commander smiled and said, "not yet. Strangely enough, you have provided invaluable service to your country—above and beyond your value as a mechanics mate. Your next assignment is to attend a funeral. I understand Captain Daniel Ludlow of the U.S. Marine Corps will be buried next week in your old hometown."

"Gainesville? I'm going home?"

"Yes, enjoy the visit. Gainesville will never be your home again. We have other plans for you, Mr. Davis."

"I'm not going to ask about those plans," Will said. "I'm pleasantly surprised that I'm not going to be killed—yet. May I be excused, sir?"

"Yes, Mr. Davis. Mr. Sullivan will be accompanying you back to Gainesville. I understand he also knew Captain Ludlow."

"Yes, we were ... all friends."

"Any significance to the pause?"

"Not really. Seems so long ago, that's all. Like I'm talking about people I read about in a fairy tale."

"Things change."

"Amen, pass the bread."

The Commander stood and then leaned against the desk. "Hurts, doesn't it Mr. Davis?"

"What Commander, The war, Danny, what?"

"Spare me the disingenuous confusion, man."

"Oh, you mean that sudden moment when you realize that good doesn't always win out against evil. That good people and good things often get the living shit kicked out of them while evil rolls on–laughing. Is that what you're rubbing my face in, Commander?"

"Not rubbing your face in, Mr. Davis. Only telling you what I see in your eyes, what you already know. The best gifts come with the highest price tags. Freedom is the gift. Captain Ludlow, you, me, the President, we're all paying full price."

"Do we have enough treasure in the coffers, sir?"

"We must, Mr. Davis. The consequences of failure are too awful to be borne by humanity."

Will scraped the floor with his shoes. "Humanity, Commander? We playing God now?"

The Commander laughed. "The war has certainly given you an edge I don't remember from our first encounter."

His expression became serious again. "I try to maintain no illusions. I try hard, notwithstanding my ... our ... business to stay in touch with reality. No, Mr. Davis we are not playing God. We are trying to preserve a system that brings the greatest amount of dignity and respect to the greatest number of individuals."

Will abruptly came to attention, saluted, and as he left, said, "I'll keep that in mind, sir."

The Commander remained in the safe room looking at the coded message for a long while after Will had left. The copy he had was on flash paper. He'd burn this paper before he left the safe room.

Captain Bates walked in carrying a pot of coffee, two cups and a small silver flask on a serving tray.

"Some liquid fortitude?"

"Normally, Marty, I'd decline, but the times grow somewhat trying. So, yes, give me a generous dollop of fortitude."

"Seriously, sir, I'm wondering why you bother."

The Commander took a large gulp of the rum-laced coffee, and then added more rum to the mix.

"Bother with what, Marty?"

"The navy kid. I was watching from the portal. You even gave him the 'greatest dignity' speech.

"I know. I remember when I believed every word. The thing is, Marty - and I say this with no malice - this country is going to need kids like Will and diamonds in the rough like Bob, and a thousand more like them in the future. You disappoint me by failing to grasp this notion. Your arrogance is your Trojan horse."

"Ouch, spray me down before I'm burnt to a crisp."

When his boss didn't laugh, Marty sipped his coffee for a moment and said, "okay, I was out of line."

"The real issue is do you know why you're out of line?"

"I'm...class conscious when I can ill afford to be?"

The Commander noted that his subordinate asked this as a question, rather then stating it as a fact. He sipped his coffee. The brew was Jamaican, rank still had some privilege.

"Consider that our dear friend Elena has now provided our government the two most vital pieces of human intelligence we have ever received from a foreign agent. In both instances, she has used Mr. Davis as her contact."

The Commander got up with his cup and walked around until he stood behind Captain Bates. Bates wanted to squirm; but resisted the urge. The Commander stood behind him until he had finished his coffee. He sat his saucer and cup back on the gray tabletop, then placed his hands on Bates' shoulders.

"We, Marty, to our knowledge, have never even seen her. Am I being too obvious?"

"No sir. I deserved the correction. So, his contact intelligence was - valuable?"

"So astounding I'm still gasping for air. Not only because the material was vital to our national interest, but also because she revealed, on purpose, the quality of her methods and sources. We have a leak on a project where we can't afford one and she warned us. Extraordinary! The risks she took to get that message to Davis can't be calculated."

"Allow me yet another moronic question?"

"Yes?"

"Why are we letting Davis leave this compound? Let alone, go home?"

The Commander sat down and lit the flash paper. Both men watched the paper burn to fine white ash.

"That is a better question than your first one. I conclude that Davis knows nothing right now. Therefore, he can reveal nothing. We will protect him if we can. I think he'll be useful in the future, if he survives. I want to see if he can and I don't want to highlight his importance by keeping him under wraps."

The Commander rocked back in his chair until it was balanced on the two hind legs only. "Besides, no effort has been spared to get Ludlow's body home. I'm not even sure who's behind that. Actually, I had a much tougher time deciding not to keep Sullivan under wraps. His talent is very rare."

The Commander laughed. "I cut you some slack though. I couldn't see tying you down in a safe house with Bob for the rest of the war."

Martin Bates grew pale right before the Commander's eyes.

"I don't think Bob would have handled that well," the Commander said. "Instead, you're going back to Gainesville with them. Wear very casual mufti and practice your drawl. Take four men with you. Stay low key but don't let them out of your sight. Try eating at the White Rose and at Dum Dora's, the pie is excellent at both places. You have reservations at the Turner. You and your team are doctors attending a conference at Camp Howze to review their research data on penicillin.

Bob and Will know that you'll be there. If something happens requiring extraction, call. If I need to get word to you, I'll send a message through the county sheriff's office. If you must contact me about something urgent, extraction, for example, say, through the switchboard, that 'my prescription can't be filled here."

"With all due respect sir, am I being told everything I need to know? Or is something going on here? Setting up covert surveillance on two guys carrying around sensitive information makes no damn sense. Lots of guys are getting killed. What's so damn special about this guy and this funeral that we're giving Sullivan and Davis this much leeway?"

Martin paused. "For crying out loud, extraction - from Gainesville, Texas? Again, what am I not being told?"

The Commander patted Bates on the back and said, "when you get back to your billet, you'll find a detailed packet concerning cover and exit instructions.

Read them carefully. Let me know if you have any questions about the arrangements. Your concerns are noted."

The Commander got up and headed for the door. This had been another grueling day, in a grueling year. Martin Bates was left sitting in the safe room wondering what he had done in a former life to merit this assignment.

"Hi, ya'll," he murmured.

No one heard.

Chapter 57
Roosevelt's Folly

The icy vodka was as thick as cherry syrup. Mindy downed the vodka and turned her glass over on the bar. She chased the vodka with two swallows of lemonade.

"Damn," Mindy said. "That burned all the way down."

"Hulen," Brad Whitford said. "You could mix the vodka and the lemonade."

"I could, Whitford, but the effect wouldn't be so dramatic. Right now, that vodka is rushing unimpeded for my blood-brain barrier." Mindy widened her eyes and held her hands to her head. "Whoa! The stuff is already there."

Brad eyed her with admiration–tinged with some resentment. "Hulen, do you *want* to be impaired for the anatomy mid-term tomorrow?"

"Already took the anatomy mid-term."

"What! You don't have to perform the practical in front of everyone? I smell a rat."

"Got to leave for home tomorrow. An old friend is being brought home from the Pacific for burial. Remember the guy I mentioned when we were having tea at the Winston?"

"Oh, no!"

"I'm afraid so."

"Mindy, I'm sorry. Petty of me to accuse you of avoiding your practical."

"That's okay, Whitford. You didn't know. Anyway, if Chamberlain thought anatomy would break me, he'd have made sure I took the practical with everyone else."

"I agree," Brad Whitford said ruefully. He considered her over the top of his beer mug. "You're probably better with a scalpel than anyone I've ever seen, including my old man - and he's gifted."

"Lay off the praise, Whitford," Mindy said. "I've already slept with you." Annoyed, Whitford said, "This isn't about sex. I know a surgeon when I see one. A scalpel moves like magic in your fingers and apparently I'm not the only one who thinks so. You're here one minute as a nursing student. The next minute you're back from the war, enrolled as a medical student. How many people manage to do that?"

"Okay, so what's eating you?" Mindy said. "Can't we have a drink or two without medicine or surgery entering the discussion?"

"We could if you'd let me in on the secret."

"What secret?"

"Word is going round that when you diagrammed the digestive process in the G.I. tract yesterday, the professor took notes."

"So?" Mindy said. "He was interested in what I was saying about pepsin production."

No wonder Chamberlain adores her, Whitford thought. Unlike any other woman he'd ever known, she could converse about Mozart or mothballs without missing a beat–even while she was up to her elbows in a cadaver. A sudden flood of emotion hit him. He realized that he loved this woman too. He was, in fact, in complete awe of her.

"Whitford! Hello!" Mindy waved her hands up and down in front of his face. "Am I that boring?"

"Sorry, I was wool-gathering."

"No, my fault. I dragged you away from what little sleep you're getting."

"Were you close to him, the guy who's coming home?"

"The answer is so strange Brad. Yesterday, I'd have said, 'no'. Now that he's gone I realize that he was my friend...too."

"Your friend too? Was he or wasn't he?"

"Danny Ludlow was the best friend of another guy, a guy who...a guy that..."

"I don't believe this. Miss Hulen, medical student extraordinaire, is at a loss for words, over a guy no less."

Mindy reached over and punched Brad hard on the arm.

"Ouch! Mind those fingers. Don't jam those jewels on my carcass."

"He was the best friend of a guy I really liked, okay?"

"Yeah, so?"

"Barkeep, another shot of vodka here please."

The Bartender came up and said, "I had doubts about giving you the first one. I don't think a lady should be downing more than one shot of vodka a day."

Mindy pulled her wallet out of her purse.

"I'm a lady only by act of Congress. What I really am is a 1st Lieutenant in the Army."

She flipped her I.D. card right into the Bar Jockey's hands. He looked at the card, looked at her, and said, "suit yourself, Lieutenant," as he poured her second vodka.

"This one is on the house. My boy's in the Army, somewhere in Holland now."

As he said this, he headed to the other end of the bar.

"Danny Ludlow was considered beneath me. I wasn't supposed to even talk to him. Sort of like what would happen if you took me home to meet your parents. They'd accuse you of slumming."

Whitford started to protest, and then stopped. He wasn't sure his parents even knew where Texas was. If they did, they probably thought the entire state was populated by tobacco chewing cowpokes.

"I'd be a scandal right? No need to reply - I know the answer."

Mindy downed her second vodka in a gulp. Her cheeks flushed.

"I have to go," she said. "I really appreciate you coming out on the spur of the moment. As she put on her coat and picked up her purse, she said, "know what? Until this moment, I never understood that old adage about not being able to truly go home again."

"Perhaps when you come back, we can test the adage at my home as well. My parents need to meet the fair Lieutenant from Texas. You and my father can practice surgical technique on the Easter roast."

Mindy stared at him with those piercing eyes. He felt he was falling right into them.

"Perhaps, Whitford. So long as you understand one thing."

"And that would be?"

"I intend to be a surgeon. Nothing gets in the way of that goal - *Nothing*. Got it?"

"Like it was branded on my forehead."

She smiled. As she turned to walk out the door, she said, "good, I won't have to heat the iron then. By the way, you never asked me how I did on my practical."

"I don't have to; I've been your partner all term."

"Be seeing you, Whitford."

The door slammed shut.

Brad sat at the bar, finishing his beer. In his mind, he practiced saying things like, "mom? I've met this girl. She's an Army Lieutenant who's going to be a surgeon too. No, her people aren't New York or even Boston. She's from Gainesville, Texas."

He ordered another beer and thought; she could have at least helped me out by being in the Navy.

Brad's older brother, Whitey, had attended Annapolis before the war. His parents were thrilled because he was close to home. In June 1942, Whitey Whitford was killed dive-bombing some Jap Admiral's flagship at the battle of Midway. Since then, his parents held the Navy in even greater esteem than the Presbyterian Church and the Republican Party. After Whitey had been assigned to the Enterprise, they even quit referring to the war effort as "Roosevelt's folly."

Sometimes Brad thought that his parents were almost grateful for Whitey's death. He ordered a scotch shooter to go with his second beer. His brother's death in combat had brought his parents tremendous prestige and sympathy within their social circle. On Saturday nights, they always got the best table at their country club. His dad never had to wait for a choice tee time. As he tossed back the scotch, Brad decided to take Lieutenant Hulen home to meet his parents the first chance he got.

"And they'll like her."
"Say something, pal?" The bartender said.
"No, sorry, I was on my way out."

He had a practical and two written exams scheduled over the next six days and here he was downing shots and beer chasers in a harbor-side dive. He headed back to his room wondering what taking his anatomy practical with a hangover was going to be like.

Chapter 58
Drinks in the Parlor

They had loaded Danny onto the baggage coach just before the train pulled out of San Francisco. The coffin was burnished silver underneath the American Flag. A Marine Corps Flag stood at Danny's feet, an American Flag stood at his head. Two tapers were lit and placed behind the coffin.

With Will at his side, Martin Bates supervised the loading of the casket. "Do Marine Corps Captains always get full military honors, Mr. Bates?"

"They do, Mr. Davis, when the Speaker of the House personally requests the honors via the Secretary of the Navy."

Once Danny had been properly situated in the baggage car, Bates said, "I'm headed forward. Are you -?"

"If it's alright, Mr. Bates, I think I'll stay here for a few moments."

"Of course, shall I tell Mr. Sullivan where you are?"

"Yeah, that's okay." Will was left with Danny and the baggage.

Will spoke. "Danny, what in holy hell were you thinking? I guess you joining the Marines was okay, but you never said one damn thing about getting yourself killed." Will lay his head atop the casket.

"My dad, Wat, now you. How can I bear it, Danny?"

Danny had no answers.

Bob stood just inside the door of the baggage car listening to the one-sided exchange. He shuffled his feet to let Will know he was coming.

Will jumped up and said, "I didn't, you know, feel right…"

Bob finished for him, "about leaving him alone in the baggage car? Guess that's what the guard outside is all about."

"Pretty dumb, huh? Danny doesn't need me. He has his own guard."

"Oh, I don't know, Will. Wherever Danny is, he's probably glad you're here. I'd be glad you were here if I was the one laying there."

They stood there listening to the clacking of the train on the rails.

Finally Will said, "let's go."

Both men came to attention and saluted Danny's casket. Once they were out of the baggage car, Will asked, "when is Betty coming back with her mom and the kids?"

"Already there. Getting the house aired out and stuff."

"I'm happy for you. Good time to have your family home."

Bob opened their compartment door and they dropped into their respective seats, unknotting their ties.

"They started packing the moment you and I headed back to Frisco with our spook escort. Things are a mess. They were headed home even if Dud, I mean Danny, wasn't being shipped back. Have you heard what Bet's old man is saying?"

"Bob, he's still Dud to me too. And, yeah, I've heard, Ralph wrote to me."

Bob made sure no one was close enough to overhear their conversation.

"We can get to him, you know that?"

"The land is arid here. Never thought about California having so much desert."

"Did you hear what I said?"

"I heard you. Let the mess play out."

Bob stared straight ahead as he spoke. "You sure? I mean look at what ..."

"I know. Your father-in-law is scum, but that alone doesn't mean he's lying. He may not be the final player. I think he's holding back information as his Ace in the hole."

"Sorry, Will. I didn't mean to force this out in the open so, so tactlessly."

"Hell, why not? Bet's your wife and, for better or worse, our paths seem joined at the hip. We can't avoid the issue. By the way when did tact become a concern of yours?"

Bob shrugged and moved closer so as to be heard over the train without raising his voice.

"Why allow him to carry on? Do you *really* want this to play out?"

"Bob, he's not worth killing. Why risk everything you've accomplished?"

"Because, I detest the bastard."

"You still scare the crap out of me Bob you know that? You don't even have a dog in this hunt."

"The man tried to kidnap my boy, now; he's called your mom a murderer." Color rose in Bob's cheeks. "You don't want him dead too?"

"Deep inside I do. But, I'm trying to compartmentalize as well as I can."

"What does that mean?"

"Think, Bob. My dad, Dud, and Wat, are already gone. Who knows what our government has in store for us? We may be gone too before this is all over. Do you really want the death of your children's grandfather on your head? No matter how evil or screwed up he is?"

Bob stared out the window.

"Guess my plan wouldn't cut the mustard."

"You still get an 'A' for effort. Believe me, I appreciate the sentiment, but his reputation is already ruined. He's out on bail but isn't allowed near his own

403

home. You, on the other hand, Bob, will be met at the train station. Your wife, your children, and, probably, your mother-in-law will all be there. And, you'll stay at the old bastard's house while you're in Gainesville."

"Will?"

"Yes?"

"After you've settled in, want to come over for a drink? We'll sit in the parlor."

"Mind if I bring, Ralph?"

"You can bring any damn person you want, except for Louis DeWitt, if that weasel's still around."

"Ralph told me Louis is on the local draft board now."

"Doesn't that take the cake? Dud comes home in a box. DeWitt decides who rolls through the grinder next."

"If I brought Louis over, we could roast him in the fireplace."

"Bring him."

Bob leaned back and closed his eyes, as a smile played across his lips. The smile Will thought, of a man who finally realizes he has worth–to himself. "We're getting close, Dud," Will whispered. "We're coming home."

Chapter 59
Closing the Books

"I don't know why you're doing this. You have a full plate just keeping up with your studies."

"I know, Aunt Shannon," Mindy said. "The dean wasn't happy with me."

"Then why go back for this funeral?"

Mindy dug around in her purse for a comb. "Thanks for coming with me. This has to be tough on you too."

"I want to look your father in the eye and say, "you stupid schmuck, I'm lucky to still be alive.""

"That's true too, isn't it?"

"What? That your dad's a schmuck?"

"No, that you feel lucky to be alive."

"I'm not the issue here. You're heading home for the funeral of a guy you barely knew!"

"My shoes are wedged under the seat and I can't go to the dining car in stocking feet."

"Don't change the subject."

"Don't be pushy," Mindy said. "You know damn well I'm closing the books on another matter."

"Will Davis?"

"Yes."

"Letter's quicker."

"A letter is also the method employed by the indifferent, the government, and cowards. I'm none of those things."

"Such high moral tone!" Shannon said. "Sound like a doctor already."

"Blow it out your tight little anus, Auntie."

"And correct anatomical terminology too! My, my, an educated trash mouth."

405

Mindy punched her aunt on the shoulder. "Want the comb before I stick it back in my purse?"

"No, and if I want to be assaulted, I can get back into real estate," Shannon said. "Quit screwing around with your shoes. Let's get to the dining car before the crush hits."

"Fine," Mindy said. "I'll go in my stockings, but they won't serve us. You watch."

"Yes they will. The Hopkins grind has really made you very cranky. Or is the crankiness due to a lack of sex?"

As they headed for the dining car, Mindy said, "yes to the first part, and none of your business to the second part."

Shannon laughed. "Thought I'd ask. I propose brandy stingers to take off the edge."

"Lead on, Auntie."

Their rack of lamb with mint jelly was superb. Mindy had one stinger. Aunt Shannon had two and, feeling frisky, winked at the bartender on the way back to their compartment.

Chapter 60
Typing With Broken Nails

"My eldest son will be arriving tomorrow. Will he have to visit me in jail?"

Chief Becker scratched his paunch. He had to admire her; he doubted Elizabeth Davis would bat an eye if he put her in the lock-up.

"No, Mrs. Davis. Notwithstanding your lack of cooperation, I don't believe you conspired to kill your husband."

"Is that so?"

"Yes ma'am. A certain dead man left correspondence behind that deflates Mr. Stevens' credibility. But, I'm baffled by one thing."

"Yes, Chief?"

"Can I get you anything before I continue? Another cup of coffee perhaps?"

"The coffee is atrocious. I'll get better coffee in prison if you all decide I'm a low-down conniving husband killer."

"I'll take that as a no."

"Please, come to the point, Chief. Mr. Chaney is waiting. If we keep him much longer, he may have a heart attack. He loves me, even though he has half a notion that I wanted Mason dead."

"Did you?"

Elizabeth turned to stare out the dingy, barred window, which sat high on the wall of the Chief's office.

"Mason was a drinker and a gambler," She said. "I did not approve and that was no secret. But, he loved his children, and he loved me. I did not want him dead. I love him still and miss him horribly. He *was* a scoundrel - and that's what I miss most."

When tears tumbled down Elizabeth Davis' cheeks, Chief Becker almost tripped over his desk offering her a reasonably clean handkerchief.

"You see, Chief?" Elizabeth dabbed at her eyes. "God has a sense of humor. The very traits I despised in him are also the ones that made me love him so. Want him dead? I dream that he's on the front porch, smoking his pipe, and spouting his usual nonsense about cards, sports, and whatever else pops into his foolish head. Damn Chester and Robert to hell! Put together, they don't equal half the man Mason was!"

Chief Becker realized if he lived three lifetimes, he would never understand women. He had no idea what made Elizabeth Davis tick. He made a mental note to recount this conversation to his wife, Mavis, to see if she had any insight.

"Mrs. Davis. I'm baffled about one thing here."

Elizabeth held up her hand up to him, saying, "I'm guessing you want to know why Stevens is trying to pin my own husband's murder on me?"

"Yes, any ideas?"

"You won't believe the probable answer."

"Try me."

"This is a long story."

"Mrs. Davis, if you can provide us with potential corroboration of motive, I'm all ears."

"Mason won me in a card game. I didn't really have to go with him, but I did. Robert Stevens was the loser. So was Chester. Both were potential suitors. I was Chester's date at a barn dance outside of Whitesboro. Robert was already mad that I had decided to go to the dance with Chester rather than him. He took Melrose, but glowered at me the entire evening. Mason showed up alone, on horseback and danced with every girl there but me. Chester got liquored up even though I kept telling him to go easy on the corn squeezings, that he had to drive. He didn't listen and drove his dad's car into a muddy ditch on the way home from the dance."

Elizabeth paused long enough to drink some water.

"Robert drove up with Melrose, claiming he didn't have a towrope. While we were discussing our options, Chester upchucked, and then passed out in the mud. Robert wanted to leave him there, but I talked him out of doing so. We managed to get him in the back of Robert's car. Well, Mason happens along out of the brush, his shirt is half - way undone. His cheeks were flushed and his hair had that tousled look you get from the wind. The moon was out and you could see every star in heaven."

Elizabeth Davis' eyes had a faraway look to them, a look that made Chief Becker realize that Elizabeth Davis was beautiful. As if she had read his thoughts, she said, "understand that in my day, I was quite the looker. So was Mason. He looked like a god sitting on that black mare."

She smoothed out her dress and glanced at her watch.

"Anyway, Robert sees Mason and gets his dander up. He says, 'Mace, clear on out of here. This soiree's under control.'

Mason looked at him and said, 'maybe so, but you have a backseat with a drunk lying across it. How is Miss Elizabeth going to get home?' "'Well,' Robert said, 'she can sit up front with Rose and me.'"

Elizabeth burst out laughing.

"Melrose didn't cotton to that idea. She piped up and said, 'like hell Robert! Let Mason take her home!'

"Well, let me tell you, Chief, the thought of riding with Mason on that horse through the brush terrified and excited me all in one go. Grinning at me like the cat that ate the canary, Mason says, 'Rob, you got a deck of cards on you?'

Stevens grabbed a deck from under the driver's seat. 'What have you got in mind, Mace?'

Mason looked at me the whole time, then said, 'high card takes Miss Elizabeth home. Miss Rose may draw for me." Then he looked at me and said, 'are you agreeable?'

I glared back at him in the dark and said, 'If you win, this'll be the only time I'll get close to you.'
He laughed. He knew I wanted him."
"*Wanted* him, Mrs. Davis?"
"Oh my Chief, have I broken a rule by admitting I wanted a man?"
Chief Becker did his level best not to blush, but only partly succeeded.
"No, I …well, never mind. Please, continue."
"Anyway, Rose drew a seven. Robert grinned. Till he drew a three.

He looked at me and said, 'don't go with him Elizabeth. Davis is lucky at cards, but he's trash and so are you, if you go.' That sealed the deal. I let Mason help me onto his mare. I rode sidesaddle until we were out of sight. Then, I got off the horse and stripped off my dress. Mason gave me a strong tug and I straddled the horse behind him in knee high bloomers. Put my arms low around his middle. He was warm and so was the mare…well, you get the idea.

The ride was glorious. We rode for what seemed like only minutes. Mason told me later, that we took two hours to get back. When we did, I couldn't let him see me soaked with sweat. I looked like I'd been rained on. When we got home, I jumped off the horse and ran around back without saying thanks, or even goodnight.

410

My abrupt departure didn't matter. Like I said, he knew. I never dated anyone but Mason after that night."

She got up and started pacing.

"I was one of them, you know?"

"Sorry, Mrs. Davis?"

"My family didn't have money like the Stevens or even the Harris family. Still, we owned a small pharmacy. My parents grudgingly put on the wedding to avoid a complete scandal, but they made the fact clear that we were on our own, and they stuck to their guns. Robert has never forgiven or forgotten the slight. He's seethed all these years. Chester went along, but apparently his conscience caught up with him."

The Chief sat and watched her for a couple of minutes.

Elizabeth watched back, not a fidget or wiggle. She simply waited the Chief out. A tap on the Chief's frosted glass door ended the silence.

Chief Becker said, "we're almost done, for now."

"That's good, Chief, because Mavis is out here with me, wondering what you're up to with Mrs. Davis. Mr. Chaney doesn't look too happy either."

The Chief turned his attention back to Elizabeth.

"If I understand you correctly, you're telling me Mason was killed because of jealousy going back twenty-five years?"

"That was only the beginning, Chief. Over the years, Chester and Robert embarrassed Mason whenever an opportunity came up. They lorded their money, their homes, their business trips, and their general importance over him.

Mason went to the bank one time to get a loan to buy a farm that was for sale out on the south side of town, you know–the old Chasen place down towards Valley View? Well, the old Chasen place should be called the old Davis place. Mason had cash money to put down, only needing about half from the bank. Chester laughed him out of the bank. Chester also made damn sure he couldn't get a loan anywhere else either."

Again, tears trickled down her face. She looked straight at the Chief.

"What kind of cruelty does it take to prevent a man who wants to engage in decent work, from succeeding?"

Without waiting for an answer, she responded. "As a result of his failure to procure the farm, Mason and I went out west. We tried dry land farming and, then, Mason went into the oil patch. First, out in West Texas, later over to Kilgore. After he got hurt, he took to playing cards. Very few men ever beat him on the felt. He remembered every card played in every hand. Every time Chester and Robert played him, they lost; even when they cheated, they lost. He was even a better cheat than they were.

A better man too, and they knew this to be true. So, they killed him. Actually, they were cowards and hired someone else while they gloated over him, as he lay dying on a Mexican trash heap. And now," Elizabeth stood, "the remaining, lousy, stinking low-life is such a coward he can't admit, even to himself, that his soul is rotten to the core. I tell you that as I live and breathe I didn't kill my husband, or have him killed. But if I see Robert Stevens on the street, I'll shoot him down like the sick old dog he is. And go to jail smiling."

Chief Becker stood and said, "you probably have cause, Elizabeth, but I'd appreciate it if you let justice run the course here. In this state, murder for hire is a capital offense, even for rich white men. And, now that we have evidence that Robert and Chester conspired to commit the murder while in Texas, I believe the Mexicans will drop their extradition demands."

"You called me in here knowing I had nothing to do with the murder?"

"Elizabeth, I called you in here knowing you probably had nothing to do with the murder. There is a difference."

Banging commenced on the door.

"Ronnie!" Mavis yelled. "For the love of God, what are you doing in there? Everybody in the damn town knows Elizabeth didn't have anything to do with killing Mason!"

The Chief rolled his eyes. He had a look on his face that said, 'throw me a rope and I'll hang myself.'

He opened the door and said, "glad you cleared that up for me dear. I was getting ready to shoot Elizabeth because I thought the town had come to the opposite conclusion."

Elizabeth suppressed a smile and said, "are we done, Chief?"

The Chief and Mrs. Chief waved her out the door; they had more important matters to discuss. Mavis wanted to sit on the reviewing platform with Speaker Rayburn when the Speaker arrived for Danny's funeral. Elizabeth closed the door behind her as Mavis said, "and another thing, Ronnie..."

She loves him, thought Elizabeth. George stood as she entered the waiting area. He looked worried.

"Relax, George," Arlene drawled out of the side of her mouth, not holding the Lucky Strike. She kept typing. Elizabeth had never seen anyone type, smoke, and yell over clattering typewriter keys all at the same time.

"I don't see any manacles, and I haven't been asked to prepare an information for the County Attorney. She isn't going to jail today, tomorrow, next week, or even next month. Elizabeth, by the way, please tell Ralph to stop throwing rocks at the Stevens' home. He's beginning to hack the Chief off. Betty's there now with the babies and Ralph probably doesn't want to deal with Bob's bad side right off the bat."

As they opened the door to the front stairwell, they heard Arlene say, "damn there goes another nail."

They walked down the courthouse steps, onto California Street towards home, George said, "I finally understand how this town works. Mavis gives the orders; Arlene types the orders and sends them out with appropriate instructions. Why are we paying all these other officials? They aren't needed."

Elizabeth hooked her arm into his. He said nothing, but his heart swelled.

"Will gets in tomorrow evening at six. You'll be there?"

"Of course, Elizabeth. Where else would I be?"

"I'm so glad Wilson is coming home. I should feel guilty because of the reason, but I can't."

"I know. The dead don't speak in normal voices, yet, they are with us. Danny Ludlow is missed and he, I think, is also loved. But, he's gone and Will remains. I don't believe loving the living is disrespectful of the dead. Love for the living and respect for the dead are two separate kettles of fish."

"You speak like a man with experience in such matters."

"Elizabeth, when this war is over, we'll talk about my experience. For now though, we shall mourn Wat Eakins and Danny Ludlow - even while rejoicing that Will and Mr. Sullivan are still alive. May they be among the living for a long time."

"Amen," sighed Elizabeth.

The ball bounced against the wall, hit the floor, and then bounced back into Ralph's mitt. He pretended that he didn't notice his mother standing in the doorway of his and Will's room.

"Ralph, put the ball and mitt down and come into the kitchen. We need to talk."

Ralph was getting pretty big for sixteen, but no one in his right mind would want to get on his mom's bad side. Ralph was no exception.

He walked into the kitchen and slumped into a chair at the table. Even in his current mood, the kitchen smelled heavenly.

His mother was actually cooking - a fairly rare event. Even when Will was home and his dad was still alive, Will did the heavy cooking, usually to get out of church. He was glad his mom was getting back to normal. He was fed up with being mothered by everyone, except his own mother.

"Ralph."

Ralph jumped in his chair and looked around. His mom had two pies cooling on the sill, and was now pan searing a roast in a huge, cast iron skillet.

"Dang Mama how many ration points did that take?"

"Mr. Chaney used his, he's is not a big meat eater. Besides, the butcher held the roast back for me; he knows Will is coming home for the biggest event this town has seen since Camp Howze opened. Our ration points are not the issue though - your conduct is."

"Oh, mom!"

"Are you aware how many people have looked the other way, while you've committed crimes that would get other kids locked up?"

"Mom, I've been good, honest."

Elizabeth took the roast off the heat and knelt in front of Ralph, placing her hand on his face.

"Ralph, remember me? I'm your mother. Not a particularly good one, but that doesn't mean I don't know

about your activities. Don't sit there and lie to my face.
Just listen."

She went back to the stove.
"I know you're angry, Ralph. I am too. Can you
imagine the hurt and anger I feel knowing my youngest
son has been deprived of his father?"
Elizabeth gripped the stove.
"Mom, please don't do this. I'm sorry."
Elizabeth turned the roast over and said, "don't
apologize, like I just said, listen." She kept her back to
him so that she could finish without breaking down.

"Today, I had to give the Chief of Police reasons
for not arresting me as an accomplice in your dad's
murder. I have come to grips with the notion that several
people believe that I actually could have been an
accomplice."

She turned to face him.
"The very idea hurts, Ralph. Some of the things
people say about me. Maybe the memory will always
hurt. Still, you can't steal things, or continue to throw
things at the homes of people you dislike. People have
short memories. Soon, people won't see you any longer
as the poor kid who lost his dad. They'll see a punk who
needs to be put away. If that happens, I can't save you.
Neither can Will. Maybe the Lord could, but He might
make you wait a long time first. Rise above the evil, son.
Let Robert Stevens spew his venom.   He will pay.
Remember, if we fall down too - he wins. Don't give him
the pleasure."
"Mom, I'm so lonely. I miss my dad. He loved me,
and now, for no reason, he's gone."
Ralph burst into tears, wailing out his grief and
sadness. His Mom cradled him in her arms at the kitchen
table.

"He loved us all, Ralph. He loved us all, baby boy. Hush now. Remember this from when you were little?"

She began to sing,

"Three winsome ladies gliding down the wings of the wind.
Three gallant men riding the edges of starlight.
Wither goest thou o' wind and where may a maiden alight?
Wither goest thou o' light and where may a man tarry with kith and kin?
Not here sweet maidens for the wind searches endlessly.
Not here noble men for the light is constantly a flight against shadow and vale;
No rest for the weary, no sleep for the dead."

Elizabeth rubbed her son's head as he lay across her lap. Elizabeth and Ralph stayed still and quiet while the moon rose.

Chapter 61
Pawns, Bishops and Queens

"Who is that crowd for, Will?" Bob said. "Danny or the politicians?"

The platform was mobbed as the train pulled into Gainesville. The station was lined in bunting and draped in black crepe.

"Danny, I think," Will said. "The politicians aren't due here until the day of the funeral. Come on, Bob, we're getting off with him. Only his parents get close. This isn't going to turn into a carnival for the locals."

When Bob and Will got to the baggage car, Brad Bates was already there with six muscular marines in dress blues.

"We waited, gentlemen. Figured you two would want to assist in escorting Captain Ludlow back onto his home ground."

"Aye, sir," Will said. "Appreciate the consideration."

Bates ducked his head in a bobbing motion. He was not used to being thanked for being kind. He was decked out in an expensive suit. Other than the honor guard, only Will was in uniform.

"Mr. Davis, because you're in uniform, you move out first. Step down the ramp in funeral march cadence. The honor guard will follow with Captain Ludlow. There's a hearse waiting at the bottom of the ramp. Step to the side of the back door, execute an about face and salute Captain Ludlow as he's placed in the hearse."

"Aye, sir."

The side door to the baggage car opened as sunshine struck the ramp. Will stepped out. The crowd was silent. At the bottom of the ramp, he heard a band play a ruffle and flourish. When the casket appeared, the band played a dirge. Will heard a collective sigh, like wind through live oaks. Then he heard sobbing. Dud Ludlow had come home, and the town wept. As Will saluted the casket, he wondered what Dud would make of all this sorrow. A woman came forward. With a shock, Will recognized Dud's mom. In a voice barely above a whisper, he said, "its okay. This is Captain Ludlow's mom."

Mrs. Ludlow bent over and kissed the top of the casket and, then the flag. Only as she turned to leave, did she stagger. Will reached out and caught her by the elbow. A man, Will barely recognized as Bert Ludlow, took her other arm. Bert had shaved, combed his hair, and put on a nice suit. Will recognized George Chaney's work.

Bert looked at Will and said, "thanks for bringing Danny home Will."

He then put his arm around his wife and escorted her through the crowd.

Once the honor guard had been dismissed, and Danny driven away, Will stood dazed on the platform. Someone hugged him and then someone else grabbed him, sandwiching him. He realized he was between his mom and brother. They were hugging him so hard he could barely breathe. His uniform blouse was wet with tears - his and theirs.

He heard himself say, "Bob and I are both home. But Danny, dear God, I just can't figure this out."

"I know son," his mom said. "No one can, except for God and He is not saying much at the moment. Grieve for the loss, but rejoice in your own life. Ralph and I have missed you and thank God that you're still with us."

They walked down California Street in a silent procession. People came up and touched him on the arm, on the cheek, on the shoulder. Most he knew, some he didn't. When he reached his home on Dixon Street, he fell onto his bed. He started crying and he couldn't stop.

Ralph sat next to him, stroking his hair and singing to him about starlight. He went to sleep. He was home, and his brother was standing guard. He was safe.

Chapter 62
Breakers

The surf was up and Will was sitting on a dune.

Dud was sitting next to him wearing his cowboy hat and a bright orange swimsuit. "Sure beats the hell out of the Red River, doesn't it."

"I don't know, Dud. I'm getting kind of fed up with the ocean."

"Well, I'm glad they brought me home rather than dumping me into the ocean. How undignified - to be fish food."

"You're wearing a black cowboy hat and an orange swimsuit and you're worried about your dignity? Anyway, guess what? Now you're going to be worm bait."

"Guess you'll know where to find night crawlers next time you need some quick."

"That's gross, Ludlow."

"Only trying to be helpful."

"Great! Why didn't you help out by not getting yourself killed asshole?"

Dud laughed. "I've really pissed you off now, haven't I?" He stood to skim a couple of shells across the waves.

"Tried hard to stay alive, but got into a bad situation. Felt like Jim Bowie at the Alamo for a minute. Too many Japs, not enough Dud."

"You got it right, I am really pissed off."

Danny smiled and said, "Will, come on man get over it. You know why I'm here and my time is short."

"Saying good-bye are you?"

"Yep. Places to go, things to do - you know the drill."

"This is a trauma - induced nightmare, isn't it?"

"Wow! Trauma - induced nightmare, huh? Maybe you ought to go to medical school too." Dud got up and brushed the sand off himself. "Damn, I feel a little dead on my feet."

I stood up too, laughing in spite of myself.

Dud reached over, grabbed me, and hugged me hard.

"When you're feeling a little less sorry for yourself, tell my mom that I'm okay."

"How am I supposed to do that?"

Danny screwed his hat down tight and began looking for something behind the dune. "Quit being a total jerk. You're my best friend, Will, and always have been. You'll think of something. Here the blamed thing is. Knew I tucked it back here somewhere. Have to go. Surf's up."

Dud picked up a surfboard and ran towards the pounding water. Just before he dove in, he yelled over his shoulder, "catch you in the funny papers. Tell Bob I said sayonara, and that the last time you saw me, I didn't have a smoke to my name." He waved his hat at me over the crest of the surf.

Will watched Dud paddle into the horizon until the sun's glare was too bright. He popped straight up, disoriented. With a start, Will realized he was in his own bed; the sun beat down on him. He glanced at his watch. It was 1:15 in the afternoon. He jumped out of bed.

He never told Bob or anyone else who knew about his dream, that when he walked into the head that morning, he had to rinse white sand out from between his toes. Some things are private, always.

Chapter 63
Parlor Window

When he entered the Stevens home, Bob realized he had no idea where to go. He'd never been in the house before. The house was nice, in a formal 'I have a corn cob stuck too far up my butt,' sort of way. When Melrose asked him what he thought, he said, "Mrs. Stevens, this is the nicest home I've ever been in."

"Bob, I'm not stupid, I know we've had our differences. I won't ask you to call me mom, but Melrose will work nicely, if you don't mind."

Bob sighed. Making nice was by no means his strong suit. "Alright, Melrose, as long as we understand one thing."

"Yes, Bob?"

"I have neither forgiven nor forgotten what's going on with Mr. Stevens right now. Betty tells me you threw a wrench in his plans, so here's the deal. I call you Melrose and smile. I see your psycho husband on the street; I kick the crap out of him. Beat him until he can't breathe. No one messes with my kids."

"I feel the same way, Bob. Robert was way out of line."

"Good, Melrose, but how do I trust you? Maybe you're still running a scam."

Melrose put her hand over his. Bob exercised a lot of will to keep from flinching. Her touch felt like a hot frying pan.

"Bob, I swear on the heads of my grandchildren that nothing bad will ever happen to them while they're in my care."

Bob slowly slid his hand from under hers, and said, "okay, we owe it to the kids and to Betty to get along. In any event, once Danny's funeral is over, the heat's off of us both for awhile. I'll be out of here again."

"Your situation *is* interesting," Melrose said. "I've noticed several well-dressed young men strolling around the block. They're taking enormous pains to blend in, even though they continue to stick out like yellow daisies in a green meadow."

"My professional shadows. People notice, that's okay. If anyone asks you about them, pretend you haven't noticed anything out of the ordinary."

"I can do that," she said. "I'm good at pretending. Why don't you grab a seat in the parlor, Bob, and relax. You don't need to stand in the entryway like…"

"Like hired help, Melrose?"

"I was going to say like a statue."

Bob laughed.

"What? Did I miss something?"

"No, Will and I were talking on the train yesterday; your parlor came into the discussion - nothing bad. He just told me to accept my success with grace, or something like that."

"Good advice, Bob. Take a load off. I'll bring you a glass of sweet tea. Betty and the kids will be back soon."

They went into the parlor and Bob sat in the over-stuffed wing chair. As Melrose turned to leave, Bob said, "Mindy Hulen is in medical school now?"

"Yes, I'd like to hear her whole story too. Her parents were thunderstruck when she went to live with her aunt in Philadelphia. In less than three years, Mindy got into the University of Pennsylvania Nursing School, joined the Army, went to the Pacific, and was sent home to attend Johns Hopkins. Word is that she has great potential as a surgeon."

"She's going to be famous."

"No more than you Bob. Who else around here has enough talent to warrant a full-time security detail? Mindy doesn't have one of those yet."

Bob snorted. "My situation is a hoot n' holler, isn't it? I'm not kidding when I say I can't tell anyone about what I'm doing."

Melrose sat on the sofa facing Bob.

"Betty says you and Mindy have two things in common."

"Really?"

"Yes, she says you and Mindy have always loved her and both of you have the kind of intelligence that shows up in your hands. The way you use them."

Bob stared out the plate glass parlor window. He had no response. The observation hit too close to home. He couldn't fault Betty for sharing observations with her mother. Still, all this attention focused on him was going to take some time to get used to.

Melrose stood up, and said, "I'll get you that glass of tea now."

"Thank you Melrose that would be nice."

Bob Sullivan looked around at the tastefully furnished parlor. He was sitting in one of the Lindsay Street 'swell' homes, and no one was going to call the police.

"Ain't this the shits, Danny? I'm getting the royal treatment because I built a little box that makes funny little squiggles on paper. And you, Danny, get a front row seat at the cemetery."

Bob looked out the window, thinking, "I never dreamed things would turn out like this."

Conor burst into the room.

"Hey, daddy!"

"Hey, big guy! Where are Mom and Megan?"

"They're coming, Bob," Melrose was back with his tea. "I looked out front. People are coming out to say hi. She's about three houses down. Megan's in the stroller."

"I was bored Dad, so I ran back to Grandma's by myself."

"Good man. How was Aunt Mindy?"

"Mom and her sure cry a lot. She kept kissing me daddy."

"I'll bet. Come sit in my lap while I finish my tea."

"Aye, aye, dad."

Bob laughed. Conor laughed. They drank the tea. Grandma promptly brought them more tea and a plate of gingersnaps. She didn't mention that Robert never allowed eating in the parlor.

Melrose figured this was only one of the rules that would change - and to her own surprise, she found that she didn't mind in the least. In any event, a new sheriff was in town and Robert wasn't around to object.

Chapter 64
Hateful Thoughts

Prather DeWitt took careful aim, and his putt rolled fifteen feet into the cup. He had installed this cup and three others in his office floor.

Robert Stevens fidgeted in a high-back chair, in the corner. "Damn it, Prather, I'm in trouble here, and you stand there putting like you were Bobby Jones."

"Robert, I'm not Bobby Jones and you're not Ben Hogan. But let's use the golf analogy since you brought it up."

Prather set aside his putter and leaned against his desk.

"Robert seems you've taken complete leave of your senses. If this were a golf game, you'd be in the deep rough, six strokes behind, with only one hole left to play. I'm being generous. I don't think you have a hole left."

"Now wait a damn minute, Prather! I–"

"No, Robert you wait a damn minute. If you're not careful, you'll end up stamping plates in Leavenworth or Huntsville for one hell of a long time. You won't end up on death row only because I've worked diligently to ensure that's not on the table."

"Setting aside why I'm being prosecuted, you really believe that silly county attorney has enough to convict me of murder?"

Prather pulled a silver flask from his middle desk drawer; he then grabbed two tumblers from his credenza. He poured two fingers of single malt scotch into each tumbler. He passed one over to Robert, his "former" friend. *Former* kept blinking like a red neon sign in his mind.

"The United States Attorney will be prosecuting this case, not the silly little county attorney. This is a federal case. Their theory is that you conspired with Chester Harris, and, perhaps, others to transport Mason out of the United States for the purpose of committing murder. They will emphasize that you, a wealthy American, hired impoverished foreign nationals to do your dirty work. I have exercised the limit of my influence by obtaining your release on bail, and in securing an arrangement."

Robert contemplated the meaning of the word 'arrangement,' but said nothing. He sipped his scotch and listened to the mantle clock ticking.

"I can't walk away from this can I?"

"You stepped on your dick big-time on this deal."

"Yeah, Prather, because of you. At the time, you seemed real interested in Chester and I getting Mason down there."

"True, I unwisely facilitated your wishes to rough Mason up. The thought of you and Chester seriously harming Mason never occurred to me and I certainly never thought your issues with Mason would end up in murder. Of course, poor old Chester is beyond caring about all of this now, isn't he?"

"Yeah, poor old Chester. Leaving me to hold the bag while he dodges *Satan's* pointy ended pitchfork."

"Really, Robert. Why speak ill of the dead? What's done is done."

"You're probably right. Besides, I find my thoughts of you dodging the pointy end of Satan's pitchfork immensely more comforting."

"All in due time, Robert, all in due time. While we're dwelling on hateful thoughts, I have one other question."

"Yes?"

"Why did you try to implicate Elizabeth Davis in her own husband's murder? Ultimately, you had to know that such an accusation wouldn't be taken seriously. Everyone knows that if Elizabeth wanted Mason dead, she would've shot him herself. "

"None of your business asshole, besides, you know the answer anyway."

Prather rocked slowly in his chair. "Really, Robert? Getting Mason wasn't enough for you? After all these years, you still couldn't resist taking a shot at her too, huh?"

Robert shrugged and said, "think what you will. What's my arrangement?"

Prather finished his scotch in a quick swallow.

"My understanding is that the U. S. Attorney will not oppose a defense motion to place you in a psychiatric ward at the federal pen in Leavenworth, Kansas. You can expect to be there for about ten years. But you must agree to plead not guilty to the charges set forth in the indictment by reason of insanity."

"I'm no crazier than you are!"

Prather shrugged his shoulders but didn't respond.

"Is my attorney aware of this arrangement?"

"No. I didn't think our discussion warranted the involvement of counsel, at least until after we'd spoken in private."

Prather looked his former friend right in the eye.

"Robert, understand me here. This is the last time we'll ever meet or perhaps even speak."

"Prather, please I…!"

"For once, shut the hell up and open your ears, Robert! If you open your trap once more, this meeting is over."

Prather waited. Robert Stevens turned beet red but held his tongue. "I have arranged this deal by expending huge amounts of political and fiscal capital," Prather said.

"I even made political contributions to several democrats. This is the only deal you're going to get."

Prather drew closer to Robert so he could talk in a softer voice.

"The feds will take this deal so they don't have to waste time dragging wet backs up here to testify and they don't have to convince a judge that Chester Harris' letters implicating you and providing motive are 'dying declarations'. But, they will if they have to. Finally, you need to understand that the fix is in to take you down hard. There's high level political interest in this case. Don't ask me why the federal government cares. I don't know. Nor do my contacts. They think the interest has to do with people Will is involved with but can't say for sure. They just know someone with serious juice is pushing to nail your ass."

"May I speak now?" Robert said, with as much dignity as he could muster.

"Yes."

"What happens if I roll the dice and go to trial? What if I tell them the slimy, smarmy truth?"

"Two possibilities arise. You are convicted and go to the penitentiary for ten to twenty-five. Or, perhaps, you plead not guilty and have an accident before the trial."

"Did you just threaten my life, Prather?"

"I'm the messenger, Robert. I've been told that no one wants a trial involving these families right now. Again, I don't know why and don't want to know."

"Why'd these mystery people come to you, Prather? *You* of all people, I don't believe this crap. Chester accommodates you by blowing his brains out, then implicating me in his fucking suicide note. Now you're the messenger? That's rich."

Prather sat back in his chair for a moment, considering what he had to gain by telling Robert the truth. He decided Stevens was no longer a player. Telling him the truth served no purpose and might be dangerous to his own legal interests.

"I have no idea, Robert. Guess they found out about our long-standing association."

Someone knocked at the door.

"Yes?"

His secretary, Mildred, poked her head in.

"Mr. DeWitt, two men identifying themselves as FBI agents are out here. Louis is here now too."

"Thank you, Mildred."

"Aren't you even going to ask what they want?"

"I know what they want, Robert. They're here to escort you down to Dallas. My understanding is that your state bail has been revoked. Apparently, federal charges have now been prepared - don't worry though. Counsel will be at the federal courthouse in Dallas waiting to represent you in the arraignment hearing in federal court. Counsel will post bail on the federal warrant."

"You son of a bitch. You knew they were coming the whole time I was here."

"Of course, Robert. Couldn't you sense the urgency in my voice? Just remember, life on a mental ward is better than life on a prison cellblock - or is it?"

"You've ruined my life, you bastard!" Robert yelled, as he jumped on Prather. "This all started because of you. I never would've touched him, goddamnit, if it…"

As the two men rolled on the floor, the FBI agents entered the office. They separated the two men and handcuffed Robert.

Prather stood and said, "take it easy with him. I believe he's quite deranged."

Robert Stevens screamed and cried, "you bloody, monstrous bastard. I'll see you in hell!"

Prather, Mildred, and Louis watched them throw Robert Stevens into an unmarked Buick sedan's backseat.

Mildred looked at Prather and said, "Sir! You're injured! I'll get a wet cloth." She hurried out of the room.

Prather got on the phone, which was picked up immediately on the other end.

"DeWitt here. He's on his way. When he left here he was acting out violently. I believe he is quite deranged. I'm no doctor, but I'd say he's delusional as well. Make sure he takes the arrangement. I'm not paying you as much money as I am to fail."

He hung up the phone. Mildred came back in and started daubing the cuts on his face. "Thank you, Mildred. I'll take it from here. Please hold my calls for the next fifteen minutes."

Mildred left. The heavy mahogany door made a soft click behind her.

"Dad, what in hell was that all about?"

"You don't want to know. Besides, I asked you here to discuss something important, listen up."

"Sure, dad. How can I help?"

Prather winced as he dabbed his forehead with the cold cloth.

"Louis, did you really show up at Chief Becker's office this morning, demanding that he arrest Bob Sullivan on the outstanding assault warrant?"

Louis stared down at his shiny Floresheims.

"Well, yes sir. He comes waltzing in here like some muckety-muck and…"

SMAAACK!

Prather hit his son hard enough to knock him out of his chair. "Jesus Christ, dad!"

Louis held his face, where a big red handprint ran along his jaw line. He managed to get back into his chair.

"Dad, I'm a grown man. Don't ever …"

"Then, act like a grown man, you damn lame brain. When you pull a stunt like this, I'm convinced the best part of you trickled down your mother's legs."

"Bob's not above the law, dad."

Prather leaned forward as Louis leaned back, as if to ward off another blow.

"Yes, Louis, he is. He's above all the law we know and can control. Right now, someone we don't know and can't touch is protecting him. He could probably have anything he wanted now, including your ass in a sling. Fortunately for us, Chief Becker is not a complete idiot. He called me first, before heading over to the Stevens house on your say-so."

Prather lowered his forehead to his cool, glass-topped desk.

"Why can't you understand how things work, Louis? Are you *that* blind? Have I taught you *nothing?*"

Louis was smart enough to say nothing. His face hurt like a motherfucker. He wished he had a cold rag too.

"Louis, games are always played, in business, and in life. The games are sometimes played for very high stakes. But, in every situation, there are winners and losers. You must be able to spot the powerful players in any situation. If you don't, you will lose every time."

Prather examined his son's face to see if anything was sinking in—nothing appeared to be. Louis was still fretting about the slap. He's so lucky Sullivan didn't kill him, Prather thought.

"Consider the game of chess for a moment. When Bob Sullivan beat you up, he was barely a pawn. We had the upper hand. If we'd caught him right after he'd beaten you, we could have done anything with him. Today, you saw first-hand what happened to Robert

Stevens. On our chessboard here in Gainesville, Robert was a bishop, who got mixed up in events bigger than he could handle. Therefore, I had to sacrifice him. He was expendable." Prather poured himself another scotch. "If we now apply the chess analogy to Sullivan, what can we say about him?"

Louis' forehead creased in concentration, but he said nothing.

Prather continued hammering him with the obvious.

"He is no longer a pawn, Louis! He's so important; he's not even playing the game on our board. We don't know why because we don't understand the source of his power. This being the case, what should we do?"

"Leave him alone?" Louis cowered. Figuring if his dad came around that desk again, he'd make a run for the door.

"Yes, leave him alone. That's why I slapped you. You don't see the obvious. Didn't you take note of the fact that some very serious men are wandering up and down Lindsay Street protecting him? You don't protect pawns, son."

"Dad, I thought he'd messed up somewhere else and those guys had him under house arrest."

Prather wheeled his chair around to stare out at his grain elevators. I have only myself to blame, he thought. My son is a moron. I will provide for him, but I must leave the business to someone else or everything I've built up won't exist five years after I'm gone.

Louis would never know - no one would ever know - that he, Prather DeWitt, had been the biggest fool of all. No one else would ever know that he'd lost his grain elevator business to Mason Davis in a high stakes card game. Fortunately, Chester had been the only other player at the table that night when the final hand had been played. Robert had been at the card table, but, had left moments earlier. The fact that Chester had blown up at Mason in front of witnesses at a card game in the hotel only a couple of nights before his loss had been a stroke of luck.

Prather had been drunk. Mason had been sober and had bet his one-eighth interest in three potentially profitable oil leases, and the Turner Hotel deed, against Prather's business. Prather should have folded. He didn't and he lost. He had begged Mason to accept a large cash sum in lieu of the business. The grinning Mason had declined. "Don't worry, Prather," he'd said. "You'll still have a job. I'll need a cracker-jack general manager."

Too bad really, thought Prather. Mason should have taken my cash counter-offer. I had to have him killed. Strange, that he still respected Mason more than any other man he'd ever known. Win or lose, Mason never broke a sweat, no matter the stakes. This made him a deadly poker player. Yes, Prather admired Mason, even though he'd become expendable.

Prather hadn't gone on the card trip to Mexico. He had merely stoked Chester and Robert's long-standing resentment of Mason to convince them to lure Mason down to Mexico with the promise of big stakes. Mason was a true gambler and Prather knew he would go - the lure of meeting new marks, taking everything they had, and then grinning at them. These things were too tempting for Mason to pass up.

Prather had also given Bob and Chester a little 'seed' money to hire thugs to 'rough Mason up.' But, that's truly all the thugs did...they didn't *kill* Mason. Although by now they probably believed that they had. Prather had hired Mason's actual killer through a grain dealer contact in Chicago.

The hitter had trailed the men to Mexico and had killed Mason while he was still laying in the alley hollering for help. The ten thousand dollar fee for the killing was a person-to-person cash transaction. The hit man was someone you wouldn't notice twice. He'd looked like an accountant for a seedy, third-rate firm.

Funny thing, the hit fee was considerably less than he'd offered Mason in lieu of the grain elevator business. He regretted that Mason hadn't been reasonable about the whole sordid matter.

"Dad? Are you okay, Dad? Should I call Mildred?"
Prather spun his chair back around.
"Sorry son had something else on my mind for a moment. Where were we?"
"You were explaining the game of chess to me. Something about this board, that board, our board, his board."
"Forget all that and remember two important things."
"Sure, dad. I'm listening. This time I really am."
"I believe you, boy. Here is what I want. Stay away from Bob Sullivan and the Davis boys. We accomplish nothing by antagonizing them. When I say stay away, you understand I mean from their families too?"
"Sure, pop."
"Stay busy at the elevator and at the draft board. I'm serious about this, Louis."
"Alright, already, dad. I understand."
With much sadness, Prather thought, no son, you don't.

Chapter 65
Kitchen Conversations

"Mindy Hulen is coming over to get you, Wilson?"

"Yes ma'am, she is."

His mother removed his dinner plate.

"Excellent roast, mom."

"I agree, Elizabeth, a superb meal," George Chaney said, while patting his ample belly. Ralph had wolfed his plate down and asked to be excused. He and some other kids were lining the funeral procession route in black crepe from the Harvey Brothers Funeral Home to Leonard Park. The city was paying him and the other boy's two bits an hour to make sure the city looked both patriotic and somber.

Once the procession was over, Danny would be laid to rest in Fairview Cemetery. Will had seen the black marble tombstone earlier in the day. The Marine Corps emblem was etched onto the stone. Several townspeople had insisted on pitching in to pay for the expensive monument. There was a rumor that Prather DeWitt had made a sizable contribution. A black marble memorial stone with Wat Eakins' name on it was going to be placed next to Danny's grave.

When word first got out that Wat was going to receive a Distinguished Flying Cross posthumously at the same time Danny was getting a silver star, from the Speaker no less; the breath was knocked out of every person in Cooke County. The initial view expressed was, "imagine that. A dead colored boy receiving a medal from Mr. Sam. What is the world coming to?"

An aftershock hit the county when Mr. Sam expressed his personal opinion that these two native sons should be memorialized together. The Klan attempted to rally in protest, but the protest never got off the ground. For once, the Klan was told to shut up. Wat Eakins had been killed defending southern white boys from a Nazi air attack. The Speaker, Mr. Sam himself, was coming to say words in memory of Wat. The town decided to accept the enlightened view, that Wat was a pilot *and* a war hero, which trumped his being a Negro.

"What are you two going to do?"

Will's thoughts snapped to the present.

"I don't know, mom," he said. "If I was a betting man–he noticed his mom visibly cringed when he said 'betting man'–I'd guess we're going somewhere to say hello and good-bye to each other."

George pulled out a pipe from his vest pocket. "Think I'll go out on the porch and smoke."

"Nah, stay here, George. The weather is still raw out. This is nothing to get upset about. Mindy and I are headed in different directions. Glad we're getting the chance to talk face to face."

His mother wiped down the kitchen table with an old rag. "Well Wilson, with your current status in the town at least there won't be any gossip about a Hulen and a Davis being seen together."

"I may not be home until late. I promised I'd stop by the Ludlow place. Dud's parents want to talk to me."

Everyone was silent as George filled the kitchen with cherry wood tobacco smoke. When Will's mother sat at the table, Will realized there was no tension in the room. Notwithstanding the pending funeral, the accusations of Robert Stevens, and the concerns about Ralph, they were all at ease.

"Will," his mom said. "You have a lot on your mind right now. Let me ease your burden on one very important issue."

Will said, "mom, you don't have to explain anything to me."

"Nonetheless, I intend to. I had nothing to do with your father's death. Someday, we will talk in more detail about how I've always felt about your poor dad. Right now, I want you to understand that I deeply loved him. Still do. Robert Stevens is a disturbed man. He has hated your father and me for years. His accusation was his parting gift of evil to me."

His mother reached across the table for his hands while George quietly left the kitchen.

"Mom, I know you're telling the truth ... but I'm still mad at you."

"I know, Wilson. Your father made me crazy. As I told our police chief today, the very things that made me love him also angered me on occasion. I only ask that you remember one thing about your father and me."

"What?"

"Don't confuse simple tears in the carpet with cracks in the foundation."

Mindy found them sitting in the kitchen holding hands, saying nothing. The scene was akin to watching sunshine through stained glass. These two people were drawing strength from one another. What she was not prepared for is how her heart pounded when Will turned and saw her at the door, she turned to liquid. Nothing had changed at all. He melted her with a glance. Will is my center, she thought. I'll always carry him around with me, even if I never see him after tomorrow.

"May I come in?"

Will stumbled on the leg of a kitchen chair in his effort to get to the screen door and fell face first onto the kitchen floor.

"Graceful, as always," Mindy giggled. Like a fine wine, he was going straight to her head. She let herself in, while he picked himself up.

Elizabeth rolled her eyes and said, "Mindy, I'm glad you made it home…"

Mindy didn't hear the rest because Will put his arms around her and kissed her. She swayed right into him. He smelled so good, like he always had, wood smoke, sweat and … he smelled like Will.

Elizabeth left the kitchen knowing her presence wouldn't have mattered if she'd left with a marching band. She figured they had a fifty-fifty chance of getting out of her kitchen without ripping their clothes off right then and there. She wasn't going to do a thing about it either… they were burying a friend tomorrow.

George was reading the newspaper in Masons' rocker in the small, cluttered living area. She moved some sewing pieces around to sit on a worn divan.

"This poor mother," George said. "Says here five boys, the Rourke boys, were all killed on one ship, the Juneau. Why in God's name would the navy assign a whole family to one ship?"

George noticed that Elizabeth seemed distracted.
"Mindy here?"
"Yes," she said.
"Thought I heard the screen door," George said. "They off?"
"George, I am afraid to look."
"Pardon?"
"Let me explain." She stood, took two steps and sat in George's lap. Before he could react, she held his face and kissed him passionately. Then, she stood, straightened her apron, and sat back on the divan.
"Glad to see each other, I take it?"
"Immensely so."

440

"Elizabeth, what would your reaction be if I said I wanted us to look for our own place?"

"I'd say find a place with better light. Always seems gloomy in here."

"I agree," George said. "Better light would set off your gorgeous eyes–a bonus."

"The things you say Mr. Chaney. You are quite outrageous."

"With two young people making love in the kitchen, I thought outrageous might be called for."

Neither had the courage to enter the kitchen.

Will and Mindy did manage to leave the kitchen–barely. "Come on, Will. I've brought some blankets. Let's head out to the river," Mindy whispered.

On their way out of town, Mindy said, "after we bury Danny, I'm not coming back. I mean, I'll be back for certain things, like other funerals."

"You're just not coming back here to live, right?"

As he spoke, Will ran his hand over Mindy's stomach, then, upward till he reached her breasts.

"Will, I swear if you don't stop, I'll run this car off the road, and Gainesville will be hosting two more funerals."

"Mindy, if we're going to wreck, I hope you're wearing clean underwear."

"I'm not wearing any underwear."

"You medical students are all alike," he said, laughing.

The car jolted along a narrow dirt road towards their favorite bluff. The car was missing badly. The rough road and the coughing engine made for a wild ride.

"I know gasoline is in short supply, but this is really bad," Will said.

"I know. I put drip gas in the car."

"You put drip gas into the Packard?"

"Only way we'd have enough to get out here," Mindy said. "Dad keeps a couple of five gallon cans of the stuff in the garage."

"Does he collect it from the pipelines himself?"

"Are you kidding? That would be beneath him. He sends the yard guy out."

When they reached their favorite bluff, they gathered wood and started a fire. As the flames blazed skyward, Mindy stepped out of her clothing, folding everything. Will followed suit. After their beginning in the kitchen, their lovemaking was languorous. When they finished, they did not separate. Will stared into her eyes and said, "Mindy it's really nice to see you again. How's your piece of the war progressing?"

Mindy slapped at his chest. "The awful truth is that the war is one of the two best things I have ever had happen to me."

Will slid his left arm underneath her as she snuggled next to him.

"I've seen horrible things, Will. Boys like you and Danny coming into the operating theater blown to bits and crying for their mothers."

Will held her tighter, but made no attempt to stop her crying. Crying was good. You were in trouble when you couldn't cry anymore.

Finally, she said, "I've been given a great gift, Will."

"Mindy, you're a gift to everyone who knows you. The word is spreading that Walt Hulen's daughter is a healer."

"Sssh!" Mindy said. "If that gets out, the town fathers, the same ones who don't want Wat's tombstone in Fairview, will advocate burning me at the stake."

"I agree," Will said. "You're a witch, one I'm completely entranced by. But, burning you would be a tad extreme. Perhaps we could dunk you in the river until you confess that your talent comes from the devil."

Mindy punched Will in the stomach and said, "why do I bother?"

"Seriously?" Will said, "because getting your MD, *being* a doctor matters. Ignore the naysayers. Listen to the smart people, like me, who know what you're capable of."

"We aren't going to be together much longer. You know that too, don't you, Will?"

"I can't go with you. You can't go with me. I too doubt that I'll come back here after the war - the war has changed everything. Bob Sullivan and I are getting involved in something I can only describe as surreal."

"Have anything to do with the G-men walking around pretending they're visiting Camp Howze?"

"Yes, and don't ask. All I'll say is that I went into a New York bar and something bizarre happened. I went into a bar in Panama and something bizarre happened. In Australia, we ended up buying the bar. What I've learned is to stay out of bars. I know this makes no sense to you."

"Are women mixed up in this?"

"Yes."

"I figured, say no more."

Will smiled. "Got me all figured out, huh? Women are at the root of all my problems."

"In case you haven't noticed, women are attracted to you. Be aware and beware."

Will laughed.

"Listen to me," she said. "You probably think this is an unqualified compliment or even a display of jealousy. This isn't an empty compliment and while I am jealous, I'm also your friend. Your effect on women is palpable. If you don't control where you cast...your net, you will make your life miserable–especially now."

"Why now, Mindy?"

"Think about the times we're living in," she said, as she got up.

"Are we headed over to the Ludlow place from here?" Mindy said.

"If the car makes it."

"Let's scrub each other off in the river, Will. We don't want to show up at Danny's house smelling like sex."

"Good idea," Will said. "Stay on the path though. The bramble will tear you up otherwise."

The days were growing longer in early April, so some light remained. Enough to illuminate their path down to the river. The dusk sky was clear and a chill breeze was rising off of the river. The sand too was cold, the water colder. They yelled and screamed when the sandy water hit them.

They heard a yowl close by. Twenty yards away, a mountain lion eyed them. She'd come down to the water to get a drink. They'd drawn her attention.

They stood close together, their teeth chattering as they watched the big cat. "We have a genuine prehistoric scene here," Will murmured. "A naked man and his mate covered in mud, stare across a watering hole at a predator. Isn't it a bit ridiculous?"

"What, Will? Getting mauled by a cat? I'm scared to death."

"I survived an armed torpedo bucking like a bronco in one of our aft tubes, now; I'm home and could be eaten by a hungry mountain lion in my own backyard."

The cat crept closer, sniffing the breeze.

"Mindy, listen to me. If she decides we're prey, you take off running straight down river. Don't look back. I'll divert her."

"Will, I'm not leaving you here. Are you nuts?"

"Don't argue, Mindy. I have a better chance of fending her off if I know you're safely out of her killing zone."

The mud must have stifled their scent. The cat yowled again, and then loped off into the brush.

"Let's not hang around, Mindy. She might change her mind."

They didn't speak again until they were safely back in the car.

"Will, she looked bent on attacking. What caused her to retreat?"

"I don't know, Mindy. Strange though, I could swear I've seen that particular cat before."

"You told me about seeing a cat up here before, remember?"

"Right, when Dud and I were here before the war. Her lair, I think, is near the bluff. This sounds really dumb, but I think she left us alone because she recognized me. I've had a couple of opportunities to shoot her before, and never have. After all, this is *her* home."

"Are you trying to tell me that cat is an old friend?"

"Yes."

"Will, that is the dumbest explanation of animal behavior I've ever heard."

"Yep."

"Problem is I believe you. She might have decided we were too large, but she looked hungry. She could've taken us."

"Mindy, our time isn't up. Look at what happened that way."

He squeezed her right thigh as she negotiated the narrow dirt road, both wishing the ride - their last together for many years - would continue forever.

When they reached the Ludlow home, Mindy said, "want me to go in with you?"

"I want you to do everything with me from now on. But, this isn't about me. See you tomorrow at Danny's funeral."

He hopped lightly out of the car, ran around to the driver's side and kissed her. She smoothed his damp hair back off his brow.

"I'm crazy about you, Will, no matter what happens. You know that, right?"

"I'd have to be dumb, deaf, blind, and stupid not to know that Mindy. See you tomorrow."

When she drove off, he forced himself not to run after her. He wanted to beg her to stay with him. But, he figured he'd lose. If she did follow him she'd resent the imposition. If he followed her, she'd end up resenting that too. Her life would take her away from him sooner or later, and that was that.

He turned and headed up the cracked walk to Danny's house. He noticed that the house had been freshly painted and that the yard was cut. He knocked on the door.

The house was not only picked up, the interior sparkled, as much as a house on Gribble Street could sparkle.

"Thank you for coming, Will," Bert Ludlow said.

That's when Will knew things were bad. Bert hadn't been sober and polite for two days in a row for as long as he could remember.

"Doris wants to see you too. It's… well, when she saw you coming up the walk without Danny beside you, she couldn't handle the torment."

"Believe me, sir, I understand."

Bert smiled. "Will, you can call me Bert, or even the old drunk. Just lay off the *sir* stuff would you? Please sit down. Can I get you a beer or a soda water?"

"A beer would be great, thanks."

Bert returned with a beer and a root beer for himself, smiling self - consciously. "You know me, Will. One beer is too many, and ten is never enough."

"Will my drinking one bother you?"

"Nah, I'll enjoy it."

Both men sat and took swigs.

"Will, I know this is short notice, the funeral being tomorrow and all. Doris and I would be real happy if you'd say some words about Danny at the church tomorrow. I'm not up to the task. Besides, what can I say? Sorry I beat and cussed you, boy. Sorry I ran you off to get killed."

Will didn't have a response. Bert was right. He swallowed more beer.

Bert smiled that small sad smile again. "Thanks for not contradicting me, Will. The truth is what it is. Can you do this thing for Danny?"

"Yes Bert, I can speak for him and about him."

"Danny would be pleased. I don't think anything mattered more to him than your friendship."

"Then, we're equal. I'm not letting myself think too much about him. I'm afraid I'll start screaming and never stop."

"I wish I could help you, Will but I don't know how. I was down to the funeral parlor today. I kept wanting him to, you know, sit up and scream at me or something."

The bedroom door opened and Doris came out with her eyes downcast to avoid eye contact with Will. She carried a small pouch in her hands.

"Will," she said. "I know you'll be leaving after the funeral. You're welcome to anything in Danny's room. I found this pouch with an old note in his room. Thought these might be something you'd want right away."

I knew the moment I saw the pouch. Over the years, Danny had won every decent marble I'd ever acquired, including my favorite green aggie. I took the pouch. Sure enough, all my marbles - including the green aggie were there. I saw the note too, but didn't want to look at it right then.

Doris headed back to her room after she'd turned over the marbles.

"You'll speak right after the preacher and before Speaker Rayburn," Bert said. "They said you'd have five minutes, but I told them you'd have all the time you wanted. Their schedule be damned. I guess it comes down to this. Danny had you to look out for him. Sometimes, you *were* the only one ..." Bert couldn't finish the thought. He sat and stared at the floor. I let myself out.

As I closed the door, I said, "see you all tomorrow, Bert."

He waved at me with his root beer. I shut the door.

The marbles clacked in my pocket as I walked the long blocks home from Gribble over to Dixon Street. As I passed the intersection of Lindsay and California Street, I saw the black crepe paper hanging everywhere. A silhouette approached me. I jumped. The shadow looked like Dud.

Ralph laughed. "Seen a ghost, Will?"

"That's not funny Ralph."

"Yeah, I know."

We walked on.

"Hear the latest?"

"On what, Ralph? The war?"

"Nah, we'll win that within the next year."

"Good, Ralph. If you have inside information, we need to get you a job on the general staff."

"For someone in the war," Ralph said. "You don't focus much on the big picture. Odessa is ready to fall. Soon, Italy will be completely in Allied hands. Where you've been in the Pacific is much tougher. You know all the island hopping, landings, and pitched battles at the end of an elongated supply line." We walked on, black crepe billowing around us.

"No, I was talking about the latest news on that scum Stevens."

"What's going on?"

"He's been indicted on federal charges. Conspiracy to commit murder and some other stuff. They revoked his bail and carted him off to Dallas earlier today."

"Where did they pick him up?"

"He was at Prather DeWitt's office when the FBI showed up."

"Prather DeWitt? I smell a rat. Why would Robert be over there?"

"I have no idea."

"My question is Ralph, now that Harris is dead and Stevens is in Dallas, are you going to quit vandalizing?"

"I think so. Mr. Chaney is putting me to work down at his store, just like you. He wants to make me respectable."

"Good for him, Ralph. I happen to agree."

"Will?"

"Yeah?"

"I'm glad you're home. We were afraid you weren't going to come."

"Sure glad I did. Seeing Mindy again was absolutely necessary and I'm proud of how you've hung in there, little brother."

"Barely, Will...only barely."

They walked in the kitchen door, where a note and folder lay on the kitchen table. His mother's note read:

Will: A Mr. Bates dropped by this evening not long after you and Mindy left. Too bad you missed him. He left the packet for you, saying the contents are self - explanatory.

Inside the packet, was a note from Mr. Bates.

Will:

Monterrey California is nice this time of year. You're headed there the day after tomorrow. Your orders and train tickets are enclosed. You've been assigned to us, but will still wear your navy uniform. The government's language school has been set up in Monterrey, so, we'll see if you can learn German and Russian at the same time. If you show the aptitude and make appropriate progress, you'll be at the school six months. Then, we have a project in mind for you. See you at the funeral.

Bates

Great, Will thought. Who is 'we'? He went upstairs, brushed his teeth and went to bed. Tuesday, April 4, 1944 would be a trying day.

Will sat on the aisle. They were in the second pew. His mother switched places so Mindy could sit next to him. On Mindy's left sat his mom, then Ralph, then Walt and Elaine Hulen. The Ludlows, The Speaker, Congressman Johnson, and other dignitaries sat in the front pew. The church was packed. Wisely, in Will's view, the Ludlows had decided against an open casket service. Dud's senior picture sat atop of the flag-draped casket. When he was motioned up to speak, Will mounted the church dais and stood behind the podium. He spoke.

"Danny was my best friend. I didn't want him to leave Gainesville before finishing high school. I thought Danny wasn't ready for the world, much less combat. I was wrong. Danny distinguished himself in a manner I would not have thought possible. He always talked about being a marine. Today, we honor his contribution. He has given everything. During his short time in the service, he fought with bravery at Pearl Harbor,

450

Guadalcanal, New Britain, and, of course, Bougainville. The only reason he was at Bougainville, was because he was the best. He went from being a slick - sleeve private to a captain in an organization that values toughness, bravery, loyalty, and love of country. I, like his parents, will miss Captain Daniel Ludlow, United States Marine Corps. His country will miss him even more. I am pleased that my best friend Danny and my good friend Wat will be together in spirit. Gainesville will be poorer for their loss. Good-bye, Danny.

Mister Sam's remarks were somber and appropriate. I heard little of them. The mourners walked behind Danny's parents up Lindsay and then left, down California Street to Leonard Park. People wept and threw flowers in the caisson's path. Danny, they sure love you now that you're dead. The town showed Danny some class and Danny had earned the respect shown. He was a native son in every sense of the word.

The group for the internment at Fairview was smaller. Bob stood next to me, so did Mr. Bates. As we walked away, Mr. Sam and Mr. Johnson stopped us to say hello.

"Those were nice words today, Will," Mr. Sam said. "No beating around the bush. You show promise as a politician."

Sir, I'm glad to see you. Thank you for all your help with Wat and Danny. I take your remarks about my eulogy as high praise."

"I agree," Mr. Johnson said. "You did well, boy. Do you know Mr. Chaney?"

"Yes sir. He's my step dad now. May I introduce you?"

I waved over Mr. Chaney and my mom. "Mr. Chaney, Mrs. Davis may I introduce Mr. Sam Rayburn of Bonham and Mr. Lyndon Johnson of Johnson City."

"Will, you didn't tell me that you had such an attractive mother," Johnson beamed at my mom.

"Lyndon, keep yourself in check," said Mr. Sam. "Mr. Chaney, I wanted to thank you for bringing Wat Eakins' case to my attention. I hope we've done something good here."

I saw Mr. Bates waving, so I said my good-byes and went over to where Mr. Bates and Bob stood.

"Ants in your pants, Mr. Bates?"

"Funny guy, Will. You got your orders and your tickets?"

"Yes, last night after I got home."

"Good, we'll see if you're this witty in three months when you can't keep the Cyrillic alphabet and German pronouns separate in your head."

"I'm leaving today," Mr. Bates said. "Bob, I'll see you in Washington tomorrow night. A car will transport you to Perrin Field over in Denison tomorrow morning at 10. Be ready to hit the ground running. We have a number of important briefs to give day after tomorrow. Godspeed, gentlemen." Martin Bates climbed into the back of his car and sped off without further ado.

"Don't worry, Will, he's even a bigger jackass after you get to know him."

"Bob, I still don't know how we got here."

"Could be worse. We could be storming Monte Cassino."

"Where's Wat's stone going to be?"

"Stone's already in place, over here," Bob replied. "Want to come over for dinner tonight?"

"Sure, mind if I bring Mindy along?"

"I was hoping you would," Bob said. "Then, my mother-in-law and wife have someone else to pounce on."

"Did I hear my name?" Mindy walked up with her aunt and introductions were made.

"I was committing you to dinner at the Stevens' house tonight," I said. "Bob and I have orders. We leave tomorrow."

"Oh Will! So soon?"

"Afraid so."

"What time shall I expect you?" Mindy said.

"I'll drop by around six forty-five. Then we can walk over, since Bob is your parents' neighbor now."

"Bob," Mindy said. "Are Bet and the kids staying here or going back to California?"

"Here for awhile. Melrose wants them here badly, and I guess that's okay with me."

Mindy smiled. "Bob, you're getting more diplomatic by the moment. You didn't even mention that having your father-in-law locked up in Dallas solves a few problems."

Shannon elbowed her niece in the ribs. Bob and I both stifled laughs with our hands, and then looked around to see if anyone heard.

"Miss Mindy, your tongue is as sharp as your hands are talented."

Excepting Doris and Bert, they were the last group to leave the cemetery. Will went up and hugged Dud's folks again.

Dinner that night was a success. When the women and children headed for the parlor, Will and Bob headed for the train station.

"I saw in the paper yesterday that the Supreme Court ruled that Negroes have a right to vote in the Texas primary," Bob said. We crossed California Street to get to the train station.

The Street was empty. It was, after all, a Tuesday.

"What about it?"

"Things are going to change in this country after the war. Two years ago, if you'd told me Wat Eakins would be killed flying over France, I would have sooner believed men had landed on the moon."

Bob lit up a smoke and handed me the pack. "You're still a mooch, Davis. Always were."

I looked down California Street and said, "they must really like Veronica Lake around here."

"How so?"

"They're still showing *I Married a Witch.*"

"I know that film. Thought my mother-in-law played the lead."

"Jesus, Bob, cut her some slack. She was trying hard at dinner."

"Guess that's what eats me - she has to make such an effort. Still, the kids seem to like her and she has helped out Bets a bunch."

"You ought to detest her," Bob said. "What, with my father-in-law and all."

"Bob, you can quit bringing that up any time now. Ain't small town life grand?"

Bob exhaled blue smoke into the night air. "It's a regular combat zone, sure enough, but what can you do? You can't make nasty people nice–not on a regular basis anyway."

"Guess all us good ones carry on the fight."

"You got that right, Will Davis. We carry on."

Bob stubbed out his cigarette. I stubbed out mine. We headed back across California Street … to the future.

2nd Tuesday Bookclub

Lyndall Stockebrand 940.668.1261	Jodelle Greiner 940.665.5511	Nadine Creswell 940.665.8154
Nita Johnson 940.668.7028	Michaela Kersey 940.736.3601	
Sherry Bain 940.759.2183	Dawn Porter 940.668.7107	
Bernie Gordon 940.668.2547	Julia Mayo 940.668.0710	
Brenda Bubak 940.637.1170	Rosanna Webb 940.665.0153	